PRIMAL
THREAT

PRIMAL THREAT

A NOVEL

Earl Emerson

BALLANTINE BOOKS

NEW YORK

Copyright © 2008 by Earl Emerson, Inc.

Published in the United States by Ballantine Books, an imprint of The Random House Publishing Group, a division of Random House, Inc., New York.

BALLANTINE and colophon are registered trademarks of Random House, Inc.

Library of Congress Cataloging-in-Publication Data
Emerson, Earl W.
Primal threat: a novel/Earl Emerson.
p. cm.
ISBN 978-0-345-49299-9
1. Cyclists—Crimes against—Fiction. 2. Cascade Range—Fiction. 3. Northwest, Pacific—Fiction. I. Title.
PS3555.M39P75   2008
813'.54—dc22   2007028740

Printed in the United States of America on acid-free paper

www.ballantinebooks.com

2 4 6 8 9 7 5 3 1

First Edition

For Sandy, who keeps me sane.

For practical purposes, we have agreed that sanity consists in sharing the hallucinations of our neighbors.

EVELYN UNDERHILL

Adapt, migrate, or die.

LIEUTENANT JAMES MULDAUR, SFD

PRIMAL
THREAT

I

February

In later years Zak Polanski found it odd that he could divide his life into chapters separated by fatal or near-fatal automobile accidents. The first occurred when he was eleven, and it reflected in the dynamics of his family even today. Wreck number two was the accident that catapulted him into an unexpected summer romance with Nadine Newcastle.

The call had come just after twenty-three hundred hours on a cold night in February. There were only three firefighters riding Engine 6, so after they arrived Zak quickly laid a hose line in the street while the driver put the transmission into pump; the lieutenant scouted the wreck to see how many patients they had, and whether or not any of them would require extrication. Then came the part Zak dreaded, the part where he flopped onto his belly and squirmed into the vehicle to tend the patient.

Everyone on the crew thought Zak exhibited an uncanny bedside manner at wrecks, displaying a sense of calm to patients that helped pull them through the ordeal in a way nobody else in the department could. It was a tribute to his ability to sequester his feelings and get the job done, because around a car accident Zak was actually the most insecure person in the fire department.

Zak wouldn't get the tremors here in the bowels of the wreck, but he would later at the station when he slipped back into his bunk. It was his practice afterward not to think about any of the auto extrications he'd been involved in, for every one of them terrified him. His auto-crash anxieties were something he would never confess to a buddy, nor to a priest, and probably not to a wife. For all of his adult life and the bulk of his childhood Zak had entertained an abnormal fear of dying in the tight confines of a car wreck, trapped, defenseless, perhaps even bawling. For as long as he could remember, his mental picture of hell was the scrambled interior of a wrecked vehicle, and here he was inside his worst nightmare once again.

It was a Lexus SUV, upside down, a car–pole accident. After Zak had crawled in and turned on his flashlight, he saw his patient's leg trapped in the crushed door and realized that the weight of her body, as she slowly slid out of the seat, would soon be wrenching her pinned leg. If the pain wasn't excruciating now, it would be within minutes. He removed his helmet and flung it outside the vehicle, then scooted under her and gave support to her shoulders, easing some of the pressure off her leg while doing his best to keep her spinal column aligned. It wasn't an elegant position for either of them, but as soon as he had his hands on her, she ceased whimpering.

She was young, and he had the feeling his touch was both a surprise and a novelty. He explained what he was doing and why, and then told her how many more firefighters and machines would be arriving, warning her there was no place noisier than the interior of a vehicle with a crew of firefighters working to cut her free. "You okay with all that?" he asked.

"I guess I'll have to be."

"Good. What's your name?"

"Nadine Newcastle."

"Hello, Nadine. My name is Zak. Now, I don't want you to worry. I've been to dozens of wrecks, and most were a lot worse than this one, so we'll get you out. Actually, this will be fairly easy."

Zak could see her breath in the dark interior of the car. Even though it was early February, she was clad in shorts and a short-sleeved blouse and was shivering, partly from the influx of cold night air and partly from shock. Her femur looked intact; her knee was aligned and normal looking, but below that her tibia and fibula were not visible in the twisted metal.

She started crying again, a desperate series of hiccuping sounds that almost resembled giggling, tears glissading off her upside-down face. "I want out. I want out of here."

"Don't worry. It'll just be a few minutes. Then we'll both be out of here, but we're going to have to be patient." He smelled gasoline, and even though the motor was off he had an ominous feeling that the car was going to flame up with them inside, a feeling he always entertained while working inside a wreck. Without letting go of her, he reached up with one hand and tried to remove the keys from the ignition, but they wouldn't come loose. Even with the car off, he would feel better with the keys in his pocket.

"Can you wiggle your toes?"

"I think so."

"On both feet?"

"Yes. I'm so scared. Please get me out, Lord. I know You know what's best, but I don't want to die like this."

"Listen to me," Zak said. "Nobody's going to die. We're getting you out, and I'm going to stay right here with you until it happens."

"Honest?"

"Of course. That's my job."

"Pardon my saying so, but I think you have a lousy job."

"Well, I'm glad I have it tonight, because it offers me the chance to help you through this." As he spoke, her cheek brushed his, her long hair falling into his face. Her teardrops cooled his neck as if they were tiny splashes of alcohol.

"Do you ever get scared?" she asked. For a moment he thought maybe she'd felt something in his touch that conveyed his own terror. "Of course you don't. You're a trained professional. It was stupid to even ask."

"No it wasn't. But listen. You're going to be fine. Let's just try to keep weight off that leg. That's our goal right now."

As they waited for help and as Zak inhaled the aroma of shampoo from the girl's hair, his hands felt a steely strength in her shoulders, and he wondered if she was a swimmer. He explained that a truck company would arrive with a Holmatro tool, which they would use to strip the door off its hinges, that the car would shake and there would be noise, and that once they had her leg free she would be lowered onto a backboard and removed from the vehicle. All standard operating procedure.

"Jesus, just please let me get out of this. Please, Jesus."

"We'll get you out. Jesus and me," Zak said, with a pinch of sarcasm she either didn't notice or noticed and refused to be offended by.

A minute and a half later a lieutenant he didn't recognize poked his head inside and eyeballed Zak and the patient. "Wha'dya got?"

"Her leg's pinned under the door. Everything else is free. Tib–fib, I'm thinking. No loss of consciousness."

"Okay."

The officer stood up and shouted something to his crew.

"I'm not feeling so well," the girl said.

"These guys will have us out of here in a couple of minutes, Nadine."

"I like how you say *us*."

"That's right. I'm not leaving until you do. You and me all the way."

As soon as the power unit for the Holmatro started up, the noise level increased tenfold. It was always somewhere around this point, always with a lot of people looking on, that Zak began to get overwhelmed with a desire to scramble out of the vehicle and run away. He had never been to an accident scene without the sense of wanting to flee, but so far he never had, at least not in the fire department; still, that didn't mean it wouldn't happen tonight. His vision of sprinting down the street was so clear and stark, it might as well have been a recent memory instead of a fantasy.

Peering around the interior of the cabin, Zak spied a Bible, some schoolbooks, a handful of CDs, and a tennis racket in a mono-grammed leather case.

"I'm going to die. I know I'm going to die," she said.

"Nobody's going to die. We'll have you out of here in minutes. After that you'll be on your way to the hospital, and everything will be hunky-dory. I'm sure your parents or your boyfriend or whoever will meet you there. You're doing just fine."

Zak wasn't sure what the truck officer's plan was, though he could hear the crew talking it over as they worked, shoving blocks of wood inside, cribbing the vehicle lest the weight cause it to sink onto Zak and his patient. Getting crushed by an SUV was just one more thing for him to think about.

"You guys were out late."

"We were at Bible study class."

"This late?"

"It goes on for hours sometimes."

"There's a tennis racket here, too. You play tennis?"

"I live for tennis."

"So you're pretty good then?"

"Third seed on the Seattle U team, but I'm going to challenge and take second. I'm pretty sure I can. By the end of the year I'm planning to be first."

"You ever play guys?"

"I play anybody."

"Good. I bet you can't beat me."

"You're on, buddy."

"What do you want to bet? Lunch?"

"It's against my religion to actually wager. But I'll play you any-time you want. And you won't win."

"Okay, then. We've got a date."

"Not a date. I have a boyfriend. Just a tennis match."

"Right."

When they began using a small electric saw to cut through the sheet metal, it got significantly noisier inside. It didn't take long before Zak saw large slabs of the night sky appear, and it wasn't much longer before Nadine's leg was free. Somebody slid a backboard partway into the car and asked Zak which direction was most appropriate for sliding her out of the vehicle. He directed them toward the passenger's side, knowing it was crucial to keep her spine aligned and immobile. Another firefighter grasped her leg, and they carefully eased her out of the driver's seat and onto the backboard, which made harsh sounds against the particles of broken glass when they slid it out. Nadine blew air through her clenched teeth but other than that was silent, holding Zak's hand until they pulled her from the vehicle.

Zak crawled out in time to see her placed on a gurney and wheeled toward the back of a nearby medic unit, another firefighter having taken traction on her neck. Even though they'd agreed to play tennis, he doubted she would remember it or that it would actually take place. She was a Bible thumper, and he'd already had one too many Bible thumpers in his life.

Perhaps because he'd grown up in a household full of women, Zak never had any trouble talking to them, which was a good thing, because Zak lost girlfriends almost as quickly as he acquired them. Muldaur, his lieutenant, once said he was so relaxed around the opposite sex it was almost as if he were gay. "Zak could pick up women in a garbage dump," Muldaur said. "And they'd be gorgeous, too."

Though he'd had plenty of relationships, Zak would have given anything for a stable situation that would endure as long as the twenty-five-year marriage Muldaur basked in. What he got instead was one unsatisfactory fling after another. Zak's routine was to meet a woman, take her out a few times—or once—before falling into bed with her, and somewhere in that twilight space after they'd become intimate but before they became friends, he would simply forget her. It wasn't exactly that he lost interest; he actually *forgot*. It was pathological and he knew it, but so far he'd done nothing to stop it.

At twenty-eight, Zak had never moved in with anybody and

never let a woman move in with him. He'd never been close enough to loving someone to contemplate it. He wasn't proud of the multiple liaisons and did not boast to his friends about them the way some men did; he was in fact embarrassed by the relentless train of relationships, viewing each as another dereliction in a long line of derelictions. In view of his history, he found it odd that he'd become so attracted to a patient he'd been with less than ten minutes.

2

August

Pedaling up into the first of the foothills, Zak felt a droplet of sweat trickling out of his helmet and down the side of his face, dangling for just a moment on the tip of his chin. The others had been sweating heavily all along, especially on this ferocious uphill. At some points on the gravel road they found themselves pedaling up grades so steep your average Joe would have a difficult time walking them, much less riding a bike—so steep that if they got off they would not be able to remount, each of them fighting hard to control his bike on the washboard fire road, each breathing in his own labored and painful rhythm.

The five riders were bonded by affection for this type of grueling exercise, intoxicated by the adventure of hard workouts, and addicted to the endorphins exercise produced. While other northwesterners spent the three-day weekend lounging around the house or semicomatose on a blanket at the beach, Zak, Muldaur, Stephens, Barrett, and Morse would be logging two hundred miles in the mountains, climbing fifteen to twenty thousand feet on fire trails, county roads, and overgrown logging roads.

For Zak and Muldaur it would be a calculated shock to their systems to help them prepare for a twenty-four-hour mountain bike race they planned to enter in three weeks. For Stephens, who lived nearby, and for his friend Morse, the ride was an end in itself. Always game for an adventure, Barrett had tagged along almost as an afterthought.

Zak had been riding last in the string of five men, a position he took up from time to time in order to size up the opposition. *Opposition.* He liked that word. They weren't actually enemies—in fact they were friends—but he knew each climb on this trip would be a contest, and the best place from which to size up the other contestants was at the back. They were all competitive and more than a little vain about their prowess on a bicycle, and thus competition would be fierce.

The Northwest was suffering through the last days of August, and afternoon highs in western Washington had been languishing in the mid- to high nineties, briefly touching a hundred in some counties. In the mountains the evenings would be cooler, but the midday sun would also be harsher. Their plan was to traverse from the western side of the Cascade Mountains to the east, ending in Salmon La Sac, a journey Muldaur had promised Zak would be similar to running three or four marathons back-to-back.

Zak, Jim Muldaur, and Giancarlo Barrett were firefighters, while the other two were businessmen, friends of Muldaur's. Besides the five years they'd put in together working on Engine 6, Zak and Muldaur had raced mountain bikes and competed in road races together, traveling to and from many of the events in Muldaur's Subaru Outback with their bikes on a roof rack, so they knew each other's habits and predilections like brothers. At 160 and 165 pounds, respectively, Zak and Muldaur were the fittest in the group. In biking the most critical single factor in climbing performance was the combined weight of bike and rider. A pound or two might not make much of a difference in football or basketball, but people paid hundreds of dollars to shave a couple of ounces off bicycle components.

Muldaur's friend Steve Stephens was the chief financial officer for a successful local biotech company; his salary, bonuses, and stock options placed him in an income category none of the others could match, although his buddy Morse, a freelance labor negotiator, came close.

Thursday afternoon before Labor Day the five of them met at Stephens's house in North Bend, a burgeoning hamlet at the base of the Cascades and the last town before Snoqualmie Pass and the ski areas. Stephens lived under Mount Si, a rocky, four-thousand-foot monolith that jutted almost straight up from the valley floor. Originally eight men and one woman had signed up for this weekend, but the woman and one of the men bailed for family reasons. The last two jumped ship after hearing that the woods in western Washington had been declared off limits because of fire danger. The drier eastern half of the state had been in a condition of fire alert for the past month, but until recently spotty rainstorms had shielded the western half from sanctions. Now *all* the backwoods in the state were officially off limits to motor vehicles, hikers, bikers, and riders on horseback. Forest fires had consumed a record number of acres in eastern Washington, Idaho, and Oregon, and the governors of the three states had asked for federal help to finance fire-suppression efforts.

"It's bullshit," Muldaur said when they gathered in Stephens's driveway to discuss it. "We've waited too long. And now comes Labor Day weekend and the weather's going to be perfect and we can't go? We're not going to have a campfire, none of us smokes, and bicycles don't throw off sparks. The ban is to keep the morons out, and we're not morons."

"I agree," said Giancarlo.

"I also vote that we're not morons," said Zak, facetiously.

Stephens added, "You're absolutely right. That is . . . Well, after all, bicycles don't set off sparks. Everybody knows . . . I mean rules like this are, uh, to keep out the vast majority of the public, because they know if they let everybody up there on a dry weekend like this . . . I'm sure you'll all agree, uh, there'll be a certain percentage of the population who don't obey anybody's rules, and of course, as we've all discussed before, at least Morse and I have, all it takes is one."

Zak was beginning to remember Stephens from a ride they'd

been on together the previous year. In his late forties, he was two years younger than Muldaur, and he had a way of stammering out his thoughts as if English were a second language. In his own clumsy way he was fond of repeating important points others had stated, but at a torturously slower pace than the original speaker. It was almost as if he thought something hadn't been said until he said it himself. Muldaur once said, "I always wondered where the center of the universe was, and then I met Steve Stephens and realized he was it." Cruel, but there was a core of truth to the remark.

"It's a very dry forest," said Giancarlo Barrett. At 220 pounds, six feet three inches tall, Giancarlo had climbed Mount Rainier half a dozen times and had done STP, the Seattle to Portland bike ride, eleven years in a row. He and Zak had been friends since drill school six years earlier, and Zak was the best man at his wedding. "The weather guys said it was going to be dry and hotter into next week. More danger of fires. This'll be our best window."

"I'm going," Muldaur said.

Giancarlo turned on his impish grin. "I'm going too, then."

They would be riding north along the face of the mountain, circumnavigating it and other sheer peaks, pedaling up into a series of low, rolling hills that stretched into the northern part of western Washington. It was an area frequented by fishermen looking to be alone, loggers, mushroom gatherers, dope smugglers, and bear hunters.

A sign cautioned travelers that the road stretched twenty-six miles on gravel before ending, though Stephens assured everyone it was possible to ride mountain bikes all the way to the small town of Snohomish on Highway 2. But that wasn't where they were headed. They would trek five miles into the hills and then turn east into the real foothills. The first climb after they crossed the North Fork of the Snoqualmie River would gain four thousand feet of elevation.

The plan was to scout for a couple of hours on the rolling county roads and then climb halfway up the side of the Cascades to a camping spot at Panther Creek, where Stephens had paid to have a local man stash their gear. Framed by the summer twilight, they would have a splendid view of Seattle and Bellevue and the Olympic Mountains eighty miles away.

They would spend the first two nights on the western side of the Cascades and then thread their way along hiking trails and back roads until they traversed the Cascade Crest Trail and descended into Salmon La Sac, a small tourist town in central Washington.

They were carrying only rudimentary repair kits for their bicycles, CamelBak water bags, GU packets, Clif Bars, sunglasses, and other necessities: traveling as light as a body could travel in these mountains. At the finish they would savor a Mexican dinner in Salmon La Sac with a couple of the wives, who would caravan across Snoqualmie Pass to meet them on Sunday afternoon.

The part Zak liked best was that there would be no cell phones, no GPS finders, and except for their bikes no appurtenances of the modern age. For one weekend they would be largely independent of modern amenities, knights errant jousting with one another on the climbs, racing down the miles-long descents at breakneck speeds, roaming a section of the Northwest where they were unlikely to see another human being for at least three days.

3

They rode easily on the five miles of pavement that preceded the first climb into Weyerhaeuser property. Traffic in the upper Snoqualmie Valley was sparse, and the sunbaked tarmac roads gave off heat in waves they could see. In front of them to the east were the low, rolling green foothills of the Cascades they would soon be climbing.

The road pointed north with the sheer, rocky base of the foothills to their right and a series of low, forested hills to their left. Even though the Northwest had been suffering a drought for months, the stark green of the foothills never faded. They passed a Christmas tree farm and a few isolated houses. Then, while they were still on the paved road, four teenagers in a Honda sped past, honking and shouting. Muldaur, who was in the front next to Barrett, turned around with a smile and said, "None of that shit where we're going."

"No sirree," said Morse. "Nothing but bears, coyotes, and deer-shit."

Morse was a jolly man, repeatedly cracking impromptu jokes and launching into witty wordplay. The three firemen took to him and his self-deprecating sense of humor immediately, which was ironic because he didn't seem too concerned whether people liked him or not, in stark contrast with Stephens who worked overtime to make friends without accomplishing a whole lot. Zak tried to recall if he'd ever met anybody who wanted to be an integral part of the crowd as badly as Stephens did.

Muldaur, the oldest rider and arguably the fittest, wasn't going to let anybody beat him to the top of a mountain if he could help it; Zak felt the same. Certainly Stephens, who had been a national champion runner in college, wasn't going to be outshone if he had any say in it. Giancarlo Barrett was tough but too heavy to be competitive on these long climbs. Morse would be at the back of the pack, and he made no bones about it. "Just wait for me, guys. I may be slow, but I'll make up for it by eating and drinking more than my share."

As they rode, Stephens dropped back and rode alongside Zak, attempting to be friendly, giving him encouraging words about how it wasn't going to be "that hard." Apparently he thought that because Zak was at the back, he was having a tough time keeping up. Stephens was six feet tall, almost the same as Zak, though built heavier, with pale skin he protected via gobs of sunscreen slapped on like paste. Zak learned as they talked that they'd been to many of the same biking events in years past: STP, Seattle to Portland; the Tour de Blast up Mount St. Helens to the observatory; and RAMROD, the one-day ride around Mount Rainier, 154 miles that included ten thousand feet of climbing. Like Muldaur, Stephens was in incredible shape, considering he was almost twenty years older than Zak and Giancarlo. Muldaur had the newest bike and, oddly enough, Stephens, who was the wealthiest, rode the oldest. Stephens also wore the tattiest clothing, most of it musty racing gear that was ten or fifteen years old. Zak wondered why a man would keep four luxury vehicles in his driveway, a speedboat, a new motor home, motorcycles, and Jet Skis—but then wear a cycling jersey that looked as if it had been in the doghouse.

At the point where the pavement ended, a sign was nailed to a tree. FIRE DANGER. UNTIL FURTHER NOTICE ALL WEYERHAEUSER PROPERTY NORTH OF THIS POINT WILL BE OFF LIMITS TO HIKERS, CAMPERS, HORSEMEN, AND MOTORIZED VEHICLES.

"Doesn't say anything about cyclists, does it?" Zak said.

"Typically," Stephens said, "they post a twenty-four-hour guard. But I don't see him." A steel gate had been swung across the road, and alongside the gate on a level piece of ground sat a black Ford Bronco coated in dust so thick, the windshield looked opaque.

"I don't see a guard," Muldaur whispered.

"I don't see a guard," Zak repeated as he dismounted and lifted his bike over the gate.

One by one the others followed. "I don't see a guard," said Morse, his voice softer than the others.

"Do you see a guard?" asked Giancarlo.

"Obviously . . . well, I mean, he's probably asleep in the Bronco, wouldn't you imagine?" Stephens asked, spoiling the joke for everyone.

As they rode up the steep hill and pedaled out of sight, they kept waiting for somebody to call them back, but all they heard was the soft crunch of tires in the dirt and the strong, hot wind blowing intermittent tornadoes of dust the height of theater curtains in front of them. The late-afternoon sun pounded their backs, and the heat flowing from the woods seemed almost too humid to inhale.

"It's going to be great," Muldaur said, speaking to no one in particular. "The whole area's closed off, so we won't have to worry about cars."

Less than ten minutes later, after they'd gotten off the steepest part of the road and onto a rolling section, Zak sprinted from the rear to the front of the group. "Car back," said Zak. "Car back."

"It's probably the guard," said Muldaur. "Maybe we should duck into the woods."

"I'm not hiding," said Giancarlo. "If he wants to throw us out, let him have at it."

They'd passed two gravel pits, a section of younger trees interspersed with hundreds of tall foxgloves gone to seed, and now were riding through a mature section of Douglas fir. If they were quick about it, they could conceal themselves in the woods alongside the road, and if they hiked far enough into the trees, they would avoid both the afternoon sun and the dust that coated everything within thirty yards of the road.

"The speed these guys are traveling," Zak said, "they're going to bury us in dust."

"There's more than one?" Morse asked, gasping for breath.

"At least two. Maybe three. Hear them?"

Traveling close to sixty and towing a gigantic plume of dust, the first vehicle, a white Land Rover, passed them on a section of small rolling hills. The fine-grained silt was light enough that even their bicycle tires were kicking it up, and when Zak looked down at his legs, his socks were tan with it. As the Land Rover overtook them, the air became saturated with a brown haze. Zak took a huge gulp of clean air and tried to hold his breath. In the miasma that was being created, the following vehicles had no way of knowing they were passing five bicyclists. It would be a miracle if one or more of them wasn't run down, crushed, or annihilated without the drivers even knowing they'd hit anything. One or more of them would be hit and dragged for a quarter mile. Any second. There was no escape. To Zak's mind, the actions of the first driver were criminal, the most reckless and infuriating driving he had encountered in a long time.

What saved their lives was Muldaur shouting "This way" as he bounced off the road, across a shallow ditch, over a log, and into the woods. All four riders followed in the nick of time as more vehicles roared past, four in all.

4

August

William Potter III's entire life was blessed with luck, starting from the moment twenty years earlier when he'd dropped into the arms of the most expensive obstetrician in the state, and continuing as he rolled out of his playpen into the lap of a trust fund his grandfather set up for him and his sister, a fund that meant neither of them would ever work a day in their lives if they didn't want to. Scooter, as he was affectionately known to friends and family, had decided a long time ago that only suckers worked for money. Sissie had taken a different tack and was in medical school, but he figured that would wear off.

Scooter squandered his time in high school partying and getting drunk, and after the family pulled strings to get him into Columbia, he ceased studying and even quit cheating on tests somewhere in his sophomore year—and eventually flunked out. His folks were furious, but what did he need school for? So he could translate his quarterly stock portfolio statements into English? He'd been explaining the paperwork to his parents since he was fourteen. To fill out his tax forms? He'd had a private accountant since he was twelve. Scooter understood finances, and when you understood finances everything else in life fell into place without a whole lot of exertion.

They'd trekked up I-90 to North Bend, four vehicles carrying five of Scooter's best friends along with one of their girlfriends, Jennifer. Scooter was riding in the Porsche Cayenne with Kasey Newcastle, his best buddy since second grade, when they were both enrolled in the Bush private school. This year alone they'd taken two trips to Mexico and one off the Washington coast in the Newcastle family boat. Scooter couldn't imagine not being best friends with Kasey. Hell, they were going to be family once Scooter settled down and married Kasey's sister, Nadine.

In North Bend they spotted a few cyclists, but no large groups and none riding mountain bikes. After driving around for an hour looking for their quarry, they regrouped at Scott's Dairy Freeze and had a flustered lunch trying to figure out where Zak and his buddies might be mountain biking for three days. Scooter had hatched the scheme to drive up into the hills and camp out, and if they happened to intercept them—well then, that would just be their good luck, wouldn't it?

Even though Nadine and Zak weren't supposed to be seeing each other anymore, during one of their semiregular phone chats Zak had told her that Thursday evening he and some friends would be riding out of North Bend and into the Cascade Mountains for three days. It burned Scooter up that she was still talking to the fireman on a daily basis, because when she broke up with *him* she'd done her best to cut off all communication and had at one point even threatened to get a restraining order against him. When he went over to visit Kasey, she wasn't even civil, and it galled Scooter no end that she didn't treat the fire dude the same way. For weeks after she told Scooter she didn't want to see him anymore, he'd assumed she was joking. Even when he heard she was seeing the fireman, he thought it was a charade to make him jealous. By the time he realized Nadine was actually dating the guy, it was too late to reverse things. To Scooter's way of thinking, Nadine had a simple mind, and that made her easy to manipulate, which was exactly what Zak had been doing from the moment he met her.

North Bend was a small town with traffic backed up on the main drag for blocks in either direction. Too much of their time had already been spent in that god-awful queue, which made Scooter abhor the town even more than he did to begin with. There were a lot of junky little houses off the main drag, and a few blocks farther on somebody had made a pathetic attempt at a swank neighborhood, but Scooter had lived in Clyde Hill his whole life, and contemplating a day out here in the sticks gave him the willies.

"Maybe they're not all hicks," Kasey said, once they'd grown accustomed to the dim light in the Sure Shot Tavern, where they'd gravitated after lunch. "I mean, look around. That guy in the corner nursing the beer, who looks like he's been sleeping with pigs, sure. But check out the traffic outside. There's a Benz. A couple of 'Vettes."

"'Vettes are all bought on credit, Kase. You know that."

The Sure Shot Tavern was a block east of the only stoplight in town, the interior filled with the aroma of suntan lotion, perfume, onion rings, and beer. Pickup trucks and SUVs shuffling along in the heat outside the door lent a whiff of exhaust to the mix. All seven of them were crowded around two tables in the tavern: the Finnigan brothers, Roger Bloomquist, Jennifer, Scooter, Kasey, and Ryan. Except for Jennifer, they'd all known each other for years, had all gone to the same private schools together. This past spring Chuck Finnigan had finished his first year at Stanford, and his brother, Fred, was slated to start this year. Kasey would be off to his third year at Columbia. It was hard to believe that for all practical purposes, everybody but Scooter would be gone in a week.

"Look at that guy over there," Scooter said. "Holding a fifty-dollar bill like he's never seen one before. You think he found it on the sidewalk? Come on. Let's go have some fun."

"Oh, boy," said Chuck. On numerous occasions over the years the Finnigans found themselves sucked into crazy schemes with Kasey and Scooter, and more than once they'd had interviews with police or security personnel afterward. No matter what happened, Chuck always thought it was a grand adventure, while Fred dreaded the fiascoes.

Jennifer tugged at her boyfriend's arm and said, "Chuck, you be good."

"I'm always good, baby. You know that."

"Except when he's bad," said Fred, sulking.

The local man wore a plaid work shirt, jeans that had seen better days, and the faded, angry smirk of a man who'd been trampled by life. He looked like a character actor in a CinemaScope western, his leathery skin a weathered contrast to a close-set pair of icy blue eyes.

Scooter said, "Hey, man. You didn't happen to find some money outside, did you? My buddy here dropped a bill."

"What kind of bill?"

"To tell you the truth, it was a fifty-dollar bill. Ulysses S. Grant. My favorite drinking president. Except for the one we got now, of course."

"I didn't find no money. And our president don't drink no more."

"Neither do I," Scooter said, hoisting a brew.

"Don't mind them," Jennifer said, stepping forward. "They're just trying to have some fun."

"She's absolutely right," admitted Scooter. "The truth is, I saw you with that fifty and was wondering if you could change a hundred for me." Scooter proffered a hundred-dollar bill as crisp as the bill the man had jammed into his jeans.

"You boys are from Bellevue, are you?" he asked without turning.

"Clyde Hill," Kasey said. "Hey. Let me pay for that beer." He slid a twenty across the bar and sat down next to the older man. "You know where we can meet some women around here?"

The local sipped from his beer, glanced at Jennifer, and said, "You lookin' for women, are you?"

"We're always looking for women," said Scooter.

"Do you prefer the kind with teeth or the kind without?"

They waited five long beats and then began laughing. They

laughed for a while and then Kasey said, "That was a good one. I guess we deserved that."

"I guess you did."

Moments later a small woman who dressed like a man trotted in, stood close to the local, and ordered the same brand of beer the man was drinking, all without making eye contact with anybody. Her short-cropped hair looked as if she cut it herself without a mirror. When her beer showed up, she gulped a couple of swigs and stared dully at the countertop.

"To tell you the truth," said Kasey, "we're up here looking for some friends. We were supposed to hook up in North Bend, but somehow we got our wires crossed. You wouldn't happen to know about the mountain biking trails around here, would you?"

"Did you ask at the bike shop?"

"We tried there. We tried all the gas stations, too."

"Are you talkin' about an overnight trip?"

"Yeah, that's right," said Chuck, stepping forward eagerly. Scooter wished he hadn't done that. Both Finnigans were huge, and they were intimidating this geezer, who just might know something. "We're looking for a group of guys riding mountain bikes up into the hills."

"Why you lookin' for these fellers?"

"They're friends of ours," said Fred.

"Two hours ago I carried all their camping gear up in them hills. Base of the falls at Panther Creek. 'Course, it's not really a creek this time of year. Barely enough runoff to keep it going."

"Is that where you got the fifty?" Kasey asked.

"They paid me fifty dollars to take their gear up, and fifty more to haul it all down Sunday morning. So far, it's about the easiest fifty bucks I ever made."

"You got fifty dollars?" asked the local woman.

"I was going to tell you about it."

"When?"

"I was going to tell you."

"I suppose you want another fifty to tell us where they are?" Kasey asked.

"I was thinking more like a hundred." He pronounced it *hunnerd*.

Scooter looked at the others. After two and a half hours of wandering around this stinking hamlet, it had just become all too easy. But then, Scooter's entire life had been too easy. He'd had one stroke of unstinting good luck after another.

They paid the man and watched him draw a map on the back of an envelope, sketching with a leaky pen he'd picked up in a doctor's office. They gulped down their beers and were on their way out the front door of the tavern when the man hollered after them. "You realize you boys just wasted a hundred bucks."

"What do you mean?" Kasey asked, holding his arm in front of Chuck's burly chest to keep him from rampaging back into the tavern.

"There was a fire danger alert posted this afternoon. You boys'll never get past the guard."

"How'd you get in?" Chuck Finnigan asked.

"I went in the main county road before the guard was posted."

"How are you going to get their stuff on Sunday?" Fred asked.

"I ain't figured that out yet."

"So we can't get into those backwoods?" Scooter asked.

"Not any way I know of."

"Thanks," said Kasey.

"Maybe you should give that money back," said Fred, who was now even more steamed than his brother. Chuck took hold of his thick arm and pulled him out the doorway. "It's like selling a car you know doesn't run," Fred said, once they were on the sidewalk. "That fucker."

"How much did it cost *you*?" Scooter asked. "That's what I thought. Let it go."

"I know these cyclists," said Kasey. "They'll get in there somehow. And so will we."

"The area they're heading into is the size of some states," said Scooter. "There must be dozens of entrances."

"I'm not so sure about this," said Roger Bloomquist. "Maybe we should forget it."

"Forget it?" said Scooter. "You get up there in the mountains with us sitting around the campfire telling ghost stories and singing 'If I Had a Hammer' and 'So Happy to Be a Webelo,' you'll be glad you came."

On the sidewalk in front of the Sure Shot, it was agreed they would retrieve their vehicles and meet on Ballarat, the road that if followed far enough through its various incarnations led north into the foothills. Scooter had to admit that the closer they got to the mountain, the more impressive it looked. Even though he'd lived his whole life in the Seattle area and driven to Snoqualmie Pass dozens of times every winter to snowboard, he'd never been this close to Mount Si except for once as a child, when Vivian and Harry had taken him and his sister hiking up it. He'd gone maybe a mile when he made them all turn back. Even as a nine-year-old, no way was he going to do anything he didn't want, and he certainly didn't want to hike for five or six hours. Harry had blown his stack, but Vivian defended Scooter the way she always did, and then a few years later Harry was history like all the others.

They drove through a narrow valley, houses in the trees off to their right, then after a mile or so headed up a short but very steep hill. First in line was Kasey's Cayenne. Next came Roger in his Land Rover and Ryan in his Jeep. Then Chuck's Ford truck, outfitted for the backcountry, the body of the truck jacked up so high that Chuck had been lifting Jennifer in and out of the cab all day. His dog Dozer and most of their gear were in the bed.

Just at the point where the pavement gave way to a steep gravel road, they found their pathway barred by a steel gate, beside the gate a potbellied security guard in glasses, a cap, and a dark green

uniform with sweat stains under the armpits and around the belt
line. On the hood of his dust-covered vehicle sat a large jug and
a cup.

"There's no way this is going to work," Kasey said to Scooter as
they slowed.

"Bet you a hundred bucks."

"You're on."

"You boys are going to have to turn around!" The security guard
wasn't much older than they were, midtwenties, full of fake bravado,
swaggering over to the passenger's window Scooter had rolled
down. "These woods are closed until further notice. We're not allowing any parties up in there."

"I appreciate that, sir," Scooter said. "But we've got a friend up
there."

"When he comes on down, I'll tell him you were looking for
him. Or you're welcome to wait."

"You don't understand. My friend's Bronco is broken down."
Scooter had deliberately chosen his imaginary vehicle to match the
security guard's. "He and his girlfriend have been waiting for hours.
He's sick."

"It's only three or four miles up the road," Kasey said, leaning
over and smiling at the guard. "We've been talking to him all the way
from Bellevue. He busted his crankcase on a rock. He's maybe three
miles in. I don't think he has anything to drink."

"We've gotta get him out," said Scooter.

"He really *is* sick," Kasey added.

Scooter could tell from the guard's face that whoever had hired
him had not prepared him for this contingency. "Here. I can get him
on the phone."

"I can't really—"

"Here," Scooter said, pushing the buttons on his cell phone.
"Jack? Are you there? Jack? Jenny? Where's Jack? What?" Scooter
glanced across at the guard as he spoke. "I'm afraid I've got bad news.

You're going to have to walk out . . . I can't help it. There's a guard here who won't let us in. Well . . . I'll let you talk to him."

Scooter could hear Jennifer's voice over the cell phone pleading, explaining that her boyfriend had diabetes and was beginning to lose consciousness—that they had no water and had been stranded for hours and she thought her boyfriend was going to die. If he didn't let her friends in, the guard was headed for a huge lawsuit. Couldn't he please let her friends come get them? They would be in and out in ten minutes.

Wordlessly, the guard handed the phone back to Scooter, then walked over to the steel gate and swung it out of their way. Kasey fired up the Porsche SUV, and the four trucks wended their way up the washboard hill. A minute later Scooter's cell rang. "Did I do good or what?" Jennifer asked.

"Oscar time, Jenn." Scooter could hear the two brothers, Fred and Chuck, laughing in the background. Soon all four vehicles were racing along the deserted county road.

Scooter clapped his phone shut and said, "That was beautiful."

"Hang on. They're right up here."

"The cyclists? Already?"

"There's a bunch of 'em. I thought there were just going to be two."

"Nadine said eight or something like that."

"I see five. Hang on. We'll smother those fuckers in dust."

"Yee haw!" Scooter shrieked as they hit a pothole that jarred his teeth. "Look at that cloud. These bastards are going to be brushing grit out of their teeth for weeks."

"I hope it's the right group."

After they passed the cyclists, Scooter added, "It was them. I saw him. Jesus, I think Fred and those guys are going to run them over. It's dustier than hell back there. I don't know how they can miss. I think we cut it a little *too* close."

"Did he see you? That's what matters."

"He was too busy spitting dust."

A few moments later the walkie-talkie squawked. *"Jesus. Can you guys slow down? We can't see a thing back here. We're going to go off a cliff or something."*

It was Roger Bloomquist in the Land Rover. "Just don't hit any cyclists," Scooter said. "I don't want to have to crawl under somebody's truck to pick a bunch of Lycra out of the undercarriage." He laughed at his joke.

5

"What was wrong with those assholes?" Muldaur asked.
"I don't know," said Stephens. "Maybe they didn't see us."

"They could hardly have missed us," said Muldaur. "I can't believe how close they came to killing us. It was like they didn't care if they did or not."

"My guess is they've already started drinking," said Giancarlo.

"Let's not get too excited about something that, uh, ended up being rather inconsequential," said Stephens. Zak had to admire that quality of reasonableness, even though he was as pissed off as Muldaur. Clearly, the yahoos in the trucks had been out to do damage; had the cyclists not ducked off the main road when they did, he was reasonably certain one or more of them would be on their way to the emergency room right now.

Stephens led them down to the rugged North Fork of the Snoqualmie, which now in late August was just a shadow of its normal self, and then along some overgrown logging roads Weyerhaeuser workmen had once used to haul logs out of the area. Somewhere on the county road to the west they could hear the caravan of vehicles racing back down the road. "Who the hell let them past the gate?" Muldaur asked.

"I wonder if they even knew we were there," said Zak.

"The first car did." Muldaur turned to him. "I saw the passenger laughing."

"They were laughing at us?"

"One of them was."

Eventually they made their way down a slight incline to where the road crossed the Snoqualmie River on a concrete bridge. Because they'd detoured into the woods, they'd bypassed a good part of the county road, as well as what Stephens called the Spur Ten gate, which he assured them would be locked and would effectively bar the Jeeps from following them.

Once they attained the bridge, they stopped to take in the panorama. Zak could see a quarter mile to the north and a bit more to the south. The water was slow and swirling with eddies and currents and moss-covered rocks exposed by the summer waterline. He could have watched the river all afternoon. The bridge had no railings, and Zak couldn't help thinking how easy it would be for a car to drive off it. They stared at the hypnotic currents, at the silvers, greens, and lazy blue colors farther downstream. A kingfisher sat on a branch thirty yards away, and Zak spotted a deer standing in the water downriver. The air was cooler here and refreshing.

"Is there snowmelt at this time of year?" Zak asked.

"Oh, no, well, you know . . . that all ended months ago," said Stephens. "Most of this water's coming from up in the high lakes. When there's snowmelt, it's all sea green and milky from . . . well, not clear like this."

Zak looked up at the close mountains above them in wonderment that they would conquer these slopes in ways that hadn't been possible when their pioneer ancestors traversed them. Stephens pointed deep into the woods where there were occasional cedar stumps eight or twelve feet across, remnants of the titans that had been logged eighty years back and that dwarfed anything they would see in the tree farms.

"Can you imagine how dark this forest was at one time?" Gian-carlo said. "We'll never see that kind of majesty again. Not unless nature finds a way to eliminate us. Oh, my God, this is beautiful. This view is worth the trip."

"I've been here many times," said Morse, "but it never fails to amaze me."

Stephens had located their first night's camp on a rare flat spot hidden from the road, near an anorexic-looking waterfall that formed a small pool before disappearing over the side of the mountain. It was the terminus of Panther Creek, because from here it ran directly into the North Fork below. They'd been pedaling up the mountain on steep switchbacks, traversing the Z-scar patterns they'd spotted from the valley floor. The roads were impossibly sheer in some places—so sheer that even with twenty-seven speeds, Giancarlo was wishing for lower gears. "Couldn't ride a lower gear," said Muldaur. "You wouldn't be going fast enough to stay upright. You'd fall over."

Morse, who was gasping, said, "Maybe we should have brought ice axes."

"Or parachutes."

The camping spot at Panther Creek was one of the few places they'd seen where they could pedal off the road—everything else had been hemmed in by sheer rock faces, stands of trees, or drop-offs. Most of the area was closed in by maturing Douglas fir planted after this section of the mountain had been logged off twenty or thirty years before. The clearing was in a small cul-de-sac that had once acted as a dumping area for logging operations, old roots and broken limbs in a giant heap, on top of which sat a red-shafted flicker canting his head back and forth curiously. As soon as he hit the flat part of the road, Morse got off his bike and leaned over to catch his breath, while the other four pedaled around slowly to flush some of the lactic acid from their legs. Morse was definitely going to be their weak link, Zak thought.

After they located their gear, Zak climbed onto a stump, where he found an expansive view of the valley and the road they'd just climbed. The stump, an ancient cedar, was nine feet across and had stubby trees and brush growing out of it. According to Stephens, they were about a third of the way up the first of several mountains they would scale.

Except for the barely discernible outlines of the tallest buildings in Bellevue and Seattle thirty miles away and a single puffy white contrail high over Puget Sound, there were no traces of civilization beyond the remains of the logging operations behind them.

In August the pitiful waterfall was all that remained of Panther Creek, but it would provide fresh water and a cold shower. Morse, who'd overheated badly on the climb, stepped under the waterfall in his cycling clothes, taking off only his shoes. Giancarlo followed, grinning until his dimples showed. "That is *really* cold."

"Feels good," said Morse. "But it's giving me a headache." He peeled his wet and now heavy clothing off and stood nude.

The original plan had been to explore some of the rolling terrain on the valley floor for a couple of hours before making camp, but after the Jeeps passed them they didn't want to remain on the valley floor.

Zak and Muldaur, after ascertaining that their gear had been cached properly, pedaled back to the road and continued climbing, anxious to log more miles. The other three, knowing there would be impromptu climbing contests in the coming days and having had a difficult time already following Zak and Muldaur up the first switch-back slopes, seemed content to lollygag back at the waterfall and let the two wear themselves out.

After climbing for another hour, Zak and Muldaur stopped at a narrow perch on one of the upper road systems. As soon as they quit pedaling, the draft they'd been creating for themselves ceased, and they were both immediately painted in sweat. The afternoon sun stood fairly high in the western sky, and as they walked out to a small landing away from the side of the mountain, a breeze kicked up. They couldn't see the camping spot below, but they could see just about everything else, including the last half mile of road they'd pedaled up. "I wonder what our elevation is," Zak said.

"We passed Lake Hancock twenty-five minutes ago. It's at twenty-two hundred, and I'm guessing we climbed at least another thousand feet. Probably closer to two."

They could see a carpet of low, rolling hills stretching out thirty miles to Lake Washington, which they glimpsed just a sliver of, and then beyond the water Seattle, Puget Sound, and the Olympic Mountains. Seattle sat in a basin between the Olympic and Cascade Ranges, so it was more or less shielded from storms off the Pacific. The basin also subjected the area to periods of air stagnation, one of which they were going through now—the sky over Seattle was brown and purple.

They were situated on the side of a mountain—or technically a foothill—and the valley floor below looked just as it had several million years ago when the last glaciers moved through and scraped the earth raw, except now it was carpeted in Douglas fir and the large scabby patches that had been clear-cut. They could see the Snoqualmie River at the base of the mountain and several small lakes dotting the landscape, a couple of which they'd passed on their way in but hadn't actually seen until now.

Zak noted his heart rate monitor, which had been registering in the high 160s while they were climbing, now registered 52. If his heart hadn't been working to cool his body, the rate would have been even lower. He was in the best condition he'd been in all year.

"What's that?" Muldaur asked.

"What?"

"Over there." Following Muldaur's gaze off to the north, Zak saw a puff of dust working its way in their direction.

"The Jeeps?"

"I don't know who else would be out here. And they weren't all Jeeps. That first one was a Porsche Cayenne. It costs over ninety thousand dollars if you get the loaded model."

"At least we won't have to contend with them. Stephens said

they won't be able to get past the Spur Ten gate. The people who have fishing cabins up at Lake Hancock have a key, but nobody else."

"I just wonder how they got past the guard."

"What would you have done if they'd stopped?"

"I don't know, Zak. Every time somebody risks my life with a four-thousand-pound vehicle when I'm on a twenty-pound bike, I get pissed. I know people who carry guns when they ride, but if I carried one I'd end up using it. So I don't."

"Shooting at a car wouldn't be a good idea."

"It wasn't such a good idea trying to run us off the road, either." When Zak turned to leave, Muldaur said, "Wait a minute. I want to see if they head back to North Bend."

"They really bugged you, didn't they?"

They watched the distant plume of dust wend its way south. From their vantage point Zak couldn't make out the individual vehicles, but he knew there were four of them. For more than a minute the dust trailed off behind the trees, then reappeared, then vanished again. Finally it stopped at a point almost exactly in line with Seattle's skyline. "They're at Spur Ten gate," Muldaur said. "Probably trying to figure out how to get through it."

The plume of dust flattened and gradually dissipated. "We're out in the middle of nowhere and I can still hear somebody's dog yapping," Zak said.

"This is America. Everybody's entitled to at least one gun, one truck, and two dogs. Geez. Feel how hot that wind is?"

The breeze came at them from two directions, from above on the mountain and from the south, skimming the face of the hills they'd ridden up. "It's so dry it sucks the moisture out of your mouth."

"In California they call them Santa Anas," said Muldaur. "Up here they call them Chinooks. The wind picks up heat as it rolls down off the mountains. And some of that heat is coming directly from eastern Washington. The pass acts as a bellows." Suddenly he noticed that the vehicles were headed straight for the base of the mountain on a ribbon of dirt road. "Jesus. They got through the gate!"

"Are you sure?"

"Yes. And they're headed straight for our camp."

They got back on their bikes and climbed for another fifteen minutes until they hit the crest of the foothills, where they turned around and headed back down. Muldaur estimated they'd reached the forty-five-hundred-foot level. They wouldn't go a whole lot higher this weekend, though they would descend and climb these hills many times more. As they pedaled they drank from their CamelBak water packs. Even though Zak's pack had held almost a hundred ounces when they started, it was nearly dry now.

Though they were both expert riders and had expensive high-tech mountain bikes with disc brakes and front and rear shock absorbers, on the downhill Zak easily sped away from Muldaur. The difference between them, Muldaur was fond of telling him, was that Zak hadn't yet had his accident. "You get in a wreck where it takes six months to heal, you'll slow down," Muldaur said. "You're just one crash away from going my speed."

Zak laughed, let go of his brakes, and disappeared around a sharp bend. Later, Muldaur told him he must have been doing forty—an insane speed, really, when you thought about the unpredictable road surfaces and the drop-offs.

The trail was bisected by short sections of washboard produced by heavy truck traffic over the years. It had the added hazard of short, diagonal dikes laid across the path to channel off heavy rainwater. All of this on a bumpy road with unexpected twists and turns and the occasional rock smack in the center.

Zak bounced onto the dirt platform near their camp and purposely skidded his rear wheel, kicking up a cloud of dust. Giancarlo came out from behind the ancient debris pile, where they were setting up camp, just as Muldaur came down the hill and kicked up his own cloud of dust. "That's all very little boy," Giancarlo said.

"Isn't it?" Muldaur said.

"They're right down there."

"Who's down where?"

"The Jeeps. Just below us. Looks like they're getting ready to spend the night."

"Are you shitting me?" Muldaur rolled his bike toward the near side of the debris pile so he could peer down the hill. Zak followed until they were both able to peek directly over the lip of the landing. To their surprise, four vehicles were parked less than a hundred yards away in a tiny clearing at the end of an overgrown spur road: a Porsche SUV, a Ford pickup with gigantic tires, a Jeep, and a Land Rover that looked as if it had never been off a paved road until today. The vehicles were parked helter-skelter and coated in dust except for muddy eyeholes polished on the windshields by the wipers. One tent was already set up, and two people were working on another. Somebody had started a small fire.

"Jesus," said Muldaur. "Of all the fucking luck. There must be fifty square miles out there, and these assholes park so close they'll hear us snoring."

"It'll be okay," said Giancarlo. "They'll be down there and we'll be up here." He smiled ironically at Muldaur. "Besides. The waterfall makes enough noise that we probably won't hear each other."

"There's a statewide fire alert," said Muldaur. "They're not even supposed to be here."

"Neither are we," said Zak.

"We'll be all right," said Giancarlo. "If we're lucky, they'll never even know we're here."

"Fat chance." While Zak pulled out the tent he and Muldaur were going to share, Muldaur took a small, folding handsaw from the items Stephens had sent up for camp maintenance and rode back up the mountain with it. Nobody questioned him, probably because everyone but Zak thought he was having a hissy fit over the other campers.

Zak set up the tent, washed the dust off his legs under the waterfall, and changed into a clean pair of cotton shorts, sandals, and a loose-fitting T-shirt he'd received as part of the entrance package at a bike race earlier in the summer. Then he began exploring. The forty-foot waterfall zippered a sheer wall very close to where they'd camped, then meandered straight to the cliffs and lapped over the edge in a sorry dribble. To the west, jutting out from the edge of the mountain with a sheer drop on three sides, stood a bluff, a narrow bridge to nowhere. The first part was the narrowest with a drop of sixty or eighty feet; then the land fell away, and the distance to the jagged rocks below grew to more than a hundred feet.

Anyone going out onto the bluff had to jump a five-foot gap with a small gully directly under it. Still in his sandals, Zak leaped to the first outcropping, strolling out onto the bluff, which, at its widest, was as wide as a man was tall and twenty-five feet long. "Geez," said Giancarlo. "What if that rock's bad? What if it crumbles?"

"Then I'll be dead," Zak said nonchalantly.

"I guess I will be, too," Giancarlo said, making the leap.

The view from the outcropping was magnificent.

Giancarlo said, "Look over there." It took Zak awhile to spot it, but off to the south, where they'd seen the last houses when they were riding up, white smoke was pouring off a hillside. "Is that a forest fire?"

"A small one. Look how it stretches along there. I don't think they're going to tap it with a pump can."

Zak heard a dog bark again, closer this time, and as he glanced at the side of the mountain where the Jeep group was camped, he noticed a man on a rocky outcropping, a pair of binoculars aimed at them. Zak waved, but the binoculars didn't budge. Thirty minutes later when Muldaur showed up, the man was gone. "Where you been?" Zak asked.

"Nowhere."

"Just thought you needed some more miles?"

"I don't want to take advantage of you youngsters by being too fresh tomorrow. Jesus. Look at that fire."

"We've been watching it."

"You know these campers below us have a fire going, too?"

"Plus a couple of boom boxes that are making a hell of a racket," said Zak, who'd been trying not to let the noise bother him. "Why is it that music is the most beautiful thing in the world if it's yours, but it's simply hideous if it isn't?"

Beyond the Olympic Mountains the sky was beginning to glow a rosy pink, yellowish at the edges, with deep purple and maroon patches in the middle. It was easy to see from the haze over Seattle that the colors were going to get only more vibrant as the sun continued to die. A small bank of cumulus clouds hunkered over the Olympics, and the waning sun was painting them a brilliant white.

"There are communities near Wenatchee that have been evacuated because everyone is choking from the forest fires," said Muldaur.

"Yes, but this is going to be a splendid sunset," said Zak, nodding at the horizon. "Thank God for pollution."

Muldaur laughed his loud, braying laugh. Few people laughed as hard as Muldaur, and even fewer found as much to laugh about. It wasn't until they hiked back to camp and saw the visitors that he stopped.

6

February

It had been almost four weeks since the wreck, and Nadine New-castle was still in a neck brace, her left ankle in a cast from toes to knee. Walking with the aid of crutches and accompanied by a horde of family, friends, and department officials, she smiled sweetly at the firefighters who greeted her at the front door of Station 6.

The first thing Zak noticed was the unmarked cast on her leg. Not a single signature, greeting, or smiley face had been scrawled on it, even though each of the three giggling girlfriends accompanying her looked fully capable of wielding a grease pen.

With Nadine were her parents, her brother, and one of her brother's buddies, a soft-looking young man introduced as William Potter III but called Scooter by the Newcastles. Zak immediately tagged him as a soul who wouldn't last ten minutes in the fire service. A lot of people came through the station because they wanted to be firefighters, and it was impossible for Zak not to regard each one the way a horse trainer eyed a colt he was thinking about taking on. Not that Potter wanted to be a firefighter. The watch he wore was easily worth a month of Zak's salary.

Twenty minutes earlier, they'd received a call on the main phone from the assistant chief telling them that the chief of the department and several other city officials would be visiting, along with a civilian who wanted to donate a good chunk of money to the Medic One Foundation. The civilian turned out to be Donovan Newcastle—Nadine's father.

Before Zak could finish polishing his boots, the visitors showed up in staggered formation: chiefs, a couple of newspaper reporters, the boisterous family and friends pouring through the front door like partygoers and, except for the girl on crutches, all chattier than magpies.

Nadine Newcastle was prettier than he remembered, with an open face, guileless gray-blue eyes, and lustrous brown hair that hung below her shoulders. And she was sweet—in fact, that seemed to be her main trait. He found himself immediately attracted to her. Her brother was a year or two older, about her height, the same stocky build as their father but with the pug nose and freckles of his sister. His name was Kasey.

The Newcastles told everybody how grateful they were for the rescue of their daughter, who, according to the doctors, might have ended up a quadriplegic had the firefighters been even the tiniest bit sloppy in their spine management.

Mr. Newcastle was dressed in a formal suit and at various intervals stood off to one side as if he wasn't interested in talking to any firefighters. Mom flirted with the chiefs, who tried not to ogle her plush figure. The Newcastles had money coming out their ears, and Zak couldn't help noting that the son, who wasn't more than twenty or twenty-one, wore an expensive-looking European-styled suit. Muldaur tried to politely engage him in conversation, but he and his friend Scooter turned their backs on Muldaur to zero in on the lone female firefighter in the station.

All in all, there were probably eighteen or twenty people crammed into the beanery and adjoining watch office. At one point the crew of Engine 6 was asked to line up in front of the apparatus with Nadine Newcastle while a newspaper photographer stood outside the open bay doors in the rain and shot photos. Mrs. Newcastle had brought a small cake, and it was served on mismatched plates from the station's beanery cupboards. It was then, while everybody was standing around holding crumpled paper napkins, that Zak stole out of the room, squeezing behind the two bulky pieces of fire equipment in the tight apparatus bay, and was startled to find Nadine Newcastle more or less hiding behind Ladder 3.

Even though their initial meeting at the accident nearly a month earlier was the genesis for all the pomp, they'd exchanged only a few words until now. "Looking for the restroom?"

"I was just standing here thinking."

"And what were you thinking?"

"That I don't like parties."

"I don't either. What's *your* excuse?"

"Do I need an excuse? I just don't like them."

"I was sneaking away myself." When Nadine smiled, it made her look even younger and prettier than when she'd first walked in out of the drizzle.

Zak made his way around her and headed for the bunkroom fifteen feet away. When he reached the door, he turned and looked back at her and thought for a moment he'd never seen anyone looking quite so blue. They were celebrating the fact that she was alive and not in a wheelchair, that her father was bestowing a hundred grand on the Medic One Foundation, but she looked like she'd just flunked a midterm. "Does that C-collar hurt your neck?"

"None of it hurts. I just want to be myself again."

"I know what you mean. I've had some injuries over the years, and they're never very pleasant." And then, with a twinkle in his deep brown eyes, he added, "Want to look around the station?"

"What's in there?" she asked, pointing to the bunkroom door.

"It's where we sleep."

"You're sure it's okay?"

"It's not okay at all, but I'll make an exception for you." While he held the door, she hobbled into the bunkroom, handling her crutches with the skill of an athlete. "As I said, this is where we sleep. Where we change clothes. This is also where we hide out when the station's full of people." The bunkroom was a long, narrow affair built onto the old station during the remodel twenty years earlier. It had a men's washroom at one end, a women's at the other, and a long corridor off which were small cubicles formed from tall banks of lockers enclosing each bunk. Firefighters assigned to the station kept their uniforms, sleeping gear, and assorted personal effects in the lockers. "This is mine."

She worked her way into his cubicle, glanced at the narrow bunk, saw the book he'd been reading atop a pillow, then turned to his open locker door and scrutinized the photos taped inside the door. "Do you mind if I ask who these people are?"

"That's me alongside my two sisters, my mother, and my father. I think I was about ten."

"You were a cute little guy. What are they all doing now? I mean, you're a fireman, of course, but how about the others?"

It wasn't something Zak had often been asked, or else he would have taken the photo down. A year ago one of the men on the other shift wondered why he didn't have pictures of girlfriends on his locker instead of ancient family photos, but Muldaur, who had been nearby, replied for him. "Modern-day shutter speeds aren't that fast. Zak doesn't keep a girlfriend long enough for anybody to get a picture." Recognizing the essential truth behind the joke, everybody had laughed, Zak included.

He hadn't shared any stories about his family with anyone at the station and was mildly intrigued that he felt like telling a stranger. "The one on the end is Charlene. She was the oldest. Six years older than me."

"She's pretty."

"Yes." Even after all these years, Zak was amazed at how much it hurt to tell somebody about it.

"You put that in the past tense."

"She's dead."

"Really? How did it happen?"

"She was driving me and my other sister somewhere, and we got hit head-on by some zoned-out woman in a pickup truck. It's a long story and one I'd rather not go into."

"I'm sorry." Nadine pointed to his other sister in the photo. "And this is . . . ?"

"Stacy. She's three years older. She's staying with me for a while."

"With you and your wife?"

"I'm not married."

"And your mother and father, how are they doing?"

"I can tell family's important to you, isn't it?"

"Family is *everything*. Family and Jesus."

Zak remembered how her mother had watched over her in the beanery, how her brother and the family friend had fetched cake for her and made sure she had a place to sit, how they'd tried to include her in their conversations even though she'd been a reluctant participant, and now she'd given them all the slip.

"My father's living with me, too, but only until he gets his own place."

"And your mother?"

"My mother died the year before I got into the department."

"I'm sorry. I don't know what I would do without my mother."

"Mine had breast cancer. She beat it back the first time, but we didn't have any insurance, so she was facing these huge bills—and then it came a second time, and she didn't take any treatment. We weren't as close as I wish we had been. I think about that sometimes and wish I could change it. But . . ."

"Why would she do that? Why would she forgo treatment?"

"She never admitted it was money, but I'm pretty sure it was."

"You must miss her."

"Yes, I do."

They thought about that for a moment or two as they stood in front of Zak's open locker, his folded sheets on a shelf, spare uniforms pressed and hanging neatly. Nadine perused the rest of the photos on the inside of his locker door and then spotted a racket hanging on the wall. "Racquetball?"

"Yes. Do you play?"

"Mostly I play tennis, but I love racquetball."

"If you have time, we could play right now," he joked. "I'll spot you five points because of the crutches."

She laughed. "Where on earth would we play racquetball around here?"

"There's a court downstairs."

"You don't have a court downstairs."

Holding the bunkroom door open for her, Zak escorted Nadine across the apparatus floor then led her down the single flight of stairs to the basement, where they stepped inside a small court with a basketball hoop at one end and a row of screened windows on the street-side wall.

As she surveyed the small court, Nadine said, "I miss sports so much."

"A couple of years ago I crashed into a horse and broke my collarbone, so I know how you feel."

"You crashed into a horse?"

"On my bike. It's a long story."

They were silent for a few moments until Nadine said, "I overheard somebody upstairs talking about a patient you had today. They said her blood pressure was three hundred over a hundred thirty? Could that be right?"

"Yes, it was right. She'd had a headache for two days."

"What did you do for her?"

"Called the medics, got her on O-two and up to the hospital."

"Why would her blood pressure be so high? Isn't normal something like one twenty over seventy?"

"Exactly, but she's traditionally had high blood pressure, which she's controlled by medication. She ran out of the meds."

"That was kind of careless, wasn't it?"

"She ran out because she couldn't afford to buy them any longer."

"So why didn't she go to the hospital a long time ago?"

"No money."

"Not even a credit card?"

"This might be hard, but use your imagination. No credit cards. No checking account. No savings. No daddy. No big-screen TV in the other room she might hock. Nothing but a crummy apartment with broken-down furniture and maybe a bus pass to get her downtown to her job five days a week and then to her other job all day Saturday. Babysitting on Sunday."

"You don't have to talk to me like that."

"Maybe not, but if you can't pay, you go bankrupt, lose everything you and your family have, and then you're in debt for the rest of your life. It's part of why my mother chose to die rather than suffer the indignities of debt collectors and all the rest of it. She'd already gone through that once. I guess I'm a little bitter over it."

"I guess. But you're making it sound as if I'm responsible somehow. I'm not." She was right. He'd lashed out at her and he didn't know why, not exactly. Zak did not reply; being fair-minded on this topic wasn't something he was capable of. "Okay. I'd like to ask another question. Do you mind?"

"Go ahead."

"Are you going to get sarcastic when you answer?"

"Sarcasm is part of my basic nature, but I'll fight it." He grinned, unable to believe he'd gotten so antagonistic with someone he was drawn to as much as Nadine. It struck him that his belligerence may have been prompted by just that: how much he liked her.

"What would have happened to this woman if you guys hadn't shown up?"

"She would have gotten worse. Maybe had a stroke. Maybe died."

"Excuse my ignorance here—and I don't want you to get mad at me again—but I thought there were programs for people like her."

"There are. Us. We're the program. The fire department. We send her to the public hospital. They treat her, give her a supply of drugs, she goes home, uses them up, and the cycle starts over. She works part time for a bank and doesn't have insurance."

"My father says nobody dies in this country because they don't have money."

"I hate to be the one to tell you this, but your father's full of shit." Nadine and her family were oozing money, and it galled him in the same way it always galled him when anybody with money showed up. Everyone had at least one peccadillo. Money was his.

She regarded him for a few moments, seemed to make some sort of decision, and then changed the topic. "I was really scared in that wreck."

"It's a scary thing, getting trapped like that. Every time you get in a car afterward, it goes through your mind."

"That's exactly what happens. But you were great. I don't mind telling you, it was the worst thing that ever happened to me. I haven't told that to anybody else. I mean, when my grandfather died it was awful, but this was so sudden. I really thought I was going to pass away. And then you came and you were right there with me. I mean, you were right there, whispering in my ear. It made me feel . . . just made me feel like it was going to be all right."

"I'm glad everything turned out okay. You're a nice girl. Bad things shouldn't happen to you."

"They shouldn't happen to anyone."

He regretted his harsh words. He fancied the way her long brown hair flowed when she moved her head, and he fancied the way she looked at him brazenly now that they were alone, even though upstairs she'd seemed about the shiest human he'd ever met. He even fancied the way she'd faced up to his insane verbal onslaught about money. He liked the strength in her arms and shoulders when she scooted around on her crutches. He wondered if her life was as simple as he thought: playing tennis, going to school, pleasing Daddy.

"What's that on your arm?" she asked, pointing to a scab that wrapped around either side of his elbow and ran under his shirt-sleeve.

"We were mountain biking in a local park, and I took a couple of spills."

"It looks terrible."

"You should have seen it before."

"Let me see."

"It's too ugly."

"No, I want to look at it." When he pulled his sleeve up, she stepped close and examined the wounds with interest. "Where else were you injured?"

"My hip. All down one side of my knee. That was the worst."

"Can I see?"

He leaned over and pulled one pant leg up carefully, exposing the thick scabbing above his knee while she stared like a kid in a spook house. "You in premed, or something?" he said.

"Social work. What are these here?"

"Old scars. I got this one at a criterium in Port Townsend a couple of years ago. These others are mostly from mountain bike crashes. This is where I got torn up by blackberry vines last summer."

"And you have one on your hip, too?"

"Yeah, but I'm not going to drop my trousers," Zak said, at the same time that the door to the court opened.

"You're not going to drop your trousers?" Lieutenant Muldaur repeated.

"We were just talking," Nadine said, embarrassed.

"We've been looking all over for you. Your boyfriend's getting worried."

"It was nice talking to you," Nadine said, looking at Zak and then squeezing past Lieutenant Muldaur, who was still smirking. "And thanks for the tour."

"Sorry about what I said earlier."

"No problem."

After she left and the door swung closed, Muldaur said, "Were you hitting on her?"

"She wanted me to drop my pants."

"So I gather."

"She wanted to see my scabs from that crash."

Muldaur laughed. "Apparently, her family's got a lot of money."

"There is that."

"Your tone of voice makes the money sound like a disqualifier."

"The boyfriend's a disqualifier. I didn't know she still had one until you said it. Besides, I'm not interested in someone that much younger than me."

"Don't try to palm it off on her age. Zak, you're pretty well grounded when it comes to most things, but she's rich and you hate rich folks. Admit it."

"Okay, maybe I do. But only the ones with too much money."

"And which are those?"

"All of them."

Muldaur laughed.

Afterward, Zak wanted to go back and retrieve those moments with her so he could be civil this time. What a perfect ass he'd been.

7

August

As he turned the .30-30 over in his hands, jacked the shells out of the magazine, and then sighted down the inside of the oiled barrel, Kasey marveled at how much he loved the precision of a fine rifle. He admired the heft of it and savored the heavy cartridges sagging in his pocket. His father had given him the carbine on his fourteenth birthday, and it was still his favorite. It wasn't hunting season, of course, and he didn't hunt anyway. He liked to drive up into the hills to shoot wine bottles scavenged from one of the several restaurants Chuck and Fred's parents owned.

All of them owned guns, even Jennifer, although only three had thought to bring them along on this trip. Perhaps tomorrow morning they would cork some empties and toss them into the river, then plink them as they floated past. Kasey hadn't done any shooting since last summer out on his father's boat in the Pacific, when he'd gone through a thousand rounds of ammo in one day. He still remembered the blister on his thumb and the ache in his shoulder, but it had been a blast.

They'd made camp where the local had told them to, uncertain if they had the right place until Jennifer spotted one of the cyclists up the hill. Over the next few minutes they saw the others in turn, although neither Kasey nor Scooter recognized Zak among the distant figures.

They'd dusted them bad. Scooter had been laughing since it happened and, energized by the incident, was uncharacteristically doing all the work of making camp: sipping from a bottle of beer and setting up the tent, lighting the campfire, heating up the LPG portable barbecue they'd brought along.

"I wish we'd videotaped it," Scooter said. "We could put it on the Internet." He drained the beer bottle and was cocking his arm to throw it at some nearby rocks when Kasey stopped him.

"What are you doing, man? We need to be good conservationists. Put the cap back on, and we'll shoot it in the river."

"Right. Conservation. That's my game." Scooter placed the bottle carefully on the tailgate of the Finnigans' truck. "We'll be recycling these items," he announced to Jennifer.

Jennifer Moore was a nice enough girl and had done her job back at the guard shack, but Kasey wished she hadn't come along. Women on a trip like this cramped his style. Besides, Chuck went apeshit if anybody so much as looked her. A guy that big, you'd think he would have all the self-assurance in the world, but he had about as much confidence as a squirrel burying a nut.

"I like that," Jennifer said, tossing her long blond hair to one side. She had a habit of flipping her hair and standing so that her breasts jutted out, and every time she did it Chuck was looking around to see who was watching. "We're out here in the woods, but at least we can leave nature the way we found it." Ironically, she picked up a piece of wood and threw it onto the fire. "How about if we go up and invite those guys down? Wouldn't that be fun? We've got enough steaks for an army."

"Uh, I think they might not want to be grilling steaks with us," Kasey said.

"Why not? We have way too much food." Turning to Chuck, Jennifer bounced up and down and said, "Come on, honey. I think we should introduce ourselves. It'll be fun."

Chuck said, "Why not?"

Kasey watched Jennifer walk away in her tight pink shorts and white deck shoes, her astonishing legs long and sleek and tanned. She was about the only one in the group who didn't know Zak Polanski was the reason they were here. When he looked back toward the camp, Fred was watching him watching her, so he winked, hoping Fred wasn't going to tell Chuck later. Maybe he shouldn't have brought the steroid brothers. On the other hand, as long as the Finnigans were along, nobody was going to mess with them, which would be a good thing once Zak and his group realized who had showered them with dust.

Zak was the first to spot them walking up the hill. They were having such a hard time, Zak wondered how he and his four friends had pedaled up the steep slope. Moments later the two were standing in front of the cyclists' somewhat disorganized encampment trying to catch their breath. They looked like brother and sister. He was tall and thick through the neck and chest, blond and blue-eyed, with legs like tree trunks. A sheen of sweat glistened on his upper lip, and his muscle shirt was damp with it. She was a long-haired blonde, also with blue eyes, also somewhat thick, though attractive. Zak recognized her as one of Nadine's friends. As Zak recalled, she'd played years of soccer, thus the legs and the lungs—she wasn't breathing nearly as hard as her companion. Zak noticed that Muldaur had slipped into his thick Coke-bottle glasses and put his bicycle helmet back on, pulling it low on his forehead.

"Hi. I'm Jennifer Moore, and this is Chuck Finnigan. We're camping just down the hill here." Finnigan nodded but didn't say anything. She gave a start when she noticed Zak. "Oh, hi, Zak. Funny running into you here."

"Hello, Jennifer. What are you guys doing?"

"We're just out for a lark."

"Odd that you should end up right next to us, huh?"

"That *is* weird."

Stephens, Morse, and Giancarlo stepped forward and shook hands with both of them while Zak busied himself with some bike gear.

Jennifer bit the inside of her cheek and said, "I guess we passed you kind of too fast earlier. Was that you guys?"

"I think it was," said Muldaur, altering his voice and staring down at his lap. "I think maybe it was."

Zak recognized Muldaur's voice and demeanor as those of Hugh, an alter ego the lieutenant sometimes adopted around the fire station as a practical joke. Why he was playing Hugh now was a mystery, though.

Stephens and Morse, not realizing what he was up to, turned in unison and stared at Muldaur. Stephens turned back to the young woman and helped her with excuse making. "You were already going so fast when you came up on us, it was probably just best to keep going."

"I got a ton of dust in my boogers," said Muldaur. Again Morse and Stephens stared at Muldaur, who was now hiding his face in a towel.

"We'd like to make it up to you," Jennifer said. "We're putting some steaks on. We've got plenty. Why don't you all come on down and meet the others?"

"Fine with me," said Giancarlo, who was easily as large as Chuck Finnigan. Morse nodded, and so did Stephens. Zak said, "Sure." Muldaur shrugged, his face still hidden in the towel.

"Are you planning to stay all night?" Morse asked.

"We thought we would," said Jennifer. "We've got a campfire. It'll be fun."

"You're not supposed to have a fire in these mountains," said Zak. "You know about the fire alert, don't you?"

Neither Jennifer nor Chuck replied.

"So you guys are just out here for the one night, or what?" Morse asked. "You have plans after that?"

"I really have no idea," said Jennifer. "Do you know, honey?" She turned to Chuck.

"We follow Kasey, I guess."

"Kasey's here?" Zak said.

"Down the hill with the others."

"How about we'll be down in five minutes?" Stephens said.

"Sounds great. We'll go back and tell the others to throw some more meat on."

"They don't seem so bad," Morse said after they were out of earshot.

"No," said Stephens. "I think that speeding thing must have been a . . . well, a miscalculation. I mean, how would they have known there would be bicyclists on the road? You have to agree, we weren't supposed to be here."

"Neither were they," Zak said.

As the five of them walked down the hill a few minutes later, Muldaur had his false teeth in, his Coke-bottle glasses on, and his helmet adjusted tight and low over his ears. Zak turned to him and said, "You sure you want to do this?"

"Abso-fucking-lutely." Muldaur strode ahead in an awkward gait neither Stephens nor Morse had seen before. The walk alone made Zak laugh.

Giancarlo smiled at Zak and said, "*He's* Hugh? The guy who's always visiting your station?"

"Yep."

"Does anybody else know?"

"Just me."

"What's so funny?" asked Morse. "What the hell is he up to?"

"Just play along, okay?"

"Yeah," Giancarlo said to the others. "You're going to have to see this to believe it."

8

As they walked down the hill Zak and Muldaur threw each other looks to show their unease over the venture, while Morse and Stephens, seemingly content, led the way into the camp at a leisurely pace. Muldaur was in full disguise and was moving in that ungainly, jerky motion he was so good at. Even his friends at the station hadn't been able to see through his modest getup, the slightly altered modulation in his voice, or the distorted body language. As far as Zak could tell, he was the only one who knew that Hugh, who had been regularly visiting the fire station for months, was actually Muldaur playing his most elaborate practical joke yet.

Every fire station has at least one learning-disabled civilian with an obsession for firefighting apparatus who hangs around the station as much as he can. With few exceptions, most crews treat him with tolerance and generosity and enjoy having someone they can think of as their station mascot. So it wasn't all that surprising that no one at the station saw through the Hugh disguise or that, undetected, Muldaur chose to keep his alter ego alive. It was unclear, however, why Muldaur had chosen to play Hugh just now, or why he'd bothered to bring the glasses and fake teeth along on the trip. But Muldaur was full of surprises.

The encampment below was far more elaborate than theirs. In

addition to the vehicles, they'd set up four tents, camp chairs, a battery-operated television, and a barbecue grill complete with sizzling steaks. The campfire in the middle of the encampment was growing larger by the minute. So was the beer-fueled bonhomie.

Nadine's brother sat in front of the grill in one of the camp chairs next to William Potter III—Scooter. Zak recognized most of the others, even if he didn't know them all real well. Roger Bloomquist. Ryan Perry. While the others made introductions and ignored the fact that an hour and a half earlier these people had come as close to killing them as was humanly possible without actually doing so, Zak stood outside the circle in a disbelieving stupor. This had to be about him. There was no other reason for them to be here.

Scooter had tailed Zak before, back when Zak and Nadine were spending time together, but they weren't an item anymore and Scooter knew that. So what was going on now?

"Don't get too paranoid." Roger Bloomquist was standing alongside him, speaking in a normal tone that Zak knew nobody else would be able to hear over the truck radio Fred Finnigan had just turned on full blast, both doors of his Ford winged open to send Oasis off into the hills. Zak had met him twice before at Newcastle family functions. Bloomquist, who was living on a trust fund, had started a number of half-assed rock bands and wanted to be a famous guitarist more than he wanted to breathe. Zak had heard him play the guitar and figured his chances were about one in ten thousand. His family was known around the region for their philanthropy involving the arts, and his grandmother had endowed the Pacific Northwest Ballet Company with enough money to keep them flush for years, but Bloomquist's greatest ambition was to play in a garage band.

Bloomquist was also a longtime, second-tier suck-up of Kasey, as was Ryan Perry. The number one sidekick had always been Scooter. After Zak had gotten to know the group earlier that summer, he realized the social tier was structured, coincidentally or not, on a hierarchy that ran from wealthiest on down. Of course, that placed Zak squarely on the bottom rung in any group function. "I mean it," said Bloomquist. "Don't get too worked up about us being here."

"How did you guys know where we were?"

"Dumb luck. Some guy in North Bend told Kasey."

"You just happened to be in North Bend talking about me to the one person there who knows where I was going?"

"Somehow Scooter got wind of it. I'm not sure how."

"Scooter or Kasey?"

"Scooter."

Nearby, Muldaur, aka Hugh, had convinced Chuck Finnigan to show him the interior of the Porsche Cayenne. Chuck patiently answered each of Hugh's inane questions, not realizing that Hugh considered it his duty to exhaust the patience of anyone who tried to treat him civilly.

"Okay. Okay. Okay," said Hugh. "Three men are in a rowboat and it's in the middle of the ocean. One is a kindergarten teacher. One is a professor. And one is a pimp with a razor knife. What do they say to each other as the boat sinks?"

"I don't know," said Chuck. "What do they say?"

"I got it right here," Hugh said, pulling a scrap of paper out of his pocket and holding it close to his glasses. "They say . . . they say . . . no . . . wait . . . this is for the turtle and the stripper. Wait. I got it here somewhere." He fumbled through his pockets. Zak knew there was no joke and no punch line and that he would perform this stunt as many times as they let him get away with it.

"So you guys found out what I was doing and came out to hassle us?" Zak said.

"Kasey and Scooter thought it would be funny," said Bloomquist. "They don't mean anything by it. We were just going to grill some steaks, listen to music, and party. I mean . . . well, you know these guys. Just go with the flow."

"In the morning are they going to chase us around in those trucks again?"

"No. Of course not. I mean . . . I don't know what their plans are. I'm just along for the ride."

"You know this is all about me and Nadine and Scooter, don't you?"

"We're just going to have a good time and go home. Nobody means anything by it."

"Sure."

On the other side of the campfire, Stephens and Morse were chatting with Perry, Scooter, and Kasey. Stephens was playing that game of "who do you know" and finding they had more than one acquaintance in common, mostly businessmen in the Greater Seattle area. Then Stephens asked about investments, and soon they were discussing the stock market and Japanese real estate and REITs.

It was interesting to watch the dynamics of the two groups mesh. Fred Finnigan, who was almost as taciturn as his brother Chuck, remained on the sidelines of the stock market conversations. Jennifer watched silently as Chuck showed Hugh various gadgets on the trucks and answered his questions. Kasey, Scooter, and Perry chatted amiably and passed bottles of beer to Stephens and Morse; Bloomquist drifted over to join them. Zak thought Stephens and Morse were finding more in common with these Jeep boys than they had with the firefighters, money apparently forging tighter bonds than bicycling. Giancarlo got along with just about anybody and had soon embarked upon an earnest conversation with Jennifer about religion, which was at the core of Giancarlo's life.

Zak was still mulling over the fact that he'd been followed into the foothills by his ex-girlfriend's former boyfriend. Maybe Bloomquist was right. Maybe it was all in fun. Maybe they simply didn't have anything better to do with their weekend.

Finding himself the only member of the group who hadn't paired off or joined a conversation, Zak dropped into an empty camp chair and stared into the fire. When Jennifer and Giancarlo drifted over, he said, "That's illegal, you know. The fire."

"I tried to talk them out of it," said Jennifer. "They wouldn't listen."

"My friends beat your friends!" Hugh said as he and Chuck joined them. "No. Really! My friends beat your friends. Giancarlo can go faster on his bike than you can go in your truck. Giancarlo's fast."

Zak wasn't sure what Hugh/Muldaur was trying to promote, but he was definitely working on some sort of scheme.

9

May

On what was the nicest day of the year so far, Zak found himself crawling across the Evergreen Point floating bridge in bumper-to-bumper traffic, inching his way toward Clyde Hill to pick up his father and sister, who'd called thirty minutes earlier to tell him they were stranded. Two bridges spanned the narrow twenty-one-mile lake that divided the Greater Seattle area, and traffic on both could be counted on to move like molasses during rush hour. Zak was tired from a long training ride earlier in the day and didn't much mind an extra thirty or forty minutes of listening to public radio and watching early-season water-skiers on the lake. Mount Rainier was glowing off to the southeast in the afternoon sunlight, and a women's crew team rowed in the glassy water on the lee side of the bridge.

Several times a year Zak's father, Al, called with the not-so-surprising news that his car had broken down and he needed a ride. Even when Zak was a kid, Al's cars were always breaking down. Part of the problem was that Al was lousy at picking used cars and refused to buy a new one. "You drive it a thousand miles, you're in a used car anyway. Let somebody else pay for that new-car smell." It wouldn't have been so bad if every used-car salesman in the state didn't have Al's name at the top of his sucker list. The Volvo he'd purchased a month ago had already broken down twice.

Zak finally made his way to Clyde Hill, directly across the lake from Seattle—a neighborhood widely regarded as one of the wealthiest in the state. For the past few weeks his father had been renovating a pool house for a man who owned a chain of restaurants, and Al had recently cajoled Zak's sister into working with him on the days she wasn't at the post office.

The sunny street was lined with houses of the sort you saw in ads on the back of the Sunday magazine supplement: the shabbiest of the lot went for a million five, the others for substantially more. There was a gate at the end of the cul-de-sac, and a sleepy, heavyset guard with a meticulously trimmed mustache checked his ID and matched his name against a list on a clipboard. Zak wondered how much these five home owners were paying for a full-time guard.

It was a slate-gray house that resembled seven or eight rectangular boxes artfully stacked in no particular order. Some of it was two stories and some of it three, and all of it took up four times the footprint of Zak's house. The garage had five doors, but Zak's father had told him they had a hoist inside with underground storage, that the old man had more than twenty antique autos and a Maserati collecting dust in the basement. Zak saw his father's dull green Volvo wagon sitting in the driveway, out of the way, hood raised.

Zak walked only ten feet from his battered van before a young man talking on a cell phone intercepted him. Without looking him in the eye or abandoning the phone conversation, the man said, "May I help you?"

"I'm looking for my father, Al Polanski."

"Yeah. Sure. Around there."

Zak proceeded through some shrubbery and around the side of the garage. He kept thinking he'd seen the young man before, but he couldn't place where. Behind the garage Zak encountered a swimming pool: a woman doing laps, cutting through the water like an eel, her tan arms moving rhythmically.

Zak stepped into the pool house, where he found his sister Stacy covered in sawdust and wrestling a plastic garbage can filled with slabs of wallboard.

"We're not ready after all," said Al, when he came out of the other room in coveralls, a tool belt hanging low under his beer gut. Zak's father had a full head of bushy salt-and-pepper hair and, at five nine, stood several inches shorter than Zak. "Sorry. After I called you, we went back to work and I guess I got carried away. It's going to be another twenty or thirty minutes before I get it all picked up. They like it cleaned up every night. Can you wait?"

"I got a choice?"

"I suppose not. Was the drive over bad?"

"The normal stop-and-go routine at this time in the afternoon. Hey, listen. I know this job pays well and you like it, so take your time. We'll grab a pizza and soda on the way home." He might have suggested beer, but one didn't mention alcohol around his father, who was a reformed alcoholic.

"Hey, Ace?" The young man Zak had spoken to earlier poked his head through the doorway Stacy had used and addressed Al. "Ace? You want to pick up that crap you left in the yard? It looks like shit."

"Sure," said Al, scurrying through the doorway. Al was a hard worker who skipped lunch, rarely took breaks, had an accommodating nature, and gave employers more sweat for less money than just about anybody around, yet what it got him more often than not was to be treated like a peasant.

Zak was still trying to remember where he knew the snotty kid from as he helped his father carry eight or ten long pieces of siding into the pool house. They'd finished aligning them neatly against a wall when the kid came striding through the room and, without getting off the cell phone, said, "Not there."

Zak looked at his father, who said, "That's the son. He means well."

"I don't think he does."

"He's like that to everybody. You should have seen him with the cable man. The guy got so PO'd, he walked out and they had to call another one. He's a good kid. He just needs a little polish."

Zak helped his father move the siding again. When they were finished, Zak stepped into the afternoon sunshine by the pool and let the sun warm his face and soak into his navy-blue T-shirt. As he watched, the young woman hoisted herself up and out of the water, picked up a towel, fluffed her long hair, and strode toward the back door of the house with the same quiet, cocky confidence the young man had. He sensed she'd been watching him since she climbed out of the water.

"You don't remember me, do you?"

He turned from the pool. "I'm sorry. What did you say?"

The young woman held the towel up to her chin and let it drape under her arms in front. "I said you don't remember me, do you?"

She was probably somebody he'd dated and forgotten, or the roommate of someone he'd dated and forgotten, but he couldn't figure it out. He put his hand up to shield his eyes from the sun. "I was just—"

"Nadine Newcastle."

"Uh, well, not . . . wait a minute." Sure. This was the young woman from the rollover on Martin Luther King Way back in February. Her wet hair looked darker than he remembered and was pulled straight back on her skull. "We got you out of that Lexus?"

"You remember the car better than you remember me."

"The sun was in my eyes."

"Sure."

"No, it was. You're all healed up, I see. Great."

"I've got pins that still need to be removed, and I still don't have the same strength in my left leg as I do in my right. The doctor wants me to swim. I usually swim at school, but I ran out of time today."

"That's right. You go to the University of Washington, don't you?"

"Nice try," she said, striding across the grass toward the house. "But it's Seattle U."

Back inside the pool house, Zak met his father and asked, "How did you get this job?"

"They called you and wanted some work done. Said they met you at your fire station and learned you did this kind of work off shift. You were mountain biking in Moab for eight days, and they were in a hurry, so I offered my services. I didn't think you would mind. I told you about it. Why? Is something wrong?"

"Not a thing."

Zak was in the sun again when the girl walked into the yard combing her hair, which hung past her shoulders. She had changed into a short denim skirt, a chartreuse blouse, and flip-flops. Unbeknownst to her, Kasey and the young man Zak remembered as her boyfriend were in the window behind her, the boyfriend making crude motions in front of his chest. Zak thought he was making fun of Nadine until his own well-endowed sister came into view.

Nadine walked close and said, "What's that on your arm?"

"It's a scar from a mountain biking accident in Moab."

"It doesn't look too bad."

"Not now, it doesn't. It's five weeks old."

"Where's Moab?"

"Utah. It's a destination spot for mountain bikers from all over the West. It's got huge rock trails. They're fun, but they're like sandpaper when you crash on them."

Nadine paused before her next question. "You wouldn't have time to play tennis with me tomorrow morning, would you? All of my friends are bugging out on me."

"I thought you were on the school team."

"I'm not healthy enough to play with them yet."

"Sorry. I'm busy tomorrow. Thanks for asking, though."

"I guess you don't remember you promised to play me."

"I guess I did, didn't I?"

"You said when I got better. I'm better now."

"Tell you what. I'm working a twenty-four-hour shift tomorrow, and we don't get off until Thursday morning at seven thirty. On Thursday morning I could be somewhere at eight."

"Perfect. My first class isn't until one. How about the courts at Green Lake? Just north of Evans Pool?"

"You have a deal." Zak wasn't sure why he was agreeing to this. He had a sixty-mile bike ride planned that afternoon.

On the drive home, Zak looked over at his father in the passenger's seat. "How long is that job going to take?"

"Another couple of weeks. They keep giving me other things they want done."

"You should probably get out of there as soon as you can."

"The old man's running things, not his son. And I admit, the son is pretty full of himself."

"I think he's cute," said Stacy, who was sitting in back with her feet propped up on a tub of spackle Zak had bought the night before and left in the van. "He's taking me to a show at the Paramount in a couple of weeks."

"Jesus, Stace. He's ten years younger than you are. Maybe twelve."

"Look who's talking. I heard you setting up something with his sister."

"We're only going to play tennis. Besides, she's got a boyfriend, so it's not a date. She just needs a tennis partner. I don't want you to go out with him. He's conceited and self-absorbed and . . . Haven't you seen the way he orders Dad around?"

"He's been very nice to me."

"I don't mind," added Al.

"Trust me on this. Don't go out with him."

"Whether you want to admit it or not, I'm a big girl, Zak. Believe me, if he's a jerk, I'll know what to do. And I saw the way she was looking at you. It's not just tennis she wants. She's like . . . what . . . sixteen?"

"She's in college."

"Just don't be such a hypocrite."

Because she was partially right, Zak found himself fuming over the tennis date. There were at least three good reasons he shouldn't have agreed to it. One, Nadine Newcastle was rich, and Zak had a habit of antagonizing rich folks. Two, she had a boyfriend. Three, he was attracted to her. He liked her spirit, and he liked her combination of boldness and shyness—he even liked the way she wanted all the gruesome details about his accidents.

His father had told the Newcastles that Zak roomed with him, but it was the other way around—a minor fiction Zak let him maintain to preserve his dignity. Zak was proud of his old man but just a bit embarrassed about the circuitous route his father had taken to reach his current position in life, and a little irritated that he had less than eight hundred dollars in savings and couldn't seem to build a large enough nest egg to move out, though there were times when Zak suspected his father's lack of savings had more to do with wanting to remain near Zak than it did with any failure to budget effectively.

Stacy was an entirely different proposition. Whether she wanted to admit it or not, she was coming off a delicate, windblown perch she'd been poised on the last few years, and Zak didn't want anything to disturb her equilibrium. After almost ten vagabond years of moving from city to city and state to state, she had finally settled down in Seattle and obtained a part-time position delivering mail for the US Postal Service, a job she was overqualified for but loved. In years past she'd been a legal secretary, a doctor's assistant, and a supermarket manager, and was now trying to finesse her way into a permanent position with the USPS. When you thought about it, her story was even stranger than Al's. In fact, when you thought about it, everyone in his family had an odd story except Zak. At least that was how Zak viewed it.

10

"Forty–love," Nadine said, after tossing the yellow tennis ball into the sky and whacking it with all her might. Zak was only able to return a fraction of her serves, though he was doing better on his volleying, but even those points were infrequent against Nadine's powerful returns and anticipation. After half an hour he noticed she was having a harder time moving to her right than her left, no doubt because her left leg still had pins in it, but the inside knowledge helped only a little.

She was surprisingly aggressive, putting him away with wicked overhands, grunting as she smashed the ball into his court. Her thighs were tan and thick with muscle, and her calves flexed as she moved in the sunshine. She rarely hit the net and almost never sent a ball out of bounds. She had one grunt for her forehand and another distinctive sound when she put both hands on the racket for a backhand. He began to find the grunts endearing.

"You're not going to win this one," Zak said, even as they both knew she certainly was—she'd won every game so far. The ball landed inside the line on her right side, and she returned it as hard as she could, but he'd run up to the net and was able to tap it inside the left corner for a point.

"Nice," she said.

"Thanks. How much longer do you want to play?"

"As long as you can stand it."

"I was just thinking it looks like your ankle's starting to bother you."

"Is that why you were hitting more to that side?"

"You noticed that?"

"Sure. It is getting sore, but I don't have anybody lined up to play tomorrow, so I'll swim and that'll give it an extra day of rest."

"Are you trying to wear me out, Nadine?"

"Your serve."

"You can't wear me out. You can beat me, but you can't wear me out."

"I'm killing you."

"And enjoying every second of it, aren't you?"

"Serve."

In Nadine's mind every minute on the court was clearly for tennis; she didn't like resting or talking. All she wanted to do was play. He knew he couldn't beat her, but he was determined to grind her down and maybe get a few points, even win a game if he could. He'd been an athlete all his life and thus admired her innate aggressiveness, her dogged determination to do him in. In many ways she reminded him of his dead sister, Charlene, who had been a high school swimmer and was just as tenacious in competition. Zak stopped mentally compiling the similarities between Nadine and his sister when he realized they'd both been in rollover accidents, and that he'd saved one and not the other.

It was May, and he was starting to put in some of the hardest rides of the year on the bike. This was going to tear his legs up for the ride later in the day. Yet she was so aggressive, and excelled so at the game, that he played for the first half hour in sheer wonderment. She'd seemed so ingenuous and gullible off court, so simple and uncomplicated, yet on court she was complex, tricky, and imbued with a killer instinct he hadn't seen often in women. Unlike a lot of females playing against a male, she didn't give an inch.

"Is this where you always play?" he asked.

"At Seattle U. They have indoor and outdoor courts. And at the Seattle Tennis Club. When I wasn't at school, that's where I always went. It was easy to pick up a partner there."

"So why aren't we there today?"

"There are too many people I don't want to run into."

"I can't imagine there are *any* people you don't want to run into."

"You have to see the tennis club to understand."

"You're talking about your boyfriend, aren't you?"

"He gets funny when I'm with another guy."

"Then why isn't he playing you?"

"He likes to win too much to play me."

"Your boyfriend was that guy visiting your brother the other day?"

"Scooter. We've been together just over a year."

At the two-hour mark Zak noticed she'd begun limping badly. "Listen," he said, "I don't want you to overdo it, and I've got things to do, so why don't we just say you won?"

"Finish this game?"

"Okay."

Afterward they packed up their rackets while two men who'd been waiting impatiently for an open court began warming up. Zak walked her to her car, a white Lexus SUV identical to the one she'd rolled in February, parked in the main lot near the paved trail that circled Green Lake, the most popular walking trail in the city. As they approached her car, she said, "No wonder you're always getting hurt."

"What do you mean?"

"You're not exactly a natural athlete, are you?" Zak smiled not at how many times she'd made him look like a fool on the court, but at how wrong she was in her estimate of his athleticism. He decided not to tell her he was planning a sixty-mile ride later in the day, that the road rashes she'd seen were the result of daredevil stunts, not the boneheaded mistakes of a novice she assumed they were.

"Oh, my Lord," she said.

"What?"

"Somebody's been in my car." There was no sign of forcible entry, but somebody had rifled through the CDs, emptied her glove box, and taken a spare racket out of the case. "The racket alone is worth six hundred dollars. At least it's still here. Everything's still here. It's just messed up. I wonder why they didn't take anything."

"Maybe they were looking for cash. You sure you locked it?"

"Yes. I wasn't even parked that far away. Half the time I could see the roof from the tennis court. How could this happen with all these people around?"

"I don't know, but you're shaking."

"I'm cold. I've got some warm-ups in the back . . . if they're still there." She opened the back door and sat on the seat with her feet in the parking lot, slipping into a pair of sweatpants. "Do you think I should call the police?"

"Of course."

"I wonder how they got in without breaking anything?"

"Does anybody else have a key?"

She was quiet for a few moments. "Maybe I'll call the police when I get to school. Gee. I'm scared to get in now. Isn't that funny?"

"Why don't we walk across the street and get some coffee at Starbucks? Give you a chance to let this wear off. We can sit in the sun and dry off, and I'll walk you back."

"I thought you had somewhere you had to be."

"I have time."

"Sure. That would be nice."

They locked her car and walked across the field past the children's playground, Nadine choosing to carry her expensive rackets rather than leaving them in the Lexus. She ordered a mocha while he had a soy latte. They paid individually and sat at a table on the sidewalk at the busy intersection, watching cars and pedestrians, joggers, bicyclists, and women pushing prams.

"Is your boyfriend the jealous type?"

"I guess you could say that." She sipped her mocha and gazed across the street at two women jogging side by side. "I don't want to talk out of school, so I really shouldn't say anything more about him."

"What? You think I'm going to tell him what you said?"

She crossed her legs and looked him in the eye. "Scooter doesn't like you. Not from that first time at the fire station. I think it was because you saved me. It makes him feel insecure. He's a complicated personality. Don't judge him too harshly. He's got a lot of good qualities that most people don't see."

11

August

Everyone in the camp was embroiled in a conversation except Zak, who slumped in the camp chair and stared into the fire. Building a fire was careless and dim-witted—but worse, each of the cyclists, including him, had chosen the cowardly path by not insisting they put it out. Certainly if he hadn't been playing Hugh, Muldaur would have reverted to his fire officer role and taken charge.

Stephens was talking to the Jeep guys about the economy and various hot market tips he'd either heard about or invested in recently. Even though Scooter probably had control of more money than Stephens would see in his lifetime, Stephens lectured the younger man on the vagaries of the market and the tribulations of investing in overseas exchanges. Maybe it was the age factor, Stephens being almost thirty years older.

Meanwhile Muldaur wandered around the camp, butting into conversations and making a nuisance of himself the way he did at the firehouse when he visited other shifts.

"It's getting real hot," Hugh said. "The fire's making me sweaty." He walked over to Giancarlo. "Aren't you getting sweaty?"

Giancarlo smiled. "Not yet. I'll let you know."

"Maybe if you took that helmet off, you wouldn't be so hot," blurted Kasey from the other side of the encampment. Hugh ignored him and stared at the fire. It was part of Hugh's act to select one or two in a group to ignore.

Nadine had taken Zak to Lake Roosevelt with most of these people, and he knew they were boy-men: their brains filled with nothing more than thoughts of drinking parties and days with no responsibilities.

"Remember that time we went to Mexico and picked up those whores?" Scooter said. "We kept telling them we were with the Mafia? And Fred's said she had crabs. Fred says, 'I don't care,' and brings crabs back to Julia and then tries to blame it on her for not using the paper cover on a public toilet seat. Then she dumps him."

"We broke up for other reasons," Fred announced, downing one Budweiser and popping the cap on another.

"You broke up because of crabs," yelled Scooter, laughing. Fred shrugged it off and swigged from his bottle, which looked, in his massive hands, as if it were designed for a child. He and Chuck were football players, and Kasey said often to their faces that he kept them around less for their witty repartee than for protection. Although Giancarlo was thirty pounds lighter, he could probably outmuscle either of them, but then Giancarlo was a freak of nature. "My favorite was when we were racing your father's Maserati all through Bellevue that night," said Kasey to Scooter, "and we found those guys in another Maserati. What were the odds? So it's like neck and neck, and then they pull into that TacoTime and we keep going and we see these cops, so you pull a U-ie in the middle of Bellevue Way, right in front of the cops, and then solo all over Bellevue making sure you don't lose the cops until right before the TacoTime, and they go in and arrest the two guys with tacos in their hands. That was hilarious."

"How about that time after you got your pilot's license and we were flying over your ex-girlfriend's cabin on Orcas Island," said Scooter, tapping Kasey on the shoulder. These boys were showing off now, attempting to impress the older cyclists with how carefree and wonderful their lives were, hoping to establish a power structure based on anarchy. Alcohol had to be playing into it, Zak thought. "Remember that? We were going to toss out some Baggies filled with flour, you know, bomb the house, but you decided to toss out the whole twenty-pound bag, and it went through their skylight and almost killed the maid."

"Hey, shut up," said Kasey. "You know they're still looking for the guys who did that."

"They're still looking for a lot of people," said Scooter. "That doesn't mean they're going to find anybody."

"Just don't be blabbing our business all over, would you?"

"Is it all right if I tell them about the time we got Ryan so sick on tequila he threw up all over his father's office downtown? We were down there to watch the fireworks, and the next Monday the suckers all came to work and booted up their computers and started smelling Ryan's dinner."

"That wasn't funny," said Ryan Perry. "My father still doesn't trust you guys."

"We're not the ones who barfed," said Scooter.

The war stories continued until Kasey said, "When you think about it, the good times are about over."

Stephens, who was in his late forties, said, "You know, you'll remember these days with fondness. We all . . . well at least I still remember crazy stuff I did when I was twenty. How about you, Zak? I'm sure you have some stories to tell." Stephens had tried earlier to get him to join in.

"Not a one."

"Well, you know. It's definitely a crazy time."

Hugh broke the silence that followed by launching into a long story about his uncle who got a hook caught in his nostril while fly-fishing. Sensing that the tale would go in circles the way his jokes had, the others began interrupting, and soon there were two or three conversations looping across each other. Hugh kept chattering while Jennifer looked on with wary fascination. Though he said nothing and was not outwardly judgmental, Zak knew Giancarlo was uncomfortable with the boasting and the tales of hijinks. Giancarlo came from a deeply religious family where everybody toed the line and family gatherings were of great importance. Zak admired his ability to withhold judgment, because Zak himself was critical of almost everything he disagreed with and wished above all else that he wasn't. It was one of the qualities he liked most about Nadine: her ability not only to tolerate differing opinions and outlooks, but actually to embrace them.

Stephens and Morse clearly felt more at home with this group than the three firefighters, turning the conversation back to the stock market and investments, dropping numbers and amounts of money, each group trying to impress the other. Morse, Zak knew, had worked his way up from a blue-collar family to his current position as labor negotiator and was proud of it, while Stephens's parents had been elementary school teachers—though to hear him talk, you'd think they'd been on the board at General Motors.

Zak looked around to make sure Hugh wasn't getting into trouble and discovered that Jennifer had placed the TV in front of him; he was raptly watching *Die Hard 2*, mouth agape, cheeks flabby and expressionless. It was uncanny how easily he could alter his appearance. Muldaur was fond of telling his crew that each of them was a bullet in the brain away from being a moron; by becoming Hugh, he'd found a way of illustrating it.

Zak found it interesting that half the time these Jeep guys were bragging about their family money and how much they were going to make in their lifetimes, and the rest of the time they were boasting of indiscretions, many of which were illegal and most of which were unethical. They seemed to be stuck midway in a netherworld between reckless brats and self-satisfied billionaires.

12

August

Trailing a drag chute of dust, the Ford Expedition looked like an official vehicle, and Zak wondered if they weren't about to be cited for trespassing, maybe even arrested. He wasn't sure who owned this land, but he knew it held tens of millions of dollars' worth of timber, and he had a feeling the owners would not be happy at the thought of interlopers starting fires.

Zak was walking toward the bluffs for a better view of the Expedition when he noticed an enormous malamute curled up beside a tree. Without raising its head off its paws, the dog bared his teeth and then lunged at Zak.

The dog was less than a foot from Zak's face when he was jerked to a halt on the end of a chain. Standing on his hind legs and straining against the chain, the dog was almost as tall as Zak. He could feel the dog's breath on his eyelashes.

"Dozer! Dozer!" Jennifer Moore said, grabbing the dog by his collar. "Sit. You silly thing." She turned to Zak. "Don't mind him. He's just hot and irritated. Aren't you, honey!" She began slapping the dog's hide while he continued to snarl at Zak.

When he got to the side of the mountain, he saw the white Expedition traverse the bridge and head up the mountain on the road the cyclists had used. If it had only been the cyclists, the Expedition would drive right on past without realizing anybody was there, but with all these vehicles and the campfire . . . there was little chance they would be overlooked.

The Expedition chugged up the steep road and turned directly into the short spur, parking near the campfire. Almost immediately four young women got out. One of them was Nadine Newcastle. Without introductions, the girls spilled into camp. Clearly they all knew Kasey and the others. Nadine nodded diffidently at Scooter, and said hello to Jennifer, a friend since long before she'd begun dating Chuck Finnigan. Then Nadine and one of her friends walked over to Scooter, and the three of them stepped behind the Land Rover and entered into what appeared to be a weighty discussion. After a few minutes, Nadine abandoned the others and walked directly to Zak.

"This is my fault," she said.

"What's your fault?"

"Them following you up here. You told me last night about this bike trip, and I guess I mentioned it to a couple of people. Anyway, Scooter found out. If I'd had any idea they were going to dog you, I would have kept my big mouth shut. I'm sorry."

"Don't worry about it."

"I'm just sorry they found you. Do you hate me?"

"Of course I don't hate you."

"Well, I don't see any major rioting. Maybe it will be okay. As soon as Mom told me Kasey and his friends were headed up into the hills near North Bend, I knew what was going on. I just had to come up and find you and make sure everything was all right. I know what Scooter is capable of, and I know how intolerant you are of anybody with money . . . I just thought it would be a lethal combination. What have they done so far?"

"Is that how you look at me? As somebody who gets angry at anybody who has more money than I do?"

"I would say that's one of your defining traits."

"And not a pretty one, either."

"Most times, no. It isn't."

Zak knew his sour attitude toward wealth had contributed to their breakup. If she hadn't belonged to the moneyed class, her reaction to his biases might have been different, but she did and it wasn't. Not that it was her fault he was a prejudiced jerk. "I was thinking about you," he said. "I'm glad you came. How long are you going to be around?"

"Not long. Our parents are expecting us home tonight."

"What are you two doing?" Accompanied by Fred and Chuck, Kasey walked over and wrapped his arm around his sister's shoulders, something Zak knew he only did when he wanted something from her.

"The bigger question is, what are you guys doing hounding my friend," said Nadine.

"We're not hounding anybody, are we, Zak?"

"I don't know what you're doing."

Kasey held his sister close and said, "Just think. If I'd kept dating Zak's sister and you'd kept dating Zak, one day you and I might be brother and sister and brother-in-law and sister-in-law all at the same time. Wouldn't that be the ticket?"

"Why don't you leave my sister out of it?"

"Oooh. I suppose I'd be touchy, too, if my sister was thirty-one and working part time for the post office."

"Leave her alone," said Nadine, shaking off Kasey's arm and holding Zak's look. "And don't you two dare get into this old argument again. Just stop this!"

"No. Don't stop," said Zak. "I want to know what's wrong with honest work."

"All I'm saying is we all have the same opportunities in life, and people who end up in menial jobs like hers are doing them because they're not smart enough or industrious enough to set high goals for themselves."

"You think you've achieved what you have in life through your own hard work? That you can avoid bad luck because you're smart? Jesus, you're twenty years old. You don't know shit about life."

"Anyone can educate themselves to make good choices, and if they don't bother to do that, I don't call that bad luck. I call it willful stupidity and laziness," Kasey said. "I've gone to good schools and I make educated choices, so things are always going to be fine with me."

"There are plenty of smart people who, given their circumstances, have made the best choices they could and will never be able to dig themselves out of the hole they're in. And there are brainless idiots in your spot who, through no accomplishment of their own, will be rich the rest of their lives. It's good to be smart, but it's better to be lucky. All you are is one of those assholes who was born on third base and woke up thinking he'd hit a triple."

"Zak," Nadine said. "Don't do this."

"You mean, don't voice my opinion?"

"No. I mean, don't be so disagreeable."

Hugh stepped forward and spoke in his most professorial and phony voice. "Okay, okay, okay. There's something I've been meaning to say. Ready?" Nadine nodded, even if nobody else did. Pregnant pauses were Hugh's stock in trade. "You have a camel, a donkey, and a kangaroo . . ." Everybody had stopped their separate discussions to watch Zak and Kasey go at it, and now they were watching Hugh. "A camel, a donkey, and a kangaroo . . . and three naked ladies." Hugh blushed and stepped directly across the fire as if he hadn't seen it, tripped on one of the logs, then danced about as if he'd been burned. "You girls don't mind a joke about naked ladies and kangaroos, do you?"

The eager look on his face cracked up nearly everyone. It was a welcome respite to the quarrel Zak and Kasey had been waging. The only one not amused was Scooter, who hadn't taken his eyes off Nadine since her arrival.

Once the laughter died down, Hugh said, "No joke. This isn't the time for jokes. I have a bet to make. I said it before and I'll say it again. My guys can beat your guys. Up this road. Down this road. Anywhere you say."

"Wait a minute," Scooter said. "Are you talking about your guys on bikes and us in trucks?"

Nodding rapidly, Hugh said, "Yeah, yeah, yeah. My guys can beat your guys. Up or down. I'll betcha a hundred dollars."

"That's just stupid," said Jennifer.

"No, no," said Scooter. "Let's do it."

"I like it," said Kasey. "Let's go."

"I'm not racing a truck up this hill," said Stephens.

"Then we'll race down," said Scooter. "We'll make it easy for you guys. We'll race from here down to the center of the bridge."

"Oh, yeah," said Stephens. "That sounds safe. My bicycle bumping up against a truck. Who's going to get killed in that scenario?"

"Then let's make it a time trial," said Scooter.

The cyclists all looked at one another until Giancarlo said, "I'll do it."

"A hundred bucks," said Hugh.

Scooter stepped into the center of the group. "Why don't we make it a thousand?"

13

May

Nadine was aware that her laughter was drawing looks from the other patrons, but she couldn't stop herself. Who would have guessed the stoic fireman who'd saved her from a life in a motorized wheelchair and who had such a dour outlook on the world would be hiding this streak of humor? She not only loved listening to his stories but found that he liked hers, which was refreshing, because until she met Zak she hadn't known any guys who were good listeners.

They'd played tennis again, their seventh time, on the indoor courts at Seattle University and now they were having brunch together, a habit established after that first match: coffee or brunch, one or the other, depending on how long they played and what each had scheduled for the day. She never did call the police about the break-in to her car, mostly because she was 99 percent certain the culprit was Scooter, who had a key and who was likely to pull just that sort of stunt if he caught her playing tennis with another man.

It had taken her more than a year to realize two things about William Potter III. First: even though he was financially secure for life, he was more adrift emotionally than just about anybody she knew. Second: he was a bully, pure and simple, and probably always would be. Once she'd cemented those facts into her thinking, she knew she had to break up with him, and she did it in May. Largely because she made the mistake of announcing it in his car, the breakup took almost four hours. They were parked near Chism Park on Lake Washington, and he told her he wasn't going to take her home until she changed her mind. They argued for hours, but eventually he relented and took her home.

Even though Zak still wasn't much of a challenge for her on the tennis court, she looked forward to her matches with him, as well as to the after-match coffee sessions. He was playing better now, and despite her strenuous attempt to skunk him, he'd managed to win a couple of games that morning. Zak was the only male she'd ever played who didn't get irked when she whipped him. In fact, despite how hard he fought to win, she had a feeling he almost enjoyed getting beat by her.

"I broke up with my boyfriend," she said, wondering why revealing this to Zak made her so nervous. Was it because she was afraid this announcement might change their casual relationship, or because she was afraid it wouldn't?

"Okay. Sorry to hear that. How about a movie?"

"I think it might be too soon to go out with other people."

"We're just friends, right? This won't be a romance or anything. I mean, I won't send you flowers or chocolates or a watermelon. I just don't like going to movies by myself."

"A watermelon?" They both laughed. "Okay. Sure, then."

Their first date was disappointingly platonic. Nadine wasn't sure what she'd been expecting, but they hadn't held hands in the theater line in the cold or done anything more than chat the way they always chatted. She liked talking with him, liked being with him, and had the feeling he liked being with her, too.

He was twenty-eight years old and lived in a world of men and women who did things she could only dream of, while she was a nineteen-year-old student who still resided mostly at home, was answerable to Mom and Dad every night, and had never done anything more thrilling than wrecking the Lexus her father had purchased for her eighteenth birthday.

Before the trailers began, Zak leaned over and said, "Would you like some popcorn?"

"Sure."

"With butter or without?"

"Without, I guess. I am supposed to be in training."

"Just a little butter?"

"No, thank you."

"Something to drink?"

"A Diet Pepsi."

"Jujubes?"

"No, thank you."

"Sure you don't want any butter?"

"No butter."

"Licorice Whips?"

"No, thank you."

"Dots?"

"Would you just go?"

"Okay, but what about M&M's?"

"I don't want M&M's. Just go," Nadine said, a little too loudly, realizing their neighbors in the packed house were glancing at her. It was hard sometimes for her to tell when he was pulling her leg. She laughed quietly. She'd never met anybody quite so bent on making everything just a little bit fun.

14

Zak and Nadine were on a jaunt to see Nadine's grandmother in Broadmoor, an exclusive, gated community in Engine 34's district where her father had been raised.

Since she was old enough to walk, her grandmother had kept up with her comings and goings and had recently been following her relationship with Scooter, though not with approval. Now, learning that she had a new guy in her life, Nana had insisted she bring Zak around so she could inspect him. Nadine thought it would be tricky to convince Zak to visit her grandmother, but after he learned she had been arrested back in the 1960s for protesting the Vietnam War and more recently for a sit-in at city hall to spotlight the city's poor treatment of the homeless, he said he would love to meet her.

Nana was going to get along famously with Zak. For one thing, they both had a no-nonsense approach to life. For another, they both believed humankind was slowly but wantonly destroying the planet. Plus, each had an offbeat sense of humor she was sure the other would appreciate.

Even though the May weather had turned nippy and clouds were rolling in, Zak and Nadine both wore shorts with light jackets and athletic shoes. Zak mentioned he couldn't recall ever wearing anything but athletic shoes, and Nadine said she couldn't, either. She wondered if it was silly to be thinking they had a lot in common because they both wore Nikes. But of course there was more; there was always more. There was what her friend Lindsey called the "indefinable chemical attraction" that either exists or doesn't exist between every person on the planet. It definitely existed between Nadine and Zak, though neither had acted on it yet. There was the way Zak listened to her talk about tennis or her religious beliefs or school, interested in what she was saying in a way nobody else in her life was interested, except perhaps Nana. There was the way he encouraged and admired her athletic ambitions—her parents condescendingly regarded her sport as nothing more than a "stage" she would outgrow, and Scooter had actively tried to discourage it.

Nadine was conscious of the fact that this was only the second time she and Zak had met without tennis as an excuse. She was also aware that Zak looked on this as a benchmark in their relationship. "Meeting relatives," he said, grinning, when he picked her up. "Big step."

"I suppose," she said. She tried not to think of the two of them as "dating," mostly because during the breakup with Scooter she'd told him she wasn't seeing anybody, and that she specifically wasn't seeing that "fireman dude." If he found out she was dating him now he'd think she'd been dating him all along, and that might cause even more problems than she already had. Scooter disliked Zak for a number of reasons besides the obvious—Zak's interest in her. To Scooter's way of thinking, Zak's secondary offenses were his job as a firefighter and the fact that he was older, as little sense as either made.

"He's a control freak," Lindsey said to her about Scooter. "Face it. He wants to control every event in your life. Everybody you see or talk to, and everywhere you go."

Now that she'd had time to review their relationship over the past year, she realized Lindsey was right—Scooter had done his best to dictate her own life to her, disapproving of her friends, her choice of college, her love of tennis, even her belief in the Lord.

Scooter had been even more demanding these past months, moody, and . . . well, let's face it, horny, which posed a problem for someone bent on remaining a virgin until her wedding night. Most of their dates had ended in some sort of argument about sex. In all the time she'd spent with Zak, they had yet to argue about anything. It was nice to know relationships didn't have to be one titanic struggle after another, or that she didn't have to be defending her honor every time she left the house.

She was casually comfortable with Zak in a way she hadn't been with anyone before, and she liked that. She liked it a lot. They seemed to be forming a relationship of equals, something she hadn't seen in her own family, where her father more or less ran the show.

Today Zak was driving his van, which was full of tools and paint cans, a complete contrast with Scooter's immaculate BMW 3 Series or her own Lexus. She remembered the day Scooter found out she'd been meeting Zak for tennis. "You're not going out with some asshole who drives a van, are you?"

"We're just friends. I can have friends. You can't run everything in my life."

"No guy is just friends with a girl who looks like you. He wants to fuck you."

"Would you please watch your language? I know that's not true."

"Of course it's true. Mark my words. Some asshole firefighter in a van. And nearly ten years older than you. Jesus Christ!" He'd been furious over the breakup and, as far as she knew, was still furious. The situation was delicate, because Scooter remained Kasey's best friend and was in and out of the house every day.

She and Zak had been talking rather casually about each other's families when Nadine said, "So what was your family life like after your sister died?"

"You really want to know?"

"I want to know."

"None of us ever really got over her death. My father started drinking and scrapping with Mom over trivial stuff, and then Mom threw him out, and later they got divorced. Mom took solace in a new life that alternated between religion and prescription drugs. When she was out of meds or couldn't talk a doctor into prescribing more, she would take up another religion. As soon as she had a fresh supply, the religion would drop away. The religion part of it pulled me into an endless series of church meetings, Sundays, Wednesdays, Thursday nights, and sometimes all day Saturday. It depended on the denomination. I figured if it was helping my mom cope, then I could put in the time. When she wasn't praying, she would get juiced up on painkillers and diet pills. Booze was a vice she relegated to my father."

"Sounds awful."

"I had Stacy, and she was great. When I was fourteen, I got into bike racing. It wasn't easy, because racing gear isn't cheap and we didn't have a lot of money, so I mowed lawns in the summer to pay for a bike and parts. Looking back, I think I got into bikes to make myself into the person I wanted to be. A lot of kids from troubled families find things to throw themselves into as a way of subsuming the self."

"You think I'm doing that with tennis?"

"Doubtful. Would you say you're from a troubled family?"

"No. I wouldn't say that at all. So how did you become a fire-fighter?"

"I graduated high school with pretty good grades, went to community college for part of a year, and then, when there was no more money for school, got a job painting houses. It wasn't bad work, and the people in the company I worked for treated us great, but one day one of the other painters got on with the fire department. I visited him at his station and thought it looked like a pretty good gig."

"What about the rest of your family?"

"After Charlene's death, my father spent fifteen years drinking. He had a pretty good job for the first few years and paid child support, but after a while the money stopped coming and he disappeared. We thought he might be dead. Later he told me he'd worked a succession of small-time jobs, mostly physical labor, making a fraction of what he was used to and barely keeping his head above water. The household was different after my mom became the sole breadwinner. We'd been living high on the hog until the divorce, but afterward a lot of my well-off friends didn't feel comfortable around a kid who didn't even have money for a movie ticket. Then, when I was seventeen, Mom got cancer. She fought through it, took the treatments, and declared bankruptcy two years later. The cancer went away, but a year and a half later it reappeared, except that this time she didn't tell anybody. It was just about two years after that when she died."

"That's so sad."

"She died a couple of days after my twenty-first birthday. She just didn't know how to fight the good fight a second time. Not without money or friends, and she'd alienated most of her friends with the drugs."

"I'm sorry. And your father? What's he doing? I mean, besides rebuilding our pool house."

"He lives with me. He's doing okay. He's a nice guy. Everybody likes him. He goes off on a bender about twice a year, very quietly, disappears for a few days, and then he's back. I don't really understand the psychology of it, because the rest of the time he won't touch a drop."

"I like him. He's nice."

"He *is* a nice man. He used to be a lot more outgoing, but somewhere along the line his confidence wore thin."

"And your sister? She told me she was on the swim team in high school."

"Placed in the districts and third at the state meet her senior year."

"She went missing for a number of years?"

"You heard this from your brother?"

"Some of it."

"What else did he say?"

"Not much. I mean, we don't talk much these days," Nadine

said, hoping he wouldn't sniff out her white lie. Out of allegiance to her brother and embarrassment for Zak's sister, she didn't want to tell Zak that Kasey had deemed Stacy poor white trash and a slut.

"I love her, but she's extremely independent and resents it when anybody gives her advice."

"She lives with you and your father?"

"I find it strange that we couldn't be a family when we were supposed to be, but now that we're adults we're all under one roof. I sometimes wonder what Mom would have said."

Nadine tried to figure out whose father was the more eccentric, hers, who slept in an oxygen sleeping chamber like Michael Jackson and who'd had seven remodels done on their house in the past seven years—or Zak's, who had once been a corporate attorney and now pounded nails for a living.

Zak drove north along Twenty-third toward Madison, which was well over a mile from the station. On Madison, the only street in Seattle to touch water at both ends, they would travel northeast until they hit Broadmoor, where the sumptuous houses were built around a golf course that included the Broadmoor Country Club.

"I bet you were always a good girl," Zak said.

"I was good to the point of being stupid. Once when I was about eleven I found a ten-dollar bill on the sidewalk outside the school. Any other eleven-year-old would have chalked it up to good luck and pocketed it, but I pinned a notice to the school bulletin board, thinking one of my fellow students had dropped it. Of course I got about four hundred replies. I guess I was kind of famous around the school for that one."

"I bet you get straight A's."

"You know I do. Actually, I never even got dirty as a little girl. It's embarrassing to admit. Even Nana urged me to do something wrong once in a while. The worst thing I ever did was once I wore a T-shirt to school that said, OBJECTS UNDER THIS SHIRT APPEAR LARGER IN REAL LIFE."

He was afraid to laugh for fear of offending her, but not laughing might offend her, too, so he settled for a smile and chuckle, making a point of not glancing at her nearly flat chest.

"I bought it on a whim, then one of my friends dared me to wear it to school, so I wore a sweater over it till I left the house and then I took the sweater off at school. In second period I got invited to the principal's office. I never did anything like that again."

At that point Zak couldn't help laughing. Nadine was so timid but wanted so badly to be bold. "You've got a good heart, Nadine. Don't ever lose it."

"I wish I could say that was true, but it's not. I was good because I was scared of getting in trouble. Now I toe the line with our Lord and Savior, but I'm really not sure if I'm toeing the line because I want to, or because I don't want to end up in a hot place."

"You believe there's a physical hell?"

"There can't be a kingdom of heaven without a hell. It doesn't make sense."

"Right."

Zak turned off Twenty-third Avenue onto Marion, much earlier than he'd planned, and began driving residential streets, making what appeared to be random turns. "What are you doing?" Nadine asked.

"You know a guy drives a BMW Three Series? Black."

Nadine swiveled around in her seat and peered out the rear window. "Oh, my . . . gosh. It's Scooter."

"Your ex?"

"He keeps pestering me. He says we're going to get married someday, and I'm just delaying the inevitable."

"You're sure you broke up?"

"I told him we were finished ten days ago. Since then he's been following me and calling and coming over to the house whenever he feels like it. Kasey was there the other day, Saturday, and Scooter came over, supposedly to see him, and stayed all day. He kept coming to the door of my room trying to get in. You don't know how creepy it is having him in the house."

"You tell your parents?"

"They're on his side. They think we should get back together. They've never seen his dark side and think I'm blowing it all out of proportion."

"Just how dark is his dark side? Is he going to pull alongside and fill my door with bullets?"

"Of course not. He's just kind of unpredictable right now."

"That's not very reassuring." Zak hadn't liked Scooter from the beginning, hadn't liked him any more than he'd liked Nadine's brother, and he knew jilted suitors, ex-boyfriends, and former husbands could be trouble. In this case he wasn't worried personally—he could take care of himself—he was worried about Nadine.

Zak drove around a block, then around another block, and still Scooter trailed them. It wasn't possible to slip away from a BMW in his underpowered van, so Zak picked up his cell phone. "What are you doing?"

"Calling the cops."

"Don't. Please?" She touched his arm lightly. "Please?"

"Why not?"

"Just . . . I don't want any trouble. He's a friend of the family, and his father and my father are friends. I don't want any of this getting out. It would be humiliating for all of us. Besides, he won't get into Broadmoor. We can tell the guard and they won't let him through."

"What he's doing is criminal harassment. Stalking."

"You would be doing me a big favor it you didn't call the police. I'll see him again today. Kasey's home for a few days, so he'll be over at the house. I'll tell him to stop it. I'll tell him you were going to call the police. That should scare him."

"How'd you get hooked up with such a control freak?"

"Control . . . How did you know that?"

Zak rolled his eyes so Nadine couldn't see. "Wild guess." What did she know about this kind of man? She was nineteen. She'd probably never run into anybody like William Potter III before. "Okay. I won't call the police, but you have to do something for me in return."

"What?"

"Every time he follows you or you see him on the street, I want you to write it down and note the time, the date, and who you were with. Build a file. Keep it somewhere he won't find it. That way if you ever have to go to court to get a restraining order, instead of saying, *He follows me all the time,* you'll have a record with times and dates."

"We're not going to end up in court."

"Promise me."

"Okay, but we've known him since I was in the second grade. I'm only doing this to keep the police from getting involved. Scooter's pushy, but he's not a lawbreaker."

"I already told you how many laws he's breaking."

"He thinks he's still in love with me."

"No. He thinks he owns you. That's an entirely different proposition."

15

August

"Okay, okay, okay. I'll bet a million bucks. Giancarlo's bike against a truck. Any one of them trucks. Pick the fastest. Myself, I'd take that Land Rover."

"Hugh, you don't have a million dollars," said Zak.

"Okay, a hundred. Bet a hundred dollars you can't beat Giancarlo down that hill."

"To the bridge?" asked Scooter.

"To the bridge," said Hugh, growing excited.

"Forget the hundred. I said a grand. You have a thousand dollars?" Scooter stepped close enough that Hugh backed away.

"Sure."

"Let's see it."

"I'm not stupid. I don't carry it everywhere I go, but I got it. *You* got a thousand dollars?"

Scooter pulled out his wallet and fanned a sheaf of hundreds.

"Why don't we just forget the money?" said Morse. "And Giancarlo, you don't want to do this, do you?"

"I don't mind."

"What's the matter?" Scooter stepped close and once again forced Hugh to step back. "Losing your nerve?"

"A thousand dollars," said Zak. "He's good for it."

"Are you going to guarantee it?"

"If that's what you need."

"Then you have a deal," Scooter said, staring at Zak with the arrogance and contempt of somebody who knew in advance that he was on the winning team. Somehow the bet had become an issue between Scooter and Zak. It was outrageous, because Zak had never bet a thousand dollars on anything in his life. They were like a couple of bragging schoolkids and Zak knew it, but knowing it wasn't enough to prevent him from playing it out. Zak could see that every man and woman in the Jeep camp believed it was inevitable the truck would win and the cyclists were fools. The bike group, on the other hand, appeared divided about the possible outcome. While Zak knew Giancarlo Barrett was the best natural downhiller he'd ever ridden with and that he thrived on competition, he also knew the bike Giancarlo was riding wasn't a full-fledged downhill model and this run wouldn't be his fastest.

Jennifer said, "Scooter, it's not a fair race and you know it."

"Hey, this retard wants to give me his money, who am I to stop him?"

"I'm not a retard," Hugh said. "I had a brain injury."

Hugh had put on a lot of great drama at Station 6, but he was on his way to an Oscar with this. "We shouldn't be gambling," said Roger Bloomquist, glancing around uncertainly at his friends. "Maybe we should keep this friendly."

"There's nothing friendlier than a thousand dollars changing hands," said Scooter with a smirk. "We'll be friends for life. Isn't that right, Hugh?" Scooter laughed viciously, spit erupting through his gritted teeth.

"We're already friends for life," Hugh said. "All my friends are for life."

"You up for it?" Zak asked Giancarlo as the two of them walked to the road and stared down the hill.

"I think so." The steepest section was the first twenty yards, with an almost sheer rock wall on the left and a knoll on the right, the knoll giving way to an open field that seemed pasted to the side of the mountain. It wasn't going to be pretty if one of them hit the rock wall or went off into the field, which was actually steeper and more treacherous than the road itself.

The smoke Zak had noticed in the distant hills had grown in volume, and the sun had sunk low and was lighting up the scattered pink clouds on the horizon, painting them umber at the edges, a filigreed brownish purple higher up.

The narrow, twisty road had been blasted out of the mountain, leaving a base of solid rock—a pity, since Giancarlo hadn't brought along the plastic knee and shin pads, the rib protectors, or arm braces he wore when he did serious downhilling. He was taking chances. So was Scooter, because if either the bike or the truck slid off the road, it could easily lead to a fatality, which made the entire affair something just short of insanity.

"We shouldn't be doing this. It's plain nuts," said Zak.

"I'm game unless you want to call it off," Giancarlo said.

"You want me to call it off?"

"I kind of want to fuck these guys over. They're getting on my nerves."

"Anything happens, it'll be on all of our heads, but I'm not going to stop it."

"You hate that Scooter guy, don't you?"

"Oh, yeah."

"And he hates you, too. I saw that right off."

It didn't take long for both parties to agree on a set of rules. The track was tight and treacherous enough that everybody agreed the race should be run as a time trial; Giancarlo would go first because he would throw up less dust, then fifteen seconds later Scooter would leave in Chuck Finnigan's truck. They would race from where they were standing to the middle of the bridge that spanned the North Fork, a distance of roughly half a mile, all precipitously downhill.

Zak thought the Ford was a poor choice because it was high and prone to tipping, but the consensus in the Jeep camp was that it had more rubber on the road than any of the other vehicles and thus would hold the track better. Fifteen seconds seemed like too short an interval, but the Jeep camp refused to concede any more than that.

There would be stopwatches at the top and the bottom of the hill, everyone in communication via walkie-talkies the Jeep people had brought with them. If the truck caught the bicycle, that would speak for itself, but otherwise, in order to win, Scooter had to reach the center point of the bridge less than fifteen seconds behind Giancarlo.

While Scooter talked to Chuck about the Ford's quirks and Giancarlo went back up the hillside to get his bike, Zak, accompanied by Nadine and one of her friends, walked partway down the roadbed.

"This is the stupidest thing I've ever heard of," said Nadine.

"I know. I know."

Kasey, Jennifer, Stephens, and Morse piled into Kasey's Porsche and drove to the far side of the bridge to do the officiating at the bottom of the mountain. As they passed Zak, Kasey leaned out the open driver's window and said, "This is going to be a slaughter."

Stephens was in the shotgun seat, talking to somebody in the back. Zak caught just enough to realize he was explaining the difference between mountain bikes that were built specifically for downhill runs and the cross-country bike Giancarlo would be riding, a generalist bike built to do almost everything but with no particular specialty. Downhill bikes were heavier, the extra weight helping to buffer the jolting. They had beefier shocks, larger brakes, and were designed to make a rider feel comfortable going down a hill, often with a smaller rear wheel to tip the bike to a more level position.

It took surprisingly little time to get everybody into position, Scooter in Chuck's Ford, revving the motor, and Giancarlo with his helmet, heavy gloves, and, just in case, a pair of long pants tied at the cuffs so they didn't catch in the chain. If he crashed, the pants might save some skin.

Officiating up top would be Fred and Chuck, Zak, Nadine, one of her girlfriends, and Hugh.

The road dropped steeply for the first 150 yards—so steeply, most people wouldn't ride a bicycle down it at any speed—then curved slightly to the left. It straightened out for an eighth of a mile, and it was on this straighter stretch that the grade was embedded with washboard ridges created by trucks spinning their wheels. The washboard would be the trickiest part. If the Ford's shocks or the bicycle's suspension weren't tuned perfectly, the corrugated sections could easily send them out of control. Zak hoped nobody crashed. If Giancarlo went down, he would never forgive himself, and if Scooter wrecked the truck, it could be fatal.

After the straight section came a sharp bend to the right, and while the road on this section was bare rock, there were still areas with gravel and smaller loose rocks that could cause a loss of control. To make matters worse, the steep corner was off camber, which would conspire to throw the contestants toward a scree studded with old stumps. It was from this corner that one had an unobstructed view out over the rolling hills toward Seattle and south toward North Bend.

Past the corner, the road had more curves in it and some gravel, but the grades were less threatening. At the bottom it turned into a chute that flattened out for eighty yards as it crossed the intersection and fed onto the bridge. Zak figured whoever got around the first sharp, off-camber corner with the most speed would take it.

"I figure it the same way," said Giancarlo at the starting line.

"You going to win?"

"I don't know." Giancarlo grinned, and the dimples in his cheeks deepened. "I've never seen him drive a truck."

Twenty feet away Scooter and Fred were whooping over the roar of the Ford's motor while Chuck spoke to Kasey on a two-way Motorola walkie-talkie.

Nadine came alongside Zak. "Zak, this is too dangerous. Tell him it's too dangerous, Lindsey."

Her girlfriend looked wide-eyed at Zak and said, "I kind of want to see it. I mean, a thousand dollars."

"Oh, honestly, Lindsey."

"Giancarlo knows what he's doing," said Zak.

After Chuck drew a line across the road with a stick, the truck and bicycle lined up on it. Chuck pressed the button on the walkie-talkie in his massive hand and said, *"Everything ready at the bottom of the hill?"*

"Ready."

"Everything ready up here?" Chuck asked. Now that they were up against it, Zak could see that Giancarlo was jittery. He hoped it was only adrenaline doing its job, because the last thing they needed was for Giancarlo to get the heebie-jeebies and crap out on one of the corners. He'd never seen Giancarlo this nervous. Not even when they were crawling into house fires during drill school.

16

"On your mark. Get set. Go!" said Chuck Finnigan, waving a makeshift flag.

Zak had been holding Giancarlo and his bicycle upright, so when the flag went down Zak gave him a good, hard shove. Giancarlo sat far back on his seat, which he'd lowered. Several of the onlookers gasped when they saw the speed he reached before the first corner. Even to Zak's experienced eye the blinding acceleration made him look like a bullet.

"My God," said Lindsey.

"I thought Scooter was going to win," said Nadine in a tone that made it clear she wasn't so sure now.

"He sure is a missile," said Hugh.

"Wait'll you see my brother's goddamn truck," said Fred.

Everybody watched Chuck as he timed the fifteen-second interval before Scooter could start. He dropped the flag a second early, and the Ford's tires squealed. "Go! Go, you bastard!"

Shooting small chunks of rock and gravel out from the wheels, the truck spurted forward and careened down the narrow trail, slewing to the left and then to the right on the first curve, heading perilously for the far edge. For a split second Zak thought Scooter was going to veer off the road, but at the last minute he regained the proper trajectory and roared down the hill and around the corner.

Everybody sprinted through the encampment and down the trail to the escarpment, from which they would be able to see the finish line. Zak was first, arriving in time to spot Giancarlo streaking down the rutted road and disappearing from view in a blur. "Where are they?" Nadine asked, breathlessly.

"Behind those trees. Watch the bridge." As he spoke, bicycle and rider flew across the bridge, kicking up a cloud of dust as fine as flour. Zak had never seen anybody go that fast on a mountain bike.

"There he is!" screamed Nadine.

Bouncing as it disappeared behind the trees, the truck reappeared on the same stretch of road where they'd seen Giancarlo. If there was one thing Zak could tell even from this distance, it was that Scooter had never fully regained control of the Ford, which was slewing wildly over the lower washboard sections. Moments later the truck zipped across the concrete bridge and shot up the road a quarter of a mile, trailed by huge pillows of dust that enveloped the finish-line observers in a sheet of brown and gray as tall as a house.

"How much did we win by?" asked Fred.

His brother stood on top of a nearby boulder and got on his walkie-talkie. *"Race start to race finish. It was my truck, right?"*

"Negatory," came the response on his handset. *"Negatory, big buddy. The bike won by three seconds."*

"Three seconds?" Fred said. "Three seconds? That's bullshit. If Chuck had been driving . . . Scooter doesn't know how to handle that rig. Did you see him?"

"Whooee," Hugh said, leaping from one rock to another. "I'm rich." They straggled back in three distinct groups, the white Ford, the Porsche, and Giancarlo pedaling alone up the mountainside in bike shorts, his long pants slung around his neck. The Jeep group was visibly morose and somewhat dumbfounded over the results, while the girls seemed to think it was marvelous that a man on a bicycle had outraced a truck. Zak continued to sit on the lookout rock while everyone except Nadine went back through camp to greet the returning racers. Nadine touched Zak's shoulder and said, "You knew that was going to happen, didn't you?"

Zak watched the colors in the sky. The sun would sink in another hour, but right now, squatting above the horizon in the haze and lacking the cookie-cutter crispness it usually punched in the atmosphere, it was simply a large, pale, unfocused yellow gap in the purple western sky.

By the time Zak and Nadine got back to the camp, Fred, Chuck, Kasey, and Scooter were huddled together. The girls were in a clump talking and watching Hugh perform a victory dance, slapping his mouth, whoo-whooing, and generally making an ass of himself.

"Shut up, you fucking retard," Scooter said, rushing over to Hugh and slapping him across the bicycle helmet four or five times in quick succession. Hugh cowered and raised his arms to protect himself. Before anybody could get close enough to stop Scooter, he'd slapped Hugh across the face and knocked his glasses to the ground. Hugh started crying, or giving a pretty good imitation of it, then dropped to his hands and knees, where he searched ineffectually for his glasses.

Nadine rushed to Hugh's side, followed by every woman in camp.

"Geez, you're a dick," said Jennifer Moore.

While Hugh was being pampered by the women, Giancarlo stepped closer to Zak and said, "He better watch himself."

Hugh, bolstered by the women's attentions and clearly feeling invulnerable now that he had the camp's sympathy, skipped over to Scooter and held out his hand. "Pay up, big daddy."

"Fuck you, you moron."

"Gotta pay," Hugh said, glancing around uncertainly. "That's my thousand dollars in your wallet."

"You deaf or something? Get away from me, fucker. That was a fluke. It would never happen again in a million years."

"It was no fluke," Zak said. "Giancarlo could race you down that hill all night and you'd never beat him."

"So what's Giancarlo, some sort of downhill prodigy? You bastards. You threw in a ringer, didn't you?"

"Calm down," said Kasey. "It's not like your driving didn't suck."

Scooter turned to Zak and said, "You talk tough when your friends are taking the risks. Let's see you get on the bike and try it."

"Pay Hugh and I'll think about it."

"You'll race me if I pay the moron?"

"You pay Hugh, I'll race."

"Another thousand?" Zak was surprised at how keen Scooter was to engage in a second wager after losing the first. "Or are you chicken? Tell you what. I'll drive with one hand tied behind my back. Better yet, I'll drive drunk."

"I thought you were already driving drunk," Zak said.

"Fuck you."

"Pay Hugh."

"Sure. Why not? You lose, the two of you pay me back the thousand tonight and the second thousand when the banks open Monday." Scooter took out his wallet and counted out ten one-hundred-dollar bills, whereupon Hugh danced away counting and recounting the bills. Even to Zak, who knew this was an act, the exuberant gloating grew bothersome. Zak borrowed Giancarlo's bike but retrieved his own helmet and shoes from camp, strapped on the gear and rode around for a minute or two, then pedaled out of sight higher on the road, turned back down the hill, and let it rip for a hundred yards in an abbreviated practice run. He hit an unexpected rock in the road, bounced, and almost crashed before regaining control.

"Sit back and let it roll," Giancarlo advised when he got to the starting line. "Feather the brakes before the first right-hand turn then don't touch them through the turn. Feather them a little bit before the last set of washboard, then case up and let it roll. Watch out for the gravel at the bottom."

Nadine and her girlfriends jumped into the Porsche while everybody else remained at the starting line. Before they left, Nadine came over and kissed Zak's cheek, then glanced over to make sure Scooter saw it. "Good luck."

Zak knew the kiss would only make Scooter angrier and wondered for the first time if Nadine was using him against Scooter in some sort of battle in which Zak had already been nominated to be the loser. He didn't think Nadine had that much guile—any guile, for that matter—but it was something he'd never considered until that moment.

Scooter watched Nadine climb into the Porsche SUV twenty yards away. "Pussy," Scooter said, winking conspiratorially at Zak as if they were best buddies. "You spend nine months trying to get *out* and the next ninety years doing your damnedest to get *back in*."

"Shut up."

"Don't tell me you don't want to fuck that."

"Just get in the truck and try not to kill yourself."

"Sure. Fine." He stepped close and said, "But I'm going to catch you and it's going to be the sorriest 'accident' you ever saw. There's not going to be a thing any of your friends will be able to do about it."

"I think I'm going to give the money to Greenpeace," Zak said. "Just to piss you off."

17

May

Zak couldn't help feeling twinges of envy during his first visit to the Seattle Tennis Club. Generally, when the outdoor courts were damp, Nadine opted to play at Seattle U, but this week the custodial staff's summer floor-polishing program had rendered it unavailable.

After four weeks of getting trounced almost daily, Zak had finally managed to win a few hard-fought points but no games. He suspected his improvement was dispiriting to Nadine, who voiced fears that she was subconsciously allowing him points. The notion that she might be easing up because he was a guy was unthinkable to her. "You do any better, I'm going to see a sports psychiatrist," Nadine said, joking.

"Don't worry about it," Zak said. "I still haven't won a game."

"But I haven't skunked you in a week."

"You *like* me. I make you nervous."

"I do like you, but you don't make me that nervous."

"Don't bet on it." Zak loved her competitiveness and knew the comment would make her try harder.

They played for an hour, during which she became more and more distracted and then finally excused herself. "I'll be back in a couple of minutes."

Zak took the occasion to get a drink of water and visit the men's room. When he got back to the court, she still had not returned. After twenty minutes he spotted her near a Coke machine on the far side of a gaggle of middle-aged women who played in some sort of June Cleaver league, all in tennis whites and with three-hundred-dollar rackets under their arms. As he drew closer, Zak saw that Nadine was talking to a man in a baseball cap and dark sunglasses. Scooter.

Zak negotiated his way around the group of women and approached the couple. "What the hell are you doing here?" Scooter asked.

"I *was* playing tennis." Zak stood close to Nadine. "You all right?"

"Scooter and I were just talking. I'll be there in a minute."

Zak turned to Scooter. "Stalking old friends?"

Scooter's face revolved through a medley of disbelief, disgust, and then antipathy. "What are you talking about?"

"I'm talking about you showing up at almost all of our tennis games."

"Fuck you, buddy." Glowering at Nadine, Scooter added, "Jesus, pal. My family were founding members of this club. I can be here whenever I want, and unlike you, I don't have to ride in on someone else's membership card. And here's a bulletin for you. Nadine's way out of your league."

"She's better off with a stalker? Is that what you're saying?"

"You keep this up, I'm going to speak to my attorneys about slander."

Zak had a feeling they were headed toward a physical confrontation. There was no doubt in his mind that he was fitter and stronger than Scooter—Zak was six feet one, slim, and muscular; Scooter was a few inches shorter and forty pounds heavier, the extra bulk consisting of the kind of baby fat some people carried into their twenties—but according to Nadine, her ex-boyfriend had taken years of martial arts training.

"You broke into her car, didn't you?"

"What?"

"You heard me. You broke into Nadine's car at Green Lake."

Zak knew and hoped Nadine did, too, that the proof of guilt was the way Scooter's face went through a catalog of feigned reactions. Even behind the dark sunglasses you could tell his eyes were flitting all around the room. He was nervous as a cornered ferret.

"What makes you think I have a key to Nadine's car?"

"How did you know it was done with a key?"

"You little firehouse fag. When are you going to realize you don't have anything to offer her? On top of everything else, your family and her family are going to fit together like fine cheese and horse turds. I mean, Jesus, your dad's working on the pool house like a wetback."

"Scooter," Nadine said. "Stop it."

"I'm not going to stop it. Somebody needs to say this. If everybody in your family's too polite to tell this guy what they're thinking, then I'll just have to step up to the plate. They don't like you, pal. None of them likes you. Nadine's parents and Kasey think you're nothing but a gold digger." Zak knew from the way Nadine tensed up that Scooter wasn't inventing these accusations. "We all know you're after her money. And don't dare tell me I'm stalking my own girlfriend."

"*Ex*-girlfriend."

"*Girlfriend*. I never broke up with her."

"Scooter," Nadine said, "I broke up with you, and you know it."

"The crux of the matter is I'm right for Nadine, I can provide her with the material comforts she needs in life, and you can't."

"I'm going to support myself," Nadine said. "I'm going to be a social worker. And you won't be around."

"The point is," Scooter continued, throwing Nadine a withering look, "I can treat her the way she deserves to be treated, and somebody like you . . . I mean, do you even know how to order wine or use a salad fork?"

"Come on, Zak," Nadine said, tugging Zak's arm. "Let's go play tennis."

Scooter and Zak glared at each other for several long seconds without moving. "Nadine, it matters where people come from. Look at his father. And that oversexed sister with the Dolly Parton boobs? Kasey said—"

Zak started toward Scooter, but Nadine pulled his arm and managed to swing him around in a half circle as if he were on a tether. He knew Nadine was strong, but she surprised him with just how strong. Scooter had crouched in a defensive stance. "Come on, motherfucker. Try me."

"You fool," said Nadine. "I told you I never want to see you again."

"You know you love me." Scooter smiled a smile that in another time and under other circumstances might have been charming.

"Get out," Nadine said. By now everybody in the corridor was watching, and Scooter, realizing he'd become the center of attention, ambled toward the door with a deliberate slowness and left the building without looking back.

When they got to the court, Nadine said, "I don't feel like tennis anymore."

"He was watching us play, wasn't he?"

"How can I stop him? He's a member here. Plus, I have to see him socially. He comes to the house to see Kasey."

After she'd gathered up her warm-up clothes, she started crying. Zak put his arm around her shoulders as they walked out of the court area.

"I'm okay. It's just . . . I ran into him at Bellevue Square two days ago. And today I saw him over there by the door while we were playing. He talks about taking care of me, but when we were going together he totally took me for granted unless there was another guy threatening to pay attention to me. He's so jealous. We hardly ever spent any time talking like you and I do. It was always, 'Let's go do something with Kasey and the guys.' Or, 'Let's go to my house and fool around.'"

They ended up on a bench in one of the unused outdoor courts as clouds scudded across the sky at intervals, exposing patches of blue behind them. The spotty sunshine warmed Zak considerably. "I'm sorry I'm such a baby," Nadine said.

"Does your family really think I'm chasing you for your money?"

"I'm sorry he said that. That was just embarrassing."

"Do they?"

"They don't know you like I do. Besides, you didn't chase me. I chased you. That's how we became friends in the first place. *I* made it happen."

"What do you mean?"

She giggled, the laughter a release from the stress and tears. "I shouldn't have said that."

"No, I want to hear this."

"I told Mom to call you for that pool house job."

"You what?"

"When we were all at your fire station I learned you did remodeling. I told Mom to call you. The only trouble was your father took the job, and he was there for weeks before you showed up. I was still going with Scooter, but I had my eye on you. Maybe it was because you saved me in the wreck. That day you showed up, I got out of the pool, took a super-quick shower, and ran downstairs to meet you."

"Is any of this true?"

"It's all true."

They watched the clouds scudding across the sky.

Zak knew she was working up her nerve to tell him something that had been bubbling beneath the surface every time Scooter's name came up.

"I don't even know how I got into this. We were just all of a sudden going together. I mean, we were dating once in a while, and then he wanted me to tell him I wouldn't see anyone else, and I wasn't seeing anyone else right then so it seemed like an easy thing to say. And after that he got so he wanted to know where I was all day. At first I was flattered. No guy had ever taken that much interest in me. He used to call my cell phone when I was in class or at practice. I started turning it off, but that only made him mad. And we used to go out on these long dates where he'd drive me somewhere and wouldn't take me home . . ."

"Unless what?"

"I didn't say unless."

"But it's there in your voice."

"Favors, he called them."

"You don't have to tell me the rest."

"No, I need somebody to hear this, and you're the only person in the world I feel comfortable talking to right now."

"I'm listening."

"The whole thing happened in increments. We got into this thing where we would go to his house or if his folks were hanging around we'd go somewhere in his car and he would ask me to touch him. At first I didn't want to, but he wouldn't take me home unless I did. He knew I wanted to be a virgin on my wedding night and he said he respected that, but he claimed what we were doing didn't have anything to do with being a virgin. He said it was a matter of healthy living and if a guy didn't get some release he could get sick. So I would touch him and then . . . well . . ."

"Please don't tell me this."

"No, I do. I have to tell somebody. He said every girl he'd ever dated had done it. He said it was what couples did. That it was no big deal. At the time, I was thinking we would eventually get married. He hadn't asked me or anything, but it seemed to be the place we were headed. I talked to my pastor, who more or less told me any expression of love short of intercourse was okay. When I tried to pin him down on definitions, he got nervous and cut off the conversation.

"It was always this struggle, this big argument, and then I would give in, if only to get some peace, and afterward he would drive me home with this self-satisfied smirk on his face. You must think I'm horrible."

"I think you did everything you could to remain within the boundaries of your faith."

"Despite how much he says he loves me, sometimes I feel Scooter really hates me."

When Zak put his arm around Nadine's shoulders, she collapsed against him. They sat that way for a long time, breathing in concert.

"One time," Nadine said, "I was getting the flu, and I told him I could hardly breathe and I was feeling sick and I didn't want to, but he grabbed me by the hair and forced me. I threw up in his car and then he got really angry. I said I was going to tell my father, and he said if I ever told anybody he would kill them and then he'd kill me. I was so upset and sick I wasn't sure I was even hearing him right. I'm still not sure that's what he really said."

Zak was sure.

18

August

"Remember," said Giancarlo. "It's wider than it looks, and it's off camber for the first part."

"Okay," Zak said.

As he waited, he could feel the blood pumping in his veins. He couldn't quite believe how nervous he'd gotten in the past few minutes, or how angry he was at Scooter for slapping Hugh, for his comments about Nadine, for his general air of contempt and superiority. There were a lot of things that could go wrong in a race. He might get a flat tire. He might screw up and fly off the road. Zak was good at descending, but he didn't have a genius for it like Giancarlo. And Scooter had already had one practice run.

"Get ready, boys," said Roger Bloomquist, who would be the starter this time. "Remember. It's a ten-second gap."

"What?" Zak said.

"Fifteen was too long. He never even saw the bike. Ten's more fair."

"That'll put us too close if something happens."

"Five, four, three, two, go," shouted Bloomquist, dropping the makeshift flag.

Stephens, who had been holding Zak upright, merely let go instead of giving him the same shove Zak had given Giancarlo, forcing

Zak to push hard on the pedals for ten or fifteen revolutions of the cranks. It wasn't a lot of lost time, but it was a short race and the start was crucial. They should have talked it over, but Scooter had been rushing things. Now, with the hot wind screaming past his face, nothing mattered except staying on the road and maintaining the highest speed possible. He knew as long as he could keep his fingers away from the brakes, he would be okay.

The key was to stay focused.

He let the speed build on the first slope, marveling at how fast he was traveling, then touched the brakes, scrubbing off more speed than he'd intended. He hit a washboard section and held on for dear life, then was out of it before he knew it, heading down the straights where he could see two blurred figures standing at the top of the first sharp right-hand curve. The road surface was all rock here, off camber, but when he put his weight to the inside and let the bike fly, he felt momentarily as if he were on rails. Vaguely, he could see the logged-off fields below.

The corner was tight and included a steep portion that was like a parachute drop, but he held on and stared at the line he wanted to take, feeling the centrifugal force of his weight carrying him farther and farther to the outer edge of the corner until he thought for sure he was going to smash into the rocks. Still, he did not touch the brakes. The worst time to hit the brakes was in a corner. You did your braking prior to the turn, then trusted your judgment. He could hear excited shouts from the bystanders who'd placed themselves at the apex of the corner. Then all he heard was the wind.

He was out of the turn, surprised that he was still alive, focusing on the next hazard, dips in the road followed by a washboard section he would fly over even faster than the previous one. He had the confidence now and was picking up phenomenal speed. The only thing left to worry about was the gravel at the bottom. And the truck.

As he floated over the washboard, aware that the shocks, both front and rear, were moving like crazy, he realized there was so much wind in his face and behind his sunglasses that his eyes were watering and he was beginning to lose his vision. He was like a kid on a runaway horse. And then he was in the gravel and touched the brakes, felt the rear tire skid, heard the noise, felt the back end kick out, and let off the brakes as the bike wobbled. He could feel himself beginning to crash. It was going to end in a bloody, tumbling wreck. *Don't crash,* he said to himself. *Don't do it.* Through sheer force of will, he held the bike upright and picked up even more speed. He could see the bridge now. More gravel patches came and went so quickly he didn't have time to panic.

He was carrying so much speed he began to veer toward the right side of the bridge and the eight-inch concrete lip that stood in lieu of a railing, and then as he hit the first of the concrete, he saw Kasey's Porsche parked at the far end, the front end sticking out three or four feet into the roadway. Zak was headed straight for the front bumper. He tried to shift his weight. Tried to straighten out. Was flying. Maybe forty, forty-five. Maybe fifty. It was hard to guess. And that damn Porsche was going to kill him. Wrestling the bars did nothing to change his line, and he knew he was going to clip it. There wasn't anything he could do but keep on. And then he was past it, had cleared it by a fraction of an inch, shooting up the road into the dust, skidding the rear tire to show off.

When he turned around, the white Ford was nowhere in sight. If they'd really started ten seconds behind, he'd beat them even more handily than Giancarlo had. "Shit!" yelled Kasey, his back to Zak as he watched the white Ford come skittering down the logging road.

The Ford was sliding sideways, overcorrecting and sliding in the other direction. For a second Zak thought it was going to run off the road, but it managed to avoid an accident, and then as the Ford came across the bridge Scooter gunned it, showering pebbles on the spectators and peppering Kasey's Porsche.

"Nice," said one of Nadine's friends sarcastically, as she shielded herself. Instead of asking if everyone was okay, Kasey went directly to his SUV to check for damage.

While the Ford turned around in the distance, Kasey walked over to Zak, who said, "That parking job almost got me killed." Kasey ignored him. Moments later the Ford pulled up behind the girls, enveloping everyone in another cloud of dust.

"We're not paying," said Kasey.

"What do you mean you're not paying?" Nadine joined the duo. "If you'd won, you'd make Zak pay."

"He played us. A guy plays you, there's no money owed."

"You underestimated him," said Nadine. "It's your own fault."

"How much did I win by?" Scooter asked, scanning their faces eagerly as he strutted toward the gathering. "How close was it?"

"Not close at all," said Kasey. "The bike won by five seconds."

"Bullshit."

"No, it's not bullshit. He came down that hill like something from Cape Canaveral."

Scooter turned to Zak. "I'm not paying."

Zak looked at Kasey and then turned back to Scooter. "Spoken like a true gentleman."

One of the things Zak had savored about his relationship with Nadine was their ability to spend time together without either of them feeling compelled to speak, and hiking up the hill after the race was one of those times. Zak was exhilarated over winning the race but quickly put it into the past. He was with Nadine now, alone, and happy about it in light of the fact that only two hours earlier he'd been of the opinion he might never see her again. They stopped twice to look at the view and assess the burgeoning sunset. As they approached the Jeep camp, Zak pushing Giancarlo's bike, they closed in on the white Ford and the group surrounding it.

"How many times can I win the same bet?" Hugh asked, placing his face close to Stephens. He slapped Chuck on the back and approached Scooter tentatively. "I think you owe me something."

"Fuck off. I wouldn't give you a wet fart in a windstorm." Scooter strode angrily across the camp toward the barbecue. The dog began barking after one of the Finnigan brothers teased it with a slab of steak. Zak looked around for some indication of outrage, but he only saw shrugs from the other cyclists and averted eyes from the Jeep crowd.

19

"I hope this doesn't get worse," said Nadine, searching Zak's face for signs of irritation. "Because it's all my fault. Everything that's happening is because I told people where you were going."

"Don't worry about it. Seeing you makes anything worthwhile."

"You mean that?"

"I've been thinking about you for weeks, Nadine."

"I've been thinking about you, too."

Nadine hoped she didn't sound too eager. It was wonderful to see Zak again, but she knew they were walking a delicate balance. They'd been together, and now they weren't, but even so she felt closer to him than ever. The dynamic that existed between them now that they'd split up was something she didn't quite have a handle on, but she certainly wanted to explore it.

Nadine counted sixteen people as she looked around the group: five bicyclists, seven in the Jeep group, her three friends, and herself. Following Jennifer's detailed instructions, they'd spent an hour driving through holiday traffic swollen with motor homes and trucks towing boat trailers. Nadine didn't like duping the guard, and she felt even lousier when they found her brother's camp and realized Scooter and Kasey had somehow located Zak and his friends.

Even though everyone in the Jeep camp was disappointed over

the results of the races, they sat around the barbecue with the cyclists like old friends while Kasey passed out steaks and burgers. They ate and waited for the sun to finish dying and talked about coyotes after somebody heard a distant howl. Dozer began barking, and the Finnigan brothers howled with him, which only made him bark louder. The brothers laughed so long and hard Nadine thought one of them was going to have a stroke. It wasn't until then that she realized how drunk they must be.

Nadine knew that in sitting next to Zak she was aligning herself with the bicyclists, but if she sat next to her brother, Scooter would view it as an invitation, and she didn't want to send that message. If she sat with her girlfriends, Scooter would try to cull her out like a cowboy roping a calf, and she didn't want to get into a struggle with him—not here, not with everyone watching. Even though she knew it was going to infuriate Scooter, the only safe place was next to Zak. And what if she made Scooter angry? He had no legitimate hold on her.

The group jabbered about everything except the races, Zak whispering details to Nadine to complement something one of *his* people had said, she adding information on a topic one of *her* people had brought up. After a while, Nadine said, "Come on. Show me your waterfall."

"It's up the hill."

"Then let's go."

Together they walked up the steep road. As they left, Nadine caught a glimpse of Scooter staring at them with those large gray eyes she'd once thought were so beautiful—all pale with tiny black pupils in the middle, so that when he stared at you, if he didn't move or blink, you thought you were watching a wax sculpture in a museum. Over the past month his eyes had become attributes she'd come to despise.

"I've got a bad feeling about them coming up here," she said.

"The only thing that's happened so far is we've pocketed a thousand bucks and are owed another thousand."

"Yes. Well, you'll never see that second thousand."

Nadine accompanied Zak to an outcropping of rocks just below and to the west of the bicyclists' encampment. From time to time they could hear the dog barking back in the Jeep camp. From the viewpoint, other than the dog and the smudges of smoke on the southwestern horizon, there were no indications anybody else lived on the planet. The distant buildings of Seattle and Bellevue had long been submerged in the haze.

She braved the first bluff and then steeled herself to follow Zak onto the farthest outcropping, to a point where they could look back at the mountain and view the steep, forested slopes. Nadine shuddered at what she believed was Zak's recklessness as he blithely negotiated the narrow rock ledges, each with a drop of more than a hundred feet on either side. She didn't want to look weak in Zak's eyes, especially in light of what she'd just seen him do on his friend's bicycle, so she followed him out onto the scariest outcropping she'd ever been on, finding it was easier to plunge ahead instead of hesitating or thinking about the possible consequences. Sometimes her mother was right. She was too much of a tomboy.

From out on the point the view extended alongside the mountain to the south as far as the small town of North Bend and beyond, with the occasional boulder larger than a house dotting the base of the mountain. At the tip of this bluff, they were as alone as two people could be.

Nadine had broken up with Zak at the beginning of August, almost three weeks earlier. During that time, she'd been busy with her tennis tournament, and Zak had gone to eastern Washington to train on the blazing-hot roads for the twenty-four-hour race he was doing in September. Breaking up with him, she now realized, had been the dumbest thing she'd ever done. Sure, he had a chip on his shoulder when it came to people with more money than him, but she would work with him and he would outgrow it. And anyway, he had never let his attitude affect the way he treated her. She missed him; in the beginning when he didn't call for a few days, she found herself in agony. How could she tell him she'd made a mistake, that she wanted to see him every day now? How could she tell him after she'd made such a point of explaining how important it was for her to finish school without any outside distractions, after telling him how her family was making it increasingly uncomfortable for her to be with him? Zak's constant arguments with her brother had been a nuisance, but really, when she thought about it, nothing more than that.

When they broke up, it had been so utterly different from the hours-long ordeal she'd undergone with Scooter. She could see Zak was hurt, but he hadn't made a scene. She wasn't sure what she'd been expecting, though she agonized over the speech for two days before giving it, and then did it in a fairly public place so he couldn't put on the same extravaganza Scooter had.

"I just want you to be happy, Nadine. If you're happier without me in your life, then I'll have to accept that. It hurts, but if that's your decision, I'm not going to fight you over it."

In the end—except for the pain she saw in Zak's eyes, which nearly broke her heart—she found his calm acceptance of her decision nearly as infuriating as Scooter's refusal to acknowledge their breakup.

Zak showed up a week later for her tennis tournament but sat apart from her family and friends, and spoke to her only briefly afterward to congratulate her on the win and tell her how happy he was for her. When her family and friends crowded in, he slipped away. Lately, Nadine had begun calling him, and it had been during one of those calls that he'd made the mistake of telling her his plans for this weekend.

"I don't know why we broke up," she said, staring at the sunset.

"You said you didn't want to be with me anymore."

"I don't know how on earth I came to that conclusion."

"I know how, and I don't blame you one bit. I was irritating. I *am* irritating. You're from a wealthy family, and I have this attitude that rich people aren't part of the world the rest of us inhabit, that they're not tuned in to reality. I know some wealthy people probably fit into my stereotype, but most probably don't. I've been trying to cure myself, but I guess it isn't happening fast enough. You were right to dump me. I wish it hadn't happened, but objectively I think you did the right thing . . . for you."

"Are you seeing anyone else now? I know we've never talked about it, but I would think you might be."

"There's nobody else. How could there be?"

It was exactly what she'd wanted to hear. Nadine sat on a flat rock, where she felt less likely to entertain the feeling of going over the cliff. "I've missed you. I made a mistake, and I've been regretting it ever since. And now I just want you to say you love me and you've missed me, and it's been pure torture not to see me every day."

"Well," said Zak, sighing. "If I wanted somebody to say something like that, I'd probably say it to them first. So . . . I guess I'll have to follow my own advice. I love you and I've missed you and it's been pure torture not seeing you every day." He sat beside her and picked up her hand. "I really do love you."

The sunset was beginning to damp down like a fire with a blanket thrown over it, and the colors from the horizon reflected in his brown eyes.

He kissed her. Or maybe she kissed him. She wasn't really sure who made the first move or if there was a first move. They kissed until she was dizzy from the combination of kissing and the altitude and the encroaching darkness. "So we're on again?" she asked. "We're a couple? Please say we are."

"What about your family?"

"You know my family is important to me, but I can't let them dictate who I'm seeing."

Zak would probably never get along with Kasey, but there was a slim chance that if he hung around long enough her father would come to accept him. After all, they were both men with strong ideals, men who'd thought through a clear and distinct vision of the world, even if those visions clashed. They'd both started off dirt poor and worked their way into something else. Nadine knew she could make this relationship work the second time.

"What the hell are you doing with my girl?" Scooter shouted.

Scooter was on the edge of the mountain with his hands on his hips. It was dark enough that Zak recognized him from his voice, a little high-pitched and narrow, even more so when he was peeved or attempting to be threatening. They'd been on the bluff awhile, had lost track of time, both aware from nearby voices that the cyclists had returned to their own camp. The sky had blued out and then gone charcoal black; stars were beginning to wink through the inky night.

Zak stared through the gloom at the pudgy young man in cargo-pocket shorts and voluminous white T-shirt. Scooter chugged from a brown bottle and tossed it casually onto the rocks a hundred feet below, where it exploded with a faint tinkling melody.

"Why don't you go back and litter your own camp," Zak said.

"Fuck you, fire boy."

"Scooter, what are you doing?" said Nadine.

"What are *you* doing? We were getting worried about you. And then I find you making out with this asshole."

"We weren't making out," Nadine said. "We were talking."

"He's got his dirty hands all over you. Get out of there, for God's sake. Or I'll tell your father what you've been doing."

"That's rich. How about I tell him all the things you made me do."

"You better not, bitch."

"Don't threaten her," Zak said.

"Quiet, Zak," Nadine whispered. "Stay out of this. You'll only make it worse. Come on. Help me off these rocks."

Zak walked her along the narrow ledge and held her hand tightly as she made the last small leap to the main part of the mountain. He could tell by the way she gripped him that she was a lot more anxious about the height than she had let on.

"You driving home tonight?" Zak asked Nadine.

"That was the plan," said Scooter. "But because of you they'll be driving in the dark. If they get lost out here, it's going to be your fault."

"We're not going to get lost," said Nadine.

"I'll have Stephens draw a map," said Zak.

"And we've got cell phones. We can always call back and ask for directions."

"None of our cells are working," Scooter said.

Nadine clutched Zak's hand as they walked up the narrow pathway to their camp, where they got directions from Stephens. On the way out, they passed the shadowy figures of Muldaur, Giancarlo, and Morse, the latter illuminated by a small camp light. A spray of stars was beginning to emerge overhead in far greater numbers than Zak ever saw in the city.

The three of them traipsed down the hill silently to the bonfire, where the flames were as high as Zak's waist. Minutes later, just as the white Expedition with its four occupants was about to launch down the hill, Scooter yelled at Nadine through the open window. "His father admitted he was hanging out with you only to see what the moneyed class was all about. Said he didn't have any intention of ever being serious."

Zak was shocked and mortified by Scooter's revelation. He *had* said that. He'd said it to his father and to nobody else, but he'd said it before he played tennis with Nadine the first time. His attitude had changed as soon as he got to know her, and he'd totally forgotten having made the cruel and stupid remark. The fact that his father had sold him out in casual conversation was overshadowed only by the disgrace of hearing his own thoughtless words repeated.

Sitting in the front passenger's seat, Nadine peered at Zak's face in the darkness. "Is that true?"

And then, before he could say anything, the SUV rolled down the hill, Nadine staring out the window at Zak until they rounded the corner and the Expedition became a distant glow on the hillside.

As they all turned to go their separate ways, Jennifer gave Zak a look that told him Scooter had just made a perhaps successful effort to scuttle Zak's chances with Nadine. To make it worse, Scooter was grinning ear-to-ear. It was the closest Zak ever came to coldcocking someone.

20

Zak laid his sleeping bag alongside Muldaur's, the bags situated on a bed of dry pine needles they'd prepared earlier. Giancarlo was on the other side of Muldaur, and twenty feet beyond him Stephens and Morse were on top of their sleeping bags reading with small trail lamps. The bags and other nonessential gear would be cached at this campsite tomorrow while they rode, then they would sleep here again tomorrow night. The last day would be the longest, when they would finally make the final push over the mountains and all the way to Salmon La Sac while Stephens's factotum retrieved all their gear.

Zak said, "Their fire is starting to get huge."

"They can't see it from the city," said Muldaur. "We can't see it from here, either."

"But these woods are tinder dry. And those idiots have no idea what they're doing."

"I don't think you're giving them enough credit," Stephens said. "They're basically intelligent, well-intentioned kids. They're not going to do anything too, uh, too . . . you know . . . half-baked."

"No, it's going to be fully baked," said Zak. "When they set fire to this mountain, all of us are going to be fully baked."

As if to punctuate Zak's fears, a gunshot went off in the camp below, followed by a chorus of whooping and then the dog barking.

"That had to be a rifle," said Giancarlo, who had hunted with his father since he was a tyke. "I'm guessing a .30-30."

"If they don't burn us out," said Zak, "they'll brain one of us with a stray bullet."

"They're not going to shoot anybody," Stephens said. "I mean, certainly, if you think about it, firing a gun indiscriminately isn't the smartest thing anybody's ever done. But there's some ground between us. And of course, all these rocks, too. And uh, you know—"

Another gunshot split the night, followed by gales of laughter. Since sunset when the wind had died, any little sound on the mountain traveled. "So, Zak? What's going on with you and those people?" asked Morse. "You seemed to know them."

When the lingering silence blossomed into something akin to embarrassment, Muldaur replied for him. "Zak dated Kasey Newcastle's sister, Nadine, for a few months this spring and summer."

"So that's how you know them?" Morse persisted.

"Scooter was her boyfriend before Zak," Muldaur added. "There might have been some animosity between Scooter and Zak."

"You were pretty thick tonight," said Stephens. "For two people who aren't going out anymore."

"Zak and I met Nadine when we rescued her from a car wreck last winter," continued Muldaur.

"Well, that certainly sounds . . . ," said Stephens. "I mean, if you looked at it the right way that could certainly be kind of romantic—meeting like that. If you thought about it. And the pair of you looked, if I didn't know better . . . I don't know . . . You disappeared for a long time tonight. I wasn't really sure . . . She certainly looks like a nice girl."

"Yeah. I liked her," said Giancarlo.

"You liked them all," said Muldaur.

Giancarlo laughed. "Yeah, I did."

"Nothing like a bunch of young women to convince you you're getting old," said Morse.

"I wasn't feeling old," said Giancarlo, who at thirty was twelve years younger than Morse. "I was feeling *married*."

"So, Muldaur?" said Stephens. "The Hugh thing. I mean it was funny in a way, and I can see why you might want to, uh, do something like that, but what's with the, you know . . . what's with the Hugh stuff? I'm not saying it wasn't funny. Because when you pull that helmet down on your head and put those glasses on . . . well . . . and those teeth . . ."

"And the way you talk," said Morse, laughing.

"But the primary question, at least in my mind, and I was thinking about this almost the whole time we were down there . . . the primary question is . . . I mean . . . why?"

"Sometimes I just do stuff."

The enigmatic response barred Stephens from asking more questions. Zak had known for a while there was more to Muldaur's act than he was willing to acknowledge, even to himself. He'd used the Hugh getup at work to pester and mock the other shifts, and tonight he'd used it to do the same to Kasey and his friends. Zak figured it was a way of confronting people using a strange combination of boldness and anonymity.

As they nestled down in their sleeping bags, Morse and Stephens conversed in low tones. It wasn't long before Zak could hear Giancarlo snoring lightly. Muldaur rolled over in his bag. "So what's going on with you and Scooter?"

"Scooter's the guy with the trust fund."

"Oh, I get it. He's rich."

"That's part of it."

"Just out of curiosity, how much money does he have?"

"Not enough to take over the world but enough not to work a day in his life."

"No wonder you hate him."

"I hate him because he's been stalking Nadine. And now he's stalking me, too. We're in this pickle because Nadine wouldn't do anything about it when I asked her to. If she had sicced the cops on him, he'd never have shown up here."

"Are you and Nadine getting back together?"

"I hope so."

"You really want it to work, don't you?"

"It took me awhile to figure it out, but she's the woman I want helping me through the rest of my life. And the one I want to be helping."

"It's gotta be hard. Somebody who hates rich people as much as you, hooking up with a girl like her."

"I don't hate rich people."

"Yeah, you do. She's a nice girl and I applaud you for trying to pull it off, even if I don't think you'll make it. But don't let my lousy opinion stop you. I keep thinking my folks are going to break up, and they've been together fifty-some years. What do I know? So how does her brother figure into the equation? You don't get along with him, either."

"No, but I need to get along with him if I'm going to keep seeing Nadine. As well as her father and mother." Below, two more gunshots perforated the night. "The truth is these guys have been getting away with crap their whole lives, and because they're wealthy, they've never had any repercussions. They come out in the woods; they think they can do anything. Driving the way they did today could have gotten all five of us dead."

"Don't blow it out of proportion," said Stephens, who'd been eavesdropping. "They're good people. Your friend, Kasey Newcastle? His father knows my company CEO. They've gone to Alaska together to fish. His family owns restaurants in ten states. He's a Mason. I mean—they're well connected in this region."

"We're not talking about his father," said Zak. "His father's not down there drinking beer and shooting off guns."

"Yeah, well, they're not shooting in this direction."

"Why don't you stick your head up and make sure? Those guys aren't here by accident. They came to fuck with me."

"Don't be so paranoid," said Morse. "Nobody's here to fuck with anybody. In the morning we'll go our separate ways, and that'll be the end of it."

"He's right," added Stephens. "I'm hearing too much negativity concerning people I consider to be friends."

"You just met them. How could you possibly call them friends?"

"I read people pretty well. I'm . . . It's part of my business. We have associates in common. They own land over on Lake Chelan near where we bought a vacation cabin. They're good people."

A third gunshot punctuated the quiet.

21

It was early when Kasey saw the retard heading down the mountain on his bike, helmet pulled low, the thick-lensed glasses replaced by a dark pair of sport sunglasses that, along with the cycling costume he must have borrowed from one of his caretakers, contributed to make him look nearly normal. When he spotted Kasey watching him, he became self-conscious and molded himself into an exaggerated streamlined position for descending, a pose that was comic in its ridiculousness, then locked up his rear brake a couple of times, kicking up gravel and throwing his bike to one side. How he hadn't killed himself before now was something Kasey couldn't understand.

For the past couple of hours he'd been dozing in a camp chair while the Finnigan brothers drank and gabbed with Scooter and Jennifer. Mouths agape, Roger and Ryan were sawing Z's in the Land Rover.

When Kasey finally got up for a call of nature, the sky was a bright blue-gray and smudged with smoke, though the sun wouldn't come around the mountain for some time. He'd surrounded too much beer, and, along with the heat, it had given him a headache and a general malaise.

He pissed onto a pile of rocks and then, zipping his fly, ambled along the spur road and back into camp in time to catch Scooter and Chuck walking in the direction of the road. "What's going on?"

"Gonna fuck up fire boy," said Scooter, who gave him a smoldering look as if the pronouncement were a challenge. Kasey had been warning him all night not to mess with the other camp. Kasey didn't particularly like Zak Polanski, but the idea of Scooter and Chuck messing him up with all those others around as witnesses didn't strike him as a particularly smart move, and he told them so.

"I'm just tagging along to make sure none of the others butts in," said Chuck.

"I'm going to put a wrist hold on that fucker," said Scooter. "Here. Give me your hand. I'll show you."

"Yeah, so you can break my wrist?"

"I'm just going to show you." Kasey dutifully held out his wrist and Scooter grabbed it, but instead of shaking hands he twisted Kasey's wrist and bent it backward, levering Kasey's arm into an awkward position that forced him toward the ground.

"Hey! Hold up there!"

"Pretty slick, huh? I'm going to make him bow down to the master and promise to stay away from Nadine. If he struggles, he might just break his own arm. Wouldn't you love to see him ride out of here with his arm in a sling?"

. "You break his arm," said Kasey, "I guarantee the others are not going to take it lying down."

"That's why I'm along," said Chuck, slurring his words. "Plus, I'm going to keep Scooter from throwing fire dude off the bluff."

"He's out on the bluff?"

"He's been out there for half an hour," said Scooter.

"Jesus, Scooter! It's bad enough we stayed up all night making a racket. You want to know the truth, I'm kind of embarrassed about the whole thing, especially after Nadine and her friends found us. But what if something happens and he falls off? That's a hell of a drop."

"If he falls, that's his tough luck. It won't have anything to do with me."

"The hell it won't."

"Don't worry," said Chuck, winking at Kasey as they walked away. "I'll make sure nothing happens." Chuck was just burly enough to back up his words. The only man in the bike camp close to his size was that downhill racer, Giovanni or something.

"You have to stop them," said Jennifer, approaching as the group dissolved. "Chuck? Stay out of it. I mean it."

"Jenn, we'll be back in five minutes, and then we'll pack up and go home, get some air-conditioning, read the *Journal*."

As he watched the two march away, Kasey felt a breeze blowing up the valley along the mountain, the warm air evaporating the saliva in his mouth. It was only seven in the morning and still shady on the western wall of the mountain, but the breeze may as well have been wafting out of an oven. Today was going to be even more miserable than yesterday. Across from him were the still-smoking remnants of the campfire. His head was throbbing, and he could tell all the beer was going to make him have to pee again.

Unexpectedly, Roger Bloomquist spoke. Until now he'd been a lump at the edge of Kasey's peripheral vision. "Remember in fourth grade when Scooter broke that kid's ankle practicing karate? Then he beat up Edgar in ninth grade and put him in the hospital? The dude up the hill is never going to know what hit him."

"It'll be okay," said Kasey, snatching the binoculars Ryan Perry had brought along. He moved to the rocks overlooking the north face of the mountain, followed by Jennifer and Bloomquist. When he climbed onto the largest rock and lay on his belly, he could see all of the bluff that jutted out from below the cyclists' camp about a hundred yards off.

The binoculars confirmed that the lone figure on the tip of the bluff was Polanski.

"What are you going to do from down here?" Bloomquist said. Jennifer had spread out alongside Kasey.

"I'm going to keep an eye on things."

It was awhile before Chuck and Scooter showed up below the

cyclists' camp. Kasey couldn't hear what they were saying. Scooter must have spoken, because Polanski turned around and took a couple of steps in their direction. Scooter and Chuck stepped out onto the narrow outcropping and began advancing on Zak, who had both hands out in a gesture to stop them. Kasey could see why. The drop on this side had to be a hundred feet. Judging by the way Scooter and Chuck were negotiating the first section, the outcropping was dangerously narrow.

Scooter stepped close to the cyclist, and then, where the bluff must have been wider, Chuck moved alongside. Kasey sometimes forgot how large the Finnigan brothers were, but when he saw Chuck outlined against the sky next to Scooter, it became obvious why he'd been an all-conference lineman for three years in high school and had gotten a football scholarship to Stanford.

"Get off the bluff," Roger Bloomquist whispered. "Get off the damn bluff, you guys."

"Like they can hear you," said Jennifer.

"Like they would listen, if they could," added Kasey.

22

"Hey, jerkoff."

When Zak turned around and saw Scooter and Chuck on the slope of the mountain, he could tell from the posture of both men that this wasn't a cordial visit. He'd been thinking about the events of last night—in particular, being called paranoid. Though he would never admit it to the others, he *was* a tad paranoid when it came to Scooter and Kasey, so the accusation had stung.

Zak stood up and took a couple of steps forward, realizing he was stranded on this outcropping. "What do you want?"

"I just came to apologize," said Scooter, grinning sheepishly.

"You stay there. I'll come over to you."

"What the heck. We'll come out."

"Stay there."

They came out anyway, Scooter looking more comfortable with the cliffs than Chuck, who had that stiff-legged gait people get when they're nervous. Zak wondered how they'd walked through the camp undetected. Now Zak was cornered, and, if he hollered for help, the wind would blow away any words that weren't blotted out by the Panther Creek waterfall near the camp.

"What do you want?"

"Like I said, I'm here to apologize." Scooter bridged the narrow portion of the bluff and moved onto the tabletop area where the drop-off was sheer. Zak walked forward to the tabletop portion of the escarpment and held his ground while the other two lined up almost side by side, twelve feet of flat rock spread out between them like a welcome mat, the rock maybe four feet across at its widest.

"I don't want an apology."

"No, I've acted badly. I want to tell you how sorry I am. Nothing else will get me to leave. I have to say I'm sorry."

"Apology accepted."

Scooter took two steps forward just as Muldaur showed up on the bank in his helmet and sunglasses.

"Let's shake hands on it." Scooter took another step toward Zak.

Scooter would have to be patently insane to monkey around on this outcropping, plus there was a change in his demeanor that signaled submission, so Zak extended his hand. Chuck, who was behind Scooter now, stepped forward at the same moment that Zak stuck out his hand. Zak, suddenly wary of the two men converging on him at once, withdrew his hand an instant before Scooter would have touched it. As he pulled back, Scooter's face underwent an instantaneous transformation from submissive to aggressive. Noting the change, Zak pulled back even farther while Scooter took a step forward and continued to reach for Zak's hand. By now Zak was convinced this was the precursor to some sort of choreographed stunt.

Knowing he had maybe two more steps before he fell from the bluff, Zak backed off the wider tabletop portion onto the narrow point.

Scooter grabbed Zak's bike jersey with his left hand and took a swing at Zak's face with his right. Zak dodged, brushed Scooter's hand away from his jersey, and moved another step backward. Both of them were now on the narrowest part of the outcropping, Zak with his back to a 125-foot drop-off.

"Hold your ground," Muldaur shouted to Zak as he began scrambling out onto the outcropping behind the trio.

The shout was the beginning of the end for Chuck, who hadn't realized Muldaur was even in the vicinity and stumbled when he heard his voice. He half turned while continuing to move past Scooter. Everything would have been okay if it had just been the one stumble, because he was teetering forward onto the rocks. But at that moment Scooter opened both arms and bumped Chuck, who was already waving his arms trying to recover from his earlier stumble.

"Oh, shit. Oh, shit."

Zak knew Chuck might have regained his balance if he had been relaxed, but he was in a panic. Oblivious to his friend's woes, Scooter tried to kick Zak while Zak evaded the blow and stepped forward, trying his best to reach Chuck, who was desperately trying to regain his balance.

Scooter blocked his way and began wrestling with him. "Stop it, would you?" Zak said. "Can't you see he's—"

Before he could finish, Chuck teetered off the ledge.

As he went over, Zak and Chuck made eye contact, maintaining it for the first forty feet of his descent. It was a look Zak would never forget.

Muldaur said, "Shit," and stood still, holding a small swatch of Chuck's shirt in his fist as they all watched him tumble and then heard him strike the rocks below. It was a horrible sound. For a few seconds Zak thought he was in a nightmare and would wake up any second. Looking like a broken doll, the body came to rest against a scrub tree over a hundred feet below. All three of them stood stock-still and stared at the body for what seemed like a very long time.

Then a woman's faint scream erupted from the rocks near the Jeep camp. It woke them out of their daze.

"You idiot," Muldaur blurted. "Look what you did."

It would have been overreaching, Zak thought, to label the look on Scooter's face as shock. It was more akin to wonderment. He flicked his tongue at his lips and peered over the edge. All Zak could figure was that it was taking him a few moments to comprehend that it wasn't Zak who had fallen.

"You fuckers touch me, I'm going to kill you," Scooter said, squatting in a karate stance. Zak didn't know when he'd ever seen anybody more panicked. "You bastards killed my buddy! Get away! Both of you!"

"*You* bumped him," said Zak.

"I never touched him."

"You bumped him, and it threw him off balance. I might have saved him if you hadn't been fighting me."

"I never touched him. Or you."

"We were trying to save him," said Muldaur.

"The hell. I came out here to apologize, and you pushed my best friend off. Jesus."

"Let's just get onto solid ground where nobody else'll get hurt."

"Tell him to get away," Scooter said, glancing over his shoulder at Muldaur.

"Back off, Jim," said Zak.

"I can't believe you guys killed my friend. Jesus H. Christ." Scooter stared down at the body for a long while without saying anything. Zak could see he'd gone into shock; if they didn't get him off the bluff, he was liable to get woozy and fall off himself.

"Come on, Scooter. Let's just get back on the mountain, okay?"

With great deliberation Scooter followed Muldaur off the out-cropping until he reached the main part of the mountain, while Zak remained on the plateau. "Why would I come up here with one of my best friends and then knock him off?" Scooter said. "I mean, you guys are both cracked if you think anybody's going to buy that."

"It was an accident," Zak said. "But you bumped him. That's how it happened."

"And I say I watched you two push my friend off."

"That's a load of crap, and you know it."

Zak and Muldaur followed Scooter through the camp past Stephens, Morse, and Giancarlo, who were out of their sleeping bags but moving in their own respective morning stupors. It was clear none of them knew what was going on.

"We're going to get even with you motherfuckers," Scooter shouted when he reached the road. "We're going to come back and we're going to kill all you motherfuckers! Every damn one of you."

Zak was trying to think of a way to convince Scooter that his version of the accident was wrong when somebody began shooting at them from down the road.

23

Kasey felt numb from the event he'd just witnessed, the distance itself making it surreal. At first he could not feel it, and then when it finally and truly struck him that Chuck was dead, he could only think he should be feeling more. It didn't help that he had so much beer in him or that he'd only had a couple hours of sleep. He'd seen Chuck waving his arms frantically and falling backward, and while he was watching it had sent an electric current down his spine, but now, aside from Jennifer's wailing, it felt more like an elaborate practical joke of the type both Finnigans were famous for.

He'd been fiddling with the focus on the binoculars at the crucial moment it started, so it was all foggier than it might have been. In the beginning he thought Polanski was in trouble, because Scooter and Chuck were advancing on him, Polanski with no place to go, and then he saw Scooter try to grab Polanski so he could break his arm, and then Chuck was in the mix and the bodies all became a tangle. With all the arm waving, it might have been that Chuck had been stepping forward to help Polanski. Chuck, despite his occasional steroid rages, had a streak of kindness in him, and it might have come to the fore in time to get him killed.

It the middle of it all the retard ran at the three men, and then Chuck was tumbling and Jenn was screaming in his ears. Afterward, she stood up, having wet her shorts, and sobbed as she ran back through the camp. Oddly, wetting her pants was the last thing Kasey expected. She was always so in control.

"Holy smokes," said Roger Bloomquist. "Is he dead? Do you think?"

"No," Kasey said, irritated. "He's going to get up in a minute and come up here and ask where breakfast is."

"What are you guys talking about?" asked Ryan Perry, who had just shown up. "What happened? What's wrong with Jennifer?" He was blinking rapidly.

"Didn't you see?" Kasey asked.

"I can't see much of anything until I get my contacts in."

"Chuck fell off the bluff," said Bloomquist. "He was with Scooter and then he fell off."

"Is he hurt?"

"There's no hurt about it," said Kasey, walking away through the scraggly fir trees. "He's broken all to hell."

For reasons he couldn't put into words, Kasey grabbed the .30-30 out of Chuck's truck and continued through camp to the side of the road, waiting for Scooter to return. The three of them were talking about going up the hill to confront the cyclists when Scooter stumbled into sight, falling to his hands and knees in the road. An angry-looking Hugh came running out onto the road behind him. It was pretty obvious that Hugh was chasing Scooter. Almost without thinking, Kasey waited until there was some distance between the two men and then levered a shell into the chamber and fired a bullet up the road. It ricocheted off the rocks. He fired once more in Hugh's general direction, and then Polanski appeared and they both moved back behind the debris pile.

Scooter fell to his hands and knees again on the way down, rolling on the rocky road, scrabbling back up again, all the while twisting around to see if he was being pursued. Kasey had never seen Scooter quite so panicked. He still wasn't sure why he'd fired: instinct, maybe. Scooter appeared to be in trouble. Maybe he was still in shock from what he'd seen on the cliffs.

By the time he reached them, Scooter's knees were bloody and his face was streaked with dirt. "Those bastards," he said, bypassing the group and heading straight along the flat spur road toward camp. "Those bastards murdered Chuck."

Everybody followed him into camp in a ragged line. "You mean he's dead?" asked Fred, going white and rigid.

"And who was that other guy?" asked Bloomquist. "Was that the special-needs guy?"

"The idiot. Right," said Scooter, plopping into a camp chair as he tried to catch his breath. "I think he's the one who pushed Chuck. But Polanski had a hand on him, too. They both did it."

"Are you saying they pushed my brother off the cliff?" Fred repeated.

"From where we were," said Jennifer, sobbing, "it looked like he lost his balance and they were trying to help. Like it was an accident."

"The hell it was," said Scooter. "The idiot pushed him, and Polanski helped. I was right next to them. I saw it."

"Are you sure?" Kasey asked.

"You saw it. You know what I'm talking about. Anybody else see?"

"We saw it," said Bloomquist, uncertainly. "We saw it happen. They pushed him."

Kasey turned and gave Bloomquist a look. All his life Roger had been a follower, someone so eager to be part of the group he would say or do almost anything to be included, and now Kasey wondered what he'd really seen, what any of them had seen.

Scooter said, "It's what? Six of us against two of them? I'm telling you, they pushed him. Jesus, a little handshake, and they overreact like that."

Kasey said, "You guys were talking, and then you were moving in, and then all of a sudden Chuck was losing his balance. Did you maybe accidentally nudge him a little? Because that's what it looked like."

Scooter turned on Kasey angrily. "I didn't *touch* him. It was those assholes who murdered Chuck. I reached out and tried to get him, but it was too late."

"I'm just saying I thought Chuck—"

"Hey, I was there. I saw them do it. They even said so afterward."

"What did they say?" It was Jennifer speaking now, her face full of tears as she squared off with Scooter in the camp chair. "Tell us what they said."

"I don't remember the exact words. I was worried about my own skin. You saw it. Kasey had to cover me with the rifle. I'm not sure what they would have done if Kasey hadn't fired those shots." When Jennifer stared at him questioningly, he continued. "The exact words will come to me. I know this. They as much as admitted they did it on purpose. And you'll testify to that, right?" He looked intently at Kasey.

"If that's what happened, I'll back you up." It hadn't looked that clear-cut to Kasey, but he'd been several hundred feet away.

"What about you guys?" Scooter asked, looking in turn at Perry, Bloomquist, Jennifer, and Fred.

Perry said, "I didn't have my contacts in."

"Jesus," said Scooter, disgustedly. "What about you guys?"

Jennifer replied through a curtain of tears. "If they pushed him, I'm going to testify."

Fred said, "Your story makes sense. There was no way they could handle my brother out on a ledge like that unless they surprised him."

"Polanski told me he was going to throw me off," said Scooter. "Chuck was coming to my aid. He's actually the hero in all this."

"But you're the big karate guru," said Bloomquist. "All you had to do—"

"Chuck was defending me."

"Then Chuck *is* a hero," sobbed Jennifer. "He died a hero."

"Damn rights, he died a hero. He saved my life."

"Why didn't you say that in the first place?" Kasey asked. "Polanski said he was going to throw you off?"

"Hey! Give me a break here. I'm still trying to get this whole thing organized in my own head."

"So why didn't those guys push you off, too?" Kasey asked. "I mean, if that's what they were doing, pushing people off?"

"Maybe they noticed you watching."

"I don't think they saw us until after. If they even saw us at all."

"Oh, they saw you. They saw you watching right after Chuck went off."

"I just watched those fuckers kill my brother," muttered Fred. "I'm going up there and—"

"Hold on," said Kasey. "Let's not do anything rash." Fred was obviously in shock over his brother's death, and Kasey didn't see any point in reminding him that he hadn't actually witnessed the event.

"Those fuckers killed my brother. I'm going up." Fred started to move, but all five of them jumped in front of him, and then Jennifer, still crying, hugged him, pasting herself to his body. After a few moments of trying to pry her off, he relented and began patting the back of her head in an attempt to quiet her tears.

Fred was the more introverted of the two brothers and not as handsome, though he had the same blond Prince Valiant bangs and the same pale blue eyes as Chuck, eyes that stood out on his sunburned face like Christmas tree lights. Kasey watched Fred as his jaws clenched and unclenched. From behind the trucks, where he was still tied to a tree, Dozer barked steadily.

"They might have a weapon," said Kasey.

"They have a whole camp set up," said Scooter. "Sleeping bags and even a small tent. You're right. Who's to say they don't have guns?"

"How'd the other guys in the camp react?" asked Ryan Perry.

"I didn't have time to stop and take a poll. What are you doing?"

Perry had a cell phone to his ear. "I'm calling the cops."

"Right. Sure. Go ahead. That's okay with me. But you guys are with me on this. Right?"

"It doesn't work," Perry said, closing his phone. "Anybody have a phone that's working?"

Kasey looked at all the pale, shocked faces surrounding him, then saw his own eyes in the reflection of a truck window and was startled at how haggard he looked. They were in a mental fog. Jennifer was bawling. Fred had gone white and looked as if he was going to pass out. Perry, the smallest of them all, was flitting about like a bird. Bloomquist was squirming. They were all in shock.

"Eventually those guys up the hill are going to come down and want to talk about this," said Kasey, thinking aloud. "What do we do then?"

"I know what I'm going to do," Fred said, marching through their makeshift camp and pulling a second rifle out of his brother's truck.

"Hey, hey, hey," said Kasey. "There's no need for that."

"You've got one."

Scooter spoke up. "Fred's right. There's no point in getting caught flat-footed when we have guns and ammunition just sitting here. It's only a precaution. Besides, who knows what they might have done to me if you hadn't fired those shots?"

"I'm scared," said Jennifer, mopping her face with the shoulder of her blouse.

"Somebody should go down to see if Chuck's alive," said Bloomquist. "I read about a guy who fell in the mountains once, and his friends thought he was dead, but he was still alive two days later."

"No way he's alive," said Scooter.

"Somebody needs to check," said Bloomquist. "What if he's down there calling for help?"

"I'm going," said Jennifer.

"I know how we can get down," said Fred, leading Jennifer through the woods toward the lookout point. "But it might be dangerous. You stay here. I'll go by myself."

"Like hell."

Fred handed his rifle to Scooter. "Here. Cover us. I don't want those guys doing anything when we're down there."

"My pleasure."

In their extremity Jennifer and her dead boyfriend's brother should have been closer than ever, yet they walked like awkward teenagers on a first date, making sure to keep some distance between them at all times as if they hadn't just been hugging, or perhaps because they'd just been hugging. Everybody remembered how jealous Chuck was, and that jealousy was still lingering around the camp as if he were still there, still alive.

After they were gone, the four remaining men stood in a semicircle. Nobody wanted to gaze down the mountain at the body. Kasey couldn't get over the idea that he was going to be a witness in a murder trial. Nor could he get over the niggling notion that Scooter wasn't telling it exactly the way it happened. There were a lot of things Scooter might have said when he came back to camp, but telling them the two men on the bluff murdered Chuck wasn't even close to what Kasey had expected.

When Kasey analyzed the maneuvers he'd seen on the bluff, he realized it might have been an accident—Chuck might have bumped into Scooter, causing him to lose his balance. Or it might have been that Hugh and Polanski had pushed him. It had all happened so quickly.

Kasey knew Scooter had never been nervy. His interest in karate stemmed from his mortal fear of getting hurt. Moreover, his karate instructors had consistently chided him for his inability to spar effectively and for his reluctance, out of fear that he might hurt himself, to practice falling on a mat. For Scooter, karate was all about injuring other people, and that was what he'd planned to do up there on the bluff.

Kasey popped a bottle of Bud, started to swig from it, and then thought better of the idea, setting the bottle on Chuck's truck with the other empties. It was going to take awhile for Fred and Jennifer to reach the body, longer for the return trip, and Kasey wondered if they shouldn't start somebody heading toward town. Get the police out here. They needed to spiff the place up first. Ditch all the empties. The last thing they needed was to look like a troop of drunken hooligans.

Kasey and Scooter had been friends their whole lives, so Kasey knew the story Scooter told this morning hadn't been delivered with his customary conviction, the shaky narrative coming more as an experiment than a straightforward chronicle, yet the more he repeated it, the more solid it became. Maybe if Kasey could watch the event over again like a slow-motion video or even if he could listen to Polanski's side of it . . . Or talk to the retard . . .

Kasey wondered what would happen if they found Hugh guilty in a court of law. Would they spare him because he was mentally challenged? Would they execute Polanski and spare Hugh? When you killed somebody, you deserved to die. It was simple, actually . . . even if you were an idiot. The more he thought about it, the more Scooter's story began to jell. Of course they'd pushed him. Scooter swore by it, and he'd been inches away. It was the sort of thing a retarded man might do. Not only that, but Polanski had been in a foul mood the night before and was no doubt in a foul mood when Scooter showed up that morning.

"I'm going for help," said Scooter.

"I'll go with you," said Ryan Perry.

"No. We need people here in case they try something."

"I don't like guns. Let me go with you."

"I'll move faster on my own," said Scooter, jumping into Kasey's Porsche Cayenne.

24

As soon as he got out of sight of the camp, Scooter realized he was agitated and needed to calm down if he didn't want to kill himself in Kasey's Cayenne, if he didn't want to die of a heart attack. His father and uncle had both incurred heart attacks at a young age, and even though he was only nineteen, for years his mother had been nagging him to change his diet. He wasn't sure what it was—the beer, the sleepless night, or the drama on the bluff—but when he held a hand out to check his nerves, it trembled like a cello string toward the end of a crescendo.

He didn't know where he was headed, but he knew he had to skedaddle before a horde of angry cyclists came swarming down the hill. By now it had to be obvious he'd gone up there intending to do Polanski harm. All that attempted grabbing he'd done after Polanski took his hand back had to have made it obvious.

Why had Chuck sneaked up on him from behind? And why had those bastards tried to blame him? All Chuck had to do was stand still and look big and tough, but he tried to squeeze past Scooter on that narrow ledge. And then Scooter grabbed Polanski's shirt, not realizing Polanski was trying to help Chuck recover his balance. Fortunately, Kasey had seen the retard rush in, otherwise his story would seem even lamer than it was. It didn't matter now, because everyone was on the same page, and just to make certain, they would rehearse it one more time before the cops showed up, although not too carefully. It was always better if there were slight variations in a story. Cops were suspicious when everybody was word for word.

Once he crossed the river, he slowed. Driving back into Seattle would give him time to think. He figured he would head for his mother's house and call an attorney from there.

There were two gates, one five miles away with a guard on it, and this one. The gate barring the main county road had been dutifully closed by the girls the night before. Idling the Porsche, Scooter stepped up to it. On their way in, Chuck had jimmied the lock, then put it all back into some semblance of order, but Scooter hadn't paid attention to how he'd done it. He remembered the lock assembly was inside a metal box attached to the gate, but that was all. He rattled it and kicked it, and then he got angry and picked up a rock and began battering it, which made the metal of the long crossbar across the road sing like a whale. If he couldn't get the gate open, he couldn't leave, because this gate was the only way in or out of these foothills.

Those bastards must have come down and rifled the lock so they couldn't get their vehicles out. After throwing more rocks and kicking the gate and cursing, he finally peered under the base of the box, which had no bottom. Inside was a simple locking device fastened by a broken padlock. What a dummy he was. The lock was still broken and still open. All he had to do was remove it and swing the gate open. He started to do so and then thought better of it.

He'd been furious when he thought the cyclists had jammed the gate, and he knew if he went back and relayed that information to the others, they would be furious, too. Maybe stirring up some more anger wouldn't be such a bad thing. He was so amped right now, he was driving erratically enough to get pulled over by a trooper, and if they pulled him over they were bound to discover that he was still full of beer. If they gave him a Breathalyzer test . . . Frankly, it wasn't safe to be on the highway. The right course of action was to stay in the hills until he was stone-cold sober. Scooter put the lock back the way he found it and turned the Porsche around.

When he got back to camp, the others were still waiting for Fred and Jennifer to return. "That was fast," said Kasey. Scooter had found them at the cramped outlook, where they were all looking down the mountain at Chuck's body.

"We're not getting out," said Scooter.

"What?"

"The gate's locked. Somebody jammed it. We're going to have to get a cutting torch or something."

"Who would do that?" asked Bloomquist. "Lock the gate."

"Who do you think?"

"I saw the retarded guy riding down the hill earlier," said Kasey. "I wondered where he was going."

"You think they sent him to jam the lock?" asked Perry.

"Why the hell would they do that?" said Bloomquist.

"To keep us here," said Scooter. "Don't you get it? They planned that thing with Chuck. They don't want any of us getting to the cops."

"That's nuts. We have cell phones."

"They know those don't work out here."

Bloomquist was in worse shape than any of them and was breathing hard now from the tension. "I mean, what kind of sense does it make? They didn't know Scooter and Chuck were going up there this morning. Why jam the gate?"

"Maybe to get even for that dusting we gave them yesterday," said Kasey.

"No," said Scooter. "It's bigger than that. This was planned. It was *all* planned."

"By Polanski?" said Kasey. "Well, he's certainly got enough motive. You embarrassed him bad last night when Nadine was leaving. Was that true? That he said my sister was just a fling?"

"Damn rights it was true." Scooter took the rifle from Ryan Perry's hands, levered a cartridge into the air, and caught it before it hit the ground. He'd gotten his nerve back, he noticed, because his hands were steady now.

"I don't think you should have that," Kasey said, pulling the rifle out of his hands.

"The hell."

"I mean it." Kasey held his hand out until Scooter dropped the cartridge into his palm.

"Here they come," said Bloomquist. "They're coming."

They watched as Jennifer and Fred climbed the final rock escarpment to the lookout point, both breathing heavily as they reached the landing. Scooter glanced down and saw that Chuck's body hadn't budged since the last time he looked. Jennifer's eyes were red and swollen and wet, though her shorts had dried in the hot wind. She had a different look and demeanor, Scooter thought. She'd gone down in a daze, but now all he saw was fury. Fred was even angrier.

"Well?" Bloomquist asked.

Jennifer wiped her eyes with the back of one hand. "They murdered Chuck. Are the cops on the way?"

"There won't be any police," said Kasey. "Not for a while. Our phones are on the fritz, and the first gate is jammed."

"We're not getting out. None of us," said Perry, stepping from foot to foot. "They've got us trapped."

"What?"

"It's true," said Kasey. "They fixed the gate so we can't get through."

"We could drive as far as the gate and walk," Jennifer said.

"Sure," said Scooter. "What is it? Ten miles from there to North Bend? Fifteen?"

"At least we've got guns," said Fred, grabbing the rifle out of Kasey's hands and walking toward camp. "We can protect ourselves."

A few minutes later in camp, Scooter heard somebody calling out to them from the main road. After Ryan peeked over the top of a tent and announced that it was one of the cyclists, the six of them gathered behind Kasey's Porsche to talk it over. "They're here," said

Bloomquist, even though it appeared only one man had come down the hill.

"Let's blast the fucker," said Fred, shaking his rifle.

"What if he's not the one who killed your brother?" Kasey cautioned.

"It was Polanski," said Scooter. "Polanski killed him. I was there."

"With the help of the retard," added Kasey.

Perry spoke up. "We need to get the police out here."

"Hey, you guys," yelled the cyclist. "Let's talk. It's me, Morse. At a time like this, we need to open our lines of communication."

"It's a trick," said Fred.

"Like screwing with the gate," added Scooter. "They're full of tricks."

"So what are we going to do?" asked Bloomquist.

"Let's go out and talk," said Kasey. "Nice and easy."

"Keep your eyes peeled for his friends," said Scooter. "They're probably up the road with guns."

"Or hiding in the trees," said Ryan.

Scooter thought they were starting to sound like kids working themselves into a panic over ghosts.

They walked out to the road warily, Scooter, Kasey, Bloomquist, and, hanging back several yards, Jennifer. Just as Scooter might have predicted, that little chickenshit Perry hid behind Fred, who was standing on the far side of the Land Rover, holding the rifle so that it couldn't be seen from the road.

They hadn't spoken to any of the cyclists since it happened, and now here was one virtually at their front door. Morse was one of the older bikers who'd spent the past evening talking money with Kasey and Bloomquist. Scooter, who'd felt a need to keep his eye on Polanski and Nadine all evening, barely remembered him.

"What the fuck do you want?" Scooter asked.

25

"What the hell's going on?" Stephens asked. "What were those shots?"

Muldaur and Zak had chased Scooter through the camp but were back now and visibly shaken. Zak looked at Muldaur, conscious that neither of them wanted to talk about what had just happened.

"Where's the big guy?" Giancarlo asked. "Two of them went out to see you. Where's the other guy?"

Muldaur took out his fake teeth and doffed his helmet. "At the bottom of the mountain."

"What? He found a trail down there?"

"Finnigan fell," Zak said.

"Which Finnigan?" asked Morse.

"The one with the girlfriend. Chuck."

"Prince Valiant?" said Stephens. "With the bad haircut? How far did he fall?"

"I thought they both had bad haircuts," said Muldaur.

"He fell about a hundred feet," said Zak. "Maybe more. And you're right. They both had bad haircuts."

"Jesus H." Giancarlo jogged through their makeshift camp toward the bluff, trailed at a much more cautious pace by Morse and Stephens.

Once they were alone, Muldaur looked at Zak. "Scooter's not going to accept the fact that he killed his buddy, is he?"

"It would be hard for even a normal guy to accept."

"If either one of us had gotten ahold of him, we could have stopped it."

"He must have still been drunk from last night."

"Of course he was. They both were. Plus the big guy was afraid of heights. People who are afraid stiffen up. It makes their balance worse."

"He had no business being out on that ledge."

"No."

"You think Scooter meant what he said about coming back to kill us all?"

"You know him better than I do. Does he calm down after a tirade, or does he just keep getting more wound up?"

"All I know is he can hold a grudge forever."

"Then we better take what he said seriously."

"He comes up the hill with a loaded rifle, how are you going to stop him?"

"Good point. Maybe we should hop on our bikes and ride out of here right now."

"Ride where?" It was Giancarlo, followed in ragged succession by Morse and Stephens, both of them pale after having viewed the corpse. Giancarlo had seen lots of dead bodies in his career in the fire service and looked somber, but just as shocked as the others.

"Maybe we should put some distance between us and that group down below," Muldaur said. "Scooter swore he'd come back and kill us all."

"That's just plain silly," said Stephens.

"Not if we're dead," said Zak.

"I'm sure he didn't . . . He couldn't have . . . It wasn't meant to be taken seriously. He was upset."

"When people with rifles get upset, bad things tend to happen," Muldaur said.

"Why was he threatening you guys?" asked Giancarlo.

"He claims we caused it," said Zak. "And he wasn't threatening just *us*. He said *all* of us."

Morse threw Zak a morose look. "People say lots of things after a tragedy. They get overwrought. We were talking to them for a couple of hours last night, and I didn't see anything to lead me to believe any of them were homicidal maniacs."

"You only need one homicidal maniac," said Zak. "In fact, with a gun you only need one homicidal *moment*."

"He was upset because his buddy fell," said Stephens. "That's all."

"He's pissed because his friend is dead, and he claims we did it."

"Well, did you?"

"No, but that's what he claims," said Zak. "It was an accident, but *he* was the one who bumped Finnigan and nudged him off."

"What were you guys doing on the bluff?" Stephens asked. Stephens had a habit of looking into Zak's eyes as if he thought he could read Zak's mind. When taken in conjunction with his complexion, which seemed too pale for somebody who spent so much time outdoors, Zak found it disconcerting; it was as if he had distant relatives who were vampires.

"I was out there enjoying the view. You'll have to ask *them* why they showed up. If you want the truth, I think Scooter came to push *me* off."

"You don't actually think that? I mean, this paranoia of yours . . . Seriously, it's gone far enough, don't you think?"

"They were there to hurt me. I know that."

"Come on. I mean, why would he want to hurt you?"

"Maybe because I'm going with his ex-girlfriend?"

"Oh, for gosh sakes. That's just . . . Let's go down and get this straightened out right now. And by the way, what were those shots we heard?"

"Gee, I don't know," said Muldaur, sarcastically. "Bullets coming up the hill kind of in our general direction. I don't know what that could have been."

"We need the cops," said Giancarlo. "We need to call them anyway, because of the accident."

"I'd call on my cell," said Stephens, "but it's not working way out here."

"We could take this down," said Morse, who suddenly had a pistol in his hands, gripping it in the careless manner of someone unaccustomed to handling firearms. Zak watched him violate two essential rules of weaponry: unwittingly pointing the pistol at Muldaur and placing his finger on the trigger.

"Where the hell did you get that?" Giancarlo stepped forward and shoved the muzzle toward the ground before relieving Morse of the weapon.

"I saw it in your gear. I was wondering why you brought it."

"And I'm wondering why you would pick it up without asking. This is a .357, and it'll blow a hole in you the size of a silver dollar."

"Let's hand it over to them," said Stephens. "We don't need it, and it would show, you know, good intent, don't you think? Kind of like . . . uh, unilateral disarmament?"

Muldaur gave him a sour look. "You mean unilateral stupidity?"

"I'm not handing my gun over to anybody," said Giancarlo. "Especially not to a bunch of yahoos who've been up all night drinking. And certainly not to a man who just threatened to kill us all."

"Are you sure he really said that?" asked Morse.

Nobody replied as they all watched Giancarlo bury the pistol in the folds of the rolled-up sleeping bag.

"Listen," said Stephens, in a moment of uncharacteristic clarity, "Morse is a professional negotiator. He does this for a living. What we've got here is a situation that needs negotiating. And whether it's a business deal or trying to talk some maniac out of a tree, every negotiation is basically the same. Right, Morse?"

"It's always about getting two sides on the same page. We go down the hill with the pistol, hand it over as a gesture of goodwill, and talk reason to them. I could do that . . . Giving it to them would be my selling point. I always like to have at least one major selling point. My persuader, I like to call it."

They walked out to the road and continued discussing their options. When they saw the Porsche Cayenne appear at the head of the spur road below, Zak thought for a moment it was coming at them, but it turned down the hill.

Stephens said, "They're going for help."

"He might be going around so he can come back on some other road and get us from behind," said Muldaur.

"I can't believe how paranoid you guys are."

Zak said, "You think about it. Scooter'll tell his story to the authorities and we'll tell ours, and they'll see how drunk Scooter is and get a blood-alcohol reading from him and the dead man. They'll test us and we'll come up clean. It'll be a no-brainer who to believe."

Muldaur looked at him. "Maybe."

Ten minutes later the Porsche climbed the steep road and turned back into the spur. It was Kasey's vehicle, but the driver was William Potter III, aka Scooter. They were still on the hill discussing things. "He wasn't gone long enough to get into town and back," said Zak.

"Maybe he told the guard what happened," said Giancarlo.

Stephens nodded. "It would accomplish the same thing."

"I don't think he was gone long enough even for that."

They decided Stephens would wait at the road and Morse would remain in camp while Zak, Giancarlo, and Muldaur went to see what was going on at the base of the bluffs, if anything. When they got there, the body was just as broken and immobile as it had been earlier. Gazing south along the base of the mountain, Zak glimpsed two people near the dead man.

It was easy to tell from the desultory way they were moving that they had checked out the corpse and were making their way back up the cliffs. Even from where he stood, Zak knew the woman was crying, that for her this day would always loom larger and lonelier than any other. He had a day like that in his past. Almost everybody did.

When they got back into camp, Morse was gone, although his bike was still leaning against a tree. Zak put on his cycling shoes, packed his pockets with Clif Bars, filled his hydration pack from the store of creek water they had purified, and checked his tires and the air in his shocks. He kept thinking about how distraught Jennifer must be and how her story would influence Nadine's thinking. Nadine might filter her thinking through Scooter's murky viewpoint, too. The events of this morning would severely impact his relationship with Nadine, possibly in ways he had no control over. It shamed him to realize he was thinking about Chuck's tragedy almost solely in terms of how it would affect his own life.

When the three of them reached the road where they'd left Stephens on watch, Morse was not there. Stephens stared at them guilelessly. "You can go back and get your gear ready," said Muldaur. "We'll keep watch."

"Where is Morse?" Zak asked Stephens.

"He's just going down to negotiate. Don't worry. It's what he does best."

"He negotiates *business* deals," said Giancarlo.

"All deals are basically the same."

"We better go stop him," said Zak.

"It's too late," said Muldaur. "He's already talking to them."

"What's in the back of his waistband?" Giancarlo turned to Stephens, who stared at him blankly, then stepped into the road for a better view. "Is that my gun?"

"It's a gesture of goodwill."

"He's got my gun." Giancarlo stepped close to the smaller Stephens in a threatening manner.

"I don't know anything . . . Okay. Yeah. Uh. I guess . . . he was thinking about it . . . I mean . . . *we* were thinking about it, and we, uh, we realized we were right and you were wrong." Giancarlo grasped Stephens by the jersey and pulled him close. "I know you guys think it's not necessary, but he thought it was, so he took the gun. Okay! He's going to hand it over. He knows what he's doing.

It's perfectly safe. It's not loaded." Stephens held his hand out, revealing half a dozen bullets.

"We have to stop this," said Giancarlo.

"How are you planning to do that?" asked Muldaur.

"We leave him alone, he might calm Scooter down on his own," said Zak. "I don't think so, but he might. We go down there, and for sure all hell will break loose."

"You guys just don't get it," Stephens insisted. "Morse is a professional negotiator. All this worry is for nothing."

Five seconds later they heard the first gunshot.

26

Kasey and Scooter were the first ones to the road, followed by Jennifer and Bloomquist. Lagging behind was Perry, who was becoming more useless with each passing moment.

The cyclist in front of them was one of the two businessmen, dressed in sandals, an old dress shirt, and Lycra cycling shorts that Kasey noticed creepily revealed the outline of his pecker. Kasey was glad he wasn't one of the firefighters, because he hadn't liked any of them. They all seemed too cocky for their own good. Kasey hated cockiness, even though he'd been accused of it himself. But he wasn't cocky. What he had was an innate self-confidence. "What do you want?" Kasey asked.

"I've come to talk. That's all. Just me. Morse, remember? I'm alone. I know some things have happened, and what we all need to do is try to get our bearings and figure out exactly where we are."

"Some *things* have happened?" Scooter burst forward. "Your fucking buddies killed my friend, that's what happened. Some *things*?"

Kasey couldn't help thinking the muscles in Morse's quads were impressive under the light of the morning sky. All five of those guys had incredibly well-defined legs that rippled every time they moved, even the retard, and it made Kasey a little envious, made him think maybe he should work out more at the gym.

"So, okay. Okay," Morse backed away from Scooter, his hands in an ameliorating position. "I hear you saying you believe my friends caused the death of your friend?"

"They fuckin' murdered him. Polanski and that retard."

"His name was Chuck, right?"

"Charles," said Jennifer Moore, quietly. "Charles Hilton Finnigan Junior."

"I'm not trying to be contentious. I only want to be sure what your side of it is. Then, if you folks don't mind, I'd like to give our side. I mean . . . that's fair, isn't it? Don't you want to hear what Polanski and Muldaur told us?"

"Why the hell aren't they down here propagating their own lies?" said Scooter. "Coupla chickenshit motherfuckers."

"Settle down," said Kasey. "Tell him our side of the story. What's wrong with that?"

"We already know our side."

"This guy doesn't."

"I don't see why I have to stand here and dignify this fucker by telling it again. I've been through a lot this morning. I've seen one of my best friends murdered right before my eyes."

"I know," said Morse. "I know, but right now each side only has one perspective. If we can share our perspectives, we can all see a broader picture of what happened. I'm on your team here."

To Kasey, this Morse guy was making a certain amount of sense. It might do them all some good to lay it out and hear the opposition's statement. He was still confused about what had actually happened and how they were going to present it to the authorities. If there were discrepancies, perhaps they should iron them out now instead of waiting for the police to pick it all apart. Besides, what kind of half-assed fabrication could they have come up with to justify pushing Chuck off the cliff?

Scooter gave Morse a version that was essentially the same one he'd been telling all along. He and Chuck ventured onto the bluff. Polanski got irritable. The moron showed up, and for whatever reason, probably on cue from Polanski, the two cyclists rushed forward and pushed Chuck off. Scooter had been unable to do anything about it, though he'd tried to fend Polanski off. He assumed he would have been next if he hadn't threatened them with karate.

"Let me get this straight," said Morse. "You're saying that without any warning, Zak and Muldaur, uh, Hugh, rushed forward and pushed your friend off?"

"Exactly right!" barked Scooter.

"What was your reason for going up there?"

"I don't see how that makes any difference."

"I'm just trying to get a fuller picture of the scene."

"I wanted to talk to Polanski. I needed to tell him I was sorry for things I said last night."

"Okay. Yeah, that sounds very considerate. And your friend? Why was he along?"

"He wanted to take a walk."

"I can understand that. It's a nice morning. He thought he'd get a little exercise to help him wake up. Fine. If you don't have anything to add, I'll give their side. But I have to warn you, it differs significantly."

"Lies are always different from the truth," said Scooter, glancing at his friends.

"Let him finish," said Kasey. "I want to hear this."

The warm winds were beginning to pick up and it must have been hard to hear from where she was, so Jennifer stepped forward beside Kasey. Roger and Fred remained behind the Land Rover. Ryan Perry was even farther back, hiding behind another truck. Scooter folded his arms across his chest, a defensive posture.

"Okay," Morse said. "Remember, it's not my story. It's Polanski's, as best I can remember it. And Muldaur's. The way they tell it, Zak was out on the bluff as you two approached. He told you not to come out, that he would come in. You kept coming anyway."

"It was just a stupid rock until he got pushy. A public rock, I might add. This is bullshit. We should shoot this fucker."

"Be serious," said Jennifer.

"I *am* serious."

Morse hadn't seen either Fred or his rifle.

Ignoring the hostility, Morse continued. "The way they tell it, Mr. Potter came out first, Mr. Finnigan behind. Potter put his hand out to shake with Polanski, but Polanski didn't want to shake. That was when Mr. Potter reached for Polanski's hand. At about this same time, Mr. Finnigan tried to pass Mr. Potter on a narrow section of the bluff. Mr. Potter, not realizing Mr. Finnigan was approaching, waved his arms, and at this point bumped Mr. Finnigan unexpectedly, knocking him off balance. Mr. Polanski and Mr. Muldaur moved forward to try to keep him from falling but weren't able to rescue him."

Kasey was thinking hard, because he realized suddenly that this could have been how it happened. But then, Scooter's story more or less fit the picture, too, didn't it? He'd replayed Scooter's version in his mind too many times now to be sure which story best reflected reality.

"Bullshit!" yelled Scooter, stepping away from the group. "They pushed him. You liar!"

"I'm not here to stir up controversy." Perspiration pimpled Morse's brow. "Remember, I'm just repeating what they told me. I wasn't out there, and neither were most of you. I think it's important we all know exactly what the other camp is thinking."

"Yeah, well, you're right about one thing. You weren't out there. But my friends all saw what happened, and they know I'm telling the truth and you're telling a pack of lies!"

Morse looked nervous for the first time. "Check this out. I brought a token of goodwill. I don't have to do this, and in fact, if you want the God's honest truth, they told me not to, but I'm going to give you the only weapon we have in our camp. My gift to you. Okay? As proof that we don't mean any harm."

Morse pulled a pistol out of the back of his waistband and offered it to Kasey, barrel first. Kasey, who thought for a split second he was about to be shot, realized Morse wasn't threatening him but was offering the gun—a revolver, large and heavy and silver, as lethal as anything Kasey had ever seen.

A rifle shot split the morning. Simultaneous with the noise Morse jumped into the air and landed in the road on his rump, a large patch of blood spreading across the front of his shirt. Kasey could see the hole in his rib cage when the wind blew the shirt aside. Kasey had never seen anyone more surprised than Morse, sitting in the road looking at Kasey as if he had fired the shot. Then, for whatever reason, Morse raised the pistol once again, and as he did so a second shot rent the quiet morning and a particle of Morse's skull flew away like a bat wing. The second bullet slammed the upper half of his body to the ground.

Fred, who had fired the shots from behind the truck, ran out to the road, pointed the rifle up the hill, and said, "You better get on back in before they start returning fire."

Ryan Perry darted out from behind his truck in a panic. "What did you do that for?"

"He was going to kill Kasey," Fred said through gritted teeth. "Maybe all of you."

"Jesus."

"He was talking shit," said Scooter, more concerned with Morse's story than his death. "Everything he said was a lie."

Bloomquist was shaking and cowering behind the Porsche. Perry appeared about to faint. Jennifer was crying again. Kasey felt like vomiting.

"Fred, I can't believe you did that," said Jennifer. "He was just trying to—"

"Kill us," said Kasey, wondering where the words came from. "Fred's right. He pulled that gun and pointed it at my apple sack. The cops would have mowed him down long before Fred did. You don't ever let a man point a loaded gun at you. Especially a man who was just involved in the death of one of your friends."

27

"Jesus Christ," said Stephens. "Did you see that?"

They'd all seen it. Morse had been conversing, standing a good ten feet away from the nearest man in the Jeep group when he calmly removed the pistol from his waistband and tried to hand it to Kasey Newcastle. Before he even had the pistol all the way extended, two gunshots rang out and he fell backward. Without going down to check on him, they all knew instinctively that he was dead. Moments later Fred Finnigan came out to the road and pointed a rifle up the mountain at them. Before he could fire a third shot, they all scrambled to take cover.

"It had to have been an accident. I mean, nobody shoots a . . . well, you know, there was no animosity in Morse. He wasn't somebody who . . . I don't think he was ever in a fight in his life . . ."

Giancarlo crept to a pile of rocks and peered down the hill through the brush. "Two accidents, in case you're counting. One to the chest and one to the brain. A third accident aimed our way right now."

"He *was* pointing the gun at them," Zak observed. "Morse was."

"They didn't have to shoot him. I mean, you think about . . . the gun was empty." Near tears, Stephens made a choking noise that under different circumstances might have sounded like laughter. "The gun wasn't loaded."

"You don't point a gun at anything you're not planning to kill," said Giancarlo. "And every gun is loaded. Simple rules to live by."

"He stole it," said Muldaur. "That's what he did."

"Hey, now wait a minute," said Stephens, creeping over to where Zak, Muldaur, and Giancarlo were peering down the slope at Morse's body from a point of concealment. "Don't you guys be putting this on Morse. Morse was a skillful negotiator. One of the best. Like I said, none of this was his fault. God."

Muldaur scampered away in a crouch toward their camp. Zak thought about following him and getting his bike, but he couldn't see riding out onto the road and exposing himself to rifle fire until he had a better idea of what the Jeep camp would do next.

Zak saw movement below, a man running in a squat across the road, only to disappear behind a large knob on the side of the hill, another man darting up the hillside toward them, throwing himself behind a log forty feet in front of the first. Both had rifles. One of them fired, and Zak heard a bullet ricochet off a nearby rock and whir into the distance.

"Good God," said Stephens. "They're shooting at *us*."

"We could shoot back, except we don't have a gun," said Giancarlo, sarcastically.

Just then Muldaur returned and knelt in the weeds behind them. Zak heard a zipping sound, as if a match had been struck, and then a fizzing and a loud pop that made them all jump. Muldaur was setting off firecrackers, big ones. In quick succession he produced four loud pops.

"What the hell are you doing?" Stephens asked.

Below, the two riflemen turned around and sprinted past Morse's body and then vanished along the spur road.

"They don't quite sound the same as gunshots," said Giancarlo. "At least not to the trained ear, but I don't think we have any trained ears down there."

"Where'd you get the firecrackers?" asked Zak.

"I always have a couple in my backpack when I'm in the mountains. I got chased by a bear once."

"Now they think we're shooting at them," said Stephens. "This is only making things, I mean . . . This is worse than . . . We're never going to be able to talk sense to them now."

"In case you haven't noticed, people who talk sense to them tend to have accidents," said Zak.

"I'm inclined to get the hell out of here right this minute," said Giancarlo. "This might be our only opportunity."

"Scooter must have them all convinced we murdered their friend," said Zak.

Muldaur looked at Stephens. "You want to sit here and wait for the sun to come around the mountain so you can work on your tan, fine, but I'm outta here."

"Me, too," said Zak.

"Ditto," said Giancarlo.

28

"What the heck are we supposed to do now?" Roger Bloomquist yelled. "Those were shots. They've got more guns."

Even though Fred and Scooter had been right on his heels after the shots erupted, Kasey was embarrassed over how quickly he'd scurried across the road to hide behind the trucks. He wasn't sure if he'd incited the flight or if the others would have fled anyway, but he could still feel the adrenaline coursing through his veins, as if he just drank a whole bottle of Jolt. Standing behind the Ford in various postures of readiness, guns cocked, trying to pretend they weren't embarrassed about their mad flight, the three of them avoided one another's eyes. Kasey was angry that the cyclists had fired on him but even angrier over how frightened he'd become. Before today, he never imagined that sort of instant fear existed anywhere.

Adding to the tension, the dog was barking at a regular clip like a broken cog on a motor. "Shut up," said Fred, who was breathing more heavily than the others. "Shut your mouth, Dozer!"

The dog ceased yapping but continued to strain against his chain.

"What happened?" Jennifer asked Scooter.

"They're shooting at us."

"Two or three shots," said Fred. "I lost count."

Scooter corrected him. "More like four or five. One of the bullets hit right near my head. I know why, too. I'm the witness they need to get rid of first."

"There were *three* pops," Kasey countered. "But I don't know, they sounded kind of like firecrackers. And I didn't hear any bullets hitting."

"Firecrackers?" Scooter was livid. "If they were firecrackers, why did you run?"

"'Cause *you* ran."

"You ran first."

"No, *you* ran first."

"Settle down," said Fred. "You hear shots, you run. It's common sense. And maybe they were firecrackers, but who's going to take the chance?"

"We know they have guns," said Scooter. "We already saw one. We don't have any evidence they have firecrackers."

"I didn't want to get left out there by myself with all four of them coming down on me," said Kasey.

"Forget the bickering," said Fred. "We need to work as a team or they'll come down and kill us one by one."

All three of them had their rifles trained on the trail, where they could see a small glimpse of the main road. The three rifles were the only guns in camp. Kasey knew he should have thought to retrieve the pistol lying in the road, but he hadn't. They were making a lot of mistakes. The bikers weren't going to get the pistol, though, because from their position, all three of them had a bead on it. "You think they might go down the mountain for help?"

"Help?" Scooter snorted. "They might be going down to make sure *we* don't get help. They want to finish us off so we won't talk."

"You really think they want to kill us?"

"It's the only way they can get away with it," said Scooter. "I'm telling you, they're out to kill us all."

Jennifer looked skeptical. "How did they talk the others into it?"

"I don't know," said Kasey. "But check out that guy on the road. They told him *something*."

"Jesus." Bloomquist's voice was shaky. "We're in serious trouble, aren't we?"

"Why are they doing this?" Jennifer persisted.

"It's simple," said Scooter. "They don't want to go to prison."

"I can't believe they're trying to kill us."

"You saw that guy point the cannon at Kasey."

"He *did* do that," Jennifer conceded.

"And they just now fired at us. My guess is he was supposed to draw us out on the road and they were supposed to get us in the crossfire. The only trouble is, they screwed up their timing."

"This is crazy," said Perry. "We're in a shoot-out with a bunch of guys we didn't even know yesterday."

"Not that crazy, if you know Polanski," said Scooter. "He's always been one tick away from tearing up a McDonald's with an AK-47. And that retarded fucker. He'll do anything they say. And now that we shot one of them, the others will really be after us."

Fred was pacing back and forth. "I just wish I could have picked off a second one. Damn!"

"Don't you think it's possible that guy was trying to give up his gun?" asked Perry.

"Come on, you pantywaist." Fred gave him a look of disgust. "Are you going to let them kill my brother and get away with it?"

"But your brother—"

"Just keep your mouth shut if you're not on our side." Scooter was yelling now. "Okay? If you want to hike up the hill and join their side, fine. Get the fuck out of here. You're either on our side or you're on theirs." Scooter turned and glared at Perry, then at the rest of them. "Any of you others want to go over to the other side, now's your chance."

"You know that's not what he meant," said Bloomquist. "We're with you, Scooter."

"The main idea here is we stick together," said Kasey.

"That's right. No turncoats."

"I'm not a turncoat, Scooter," said Bloomquist.

"Me neither," said Perry.

"Wait here." Fred was heading down the trail toward the road with his rifle at the ready. "I'm going to see what's happening."

Scooter followed tentatively, rifle locked onto his shoulder in firing position. Kasey followed Scooter. When they got to the main road, Fred peered up the hill for a long time, then jogged twenty feet up the road and climbed up onto a stump. "What are you doing?" said Kasey.

"They're taking off."

Kasey ran forward and climbed up next to Fred, catching a glimpse of color and movement through the trees above the cyclists' camp, bicycles and riders in full flight. "They're getting away."

"Not if I can help it," said Fred, firing several shots. Kasey sent a round up the hill, too. It felt good: the noise, the bucking of the gun against his shoulder, the smell of gunpowder. Even ejecting the hot shell into the rocks at his feet felt good. Then it occurred to him that his bullet might have hit somebody, that it was possible he'd just killed a man. He felt sick about what he was doing but at the same time was angry enough to keep doing it.

"How many were there?" asked Scooter.

"It looked like all four," said Fred.

"You sure? They might have placed somebody below to ambush us when we leave."

"I thought I saw all four of them, but I wouldn't swear to it. What are you talking about?"

"An ambush. You know? They jam that gate and then ambush us when we try to get out."

"Then why didn't he shoot at you when you were down there?" asked Jennifer.

"He probably wasn't in place yet."

"You really think they have that gate staked out?"

"It's the only thing that makes sense. Any of us touches the gate, we're dead."

"Jesus," said Fred. "Those fuckers."

If there'd been anybody left above to shoot at them, they would have been sitting ducks, yet the only ones who seemed concerned were Bloomquist and Perry, who had taken up their earlier positions behind one of the trucks. Scooter laughed when he saw them, then nudged Fred, who also laughed. Today was a time for reckoning, for boldness, a time Scooter and Fred would remember because they'd taken a stand.

"What are we going to do now?" Jennifer asked.

"First thing is we need to get organized," said Kasey.

"What we need," said Fred, "is to go up and kill them before they kill us."

The silence spread like oil on a puddle until Kasey realized they were uncomfortable with it, not because Fred had said something beyond the pale, but because he'd articulated thoughts most of them had been entertaining on their own.

Scooter was counting on his fingers. "There's what? Four left?"

Kasey started up the hill. "If you're right and there's one posted at the gate, there's only three up here. Let's go check out their camp. Maybe we can figure out what they're planning."

Scooter walked over to the dead man in the road and took the pistol out of his hand, then went up the hill. Fred followed with Jennifer. Bloomquist and Perry remained behind, while Kasey, rifle at the ready, followed at a distance, his earlier panic still fresh in his mind.

Kasey clambered up the steep, rocky road at a measured pace, keeping his eyes on the track as it disappeared farther up the mountain. He couldn't help thinking that the cyclists had climbed higher the way a hawk climbed higher—to gain altitude for an attack—and at any moment they might come speeding down.

When he reached the cyclists' camp, he saw Scooter, Fred, and Jennifer in front of him kicking through bags of clothing and sleeping bags, looking for contraband, cell phones, or evidence of more hand-guns. Scooter found a small Bible with the toe of his sneaker and squashed it flat with a vengeance. It hadn't occurred to Kasey until that moment that they might be religious, and the knowledge somehow made them all seem more human.

"Four bikes missing," said Scooter. "Four guys trying to kill us. The question remains, did they all go up? Or did one go down?"

"We're not the police," said Jennifer. "We shouldn't be the ones to track them down."

"I'm sorry, but when you get in a situation like this, you *are* the police. If there's no law nearby, that's exactly what you are."

"They killed my brother," said Fred.

"But we can't set out to deliberately kill them," said Jennifer.

"Why not?" Scooter scratched his nose with the sight on the lever-action rifle he was carrying. "They're doing it."

"But if they're trying to kill us, why are they running?"

"Are they? They sent Morse down to kill us. They fired four rounds at us. And they've got a guy at the gate waiting to ambush us."

"I've been thinking . . . that Morse guy had time to shoot," said Jennifer, "but he didn't."

"It's his tough luck that he hesitated," said Kasey. It was easy to know why Morse had flubbed his assignment. Remembering his own fear made him furious again. "Don't be counting that screwup as a point in his favor."

Kasey was anxious to see where Chuck had fallen. He was talking tough, but he was still confused by what he'd witnessed, confused enough that it hadn't fully jelled in his mind yet. He walked past the thin waterfall and stood on the rocks overlooking the bluff. The view was incredible, thirty miles of old glacial wash spread out as if he were sitting on God's shoulder.

The ledge was narrow enough and high enough that Kasey mar-veled that Nadine, who had always been afraid of heights, had gone out on it the night before. It said something about her relationship with Polanski that he could talk her into it. Below, Chuck's body looked broken and even more hideous from this vantage point. The sky was growing lighter, and most of the valley beyond the bluff was delineated by a low but quickly rising sun. A gaggle of crows cawed and flapped on the air currents alongside the mountain. Kasey wondered if the birds were waiting for them to leave so they could get at Chuck. Maybe they should have sent a blanket down with Fred and Jennifer so they could wrap him up.

When Kasey got back, he found Scooter had piled the cyclists' possessions into a heap and set fire to them. The synthetic material in the sleeping bags pushed dense smoke skyward. Kasey tried to stomp out part of the fire, but a cinder burned a hole in the top of his running shoe and forced him to quit. He realized, much to his dismay, that he'd stepped on a photo of his sister and Polanski taken at a street fair earlier in the summer. They'd broken up, but Polanski was still carrying photos of his sister.

"That's a stupid idea," said Jennifer. "This whole area is so dry."

"Last night was Chuck's last campfire," said Fred. "He had a right to it, and we have a right to this."

"It's a brilliant idea," said Scooter. "Burning their shit. They come back and want something, it'll be gone."

"You find any guns?" Kasey asked.

"Nada," said Fred. "They obviously took them."

"What about that revolver?" Kasey held his hand out. "Maybe we can tell something from that."

"I'm keeping it," said Scooter.

"Just let me see it, for cripes sake."

"I told you, I'm keeping it."

"Does everything have to be a struggle with you? Jesus, no wonder they tried to push you off."

Reluctantly Scooter handed the pistol to Kasey, who thumbed the cylinder open. The fact that there weren't any cartridges in the gun shocked him. Scooter, who had been watching over his shoulder, said quickly, "I emptied it."

"Let me see the shells."

"Why do you want to see the shells?"

"I just do."

"Why?"

"Give me the goddamn bullets."

"I tossed them."

"Where?"

"Off in the trees over there." He gestured vaguely with a nod of his head.

"They were evidence."

"Are we going to chase those fuckers?" said Fred. "Or stand around all day talking about bullets in the woods?"

It was with a renewed determination to make things right that they marched back to their own camp, Kasey once again taking the rear, casting looks back up the trail lest the bikers swoop down on them. Above, at the cyclists' camp, the smoke continued to spiral up alongside the mountain. Jennifer was right. They didn't need to be setting fire to the woods.

Leaving Perry and Bloomquist alone had been a mistake, because as soon as they arrived back in camp, Bloomquist said, "We're not going to . . . uh, we've decided if you guys want to run around trying to shoot somebody, that's your business. But we're not going to participate."

To Kasey's surprise, Jennifer laid into them. "You raggedy-ass backstabbers. Chuck is at the bottom of that cliff . . ." She began weeping, then regained control. "Don't you dare chicken out on us. We're going up that hill, and we're going to shoot them before they shoot us. We are going to do that, and you are coming with us."

"You don't," said Scooter, pointing his rifle at Perry's head, "we might as well shoot you ourselves." After a few moments of silence, Scooter pointed his weapon at the ground and laughed.

"Jesus," said Fred. "For a minute I thought you meant it."

"For a minute, *I* thought I meant it." Whether he'd meant it or not, it was settled. Perry and Bloomquist were coming.

Kasey had a feeling they'd find the cyclists halfway up the mountain, exhausted from pedaling, and that they would quickly surrender. They would take them back to town and turn them over to the police. Simple.

He was in the Porsche waiting for Scooter to take a leak when he saw the dog dash out to the road and race up the mountain. Fred passed Kasey's open car window, halfheartedly chasing the malamute. "He was Chuck's. I don't see how he could know Chuck's dead, but he knows something, because he's been going crazy all morning."

"Where's he going?" asked Scooter, stepping into the Porsche Cayenne.

"I don't have a clue. But I know he hates bikes."

29

June

Zak was relishing the stillness of the warm summer night when Stacy got out of a Carrera and slammed the door. Her exit was almost like an ejection, the car radio so loud it caused a German shepherd up the street to start baying. She'd been on a date, one of her rare social interactions since she'd moved back from Florida, and not a very successful date by the look of things.

Zak, his father, and his sister all lived in the home Zak had bought five years ago deep in the heart of the Central District, a location that missed a grandiose view of Lake Washington by a few blocks. At the time he'd purchased the house it was in ruins, so he bought it for a song compared with the other properties on the block. He'd rebuilt most of the main floor: the living room, dining room, kitchen, one bathroom, and a back bedroom, which he'd turned into a den. Upstairs he was gutting the bedrooms one by one. For the next two months he would sleep in the downstairs den while he tore his bedroom apart and restored it. Zak had done massive amounts of work on the foundation, scoured and cleaned the basement, and put on a new roof. He'd put in new walls, wiring, plumbing, hardwood floors, and fixtures. He would be doing more work this summer. The fire station was about a mile away, so most mornings he walked to and from work. What with the fire department, this house, and his bike racing, his summer plans didn't leave much time for romance, which was one reason the unexpected affection he felt for Nadine had buffaloed him.

Tonight his sister had been out with Nadine's brother.

Stacy was almost as tall as Zak and had been a star on the swim team at Chief Sealth High School in West Seattle. As he watched her make her way up the concrete walk and onto the wooden porch, he thought she moved more like a woman on her way to the gas chamber than an ex-athlete. He switched on a lamp just before she opened the front door.

"Hey, Stacy," Zak said, without moving from the chair. Her eyes were swollen from crying, and her mascara was smeared on her cheeks as if wet kittens had been pawing her. Stacy closed the door but remained in the shadows. He could see she had on her best shoes, a skirt, and a blouse, a sweater clutched in one arm. The blouse had a button missing at the level of her navel. "You look nice," he said.

"I did earlier."

"What happened?"

"Zak, honey, I don't want you grilling me right now, okay? I know you don't like him, and I guess I don't, either. Can we leave it at that?"

"Sure."

"What are you doing up?"

"We had a car wreck last night at work. A rollover. An Explorer."

"And you had another dream about Charlene?"

"Yes."

"Zak, it's so strange that you managed to find a job that puts you right in the middle of your worst nightmare. I mean, if you die and go to hell, this would be it."

"What happened to your lip?"

She touched her face. "I didn't think it showed."

"He hit you, didn't he?"

"It was what you might call a mutual love fest."

"How do you get into a fistfight on your first date?"

She walked into the room and sat heavily on the sofa across from Zak. As more light blanched her pale face and it became even more obvious that Stacy had been crying, Zak thought of several things to say, but discarded each as it came to mind.

"Life is full of disappointments," she said. "Some just a little uglier than others, but it's not the end of the world. In the morning I'll get up, have my coffee, and go to work."

He felt like driving to Kasey's house and beating the crap out of him, but all that would get him was a night in jail, maybe more.

"Zak? I know you think you have to take care of me, and I love having you for my brother because of that. What I'm trying to say is I'm grateful for your concern, but I only need so much help."

"I know."

"No, you don't, Zak. You found yourself a good job and you've stuck with it and you've got a house that's going to be gorgeous when you're finished. You haven't made any major mistakes with your life and I don't guess you will. I'm just saying I love you and I know you love me, but don't wait up for me again."

"I told you I had a nightmare."

Stacy gave Zak a tiny beauty-pageant wave and proceeded upstairs, where he heard the bathroom door close. The nightmare was bad enough, but seeing his sister step out of Kasey Newcastle's car had put him into a black mood. That they'd gone someplace and had sex, or something like sex, before slapping the hell out of each other was almost too much to think about. He had no doubt she'd given as good as she'd gotten, though. His sister had a temper and was incredibly strong.

He was eleven when Charlene died at sixteen; Stacy was fourteen. Once again, sitting in the dark, he knew he would give anything to be able to go back and replay that night, that he would give anything if he could erase those thirty seconds of cowardice. It didn't matter how many times he told himself he'd been a child, because the assurances never dissolved the cold, hard kernel of fear he'd cached away in the pit of his stomach, the fear that reminded him almost daily that his family's implosion was all his doing. They all knew Charlene would be alive today if not for him.

They'd lived in Tacoma. It was raining that night. Zak was in the front seat next to Charlene, who'd only been awarded her driver's license a month before. Stacy was in the back, a fact that probably saved her life. She'd been battling her older sister for some time and refused to sit up front. They were about to drop Zak off at a chess club meeting, driving up Sixth Avenue toward the library, when a truck in the oncoming lane blinded Charlene with its headlights, crossed the centerline, and hit them head-on. Zak didn't remember the initial details, only that there was a loud noise, that Charlene said, "Oh, shit," and then they were spinning in the road. There were more loud noises, and then Zak was crying. He'd broken his wrist. Stacy escaped relatively unscathed and got out of the wreck on her own. The car was upside down, and Zak managed to get his seat belt undone, which dropped him onto the crumpled roof of the car. Charlene, still hanging upside down, said, "Zak, help me. I'm stuck."

It had been a simple request, delivered in a tranquil voice, and Zak would remember her calm resolve for the rest of his life, making it a model for everything he did. The smoke began to grow worse, but Zak crept toward her and then reached up and tried to manipulate the belt mechanism with his good hand. As he fumbled with it, he felt a searing heat and without thinking, slithered out of the car backward. The smoke flared up until he almost couldn't see Charlene. Just as he cleared the car, a young man he'd never seen before knelt and began to squirm into the smoke until one of his friends pulled him back.

"Zak?"

Hearing her voice and realizing he still had time to get the seat belt loose, Zak crawled back in. Nobody pulled *him* out; nobody tried to stop *him*. He never did figure out why. Crawling on his belly, he reached his sister and began to fumble again with her seat belt. And then, without the heat becoming appreciably worse, without his sister coming free, without anything changing, he was once again overwhelmed with panic. The earlier terror had been a mustard seed compared with this. He didn't know it was possible to have so much adrenaline in his body or to be so single-minded about saving himself.

Again he scooted out backward. There was still time, he thought, as he lay whimpering on the ground beside the car looking on as his sister tried to unloosen the seat belt herself. There was still time to venture in and try again. The worst thing about cowardice, he later realized, was that in even the most egregious cases, there were often multiple opportunities to redeem oneself, opportunities one could look back on in future years with something a lot worse than mere regret. "Zak? Zak are you still there?"

Zak didn't answer. He could have, but he didn't. While he waited for Charlene to save herself, the car's interior burst into flames with a whooshing sound. Having already been escorted to the far side of the street by a middle-aged woman, Stacy screamed when the fire broke out. Zak didn't budge. He didn't scream and he didn't move, not until somebody took him by the shoulders and moved him.

The fire department showed up a minute later and doused the flames, but it was too late. On the day of the funeral, Zak got dressed, went downstairs, and, after a long, tearful struggle, made the family leave him alone in the house while they went to the service. When they came back four hours later, he was still in his Sunday suit, sitting in front of the television, which he'd turned on only moments before, fearing they would find out he'd been staring at a photo of Charlene and crying the whole four hours.

"Are you having a good time?" said his mother, with sarcasm she was never to repeat quite so openly, though for the rest of her life he would know she blamed him for her eldest daughter's death. If Zak's father blamed anything on him, he never let on. Nor did Stacy. Still, during the next few years his mother reminded him of it by the way she tiptoed around the topic of Charlene, always with a brief look directed his way when she mentioned her dead daughter, always subtle enough that nobody noticed but Zak.

Since that night on Sixth Avenue, Zak felt in his heart that he was responsible for Charlene's death, his parents' divorce, Stacy running away from home, his mother's pill-popping and religious binges, all of their financial woes. If he'd been a man instead of a baby, he would have worked that seat-belt buckle loose, Charlene would have crawled out of the family car, and they would have gone about their lives with an interesting yarn to spin about the time the three kids were involved in a car wreck. The tragedy so dominated his thinking that there were times when Zak believed the only reason he'd joined the fire department was to prove he wasn't a coward.

Zak was never far from the panic of that night, and it had a way of coming back, tormenting him in the form of a recurring nightmare. He daydreamed about it on the freeway when he least expected it. House fires, shootings, heart attacks, suicides he could handle as casually as posting a letter, but car wrecks turned him into a frightened boy. Outwardly, though, he never let it show, and his determination to handle every car wreck in a manly way was what gave him a rep in the department as being some sort of car-wreck guru. And now he was falling in love with a woman he'd met in almost identical circumstances to those in which he lost his sister.

Nadine. What did the two of them have in common except their competitive instincts? She was religious, and he was not. She was from a family of wealth and privilege, and he was not. She was headed for a college degree, which he had no interest in achieving. She was from a loving, tightly knit family, and he was from a home that had shattered into a thousand pieces. The best part was that she thought he was a hero. When you put it into perspective and thought about how Charlene had died, he couldn't help but wonder if there wasn't something Freudian and ultimately twisted and scarred and maybe a little bit scary about his attachment to Nadine.

The afternoon after Stacy's date, Zak found himself on the front porch of the Newcastle estate in Clyde Hill, having been asked by the Hispanic woman who answered the door to wait outside for

Nadine. During the few moments the front door was open, Zak heard shouting inside, one voice that was distinctly Nadine's, another just as distinctly her father's.

Moments after the maid closed the door, Kasey Newcastle exploded out of the house and stomped over to his Porsche, picked up a garden hose, and began spraying the windshield. If he noticed Zak, he didn't let on. Zak couldn't help noting he had a black eye.

Finally, Kasey spoke without looking at him. "Nadine used to collect lost pets. We had a stray parrot in the house for almost a year. She grew out of it. She'll grow out of you, too."

"Where'd you get the shiner?"

Newcastle reached for his eye. "Caught an elbow playing basketball, if it's any business of yours."

He left the water running, fired up the Porsche, and roared out of the driveway, narrowly missing Zak's van. Moments later Nadine appeared and chirped, "Have you been waiting long?"

"Not long at all. I was having a nice little chat with your brother."

Nadine walked over and turned off the water faucet. "He's been in a foul mood all day."

"I thought I heard arguing inside."

"Yes, you probably did. Everybody's in a bad mood. I won't dance around it. My dad and I were fighting. Daddy doesn't want me going out with you anymore."

"Why not?"

"He thinks we're not right for each other. How would he know? He hardly knows you. Plus, he thinks you're after my money. I don't even have any money."

"You will have."

"But that's not why you're going out with me."

"No? Why am I going out with you?"

"Because you like getting slaughtered at tennis." She laughed at the look on his face, and after a few moments he laughed, too.

"You still want to go out with me?"

"Daddy says he doesn't think you're good enough for me and that any other guy in your position would bow out politely. He said you simply don't have the common sense to select yourself out. He thinks life is this Darwinian thing. Well, it's not worth talking about, because I don't listen to him anymore. Of course I'm going out with you."

30

August

Zak felt something whir past his ear and then heard a sonic-boom crack open the morning; it was a moment or two before he connected the events. Somebody was shooting at them, and the bullet had passed so close he wondered why it hadn't ripped through the back of his brain at two thousand feet per second.

After the first shots resounded, Giancarlo sped ahead as if scalded, and so did Stephens. Muldaur was already in the lead, which gave Zak the number four position on a road that cried out to be ridden single-file: steep, barely negotiable, full of loose rock and off-camber grades on either side. Without hesitation, he tried to pass Stephens, who now was slowing him down. Out of some sense of fair play, he took the worst part of the track and left the better section for Stephens, but Stephens felt him coming and swerved in front of him, rubbing Zak's front tire with his rear. For a moment Zak was on the verge of crashing.

Regaining his balance, he tried to move up once more, but again Stephens swerved in front of him until it became obvious that his plan was to hold Zak back. Although Zak was the stronger rider, he was being forced to linger behind Stephens, who didn't want to be the last man in line and the first target any more than Zak did. Apparently it wasn't strength that would decide the last man, but dirty tricks.

After they rounded the bend, they continued to press on at a rapid pace, knowing that this next stretch through the trees was steep and straight for almost an eighth of a mile; if the Jeep people got motivated, they might sprint up the road on foot in time to pick them off one by one.

As the road opened, Zak pushed harder on the pedals until he pulled alongside Stephens, who gave him a leering grin, and then alongside Giancarlo. Both were breathing hard, maybe too hard.

Zak knew he wouldn't catch Muldaur, at least not on this first stretch—he was already fifty feet in front—but he tried anyway. He felt sick to his stomach, both with the effort and the thought that his friend Giancarlo was now last in line and in the first position to take bullets. *Devil Take the Hindmost* was the informal name of a race on the bike velodrome. The last guy around on specified laps had to drop out. This could turn into the same game, except here the last guy might be dead.

By the time they'd ridden the long straight stretch, Zak realized they were probably safe for a while. "They think we have guns. That we're waiting for them."

"That's why they're not rushing us," said Muldaur, from up in front. "If I hadn't set off those firecrackers, we'd be dead now."

As the road climbed to the right, the surface turning into hard-packed clay, Zak took a quick look behind him. He saw Giancarlo and, tight on his tail, Stephens, who was trying to edge him out the same way he'd edged out Zak.

"Okay," said Muldaur. "We're out of sight, so it's time to slow down. Riding like this screws up your system." Muldaur had dressed as Hugh once again, the helmet loosened so that it rode low, the sunglasses askew, false teeth in place. They carried water packs on their backs, enough to drink for at least a couple of hours in this heat, the plastic feeding tubes dangling near their cheeks. Their pockets bulged with gel packs, Clif Bars, small bags of raisins and dates. The three slowed their pace and pedaled more or less as a trio, while Stephens steamed up the road ahead of them and around the next bend.

"I thought we were going to slow down," said Zak.

"Don't ask me," Muldaur said. "He wants to blow up, that's his business."

Giancarlo came up alongside them. "What was with all the pushing and shoving?"

"He gets like that if there's any competition," Muldaur answered.

"Or if somebody's shooting at us?"

"I should have warned you."

"I was on the verge of smacking him," said Giancarlo.

Two minutes later they found a tree down across the road, Stephens sitting on it, his hands shaky when he pushed the Camel-Bak tube into his mouth. The tree hadn't been down when Zak and Muldaur traversed this road the day before, and it confounded Stephens. It confounded Zak, too.

Muldaur dismounted, lifted his bike over the tree, and continued to pedal up the mountainside at a measured pace. "I left it attached to the trunk, so they're going to need a saw or an ax to get it loose."

"You did this?" said Stephens.

"Yesterday when I took that ride by myself. I had a feeling they were going to haze us for the whole trip, and this was one way to stop them."

Zak knew even with the aid of a truck and ropes, the tree was too big and too heavy to move. He doubted Kasey and the others had a chain saw, though most locals would probably carry one. Muldaur had taken them on this route because he knew it was the only direction where they couldn't be followed.

"Any more roadblocks?" Giancarlo asked.

"As many as we have time for," Muldaur said, pulling a folding camp saw out of his jersey pocket with one hand and waving it. Zak and Giancarlo lifted their bikes over the log and remounted. Stephens, who appeared too tired to get up, said, "So this is why he said to slow down?"

"You should have listened," said Giancarlo.

"Yeah, well, uh, he should have explained himself. I thought they would get their trucks and be on us any second. I figured the last one in line—"

"We know what you figured," said Zak.

"Well, wait, uh, wait a minute. Aren't you going to wait for me? I need a breather."

A few minutes later they were climbing through trees so dense they could no longer see the contours of the mountain. The road surface was smoother, almost like a clay tennis court, and from time to time Zak saw the sunlight glinting through the branches of the Douglas firs to the southeast as they traversed another of the switchbacks. Zak knew that after they reached Lake Hancock there were two separate and very long climbs above it, one south of the water and one north. But they wouldn't reach the lake for another twenty or thirty minutes. "So what's the plan?" asked Zak.

"To get up this mountain and out of range of those rifles," said Muldaur. "After that we'll figure out something."

"You want to ride as slow as you can and still stay ahead of them," Zak said, directing his words at Stephens. "You start filling your legs with lactic acid, you'll be a goner. That means you need to keep your heart rate as low as you can."

"I *was* keeping it low," Stephens said, defensively.

"No, you weren't. Listen, the body produces lactic acid in everything it does. Under normal conditions your body clears the lactic acid, so it doesn't accumulate. But when you're working out, you can go past your lactic threshold, which is the highest point at which your pumping heart is able to clear the poisonous by-products. Above that point your muscles produce lactic at an accelerated rate, and the buildup retards your ability to transport oxygen from your bloodstream to your muscles. You rapidly get weaker. When you stay below the threshold, you can maintain most of your strength. Once above it, I'd guess you'll have twenty minutes, after which you'll be worthless.

"I know you don't have a heart monitor," added Zak, "so just try to go hard, but not so hard that you can't carry on a conversation. You get to that point, you're overdoing it."

"I'll try," Stephens said. "Thanks for the pointers. And I'm sorry about getting pushy."

"Don't worry about it."

The hills were beautiful this morning, Zak thought, as he caught a sliver of a view out over the valley cradling the towns of North Bend and Snoqualmie, and as he felt the warm winds wafting down from Snoqualmie Pass forty miles distant. It wasn't yet eight o'clock, but the temperature was in the high eighties.

Giancarlo rode at the end of the train almost out of habit now. He was the tallest and heaviest rider in the group, and total weight of rider and bicycle was the most significant factor in how fast a person could ride uphill, so he would most likely be last all day. As it circled Lake Hancock, the road flattened. Other than that, all of these old logging roads shot upward with a vengeance.

"I sure as heck wish I had my gun back," said Giancarlo.

"A gun's not going to solve anything," said Stephens. "We need to talk to them."

"It was that second shot that shocked me," said Giancarlo. "The first one could have been a mistake. But after he went down, Morse was clearly incapable of harming anyone. That second shot was pure spite."

"They waited on that second one," said Zak. "Like they were taunting him. Or us."

"There has to be some legitimate explanation," said Stephens.

Zak had been worried about so many other things, he barely had time to recognize the charcoal tang of smoke threading through the wind. Whether the smoke was traveling over the mountains from eastern Washington or from someplace closer, he had no way of knowing.

Muldaur, who had been riding in front, emitted a loud fart, then another, the latter lasting as long as any fart Zak had ever heard. Zak, who was directly behind him, moved over. "Thanks for the warning. Jesus, that was ripe."

Muldaur's reply was another fart. "Oh, my God," said Giancarlo.

"Christ!" said Stephens.

"Hey," Muldaur said, in Hugh's best voice. "I'm up here breaking wind for you guys." He laughed moronically. The phrase had a special context in cycling, for the riders in front did the most work—and it was called "breaking wind." Still laughing, Muldaur turned around to grin at them. This was so like Muldaur, Zak thought, to make infantile jokes while they were riding for their lives. As Hugh, he would sometimes visit the other shifts at Station 6 and cut the cheese loudly, giggling as they escorted him and his battered old Schwinn Varsity bicycle out the front door. "Oh, fuck," said Muldaur.

"What?" said Zak.

"Look behind us."

Fearful of losing his balance, Zak waited until he reached a pitch on the road that was slightly less steep before turning his head to scan the road. The four of them were near the top of a long, straight stretch, one of the steepest they'd traversed this morning, and had maybe fifteen more minutes before the Lake Hancock plateau. An animal was coming up the road behind them. A bear? No, it was moving with too much agility for a bear.

"It's Dozer," said Muldaur.

31

"Shit," said Stephens, revving up his rpms. Muldaur took the lead, Zak second, Stephens a distant third, and behind him Giancarlo.

"Fucking dog," said Muldaur.

"Is he catching us?" asked Zak.

"I can't tell."

"He wasn't running when I saw him."

"That's because he had his nose to the ground."

"Is he running now?" Zak turned around to check. The dog was moving in a lope. Dozer was a large dog—120, 130 pounds—so traveling uphill wouldn't be easy for him, but that didn't mean he couldn't run down four men on mountain bikes. The mechanical advantage of a bike extended only so far.

"What the hell?" gasped Stephens, who was still a couple of bike lengths in front of Giancarlo. "Wait for me. You guys? Wait for me!"

For half a minute they pedaled as hard as they could. As the effort began to eat into their reserves, Muldaur and Zak gained more ground on the other two until Zak realized that by the time the dog reached them, he and Muldaur might be out of sight. "We need to talk about this," said Zak, making a superhuman effort to get alongside Muldaur, who was slightly in front. "We can't leave them."

"You're right. I think we better face him down, the four of us together. If we get strung out, he'll take one of us down. Then the next. Maybe all of us one at a time."

By now Dozer had halved the distance between them.

"There's a bunch of rocks ahead," said Muldaur. "Let's stop. We can use the ammo."

Zak and Muldaur headed for a cluster of stumps and new-growth trees on an embankment. In the ditch stood a row of stringy foxgloves, seedpods heavy on the stalks. On the other side of the road was a steep downslope; they could see the tops of dozens of trees and, over the trees, a skimpy view of the valley floor to the west.

They'd just gotten off their bikes when the animal hit Giancarlo, who kept pedaling despite the fact that Dozer had hold of his leg and wasn't letting go. Towing the dog slowed his progress, but to his credit he managed to come to a full stop just below Zak and Muldaur, who began pelting the dog with the largest rocks they could heave. Zak hit the dog twice in the hindquarters, hard, while Muldaur hit him once directly across the middle of his back, but Dozer did not relinquish his grip. Three more solid strikes convinced the dog they meant business.

The moment he released Giancarlo's leg, Giancarlo put the mountain bike between himself and the dog, a row of flashing spokes in front of the dog's teeth. Slobber zigzagged through the air in silvery arcs as the malamute yelped and lunged.

As the others rained rocks down on the dog, Dozer switched targets and made a lunge for Zak, who backed up and used his bicycle as a shield. Soon the three found themselves trapped behind a line of bicycles, each holding his bike to fend off the attacks. Giancarlo worked his way around and was behind the barricade of bikes.

It didn't take long for the four men to realize they'd achieved a draw, at least for now. "What we got here is a Mexican standoff," said Zak.

"Somebody help me get a dressing on this?" said Giancarlo. Zak hadn't really looked at it until now, but a flap of skin the size of a woman's glove was hanging from Giancarlo's left calf, muscle and tendon exposed to the air. It looked grisly, but it was mostly damage to the skin, and Zak had patched worse. While Stephens and Muldaur kept the dog occupied, Zak wrapped Giancarlo's calf with several cotton four-by-fours and a roll of sterile cotton wrapping Muldaur kept in the pockets of his backpack. "We'll have to disinfect it at the hospital," said Zak. "It's going to need stitches, but there's no serious bleeding, and I don't think he got any of the muscle. You were lucky."

"Ordinarily I like dogs," said Giancarlo. "But this one's beginning to get on my nerves."

Stephens gave him a puzzled look and heaved another rock. It had been awhile since anybody had connected solidly, and the dog was beginning to regain his courage, moving in for another surge.

"You guys try to hold him at bay," said Giancarlo, hobbling up the embankment with a folded knife. Muldaur tossed him the camp saw he had tucked in his jersey pocket. Twice Dozer tried to circle and get into the trees so he could reach Giancarlo, and twice their bombardment deterred him.

"I think I know how to do this," said Giancarlo moments later as he stumbled down the slope with a sapling in his arms. He'd already stripped most of the branches and shaped it into a spear, whittling until he had a sharp point on the thick end. "I read about this in a hunting magazine."

"Thank God I thought to cut down that tree last night," said Muldaur. "Or they'd be up here shooting us by now."

"Yeah," said Zak. "We're lucky it's just this good-natured animal."

Giancarlo set the makeshift spear in the triangle of Zak's bike frame, its shaft between Zak's outspread legs. "What are you doing?" Zak protested.

"Just keep your legs like that. Don't move. Now I want you to get him really pissed."

"Isn't he already pissed?"

"Do it," said Muldaur. "We've been here too long. For all we know they're walking up the hill. Think about it. They're not going to leave him."

As soon as they stopped throwing rocks, the dog began inching forward, growling at Zak. "Come on, you egg sucker," said Zak. "Try me."

With the bikes in a semicircle, the four of them huddled inside, Zak the centerpiece and bait. Directly behind Zak, Giancarlo squatted with the six-foot pole between his legs, the sharpened tip resting on Zak's bicycle frame.

"Whatever you do, don't move," said Giancarlo.

"Don't move? Jesus, look at him!" The dog had closed in, locking eyes with Zak. From the sounds of the snarling, Zak knew he was readying for an attack, coming in low, ears flattened, haunches skimming the ground, muscular flanks rippling with tension. Zak's fear was that he would leap at his face and bypass Giancarlo's spear entirely.

Zak could feel the dampness in his short-fingered cycling gloves, a trickle of sweat wending its way down his spine. He wished he had something in his hands besides a twenty-three-pound bicycle. Both Stephens and Muldaur had rocks, but every time they cocked their arms to throw one, the dog backed off. Now, in accordance with Giancarlo's instructions, they let their arms hang slack.

The dog moved to Zak's right, then his left, scouting for weaknesses, for a moment of inattention, leery about absorbing another fusillade of stones. He would have already attacked if they hadn't made him cautious with all their rock throwing.

"Easy," said Giancarlo. "Get lower."

"Why am *I* the staked goat?"

"Because you're the cute one. He's stalling. He thinks it's a trick. Bark at him. Piss him off."

"Bark at him?"

"Do it."

Zak barked. "Act like a poodle," said Muldaur. "Like you're in heat."

"Next time you're the goat. Arf. Arf."

"There isn't going to be a next time," said Giancarlo. "A dog like this gives you one chance."

"What are you guys doing?" Stephens said. "You can't even get him to attack?"

A moment later the dog lunged, thrusting through the triangle in the bike frame. Zak felt Giancarlo's shoulder against his back, and for a moment he thought he was being pushed into the dog. Then the snarling animal let out a sound that wasn't quite a yelp, more like a cushion having the air squeezed out of it, and all three of them toppled forward, Giancarlo on Zak, Zak on his bike, the bike on the dog. Somehow Giancarlo had punched the shaft of the sharpened Douglas fir between the dog's open jaws and was skewering the animal, Giancarlo's thick shoulders and muscular arms tensing with the work.

"Move! Move! Move!" Giancarlo said.

Before he knew what was happening, Zak was jerked out of the fray by Muldaur. "Jesus," said Muldaur. "What do you want us to do?"

"Just leave me be. It's going to take a second."

Astonishingly, it took almost half a minute to kill the big dog. All Zak could think was that if *he* had a spear rammed down his gullet, he'd be dead in seconds. After it was finished, Giancarlo snapped the haft off his makeshift spear, grabbed the dog by a hind leg with one hand, and dragged him across the road, tossing him down a scree into the trees.

"That was just vicious," said Stephens.

"Zak'll be fine as soon as he changes his shorts," said Muldaur, laughing.

Zak started to laugh, and then Muldaur laughed louder. Giancarlo joined in. Stephens glanced from one fireman to another before trying on a weak smile. "I suppose, really, when you think about it, it was basically, uh, the dog or us . . . right?"

All four of them listened to the rush of the wind in the treetops and their own hearts thudding—and then, in the stillness of the mountains, the noise. It was a long way off so it took each of them a moment to recognize it, but within seconds they knew they were listening to the distant sounds of a chain saw.

"God, this is turning into a crappy trip," said Zak.

"You just noticed?" said Muldaur.

"The trouble with you guys," said Giancarlo, "is that you're pessimists."

The others followed Muldaur, Zak pulling alongside Giancarlo as they rode. "Does your leg hurt?"

"Yes, but the good news is it's not bleeding much."

"Can you handle the pain?"

"Why? Do you have some morphine?"

"No, but . . ."

"Then I can handle it."

"It'll feel better when they start shooting at us again," Zak said.

"Yeah. I can hardly wait."

Everything they'd said about pacing themselves went out the window now. The chain saw was still running, so they knew the crowd below wasn't moving yet, but Stephens was going for broke anyway. He passed Muldaur, who would, Zak realized, ride slowly only long enough to get warmed up again. The objective here was to protect the machinery for as long as possible. Warm up the motor. Run within its limits. Save your engine as long as possible.

By the time they got to the level part of the road that bordered Lake Hancock, Stephens had vanished ahead of them through a thick stand of trees. The three slowed near the top, cocking their heads trying to hear whether the saw was still running. "Is it?" Muldaur asked.

"We're too far away," said Zak. "You got a plan now?" he asked Muldaur.

"I think so."

"You going to let us in on it?"

"In a minute."

Riding as a trio, they increased their speed significantly, Muldaur leading, Zak and Giancarlo drafting, their speed picking up as Muldaur, the strongest rider, began doing the majority of the work. By the time they caught Stephens at the three-way intersection, they were flying, and Stephens, who had slowed and was balancing in the road waiting for them, couldn't sprint hard enough to catch their train. He shouted at them to stop, but Muldaur hooked a left at the intersection without losing any speed. From the reconnoitering they'd done the day before, Zak remembered another quarter mile of relatively flat road prior to the lake and then a spot where, despite the drought, there were puddles in the road, probably from an underground spring. The puddles were near a turnoff that led down to the lake. They were on the same route Zak and Muldaur had taken to the top of the mountain the previous day.

"Where are we going?" Stephens asked as they slowed and he caught them, then splashed through the springwater the rest of them had circumvented.

"Well," said Muldaur, "the plan was to go around that puddle so we wouldn't leave any tracks, but now that you've tracked it, we need to turn around and go the other way."

"Why?"

"Because you left tracks telling them which way we went. There's only two routes off this plateau, and you've muddied one."

"Oh. So we were going to make them think we took the other road?"

"Right. Now we're going to make them think we took this one," said Muldaur, circling in the road and making his own tracks through the spring, then riding north until his tires stopped printing mud. Zak and Giancarlo did the same thing. Then, before they could stop him from making a fifth set of tracks, Stephens did it again. Once their tires had been ridden dry on the rocky trail, they turned around and bypassed the mud hole so as not to leave tracks going in the other direction. If they were lucky, the others would think they'd taken the northern route. They rode fast, Muldaur in the lead again. Zak had a knot in his stomach, knowing this was the most dangerous part of their ride so far, because they would be backtracking for a while and might easily run into the trucks. After two minutes of hard riding Zak pulled forward and towed the pace line, giving Muldaur a breather. They reached the three-way inter-section and turned left, working their way down a continuation of the road they'd been on a few minutes earlier, then crossed a short bridge that spanned a stream coming out of Lake Hancock, the headwaters of Panther Creek, according to Stephens.

As they pedaled along the base of the mountain that sat at the south end of the lake, they heard a truck in the woods behind them and began pedaling for all they were worth, Muldaur and Zak changing leads while Giancarlo and Stephens drafted. The hope was that the trucks would go north, discover the muddy tracks, and keep going.

32

Driving the Porsche Cayenne, Kasey took the lead, Scooter riding shotgun with his rifle wedged upright between his knees, another rifle in the rear seat, which Kasey could appropriate as needed. Fred and Jennifer followed them closely in Chuck's Ford pickup truck, Fred manning a rifle out the passenger's window. Bloomquist followed in the Land Rover; tailing the trio of vehicles, Ryan Perry drove his Jeep with the enormous car-crushing wheels and tires. Why timid little Perry had ever bought that white-trash Jeep was a mystery to Kasey. It wasn't even his second vehicle. It was his primary set of wheels.

Kasey soon discovered that the road was so narrow, you had to find a turnaround to do any maneuvering, certainly in order to reverse course and head back down. In one sense they were like rats trundling through a series of very narrow pipes. If the cyclists were canny enough to hide in the woods until they went past, it might take forever to get turned around and mount a chase. On the other hand, there were damn few places where four cyclists might conceal themselves in these woods, which tended to be either impenetrable, sloping down the mountain at impossible angles, or all canopy and no underbrush, with nothing but skinny tree trunks showing for hundreds of feet. They found a couple of dead-end spur roads and explored them quickly, finding no trace of the cyclists.

When Kasey spotted Dozer running up ahead, he accelerated and was beginning to close in on the dog when the animal squirmed under a downed tree that lay across the road. All four speeding vehicles came to a sudden halt. Dozer's nose was to the ground, and judging by his body language the cyclists had not ducked into the woods yet and weren't far ahead. In fact, at the speeds they were driving, he'd expected to see them before now.

Luckily for them, Fred and Chuck had been toting the chain saw around for weeks to clear some motorcycle trails on the property their family owned near Cle Elum. While Fred pulled it out and fired it up, Scooter ducked under the tree and walked up the road with his rifle. Meanwhile Kasey scouted around and discovered the tree wasn't a blowdown at all but had been deliberately dropped across the road.

When Scooter came back, he spoke over the cacophony of the chain saw. "They were all in on it. The big guy. The retard. All of them."

"They must have planned this last night," Kasey said. "That's when this tree was cut down."

Jennifer's shock was quietly metamorphosing into rage. "They were planning to kill Chuck all along?"

"And me, too," said Scooter. "Don't forget they wanted to shove me off the cliff."

"Are you sure they didn't do the tree just a few minutes ago?" asked Bloomquist.

"That's impossible," said Fred. "It had to take a good long while to get this thing down with a handsaw. Bicycles. Handsaws. Seems like they do everything the hard way."

"But why did they kill Chuck?" said Jennifer. "What on earth were they thinking? And sending that guy down to get us with the gun? It seems . . . insane."

"All I know," said Scooter, "is Polanski's a psycho. You wouldn't even believe the lies he told Nadine to get her away from me."

"I wonder what other surprises they have waiting for us," said Perry, beginning to shiver with the excitement and terror of it. Kasey wondered if he was going to make it through the morning without fainting. Kasey wasn't worried about more surprises. The cyclists wouldn't be expecting a chain saw, so they were probably lollygagging now in the belief that they were home free. And just as *they* hadn't been expecting the felled tree, the cyclists wouldn't be expecting Dozer, either. He had no doubt the dog would cause his fair share of grief farther up the mountain.

After they cut the log away, Kasey drove slower while he and Scooter scrutinized the road above them. He knew there was a chance the cyclists had heard the chain saw, which meant they might be lying in ambush. Kasey sensed the renewed fear inside the Porsche, both from himself and from Scooter, who now fondled the rifle like a compulsive masturbator. It was mind boggling that those maniacs had downed a tree in order to block the chase and that they had done it the night before.

If they had tried to conceal the dog, they hadn't done a very good job. Scooter saw it first. "Shit! Look what they did to Dozer!"

Stopping close together, the four vehicles idled in the road. Kasey wanted to tell the others to back off, that they shouldn't congregate, but he was too upset by the dead dog to bother with tactics.

Scooter took a good long look at Chuck's dog, then peered up the road through the scope on the rifle, shoulders tight, squinting, cursing under his breath.

The others lined up along the road and stared at the skewered cadaver in the ditch.

"Jesus," said Bloomquist. "He was such a nice dog."

"He bit me once," said Perry quietly.

"Shut your fucking mouth." Fred was near tears. First his brother and now Dozer. "He never hurt anyone."

"These people are capable of anything," said Scooter, who hadn't taken his eyes off the road.

The whole morning had turned into a nightmare. All Kasey wanted to do now was drive back home.

"Damn it," said Jennifer, bursting into tears again. "Why is this happening?"

"Nothing else is going to happen," said Scooter, pointing his rifle up the hill. "We're in control here. *They're* running from us. We should take that dead guy and hang him in a tree. Show them we can be brutal, too." They'd wrapped Morse in a sleeping bag and thrown him into the back of the Porsche. Kasey hadn't approved but he couldn't stop them. Nobody thought it was appropriate to leave Morse in the road even though they had been forced to leave Chuck's body on the mountain.

"We're not hanging any bodies in any trees," said Kasey. "It's bad enough I'm driving him around like he's a sack of groceries, okay?"

"They left the dog as a message. We should leave them a message. The Indians used to do it. It was a way to terrorize your enemy. You'd be surprised how bad you can scare somebody by pretending to be crazy."

Kasey walked around to the driver's door on the Porsche. The rest of them piled into their vehicles and proceeded up the mountain, scanning the slopes that swept up from the left-hand side of the road. When they got to a plateau where the road flattened out, they sped up, hoping to catch the cyclists in short order.

"How fast do you think they can ride?" Kasey asked Scooter. "On a flat road like this? How fast?"

"Thirty-five miles an hour?"

"I was thinking more like ten."

"Hell, people can *run* ten miles an hour."

Their conversation drew to an abrupt halt when they reached an intersection, one branch leading straight ahead, the other veering to the left. Scooter got on the walkie-talkie. *"Which way, people? Let's have some ideas here."*

"Your guess is as good as ours," said Bloomquist.

"I'm thinking we go straight," said Jennifer. *"It seems like they would stay on the main road."*

"Seems like they would take a side road," Bloomquist countered. *"Remember, they're trying to be deceptive."*

They ended up taking the road that branched to the left. A minute later Scooter spotted tracks where the bicycles had splashed through a wet spot on the roadway. They stopped and everybody got out except Perry, who was anxiously looking around the woods from inside his Jeep. The woods were deep, one staggered tree trunk after another in the shaded canopy, and Kasey half expected to see somebody in a bright cycling jersey step out from behind the bole of a tree and unleash a flurry of gunshots.

"Okay," Kasey said, kneeling in the road next to the bicycle tracks. "I think there's a lake up here somewhere. I saw a sign back there—"

"Lake Hancock," said Jennifer.

"There are tracks from five bikes here," said Bloomquist.

Fred scratched his scalp. "There were five to start off with. We burned one bike back down the hill in the fire. There should only be three tracks if one of them is at the gate. What's going on?"

"We, uh . . ." Bloomquist didn't have an answer.

"No, somebody rode through this mud twice. Two somebodies. Hell, for all we know, only one of them went this way and the other three are behind us."

The two men with guns turned them toward the trees while the rest surveyed the landscape nervously. They watched the shaded woods for a long time. The only open space was the road behind and in front of them. Everything else was forest.

"Okay, okay," said Bloomquist, finally. "Let's get going. I don't like this."

Fred levered a cartridge into his rifle. "Jennie and I are going to check out that road to the lake. We'll catch up."

"Keep in touch on the walkie-talkie," said Kasey.

"If they start shooting," Fred said, "leave a couple for me."

33

By the time they got to the east end of the basin Lake Hancock lay in and found the old logging road that ran up the mountainside above the south shore, Zak decided the guys in the Jeeps had taken the other road. Perhaps the tracks they left had fooled them. Or maybe they'd found the dead dog, gotten scared, and turned around when they found room at the top of the ridge. Whatever it was, Zak suspected they now had a period of respite and should make use of it.

Even though he'd caught only a glimpse of blue water through the tops of the trees to their left, Zak knew the lake was there by the fact that the relentless stands of Douglas fir they'd been passing were now integrated with deciduous trees, saplings, brush, and other plant life that usually grew near water. Paralleling their path, a bald eagle soared over the lake. There were slopes to their right so steep a man could not walk up them. Some were solid rock, others loose rock anchored by scrubby trees. When they got to the end of the lake, the road took a sharp bend, nearly but not quite doubling back on itself, gaining altitude so quickly that Muldaur warned the riders behind him to drop their chains onto the small rings in front before they lost momentum and fell over.

As the clanking of chains on four bicycles sounded, Stephens looked up the hill and said, "Jesus, boys. We're going to have to walk."

"If a logging truck can make it," said Muldaur, "we can, too. Once you start walking, you're giving up the mechanical advantage."

Zak pushed the thumb selector on his handle grips and began going through his gears until he settled on the smallest of the three chain rings in front. It was a twenty-seven-speed bike, but when he looked down through his legs to see what gear he'd ended up in, he was in his second lowest.

"I think I'm going to have to get off," said Stephens, grunting with the effort.

"You get off, you won't get back on," said Zak.

"How far is it?" Giancarlo asked.

"I've no idea."

"There's some small lakes at the top," said Stephens. "And then the road actually goes back down to the river. It's kind of a big loop. We could actually make it back to town this way."

"Then that's what we should do," Muldaur said. "We circle up and around and back into town."

They were traveling a little slower than a fit man could walk. This side of the mountain was shielded from the wind that had been drying them on the first climb, and Zak found himself sweating heavily. He knew that if he turned around to see how the others were doing, he'd tip over, so he gauged the other riders' distance by the sound of their breathing and the noises their tires made on the hard rock. At least they were in the shadows and didn't yet have the sun beating down on them.

After a few minutes the road swerved to the right, giving Zak a view out over Lake Hancock, a beautiful blue puddle already several hundred feet below. It was a small lake encased by mountains on all sides, a row of cabins on the northwest lip; a strong man in a rowboat could cross it lengthwise in a few minutes. From here the cabins looked like Monopoly board pieces, and the water looked deep. The blue was enriched with swatches of green at either end and

traces of violet and jade in the middle. The bald eagle he'd seen earlier was still above the water, though they had now climbed above
him. Sounding mechanical, a hummingbird buzzed them, swinging
high above their heads and diving at them a second time like a
miniature warplane.

"God, they're aggressive," said Giancarlo.

"Up here they're very protective of their territory," Muldaur said.

The road grew steeper, and Zak pushed his thumb shifter until
he was in his lowest gear, traveling less than two miles an hour now.
Any slower and they'd tip over. A stand of trees came up on their
right, and the lake disappeared behind them. They were riding
single-file, each following the bike in front while searching out the
best part of the road. Zak couldn't see evidence of any vehicles having traveled this logging road in years, though there were some rust-
ing cables by the wayside in several spots.

The hillside here was so steep, Zak reminded himself to be careful in case they had to come back this way. At speed, a momentary
lapse of concentration could cause a bike to rocket hundreds of feet
off a bluff.

When they came out of the trees, they were in direct sunshine
for the first time in a long while. The shadows hadn't exactly been
cool, but now the road was baking. They were high on the mountain
on the south side of the lake. Zak had a hard time judging just how
much time it would take to reach the summit, or where the summit
might even be. Hazarding a glance behind, he saw Stephens almost
fifty yards back, Giancarlo behind him. Muldaur was still twenty feet
in front, which was close enough to keep in voice contact but not so
close they were in each other's way.

"How are they doing back there?" asked Muldaur.

"Okay so far. You see the top?"

"No, but from what we saw yesterday on the other side of the
lake, I'm willing to bet we're about a third of the way up."

They heard a popping sound from somewhere far below, the
lake and the basin it sat in acting as a natural megaphone in the quiet

morning air. When they heard a second pop, Zak said, "You think that's them?"

"It has to be. Probably trying to bring down that bald eagle. Everybody else was ordered to evacuate the area because of the fire danger. And we haven't seen anyone else."

Another hummingbird flew over their heads, and then another, whirring straight off the rocks to their right. It was a moment or two before Zak realized they were actually bullets. "They're shooting at us."

"Fuckers."

Muldaur moved to the far left side of the road, Zak following, each trying to minimize exposure to the riflemen. Zak could still see the lake and the cabins, which meant the shooters could see him.

"What's going on?" It was Giancarlo yelling from down the road. He'd dropped even farther back.

"They're shooting at us. Move over."

Zak lowered his upper body as much as possible, then heard a bullet thunk the earth embankment behind him. "They must be a quarter mile away," he said. "Maybe farther."

"More like a thousand yards. I wonder how long we're going to be exposed here."

It took another minute and several more bullets before they reached a mound of dirt and rock on the right side of the road that screened them. Zak stole a look behind and glimpsed Stephens and Giancarlo riding even farther to the left than he and Muldaur. The surface of the road was more uneven where they were, and as he watched, Stephens lost his equilibrium and was forced to snap out of his quick-release pedal and put a foot down. Without batting an eye, he began running his bike up the hill, pacing Giancarlo.

Then they hit another long open stretch where they would be exposed to gunfire. It gave Zak the creeps thinking that at any moment a bullet might puncture one of his lungs. It wasn't as if they could get medical help up here. Anybody wounded would probably die on this road, the others forced to leave him to his fate. He kept mentally replaying the gunshots that had killed Morse, especially the second bullet—the one that tore his brain apart. Any injured rider left on this road would most likely be finished off the same way.

They were like ducks in a shooting gallery, traipsing up the steep road one by one, two bright orange jerseys in the lead, followed by Stephens's red one and the royal blue on Giancarlo. They were wearing the brightest colors in the mountains.

They heard another shot, then another. Zak felt his heart thumping and looked down at the wristwatch heart monitor strapped to his handlebar: 180 beats per minute. If he kept this up much longer he wouldn't be able to ride at all. A bullet hit a wall of rocks to their left and whirred off into the distance like a Fourth of July firework. "You think from that distance a bullet still has any punch left? You think it would kill someone?"

"Not real dead," said Muldaur. "Just sort of dead."

"You see the top?"

"No. Do you?"

"I don't think there is a top."

Making a tremendous effort on foot, Stephens had almost caught Zak, while behind them Giancarlo was steadily losing ground. Breathless and choking on his words, Stephens pushed his bicycle alongside Zak. "There's a couple of old roads that veer off to the left. They go to old mining claims. There won't be anyplace to hide."

"Hide?" said Muldaur. "I was thinking more along the lines of climbing up this wall and dumping boulders down on them."

Stephens didn't have enough breath to reply. Zak said, "You find a spot, I'm with you."

"Shit!" gasped Muldaur. "Shit! Shit! Shit!"

"What is it?" Zak asked, pedaling harder, putting the pressure on until he caught Muldaur, who was twenty-five feet ahead now. The road was especially rutted here. Finally, he pulled up alongside Muldaur. They were beginning to sound like racehorses running themselves to death.

When Zak saw the Styrofoam shards sticking out of Muldaur's

helmet, he realized his friend had been hit. He didn't see any blood, but something had obviously nicked Muldaur's helmet above his right temple. "You okay?"

"Those fuckers almost got me."

Another bullet slammed into the rocks above their heads. After that it was all pumping legs, heavy breathing, and their own heart-beats thumping in their ears. After several more minutes the pitch of the road decreased, and Zak and Muldaur were able to drop down a couple of cogs, quickly outpacing Stephens, who was still pushing his bicycle.

34

Just when Jennifer thought things couldn't get any worse, Fred ran down to the water, where he knelt next to a thick tree, lined his rifle up alongside the trunk, and fired across the narrow lake and high up at the mountain. She couldn't get her mind off the dead dog in the back of the truck or the way his eyes seemed to be looking at her. At least the dead man in the back of Kasey's Porsche was wrapped in a blanket so she couldn't see his eyes. Fred fired again and again, saying "bastards" after each shot. "Bastards."

While the others headed up the mountain on the north side of the lake, she'd driven the Ford down a side trail that led seventy-five yards through a thick stand of trees to a small, muddy beach near the west end. The lake was so blue and gorgeous and pristine, she could hardly believe it was up here amid all this awfulness. Judging by the marks in the dirt, plenty of other trucks had at one time or another parked where she put the Ford. Along the shoreline she saw bits of fishing gear, a sinker with some line attached, a forgotten cherry bobber.

"What are you doing, Fred?"

Squeezing off another shot, then another, he said, "Bastards."

"What?"

When she stood behind him and traced his line of vision onto the mountainside, she realized he was pointing the gun at a scar on the mountain that traversed the slope on the other side of the lake at a steep angle from left to right, a scar she at first thought was maybe made by glaciers. Then she saw four dots moving up the mountain, two orange, a red, and a blue: the cyclists.

"Bastards!" Fred said, firing again. "Bastards."

"Stop it, Fred! Stop it. Let's just get on the walkie-talkie and tell Kasey we found them."

Without taking his cheek off the rifle he said, "They killed my brother."

It was clear from looking at the road and judging the cyclists' slow progress that Fred was going to be able to shoot at them for many minutes, and just as clear that they were so far away, hitting one would be next to impossible. Jennifer found a half-submerged log and sat on the dry end, trying to discourage Fred as he continued to crank off bullets at the hillside.

For the first time since he began shooting, Fred relaxed his massive shoulders and lowered the rifle, turned, and looked into Jennifer's eyes. He had the same starlit blue eyes Chuck had, the same blunt-cut blond bangs, and it gave her a pang to look at him and realize she'd never look into Chuck's eyes again. She and Chuck had been together for two and a half years, and sure, they'd had their share of ups and downs, but lately it had been more ups than downs. Along with his brother, he had a football scholarship to Stanford and had been looking forward to the next season. After college, he was slated to take a job in her father's brokerage house. Chuck hadn't been the sharpest pencil in the box, but Jennifer loved him and for a while now had assumed they would be married by the time they both finished college.

Fred had gone through most of the cartridges in his pockets when Kasey and Scooter located them on the water. "We heard the shooting," said Kasey. "What the hell are you guys doing?"

"We found them," said Jennifer.

"Where?" It took awhile for Scooter and Kasey to spot the riders maybe three-quarters of the way up the mountain.

By the time they got to the road behind Kasey and the others, all Jennifer and Fred could see was a trail of dust. Fred drove this time, handling the truck with the rough-hewn manner of someone who'd driven a lot of back roads, manhandling the steering wheel with those big freckled forearms that were so much like Chuck's. When they caught the others at the three-way intersection, Fred made a dangerous maneuver and passed Perry in his Jeep; driving along the flat road at the south side of the lake, they were now third in line. Fred kept swerving to the side of the narrow road looking for places to pass Bloomquist's Land Rover next. "The road's too narrow," Jennifer said. "Just stay here."

"I'm going to kill those bastards."

"If you don't watch what you're doing, you're going to kill *us*."

The Porsche had trouble maneuvering the tight uphill corner, slowing all of them before they began the long drag up the mountainside on the same road the cyclists were presumably still on. The view from the passenger's window was scary, extending hundreds of feet down the rocky slopes with only an infrequent tree here and there to slow their fall should they inadvertently drive off the edge, which is what it felt like they were about to do every time they hit a bump, Jennifer thought. At any rate, they would soon overtake the cyclists.

35

By the time they heard the trucks, Zak and Muldaur had gained a hundred yards on Stephens, and Giancarlo was so far back he was barely visible. It was hard to tell if the trucks were on the same slope they were scaling or alongside the lake, because the megaphone effect of the basin below and the molten-glass water surface magnified noises. A pair of crows cawed from a nearby tree. Hummingbirds continued to dive-bomb them. For almost half a minute an impossibly fat bumblebee buzzed alongside Zak.

Glancing at the heart monitor mounted on his handlebars, Zak saw they'd been climbing twenty-two minutes since the lake, riding as hard as they could for the last fourteen. At this rate he and Muldaur had only another fifteen or twenty minutes in their legs, perhaps a bit longer if they could find some more adrenaline. There was no telling how much longer Giancarlo and Stephens would be able to struggle on. Stephens was now suffering more than any of them. In cycling it was called blowing up, and anybody who blew up under these conditions would likely collapse alongside the road for a good long while.

Stephens found a shallow culvert engineered across the road to divert rainwater. By standing on the raised portion of the culvert, he managed to remount his Iron Horse bicycle and keep it pointed up-hill, so now all four of them were on their saddles.

The trucks had to be on the slope now. Zak had seen a plume of chalky dust billowing slowly over the east end of the lake, a sign that the trucks were moving fast on the dusty road. Surely they would be cautious on the climb, where any misstep on the narrow platform might propel a vehicle over the edge.

"They're on our heels," said Zak, pulling alongside Muldaur.

"What do you want to do?"

"You were the one with the plans."

"You see the top yet?"

"No. See anyplace to hide?" said Zak, joking. There was clearly no hiding here. The stretch of road they were on had a gravel scree running up from their left for fifty yards, rocky bluffs above that; the drop-off to their right was so sheer, even hiking down it would be insanity. Zak could feel his entire body bathed in sweat, could hear both Muldaur and himself gasping.

Realizing he was at his outermost limit of physical function, Zak found himself half a wheel in front of Muldaur, then a bike length in front. This year Muldaur had beaten him in most of the races they'd participated in, but today he was running out of steam and Zak was slowly pulling away. As he pressed on, the burning ache he'd been feeling in his quadriceps for the last fifteen minutes grew worse, until he thought he wouldn't be able to abide the pain any longer.

36

Ryan Perry stood on the edge of the universe. At least that's what it felt like when he took his first breath of outside air. His Jeep had developed universal joint problems and he'd been forced to abandon it near the second of the three small trout lakes they found at the top of the mountain. He hoped some local tow truck driver would be able to find the spot, because Ryan wasn't sure he could. The worst part was that he had so many personal possessions in the Jeep: electronic gear, radar detectors, hundreds of his favorite CDs, his new coat, and notes he'd taken while working a summer job in his uncle's real estate development firm. The Jeep was worth a small fortune, especially when you took into consideration the improvements he'd made: the suspension, the wheels and tires, and the sound system, which alone cost eight grand. On top of that, it had been a birthday present from his grandfather.

After it broke down, they redistributed the occupants of the remaining three vehicles, assigning Ryan and Scooter to the Land Rover. Fred and Jennifer were still in the Ford, while the Porsche Cayenne now carried Kasey and Bloomquist. The stated goal was to keep one rifle in each vehicle, but Perry suspected Scooter's covert reason for riding with him was to keep an eye on him. They hadn't seen a trace of the cyclists since Fred shot at them. They'd simply disappeared.

Disoriented after coming back down the road from the lakes, they traveled in circles for more than an hour, confused by roads and intersections that all looked alike, and bedeviled by trees that were so tall they obscured the sun. When they arrived at an intersection they'd already seen twice and realized they were going in circles, they decided to split up. The first couple to find a path out of the maze would mark the trail with broken tree branches and give directions to the others on their walkie-talkie.

In the past few minutes Ryan and Scooter had driven through a dark forest and come to a long, rocky descent they hadn't seen previously. It was frightening to Ryan, because they'd been crisscrossing all through these roads for almost two hours, and all they knew for certain was that this road went down the mountain in a west-northwest direction and that the aerie they'd located looked out over the same valley they'd seen the night before, albeit from a vantage point several miles south. Perry was more confused than an orphan at a family reunion. When they hit this small plateau, he could have sworn they were heading east, yet it turned out they'd been headed due west.

Perry wasn't happy to be with Scooter, whose black mood was matched only by his incessant cursing. Scooter's foul mouth had always bothered Perry, more so today than ever. It would have been a simple thing for Perry to hop into the Land Rover with Bloomquist, and he'd suggested as much, but after a private huddle with Scooter, Kasey had nixed the notion.

The Land Rover idled behind them on a flat overlook filled with broken rock from one of the nearby mines. Perry stood in the sunshine on a large boulder that looked out over the valley, a shadowy mountain to their left. They were four thousand feet above the flat valley, and the view was almost the same as from his father's Cessna. Keeping a grip on the rifle, Scooter climbed up onto a horizontal gray log that appeared to be about a year older than God. Every time he wanted to see something below, he put the rifle to his cheek and peered through the scope.

The air was warm and moist and so stifling without the air-conditioning that Perry had a hard time filling his lungs. To their left was a somewhat taller mountain they assumed was Mount Si. Some relatively cool air currents were flowing down the steep sides of the mountain, but they didn't alleviate any of the oppressive heat, which had reached the upper nineties and in some places triple digits. He could see a town in the distance, although he couldn't make out the details in the pudding-like conglomeration of smoke and haze that had settled over the area.

More than three hours had elapsed since Chuck died.

Using his riflescope, Scooter discovered a series of wildland fires off to the right, where the smoke was blowing along the ground. The landscape was murkier to the north, a whitish haze obscuring the panorama that had been visible earlier that morning.

"Is that a forest fire?" Perry asked.

"Looks that way, doesn't it?"

"There's haze everywhere."

"It was like this yesterday, too, only not as bad. It's those fucking forest fires."

"I know you're going to get mad at me for saying this, but we should get out of here before somebody else gets killed."

"It's just that sort of attitude that's the reason you're with me. Don't worry about it. We're not leaving until we find the bastards who killed Chuck and Dozer."

"I don't want to be an accomplice."

"Fine. There's a town right down there. Start hiking."

"You know I can't do that with my bad feet. Besides, it must be what, fifteen or twenty miles?"

"Then shut the fuck up."

Perry didn't say anything for a couple of minutes. Below them, he watched a helicopter hover over the fires in the distance, probably a news chopper. Knowing Scooter could go all day without breaking the silence and hating the tension between them, Perry spoke. "Those fires don't seem connected. I wonder how close they are to the road we came in on?" When Scooter didn't reply, he continued, "I hope we don't run out of gas. Maybe you shouldn't let the car idle every time we get out."

It took a few moments for Scooter to lower the rifle. "Fuck you. You know how hot it would be if we got back in and the air-conditioning wasn't running?"

"I was just thinking out loud."

"Come on. Let's see where this road leads."

Scooter got into the Land Rover, picked up his walkie-talkie, and said, *"Commando Three to Commando One."*

After a moment, the walkie-talkie hissed. *"Commando One, over."*

"We found a road that goes down the hill. I'd say it's about half a mile to the west of where we last talked. Just stay on the main drag we took and you'll find it."

"Roger. We'll be up here awhile longer. Bloomy found some bike tracks. We're trying to figure out which direction they went. We'll get back to you."

"Over and out."

37

They'd been dodging the trucks for hours now, trying to make their way to safety. Zak knew that Stephens had a fair idea of which direction they should be heading, but it seemed as if every time they began making progress, the trucks would trundle past, a rifle bristling out the passenger's window of the big white Ford. Each time they dived into the woods with their bikes and hid as best they could; after the trucks passed they returned to the road and pedaled for a while, ears cocked. It was dodgy because several times the trucks had doubled back within a few moments of passing them.

Having stumbled upon one of the primary routes back down the mountain, they'd stopped at a ledge and gazed out over the panorama of Seattle's skyscrapers far in the distance, unsure whether the trucks were below them or in the woods behind them and not knowing which direction to take.

They'd spent most of the morning climbing, getting shot at, and then meandering around this huge, forested plateau on various logging roads in an effort to keep one step ahead of the Jeeps. After escaping from the Lake Hancock basin a mere thirty seconds ahead of the trucks, they'd climbed one of several offshoot roads Stephens later said ended at three of the best fishing lakes in the state. They had been forced to hide, and not very well, when the trucks came roaring up behind them. Although the trucks didn't stop, Zak could have sworn they'd been spotted by the guy in the Jeep who'd been last in line, Ryan Perry. He looked right at Zak, eyeball-to-eyeball, but kept going. It was the closest they'd come to getting caught, and Zak wondered if he'd really been spotted and Perry, for some unknowable reason, was covering for them.

Once the trucks had passed, they descended the twisty mountain road at breakneck speeds, expecting the vehicles to be on their heels, yet they didn't come back down for quite some time. Had the cyclists continued to the top, they would have been trapped where the trees thinned out at just over five thousand feet. Two hours had passed since the close call, and now they were on the lip of the Cascades looking out at most of western Washington, including Seattle, Bellevue, and parts of Puget Sound. "We could go down the hill here," said Zak, "but we might be riding into their laps."

"I think we should stand in the road and talk to them," said Stephens. "They're not going to shoot us. At least not with us looking them in the eye."

"You want to bet your life on it?" said Muldaur.

"They're not psychos."

"No, they're not psychos," said Zak. "But for some reason they're acting that way."

"What they are," said Giancarlo, "is a bunch of out-of-control, spoiled rich kids who got pissed off and decided to take the law into their own hands."

"Easy there on the rich-kid stuff, Giancarlo. You're starting to sound like Zak." Muldaur laughed.

Muldaur had, over the course of the past hours, become the de facto leader of the quartet. It was natural for Zak and Giancarlo to take orders from him—they both knew him as a lieutenant in the fire department—but where Stephens worked *he* was the boss, and he clearly resented taking a backseat. Still, in the last hour they'd worked as a cohesive unit under Muldaur's leadership.

Stephens looked around the group. "I think they're behind us."

"There are no recent car tracks anywhere here," said Giancarlo, stooping over the road. He'd become their unofficial tracker by virtue of his hunting experience and had already twice shown them where they needed to cover their tracks in the dust to keep from giving away their route.

"No tracks doesn't mean they're not below us," said Zak. "They could have taken another road." Zak figured they could see at least fifty miles to the west, south, and north. To the east behind them lay an area clogged with old stumps that stretched for fifty yards before the dark woods began.

"Hear that?" said Zak. "A truck!"

"Which way's it coming?" Giancarlo asked, mounting his bike.

Muldaur glanced down the hill and said, "Not from down there."

"Which way do we go?" Stephens was on his bicycle. "Down or back? I have to warn you, this is a nasty downhill."

"Let's head for those trees over there," said Muldaur, running with his bike and mounting it on the fly. The four of them barely made the trees before the Land Rover hove into view from the shadowy road. They found a hollow where they were all able to duck down and hide.

Peering through a stack of dead trees and stumps the logging companies had dumped twenty years earlier, Zak found a perfect spy hole from which to observe the Land Rover 150 feet away. He watched as Scooter and Ryan Perry got out and took up the identical positions Muldaur and Zak had abandoned moments earlier. Scooter had a rifle in his hands.

Zak looked down at his crocheted cycling gloves and realized his hands were shaking. He couldn't believe how angry he was.

From time to time Scooter would jerk the rifle to his shoulder and peer through the scope as if practicing to shoot at a moment's notice. Zak turned to Muldaur and whispered, "You fart this close, they're going to hear it."

"I'll make it sound like a 12-gauge," said Muldaur. "We can get away while they're ducking for cover."

"You guys are gross," said Stephens.

"I have an idea," said Muldaur. "If they go down the hill, we'll follow them. It's a narrow track, but if we can get in front, we might get them to chase us."

"Chase?" whispered Stephens. "Are you nuts? Why would we put ourselves in the line of fire?"

"Look how steep that road is. Scooter'll crash trying to keep up."

"What if he doesn't? What if we crash?"

"It's too chancy," said Giancarlo, who was their best descender and whose opinion in this matter Zak valued above the others'. "Maybe one guy could pull it off, but even that would be dicey."

"That's why they won't be expecting it," said Muldaur. "It'll drive Scooter insane to see two of us come past. And that Land Rover is high and tippy. You saw him last night. He's a crappy driver."

"He got super-pissed when we beat him," said Zak. "If we did it again, he would really be mad."

"I think it's a bad idea," whispered Stephens. "You can beat them down, maybe, but at the bottom the road runs flat along the river for a good bit before it gets to the bridge. If they don't crash, they'll catch you on that section."

"If we do it right they'll crash," said Muldaur. "Somebody come with me."

"It's suicide," said Stephens.

Muldaur looked at Giancarlo, who said, "My leg. I can't do it."

"Zak?"

"Chase them down the hill?"

"One of us on either side. Scare the piss out of them."

"They'll shoot at us when we come by."

"They'll be lucky if they keep all their teeth in their mouths going down that mountain."

"So will we."

"Are you coming with me?"

"I wish we knew the road better."

When Scooter and his companion got into the Land Rover and

disappeared slowly over the lip of the mountain, Muldaur pedaled through the weeds and rocks to the road. By the time Zak caught him, he'd already reached the juncture where the road headed downhill. Zak took the wheel rut on the right side of the road, while Muldaur took the one on the left.

38

"This thing just doesn't seem right," said Perry, holding the armrest on the door with one hand, bracing himself against the dashboard with his other. In an attempt to further wedge himself in, he had one foot on the seat and his knee in his chest. The Land Rover was rocking so violently Perry felt like a shoe banging around inside a washing machine. He'd already bit his tongue and smacked his elbow on the window, and now that Scooter was beginning to pick up speed, he'd fumbled for his seat belt so many times he gave up. It was all he could do to keep from bouncing through a window and landing on the road.

This was by far the worst road they'd seen so far—and they'd been on some doozies—rocky as heck, the pitches changing every fifteen or twenty feet, off camber at the worst times, with more frequent and rockier rain diversions across it than anything they'd seen until now. Much of the road surface seemed to be granite, slick and hard, and there were loose rocks everywhere. There was no telling how many months or years since anybody drove it.

The only good part was that Perry was able to see the panoramic view out to the west, at least when his teeth weren't clacking together. Scooter had his eyes glued to the road, wrestling the steering wheel as if it were alive, cursing every time they hit a bump, pumping the brakes and letting them go and then jamming them again, engaging the ABS system four times in just the first hundred yards. It was almost as if he were deliberately trying to pitch Perry through the windshield.

And then in a flash their situation changed. Whooping like wild Indians on a raiding party, two orange-clad cyclists passed them, one on either side, flashing down the hill at almost twice the speed of the Land Rover.

They'd come so close to their windows and had startled Scooter so badly he momentarily lost control of the vehicle. Perry smashed his head against the roof and yelled, "Shit!" It came out *thit*.

"Jesus! What was that? Bastards!"

"Don't chase them," said Perry. "They're going too fast."

Scooter sped up anyway. It was reckless, and Perry was about to tell him to slow down when Scooter thrust the rifle at him with one hand. "Pump some lead into those assholes." Incredibly, without losing control of the vehicle, Scooter had snatched the rifle from the floor in the back. They hit another bump and Perry's head made contact with the roof again, causing him to see stars. The rifle smacked him in the face and then flew into the backseat, where it bounced into the cargo area in the far rear.

"Shoot those fuckers."

"Are you kidding? It's all I can do to keep from going through the roof."

"Ass wipe."

They passed a small waterfall, the water rushing under the roadway through a culvert. Then the road flattened and turned left, gigantic rocks on either side. It swung right and began descending along the edge of the mountain again. Somewhere between the time Ryan lost his grip on the rifle and the waterfall, they lost sight of the cyclists. When they came back into view there was only one rider, and he'd lost most of his speed. "Where's the other fucker?" Scooter asked.

"I don't know. Slow down and quit swearing. Maybe the other guy went off a cliff."

"We can only hope."

"*We're* going to go off a cliff if you don't slow down."

"Quit being such a pansy. We almost have him."

Perry's tongue was swelling where he'd bitten it, and he could taste iron as his mouth filled with blood. Twice in the last hundred yards the suspension had bottomed out with a horrible metallic clunking, and twice they'd hit so hard Perry thought he'd sprained his neck. He was being jostled so that his voice came out in a warble. Whatever else was going on, they must have been making the cyclist nervous, because the remaining rider kept turning his head half a notch so he could chart their progress in his peripheral vision. Perry could see no obvious reason for the cyclist's sudden decrease in speed. Whatever prompted it, the cyclist looked to be in complete control, while Scooter was barely able to keep the Land Rover on the narrow, snaking track.

Gradually they drew close enough that Perry could see it was the retarded guy. As soon as he realized who it was, Scooter began driving even more recklessly, edging closer to the rear wheel of the bike. "Stay still, motherfucker! I'm going to run you down."

"Quit cursing," said Ryan.

"Go fuck yourself."

"You're going to get us killed!" Just as he spoke, they slid partially off the road and sideswiped a sheer wall. Perry was surprised he'd yelled, and even more surprised at how high-pitched his voice sounded. He hadn't flung such anger at anyone in years. The noise the Land Rover made when it contacted the rocks merged into the excruciating staccato cacophony coming from Perry's mouth when he realized they were both about to die.

"Look. We can tag this bastard. Watch me tag him."

"Can't you see he's toying with you?"

"No way. All I have to do is put on a little pressure and he'll go off into the trees. If we catch him, I bet I can make him tell me where the others went."

The cyclist slowed on a piece of road about twenty feet long, a section less steep than the rest. He raised his left hand above his head and gave them the one-finger salute, then shot down the hill like a guided missile. Scooter gunned the accelerator.

Ryan stopped talking as they went around a curve that had a drop-off on the left. He could feel a knot growing on his forehead like a unicorn horn. All he could see was air, haze, and blue sky. Scooter turned the wheel too hard, and they went back across the road to the right, where the Land Rover nudged a barrier of rocks, bounced, hit it again, and then without Ryan knowing how, spun around 180 degrees. They were suddenly sailing down the hill backward, the cliff on their right.

Scooter was screaming a torrent of curse words, and then Perry was yelling, too. He heard metal on metal. Metal on rock. Metal on dirt. Metal on trees and brush. Bushes rushing past the sheet metal and windows. He was tumbling inside the car. They seemed to tumble forever. When they finally stopped, all he could hear was steam hissing out a broken engine hose and the stereo, which was still blaring. Scooter was moaning. At first Perry figured Scooter was surely dead, or about to be, while he himself was going to be okay.

Considering what he'd just gone through, Perry felt surprisingly sound. It seemed as if they'd been sliding and rolling and careening forever. It was only when he tried to get out that he realized he couldn't move. Not an inch. Not his arms or legs or head. Not even his pinkie. In fact, now that they'd stopped tumbling and he'd stopped holding his breath, he came to the sudden realization that he couldn't breathe, either. He was in a vise of crushed metal, and the vise was so tight he couldn't expand his lungs or close them. He was so constricted, he could barely squeeze thoughts through his cranium. One thing was certain. If he didn't get out of this in just a few seconds, he was going to suffocate.

"Somebody help me," he wanted to say, yet, when he tried to speak, the only thing that happened was a little bit of warm blood trickled down his chin.

39

Muldaur heard the crash behind him and began to decelerate. It had sounded like a house rolling down the road, metal grinding, trees snapping, glass breaking, and, buried in the middle of the insanity, one man screaming.

He coasted another 150 yards before he found a widening of the road where it was flat enough to turn around, then began riding back up toward the accident site.

The grade was like a wall in spots, and he marveled at how recklessly he'd been descending. He used his lowest gear and slid forward on the saddle so he wouldn't tip over backward. The slopes on the left side of the road were peppered with Douglas fir, and there were trees off to his right amid the gullies. Farther up there'd been bluffs and death-defying drop-offs, but they'd crashed at a spot where a screen of trees caught them.

He and Zak had separated earlier at a place where the road dropped like the dip in a roller coaster, and at the bottom of that dip was a hairpin curve to the left, a turn Muldaur had barely negotiated. There'd been a bailout road mostly overgrown with grass and saplings, which Zak had taken partway back up the hill while Muldaur continued left. Neither said a word. It was simply understood that Zak couldn't make the corner.

Now Muldaur saw a long strip of chrome on the edge of the road and found scuff marks in the dirt where the Land Rover had gone into a stand of immature trees. The trees had netted the SUV, bringing it to a halt before it could tumble farther down the mountain. It was on its roof, nose pointing toward the road, small trees crumpled under it.

Muldaur laid his bicycle on its side, then carefully picked his way down the rock scree toward the crash site.

They'd all been flirting with disaster, but for some reason the reality of the accident hit him now like cold water. His heart was in his mouth, sweat dripping off his nose and out of his helmet. It was a weird feeling, walking down to this wreck he'd precipitated, almost as weird as seeing Chuck Finnigan step off the bluff this morning and not being able to do anything about it.

The Land Rover's roof was caved in, the undercarriage facing up. Muldaur lay on his belly in the rocks and peered inside. As his eyes damped down from the bright sunshine, he recognized a man inside, his shoulders and head showing. He was pinned in the twisted sheet metal.

"You okay, buddy?" Muldaur said. "Hey, buddy. Buddy?"

"Can't breathe," gasped the man in the car. His lips and face were dark with loss of oxygen, his features bloody, battered, and unrecognizable, his eyes open but filled with blood and earth from the crash so that it was impossible to know if he was gazing at Muldaur or his maker. The interior of the Land Rover reeked of gasoline, beer, fresh pine needles, and mountain dust. Muldaur knew there'd been two men in the Land Rover, Scooter and Ryan Perry, but he had no clue which this was.

"Listen, we're going to get you out of there."

"Can't breathe."

"Get up, motherfucker!" Muldaur looked up from the position he'd taken on his stomach to see Scooter standing over him with a rifle. Scooter's forehead was bruised and swelling, and blood ran down his face from his scalp. "Get up, you idiot! Move!"

"He needs help."

"And you're going to give it to him?"

"Look, the two of us can get the jack out and pry some of this loose. We can at least give him some space so he can breathe, but we have to move fast."

Scooter considered the notion for a few seconds and then pumped a cartridge into the chamber of the rifle. "Stand up before I do you right here."

"But he's suffocating."

Scooter fired the rifle into the rocks behind Muldaur, then motioned for Muldaur to move away, kept motioning until Muldaur was fifteen feet from Scooter. It was an effective tactic, Muldaur thought, because the rocks would slow him considerably if he tried to rush the other man.

After Muldaur had moved away, Scooter peered into the crushed SUV. "Ryan. Ryan? You all right?" He reached inside with one hand, came out with a handful of dirt, then a shoe. He looked at Muldaur. "You killed him."

"He's not dead. We can get him out. I'm telling you."

"You're not telling me anything, you moron. Get up the hill."

"No, let me check. I can—" Scooter fired another bullet into the rocks, this one closer than the last. He did it carelessly, as if he didn't mind kneecapping Muldaur or shooting one of his toes off.

As they climbed through the rocks to the road, Muldaur conjured up several stratagems to take the gun from Scooter, but Scooter kept his distance, and the muzzle remained trained on his target.

Scooter gestured for him to kneel in the road in the classic assassination pose. "Get down, motherfucker."

Before he could comply, Scooter walked behind Muldaur and struck him across the shoulder blades with the butt of the rifle. The blow knocked him to the ground on his face, the Styrofoam helmet crunching against the rocks. "Up! Up, you bastard!" As soon as Muldaur got to his knees, Scooter hit him again. He smacked Muldaur in the head until the helmet came apart, leaving only a system of straps and a couple of strands of Styrofoam. One of the lenses on the sunglasses popped out.

The gun came down again on the back of Muldaur's neck and threw him to the roadway. For a moment he thought he wouldn't be able to get back up. The blow could easily have paralyzed him. Scooter kicked him in the ribs. "Where are they?"

"Where are who?"

"Your friends."

"I don't know."

Scooter kicked Muldaur again, and Muldaur, thinking about the appropriate time to make a grab for the rifle, covered his head with his hands and curled into a fetal position. "Just tell me where your friends are hiding!"

Scooter barraged Muldaur with blows, kicking and slapping and swinging the rifle down hard while Muldaur slapped back ineffectually, hoping to grab the rifle but coming up empty each time.

ak knew the Land Rover had crashed but didn't know how badly, and a minute after he heard all the noise, he managed to find a vantage point in the road where he spotted Scooter wandering in the trees with a rifle. The Land Rover was wrecked. Muldaur and the other occupant were nowhere in sight, and Zak knew that if he exposed himself, he'd be shot at. So he waited. Seven minutes later, when he saw Scooter marching Muldaur out of the trees at gunpoint, something in his gut rolled over.

From his vantage point he couldn't see all of the beating, but what he did witness threw him into a state of disbelief—Scooter swinging the rifle at Muldaur and knocking him to the ground, then knocking him to the ground again.

Zak made his plan as he rolled down the hill and saw a natural ramp on the road directly above Scooter. If he picked up enough speed, he might get airborne, and if he got airborne and timed it properly, he might take Scooter down. At the very least, he would crash into him, and if Zak kept to hard surfaces, Scooter might not hear him coming until it was too late.

When Scooter did hear him, Zak was already barreling down the mountainside at almost thirty miles an hour, Scooter jacking a cartridge into the chamber, sighting along the barrel, pointing the

Winchester toward Zak's chest as Zak bounced down the road. Somewhere in the middle of it the gun went off.

The crash was a blur, and strangely it was silent in Zak's brain. He was in midair when the explosion occurred, and he definitely felt the heat of the gunshot on his bare leg, but he didn't hear it. Later he figured the bullet had gone harmlessly between his legs. He must have hit Scooter with one of his pedals, because he felt a jolt in the crank arm. The force twisted Zak and the bike around in midair and flipped him. It was a rough fall—he'd been higher than Scooter's head when it started.

Now Scooter was on the ground cradling his bloodied head, Muldaur standing over him with the rifle, while Zak lay on his back trying to assess the damage he'd incurred. The wind had been knocked out of him, and his left hip and rump burned with road rash. Both shoulders were sore, but the helmet had protected his head, even though he had a headache. His right ankle was scraped, and he could feel blood seeping through the sock.

Zak rolled over and then got to his hands and knees slowly, bending his joints, counting his digits, inspecting himself for wounds. He stood slowly and limped over to his bike and found that, miraculously, except for a bent brake lever, it was mechanically sound. Zak picked it up and walked it up the hill toward Muldaur, testing his legs and glancing down at the blood oozing out his arm. A crash at such a speed should have been a lot worse. Fortunately, the impact with Scooter had absorbed much of his momentum.

Except for a large tear in the left leg of his cycling shorts, Zak's kit was intact, as were his sunglasses.

Lying on his side, Scooter groaned and said, "Don't hurt me. Please don't." Muldaur had the rifle now.

Following Muldaur's directions, Zak headed down the dirt scree toward the flipped Land Rover, aware that the closer he got to the vehicle, the more nervous he became. It was as if he were walking through a trapdoor directly into his childhood. This wasn't anything like coming up on a wrecked car while riding Engine 6. He didn't have a crew backing him up. He didn't have protective equipment, and he didn't have the profession propelling him forward. Here he was free to let fear take full rein. And for reasons he would mull over for years to come, take over it did.

Ten feet away from the wreck, he froze.

Zak peered into the half-crushed Land Rover. He edged forward, his legs quivering. He was having a difficult time breathing. He wanted to move forward. He wanted to squirm into the crushed passenger's compartment and find the occupant, but, hypoxic and shaking, he stared into the vehicle in a daze.

There was no telling how long his stupor lasted. When he finally came out of it, he forced himself to creep forward and touch the Land Rover. If he could touch it, perhaps the feel of warm metal in the August heat would bring him back to his senses. When he put his palm on the Land Rover and pushed gently, the vehicle tipped slightly. He knelt and peered inside at a man who, if he was alive, probably didn't have more than a few minutes left. Zak had met him a month earlier at a picnic at the Newcastle estate: Ryan Perry, one of the tagalongs who followed Kasey and Scooter everywhere. Nadine once told him Kasey divided his friends into two groups, those he genuinely liked and those he tolerated but made fun of when they weren't around. Perry was firmly in the latter camp and always had been.

He appeared to be dead, but Zak would have to check for a pulse to be certain, which meant crawling inside.

Okay, he said to himself. *Get inside, check his carotid artery, and then get out. No problem. You've done it a hundred times. Just do it.* Perry's eyes weren't exactly open, but they weren't closed, either. Zak knew if he were in uniform, he'd be inside by now, but he wasn't in uniform and he'd fallen into a well of fear he couldn't climb out of. It was impossible for him to put into words why he couldn't go into the wreck, what the fear was all about.

And then he was astonished to see a drop of liquid splash in the dust at his feet. Then another. Liquid was running off his face, which he mopped with the back of his cycling glove.

As soon as he realized he was crying, he entered into a transcendental moment in which he wasn't quite sure if he was kneeling beside a car with his dying sister inside, or kneeling beside a car in the woods seventeen years later. A good portion of his brain wasn't sure if he was twenty-eight or eleven. What made it worse was that his situation gave him a flash forward into the rest of his life. From now on there would be a hundred things he wouldn't be able to do. The car was only the first of myriad successive cascading dominoes. In the future he might not be able to go into fires. He might not be able to climb tall ladders. Zak Polanski—the sniveling coward who let his sister die because he couldn't crawl into the car to unfasten her seat belt.

"What are you doing, Zak?" Muldaur yelled from the road. "Hurry up. They're on the walkie-talkie. They're headed this way. We have to get moving."

Zak heard himself say, "He's dead."

"You already went in?"

"Yeah," Zak lied. "He's dead." Zak headed back up the hill, stepping carefully over the rocks so he wouldn't twist an ankle. In the space of two minutes he'd turned into a coward *and* a liar. He'd been waiting for it his whole life, it seemed, and now it was here, the fait accompli. As he walked up the hill, he wondered if it showed on his face.

Scooter was standing now but didn't look like any kind of threat, blood gushing from his nose, his shoulders hunched as if he'd been beaten. "You're going to pay for this, Polanski, you fuck. You broke my goddamn collarbone. You almost killed me. You're going to pay big time."

With the rifle laid horizontally across his handlebars, Muldaur headed down the hill. "Come on, Zak. They're right behind me."

Giving Scooter one last look, Zak caught Muldaur a hundred yards down the mountain. "Are they really coming?"

"Yeah. I got one of their walkie-talkies in my pocket."

"Com One to Com Three. Where are you? Come in?" When nobody

replied, the speaker said, *"Com One to Com Three. We're halfway down the mountain. Where are you?"*

"If they're halfway down the mountain, they're right behind us," said Zak. "You think they'll stop at the wreck or keep coming?"

"They'll pick up Scooter and check on the dead guy."

"I hope so." Zak wondered if Ryan Perry was really dead.

"Back there. That was the most awesome piece of riding I've ever seen. Scooter came damn close to blowing your nuts through the roof of your mouth when you came down the hill."

When they got to the bottom of the mountain and the road leveled out, they heard the white noise of the river. Stephens had told them it was a mile from the bottom of the mountain to the crossroads, but Zak wasn't thinking about the crossroads. Freezing up outside the Land Rover scared him in a way nothing else had in almost two decades. It scared him more than any of the close calls he'd ever encountered in the fire department, and he'd had his share.

Even if it hadn't cost Ryan Perry his life—which it might well have—in his own mind his failure would always stand between him and Nadine. Zak had been waiting for the day when the cowardice he'd discovered in his childhood would infect his adult life, and this was that day.

41

Having taken first-aid training with the ski patrol, Kasey was the only one who knew how to cut a blanket into strips to make a sling and swathe for Scooter's fractured clavicle. He worked on the sling while Fred hiked down through the rocks and broken trees toward the Land Rover. Kasey handed his rifle to Bloomquist. "Here. Keep an eye on the road. There's no telling where those guys are."

"Plus, they took my gun," Scooter said.

"What?"

"What do you mean *what*? Take a look at that car. I was lucky to get out alive. Next thing I know that retard grabs my Winchester."

"I don't understand why they didn't shoot you," said Bloomquist. "I thought they wanted to kill us all."

"They might shoot me, still. They might shoot us all, still. Right now the retard has the rifle."

All of them peered down the road with varying degrees of trepidation. Kasey could feel the paranoia in the group as if it were being passed from one to the other like a bottle of tequila. It was an eerie feeling to think somebody was watching him, eerier still to think they might be doing it through the telescopic sight of a high-powered rifle. They all crouched down, and Roger, who'd been holding the weapon as if it were a broomstick, began taking an interest in its working parts. Kasey noticed that the only one who didn't try to make himself into a smaller target was Scooter. It must have been the pain that kept him from being more diligent.

Moments later, Fred called up from thirty feet below the road. "Perry's in there."

"How is he doing?" Kasey asked.

"I think he's dead."

"What do you mean you think he is dead?"

"Read my lips. I think he is dead."

"Did they kill him?" Kasey turned to Scooter.

"I think the crash did," yelled Fred.

"Oh, my Lord," said Jennifer.

Bloomquist, who had a rich chocolate tan from lounging around the Newcastle pool all summer, turned pasty and began to look faint. He and Ryan had been friends since grade school, and Kasey knew it would take awhile for him to digest this turn of events. Hell, it was going to take them all awhile. They'd lost Chuck *and* Ryan. Jesus, how were they going to explain this to their parents? They could blame Chuck's death on Polanski, but this was partly their own doing, wasn't it?

After Kasey finished the sling and swathe on Scooter's left arm, he walked over and lifted the rifle out of Bloomquist's hands. Down the hill he could see the Land Rover pancaked on its roof, the upper half of the vehicle caved in. Looking at the wreck, it seemed a miracle that Scooter had been able to get out.

It was bad enough that Chuck was dead and the cyclists had sent their gunslinger down the hill with that pistol. It was bad enough they'd mutilated and killed Dozer. But now, to make things worse, poor little Ryan Perry was dead, Scooter was walking wounded, and the cyclists were armed with a loaded Winchester and a scope. All they'd meant to do was drink beer in the woods and have a good time. Who could have guessed they would spend the rest of the weekend running from a bunch of maniacs?

"They're going to kill us all," said Jennifer, staring at the road.

"No, they aren't," Kasey said, dropping an arm across her shoulders and hugging her close. Kasey was rather proud of the way he'd come to be the leader here, and now it was his responsibility to keep things together, to forgo a panic. "Listen to me, honey. They aren't going to get anybody else. What happened here was a fluke. We've still got two trucks and two guns, and we're mad as hell. They think they have the advantage, and that's going to be their undoing."

"I can't believe we got Perry killed," Bloomquist said.

"Bullshit *we* got him killed," said Scooter. "*They* killed him just like they killed Chuck and the dog. If Fred hadn't been alert enough to pop that dude who came down with the revolver earlier, we'd all be roasting in the sun. And I can tell you this. If you'd taken another minute to get here, you would have found *two* bodies instead of just Perry."

"Ryan wanted to try skydiving," said Bloomquist. "But he was too scared to sign up. He must have been terrified at the end."

"He was terrified his whole life," said Fred, not unkindly. "How did you guys end up crashing?"

"They must have put something in the road. Whatever it was, it blew a tire. There were two of them riding their bikes, and then all of a sudden after a bend there was only one, and he was going slower. It was like he was trying to slow us down. One of them must have gone ahead to set a trap. Next thing I know I'm climbing out of the wreck."

"They're murderers," said Jennifer. "If we weren't sure before, we're sure now. Chuck. Dozer. And now Ryan. They're out-and-out murderers."

With only the wind and the sound of Chuck's idling truck as background noise, everyone grew quiet. It was weird the way tension catapulted them into these quiet moments, Kasey thought; this was the third or fourth period of total stillness since they'd reached the crash site.

Kasey said, "When I wrecked my first Carrera in high school, there was a two-by-four in the road. Remember?"

"You were drinking," said Bloomquist.

"Which doesn't mean there wasn't a two-by-four in the road."

"I don't want to lose any more of my friends because we were too timid," said Jennifer. "We've got to stop them before they stop us. Is everybody in agreement?" Standing nose-to-nose, as she was wont to do, she addressed the question to Bloomquist, who didn't flinch but gave the appearance that he was about to.

"I'm with you guys," Bloomquist said. "Perry never hurt anyone."

"Oh, shit," said Fred, running for his truck, which he'd left idling. A small clump of dry grass had caught fire on the side of the road, apparently ignited by something on the vehicle's underside.

Fred jumped in and moved the truck down the road, then ran back and stomped the burning grass with his sandaled feet. He worked at putting out the small fire until Scooter pulled on his arm and said, "Fred, let it go. They're up there somewhere. At least two of them are. Let it burn their asses."

Fred and Scooter looked at each other for a few moments and then gazed down as the flames emitted a soft crackling noise and began to spread.

"We can't do this," said Kasey.

"Why not? It was an accident. Nobody can control accidents." Kasey noticed that Scooter's gray eyes were almost as bright as the time they tried coke.

"Besides, the whole valley's on fire. Nobody's going to notice."

"It's worth it to flush them out," said Fred. "At least they won't be behind us. There's only a couple of ways off this mountain, and we're sealing one of them off."

While Roger Bloomquist stood staring at the wreckage of his Land Rover, the others watched the fire creep through the long brown grass above the road. Within moments, a hot wind began pushing it up into the dry brush and twigs on the other side of the

ditch and assisting it as it fingered its way up the side of the mountain. Soon it looked like a series of huge orange zippers flying up the
mountain.

"Jesus, that wind is dry," said Fred.

"That's the same Chinook we had yesterday," said Bloomquist.

"The fire sure is hot," said Jennifer. "Even from here I can feel
the heat."

When the flames reached the first of the trees, they began racing
up the side of the mountain with a ferocity Kasey found hard to
fathom. It was as if a plane had napalmed the slope. "We shouldn't
have done this."

Scooter snorted.

"Too late to stop it now," said Jennifer, who was plainly having
her own doubts.

Like a series of match heads igniting, a stand of scraggly trees on
the hill caught fire and one by one began crackling and popping with
little explosions caused by pockets of pitch. Burning debris began to
rain down onto the road.

Kasey knew they had to leave or they would be caught up in it,
and he knew the others were looking to him for a sign, but he
couldn't tear himself away from the spectacle. He watched for another minute, then turned and surveyed the valley below the mountain. Even though he should have been able to see the contours of
the valley, he saw nothing but white smoke blowing through the
trees they'd driven past the day before. There were multiple fires below them, and now there was at least one above them.

"Remember," said Scooter. "This was an accident. Fred's truck ignited some grass. We couldn't do anything about it. Right, Roger?"

"Right."

"Right, Jenn?"

"Right."

He turned to Fred, who said, "Fuckin' A."

"I just thought of something," said Bloomquist.

"What?"

"That fire's going to go up to the lakes. It'll destroy Perry's Jeep."

"Those three little lakes are miles away."

"What's going to stop it from getting there?" Kasey asked.

"Yeah, well. Perry's beyond caring about that."

"Still, it's sad," said Jennifer.

"A lot of stuff is sad," said Fred, striding toward his dead brother's truck. "But there comes a time when you have to do something about it, and that time is now."

42

During mountain bike races both Zak and Muldaur had crashed and remounted to finish the race often enough that they were used to riding with injuries, so they both knew they could gut it out now. At least for a while.

"What took you so long?" Muldaur asked.

"He was having such a good time beating you to a pulp, I didn't want to spoil it for him."

"That's what I figured."

"Plus, it took awhile to figure out what to do."

"You didn't have a lot of choices. Man, that took some guts. You could have been hurt bad coming down the hill. Or he could have shot you."

"I *was* hurt bad."

"Thanks for bailing me out, though. I really mean that. I think you saved my life."

"You're welcome."

Eventually the ground leveled out and they found themselves side by side on a single-lane logging road, clear-cuts and gentle uphill slopes to their right, sporadic glimpses of the North Fork of the Snoqualmie River through the dense firs to their left. According to the directions Stephens had given them, they would soon be approaching the intersection at the bottom of the hill below which they'd camped, and would soon see the little concrete bridge where the races had ended. That morning they'd gone up the mountain and then had circled back almost to their starting point. They should be within five or six miles of the beginning point of their trip and the guard at the gate.

After half a mile Zak broke a protracted silence. "You think we should go back to town? We could send help back for Giancarlo and Stephens."

"I think we should try."

"What are you going to do if we see the others?"

"I don't think they're going to trade shots now that I have a gun."

"That gun is not going to deter Scooter. In fact, it might make him more likely to fire at us."

"Even with a broken collarbone?"

"If he can fire a gun, he will."

After riding a mile on the flat road, they arrived at the junction near the bridge. On the far side the landscape was cloaked in wind-driven white smoke, which they knew signaled burning vegetation; it was shifting like a series of rapidly moving fog banks. From time to time wind currents picked it up off the ground and allowed them to see the terrain, but from their vantage point along the river it was generally impenetrable. Every once in a while a gust would send enough toward them to cover a football field, and they would be riding in a fog for a few minutes.

"Are we going to be able to ride through that crap over there?" Muldaur asked.

"Doubtful."

"Which means we won't be going back into town anytime soon."

"It might get better farther on."

"It might get worse, too. It's a good seven or eight miles into town from here."

"More like eight or ten."

"That's a lot of smoke to be pedaling through. If we keep heading north in the hope of finding a clearing and we don't, we'll be in that much deeper. And I don't think we're going to find a clearing."

"Neither do I." Looking dazed and confused, several deer wandered down the center of the road, noses high. "Why's it so low?" Zak asked.

"The wind's holding it down."

"Let's climb the hill. We get some altitude, maybe we'll be able to see a route out of here."

"Fine by me."

They had climbed at least 6,000 and probably 8,000 feet already in their journeys, which made this 250 feet of altitude gain seem paltry, yet Zak could feel his quads burning and his back getting stiff with the work. His injuries didn't help. The higher they climbed, the better the view to the south, until they stopped at the washboard corner that had given them so much trouble in the race.

Most of the roads below were masked in billowing white smoke. Obviously, the road back into North Bend would be impassable for hours, perhaps days. Muldaur stared at the burning valley. "It's everywhere."

"The wind must be twenty, thirty miles an hour in places."

"I don't see any firefighting crews."

"Seems like all of eastern Washington is on fire. Two days ago the governor said crews were stretched to their limit and they were thinking of using inmates to work the fire lines. You don't think they ran out of manpower and are planning to let this one burn, do you?"

"All I know is the best air's going to be higher on the mountain."

"Eventually Kasey and Scooter and the others are going to figure that out, too, and come up behind us."

"That's why we better go up now. Hopefully, Giancarlo and Stephens aren't coming down, because I'm not sure they'll have the strength to make the climb back up."

"I'm not sure *I* have the strength to make it back up," said Zak.

"Now, *that* I'm not worried about."

They rode the next short, steep section and stopped at the Jeep camp, catching their breath while riding in circles around the abandoned barbecue. "I don't get it," Zak said. "Where's Morse's body? You don't think they threw him off the cliff, do you?"

"Maybe they took it with them."

When they went to refill their hydration packs at Panther Creek near their own camp, they found that their belongings had been stacked in a pile and set afire. Luckily they had their water purification kit with them. Zak kicked through the charred remains. He was sore from his crash and could feel air cooling the pus on his left hip and his left arm. As he walked, he felt pain in his right ankle he hadn't noticed while pedaling. Three people and a dog were dead, yet seeing his own charred sleeping bag and Giancarlo's scorched Bible made him feel as bad as any of it. Camp jays, crows, and chipmunks had been carrying away the scattered food.

Because Muldaur still had the relatively heavy Winchester braced across his handlebars, Zak offered to carry the walkie-talkie, which began crackling in his jersey pocket. *"Commando One to Commando Two."*

"Two, over."

"Did we ever find out what happened to Scooter's walkie-talkie? 'Cause Scooter doesn't have any recollection of where it went."

"That's a negative, Commando One. All I saw was Perry."

"So for all we know they're listening in."

"For all we know."

After a few moments of silence Scooter's bombastic high-pitched voice came on the air. *"Hear this, you redneck peckerwoods. We're coming, and this time we're not handing out any tickets for second chances. So you better start pedaling your asses off."*

"Do you think we should answer?" Muldaur asked.

"Like he said, I think we should pedal."

They climbed six more minutes on the same road they'd already climbed once that morning, hoping all the while the Jeeps weren't coming up right behind them, because this time they wouldn't have a felled tree to stall them. There was no telling what Stephens and

Giancarlo were doing. Zak hoped they were somewhere on top of the mountain, perhaps near the lake, and that they would run into them at the top.

Zak looked at Muldaur. "You know how to use that rifle?"

"When I was in the army, I was rated top marksman in my unit."

"Let's hope those rich boys behind us didn't have private shooting tutors like they had for everything else."

43

By the time the walkie-talkie crackled again, they'd climbed another mile on the single-lane dirt road, most of it in the sun, which now bored through the high haze. *"Commando One from Two. We're turning around. I just hope to God they aren't hiding in the smoke, because we'll be sitting ducks."*

"Don't be coming back here. Keep looking!"

"Bullshit. You come over on this side of the river and look. It's too smoky."

"Okay. We'll go up the hill and search. You come back and go along the river and look for a way out. That way, if one of us gets caught in an ambush, the others can flank them."

"Sounds good. I haven't scored yet, and I need to bag one."

"It'd be nice if we could each bag one."

The walkie-talkie in Zak's rear jersey pocket grew quiet. "You think they meant that last bit?" Zak said.

"Naw. They were just trying to throw a scare into us."

"It worked."

"Have you noticed there are only two units talking? There should be three."

"Maybe the other one's up top laying for Giancarlo and Stephens."

When they finally reached the plateau that couched Lake Hancock, Zak wasn't as exhausted and maimed as he thought he would be. It gave him hope he might get his race legs back. It had taken more than thirty minutes, but they'd come up at an even pace, and now the woods on the plateau afforded more shade than the hillside had.

Zak said, "The air's better up here."

"It's starting to get hazy toward the lake, though. In another couple of hours, we won't have any clean air at this elevation, either. We better find Giancarlo and Stephens."

Dreading the climb out of the lake basin, where they would have to traverse the same road that had exposed them to gunfire earlier—it seemed like days earlier—they trekked around the south end of Lake Hancock, riding with no hands while they munched Clif Bars and sipped water from the bite valves on their backpacks, gathering strength for the next climb. It was the nastiest mountain they'd done all day, but it surprised Zak to see how anxious Muldaur was. This was the area where a bullet had chipped his helmet, and until now Zak thought it hadn't affected his friend.

It occurred to Zak that all that chatter on the walkie-talkies might have been a ploy and that the Jeep gang might be circling to surprise them at the top. Or that the third remaining vehicle might have been up there waiting all along.

They kept a watch out over the lake, which had now acquired a nappy surface from the wind. The breeze was hot and laden with the perfume of distant fires. It was just past noon, and even up here the air was beginning to get smokier. By six o'clock nothing on the mountain would be breathable.

Zak said, "You think the fire's going to jump the river and creep up this mountain?"

"If it comes up the mountain, it won't be doing any creeping. In steep country like this it'll travel faster than a man can run."

"I wonder if it travels faster than a man can bike?"

"None of these roads go straight up. Chances are, even if we outrun it, we'd get cut off."

"Scary."

"Most definitely scary."

Several times Zak almost tipped over while gazing out at Lake Hancock and the surrounding mountains. He wasn't sure what he was looking for, but he wouldn't be surprised to see a Porsche Cayenne or a white Ford pickup, or muzzle flashes from a rifle barrel. "We better keep our minds on our work," said Muldaur. "If they start shooting, we'll know soon enough."

They rode uphill for another twelve minutes before they spotted Giancarlo and Stephens coasting toward them, their fingers tight on their brake levers. As they closed in, Stephens said, "Where are you guys headed?"

"We were coming to save your butts," said Zak.

"We were going down to save yours," said Giancarlo. "Why didn't you guys go back into town?"

"Way too much smoke," said Zak. "We figured the best place to wait this out was up top."

"We thought so until it got too smoky. There's a fire right below the ridge a couple of miles back. The whole ridge is layered in smoke. It's bad."

"It's true," said Stephens. "My asthma was kicking in. Are they behind you?"

"Not that we know of."

"So are we going down or up?"

Zak looked at Muldaur, who shrugged. "Down, I guess."

Zak didn't like the thought that they'd climbed almost a mile up a mountain without cause. That was the initial idea for the weekend—to ride their butts off—but now that the situation had changed, they were trying to husband as much energy as possible, to hold something in reserve in case the others got close. Zak and Muldaur turned around and lowered their saddles for the descent, then gazed down at Lake Hancock, surveying the woods and the ancient logging scars on the mountain opposite, reviewing the roads for trucks or small movements that might turn out to be angry young men with scoped rifles.

"Beautiful, isn't it?" said Muldaur.

"I could think of worse places to die."

"Me, too."

By the time he and Muldaur began their descent, Giancarlo and Stephens were halfway down the mountain. At the bottom the four of them regrouped and rode back around the lake. When they reached the three-way crossroads at the head of the lake, they stopped while Giancarlo searched for signs that the trucks had passed by. "Hard to tell," he said after scanning the road surface. "There're so many tracks. I know they came by a couple of times earlier, but I can't tell for sure if they've been around recently."

"Okay. So here's my take on it," said Stephens, looking around at the other three. "This probably isn't going to surprise anyone. I think we should ride down the hill and head back into town. If we run into them, we'll just stop and put our hands up. What are they going to do, murder us?"

"That's exactly what they're going to do," said Muldaur.

"Murder us?"

"Have you not been paying attention? Look at my helmet."

"Gimme a break, you guys. They're not going to murder us. *We're* civilized. *They're* civilized."

"The problem with riding back into town," said Zak, "is that we were down by the river and we got a good look at the roads. They're not passable, and they won't be for a long, long time."

"So we're going to have to hide out up here until it is passable?" said Giancarlo.

"That's how it looks."

"I was wondering where you got that rifle," said Giancarlo.

"I'll tell you all about it after we find someplace to hide."

They took the road on the north side of Lake Hancock, this time skirting the spring entirely. When they reached the turnoff to the lake, their choices were to either continue up the mountain on the same route Zak and Muldaur had taken the previous evening, venture through the trees in the direction of the lakefront itself, or pursue the narrow, gated road that ran along the north side of the lake, where there were a dozen or so small cabins.

"We could hide out in one of those shacks," said Stephens. "Of course we would leave money and a note for whatever we took."

"I'd rather be out in the open," said Muldaur. "What about you, Zak?"

"I want to be able to run in more than one direction."

"Giancarlo?"

"The only reason I'd go to those cabins would be to look for firearms."

"You guys are turning this into a war," said Stephens. They ended up climbing the switchback road that rose up out of the plateau to the north, the same road Zak and Muldaur had ridden the afternoon before, a mountain on their right-hand side. As they began the ascent, Stephens pulled alongside Giancarlo. "It could be worse, I guess. At least if those fires get close, I'm with three firemen."

"What do you mean?"

"You know. I'll be with professionals."

"These are wildland fires."

"Yeah. So?"

"So we work in Seattle. We're structural firefighters. We don't know anything about wildland fires."

"Same principles, right?"

"Are you kidding? You know as much about what's going on out here as we do."

44

The road climbed for almost an hour before feeding onto a rolling plateau at about four thousand feet, which was essentially the top of the foothills butting into the Cascade Mountains. The plateau was laced with an intricate maze of logging roads, many of them overgrown dead ends. Once on the plateau the worst of the climbing would be over, especially now that they weren't following the original plan to forge a path all the way to Salmon La Sac on the other side of the Cascades. Riding north out of the basin put the sun at their backs, the wind sucking the moisture out of their mouths, blowing sweat off their chins and noses. They were sweating so heavily they looked as if they were biking through a fine mist. When they stopped at the last crossroads, Giancarlo strapped his helmet to his handlebars, and the others followed suit. The hot breeze on their bare heads felt good, though Zak worried about sunburn on his scalp.

The road started off steep and grew steeper, running in a straight line for a quarter mile through a gauntlet of dark green Douglas fir. There were at least two other major roads that connected to this, one coming up from below from the left—probably from the river—and another joining from above. They wouldn't reach either for a while, though. As they climbed, the group once again separated into a hierarchy based on leg strength and conditioning, with Zak and Muldaur in the lead, Stephens farther down the grade, and Giancarlo out of sight behind. Not being a complainer by nature, Giancarlo hadn't said anything, but it was clear the dog bite was hampering him, and all of them knew that if the truckers came from below, they would reach him first. They might have given him the rifle, which he was fully capable of using, but the extra weight would have hampered him further, so he said he didn't want it. At this point, they had no idea where the trucks would be coming from, or even if they were on the mountain.

They had briefly considered riding as a foursome, but Zak and Muldaur thought it better to go ahead and use the extra time to scout, which they did, finding several overgrown side roads, most of which petered out quickly when they followed them. About a third of the way up the mountain, Zak found a road and explored it while Muldaur waited for the others. "Looks like a good place to hide out," Zak said when he came back. "It leads to an old mine."

"Do you think we need to stop?"

"I think these two are doing the dying swan."

"I don't know how they thought they were going to make the whole weekend."

"They would have made an ordinary weekend, but not in this smoke, not with all this stress. Plus, Giancarlo's got that leg wound from the dog."

"I suppose so." Stephens was laboriously making his way up the hill, head bobbing with each pedal stroke, while Giancarlo wasn't in sight yet. "Let's go in here, then. I doubt they're going to check every little dogleg, and if they do, I have the rifle."

"For all we know they went back to town."

As if on a signal, they heard the first walkie-talkie transmission in twenty-five minutes. *"Kasey? You guys check that one, too?"*

"Already got it. Stay off the air."

"Right."

"They're at the cabins," Muldaur said. "Right behind us."

The four of them ended up walking their bikes through a stand of reedy saplings that had grown through the rocks. Then 150 yards of overgrown road fed them into an open mine pit just large enough to use for a shooting range, which people had obviously done in the past, for there were hundreds of broken bottles and other consumer items filled with bullet holes against the far wall, and thousands of spent .22 brass cartridge cases under their feet. It was a horseshoe-shaped pit that might have been scooped out by a meteorite instead of miners with shovels. Trees rimmed the crater, and there was at least one spot to the east above the pit where they could see a piece of an old logging road on another face of the mountain. Here and there on the floor of the pit lay rusted chunks of abandoned machinery.

The road had a hump in it just before it reached the mine, and it was from this hump that they turned around and discovered the best view into the valley from this side of the mountain Zak had seen yet. If it hadn't been so hazy, they would have been able to glimpse Seattle and the Olympic Mountains beyond the sound, but as it was all they saw was a cotton-candy haze that stretched for thirty miles.

"Jesus," said Giancarlo.

"Your leg?" Muldaur asked.

"No. The whole valley's burning. That fire line must be five miles long. It jumped the river. It's coming up the side of the mountain. There's nothing but smoke."

The others stepped over to where Giancarlo was standing on a mound at the side of the road. From here they were able to see the distant lower parts of the mountain to the south; fire was indeed running up the sides of the lower slopes in massive sheets.

"That's about where the wreck was," said Zak.

"Shit. There's another fire."

"Where?" Stephens had climbed higher than the others, was standing on an old cedar stump eight feet across. When the others joined him, they could see directly down the mountain to some of the cliffs near where they'd slept the night before. Flames were coming up the side of the mountain close to where their camp had been.

"Three different points of origin," said Muldaur. "Out in the valley. By the wreck and one at our camp."

"They had a fire in our camp earlier," said Muldaur. "They must have come up behind us and lit something in that area again. Now they're searching the cabins at the lake. They're right behind us."

"If we'd stayed on the main road, they'd catch us for sure. This detour was good."

After some time had gone by, Stephens lowered his voice and said, "Did you see Morse when you were at the camp?" Zak could tell it had taken a good deal of effort to get the question out. He and Morse had been friends for years.

"The body was gone," said Zak.

"Gone where?"

"No idea. There was no trace of him."

"They probably took him back to town."

"Yeah, that's right," said Muldaur. "They probably have him all spread out in a funeral parlor with gardenias in his hair and wearing a nice new tuxedo."

"There's no need to get snide."

"Maybe not, but there's no fucking way they took him to town. You need to get your head out of your ass."

Stephens was too tired to take umbrage at the remark, even as Muldaur was too exhausted to guard his words. They were all exhausted.

One by one they grew weary of watching the progress of the fires and wandered into the abandoned mining area. Giancarlo sat on a small boulder and tended to the bandages on his leg while Zak dropped to one knee and helped him.

Stephens hunkered on the ground and bit into an energy bar.

Leaving the rifle next to his bike, Muldaur sat on a patch of brown grass that poked through a slag heap. "The Land Rover crashed. The little guy. I forget his name . . ."

"Ryan Perry," said Stephens.

"He's dead."

"What?" Giancarlo stopped fiddling with his bandages.

"Scooter crashed the Land Rover," said Zak. "We're pretty sure Perry died in the wreck. If he wasn't dead when we saw him, he is now."

"And Scooter?"

"Scooter was fine," said Muldaur.

"He had a broken collarbone when we left him," said Zak. "Along with some scrapes and bruises."

"So how did you two get beat up?" Stephens asked Muldaur.

"Scooter and I had a disagreement," said Muldaur. "It went on for a while."

"I crashed," added Zak.

"It must have been a doozy."

"It was."

Stephens continued to make inquiries, as if more information could somehow make their circumstances less dire. Zak had seen the same psychological mechanism at play in the fire department whenever anybody got hurt badly. Glean the details—the more, the better—and once you had them, digest them, make your assessment, then convince yourself it couldn't have happened to you because you would have done things differently. It was part of the universal human impulse to distance oneself from tragedy using rationalization and self-deception. Zak wasn't very good at it simply because every tragedy he'd seen in the fire department was one he quickly became convinced would visit him at some future date. He knew he was at heart a pessimist, and he knew his pessimism was rooted in the car accident when he was eleven, yet he felt helpless to change his nature or even try.

They would rest in the mine pit until the coast was clear or the fires came too close and forced them to move farther up the mountain.

45

Muldaur stretched out in the shade and took a nap. Giancarlo choked down an energy bar, drank most of his water, and began praying. Zak emptied his jersey pockets and lay on his back, his brown legs in the sun, his upper body in the shade of the trees near the pit. He hadn't realized how frazzled he was until he was horizontal. He figured they'd ridden, he and Muldaur, more than seventy miles, and including yesterday had done at least ten thousand feet of climbing.

All morning they'd been moving so fast he hadn't had time to think through the repercussions the day might impose on the rest of his life, but with this respite, the rest of his life was all he could think about.

Zak couldn't escape the feeling this entire mess was his fault. Scooter had engineered the Jeep trip so he could harass, embarrass, and possibly do physical harm to Zak—but Scooter's belief that he could get away with it was rooted in Zak's inaction during the past two months when Scooter had been stalking Nadine.

The moment he saw Scooter and Chuck on the side of the mountain that morning he should have retreated to a safe haven. After Nadine left the night before, he should have convinced the others either to ride back into town in the dark or move the camp to another location—anything except remaining passive and letting events dictate their destiny.

Zak couldn't help seeing this from the point of view of the authorities, for surely everything that had happened would be judged by outsiders: police, district attorneys, defense lawyers, judges, relatives of the deceased—the ever-growing number of deceased—and newspaper readers and television news junkies all over the Northwest. Eventually this would be graded by strangers, and there would be two competing stories, of that he was certain. He didn't know precisely what Scooter's story would entail, but he knew it would be attested to by every one of his friends. Their clique stuck together.

As he lay on the ground in a dizzying stupor, Zak underwent a series of epiphanies, recognizing behaviors and parts of his history that looked and sounded to outsiders totally different from the way he had always pictured them in his head. Certainly he was a dedicated firefighter, an athlete a couple of notches below national caliber. He was socially skilled but uninterested in pursuing much social interaction. He cast girlfriends aside with a casual abandon that amazed his friends and sometimes himself. Even though his sister had lived with him for more than a year and his father for almost three years, he was basically a lonely individual, or at least he had been before Nadine showed up. Even during the times when he had a girlfriend, he'd been lonely, yet he never quite knew why.

In many ways loneliness was his defining characteristic. And now that the chase across the face of the mountain had eased, he realized the only time he hadn't felt lonely was during the weeks he'd known Nadine. Funny how one person could become the whole world. Zak recalled what Muldaur had said earlier in the day while they were climbing. "That girl's the best thing that ever happened to you."

"What makes you say that?"

"Just the way you've been since you met her. It's like you've bloomed."

"I've had girlfriends before."

"Yes, you have, but they never made you happy."

"No, they never did, did they?"

Muldaur was right. Zak never found anybody who would make him happy, probably because he never thought he deserved happiness. In the year after Charlene's death, when his parents' marriage dissolved, he'd become a believer in the fragility of relationships. Zak had always marveled that so many of his friends, co-workers, and acquaintances lived their lives in the sure knowledge that somewhere a mate was waiting for them, thinking that if they hadn't found that mate yet, it was only a matter of time, while Zak had grown up assuming he would live the bulk of his life alone.

Prior to Charlene's death, his family was so normal and centered that in retrospect it seemed to Zak like a fantasy: two devoted parents, a stable home, meals lovingly served, happy moments shared. They even had family night once a week. They would order pizza, play games together, and enjoy one another's company. Zak had forgotten about family night until a few weeks ago when Stacy mentioned it.

The whole thing got sucked down the drain after Charlene died. Zak couldn't count how many times his mother talked about that night, never once openly accusing him, though he knew what she was thinking. He always knew what she was thinking. And what made it even worse was that she knew he knew what she was thinking. Over the last eighteen years, Zak had relived those minutes thousands, if not tens of thousands of times—though, curiously, he hadn't thought about it much since he'd pulled Nadine out of her overturned Lexus. But then, this morning when he failed to check Ryan Perry for a pulse, it all came back in an avalanche of personal recrimination. He'd failed Charlene and he'd failed Ryan Perry, too.

Charlene had always been the good-natured sister who tried to put a damper on any strife in the household, and after she was gone he'd missed her badly. That night she begged him to help her, and then, when she realized he was too terrified to crawl back into the car again, she'd given him a look that imbued an expression of pity so pure, so unrelenting and immediately forgiving that Zak never forgot it. Nor had he ever forgiven himself for being on the receiving end of it.

Everything that had gone wrong in his life, his father's life, his mother's, and Stacy's could be traced to that one simple act of cowardice.

Zak had gone to a psychologist several years back to work it out, and the psychologist told him all the things he already knew on a rational level: He was a child when it happened. He couldn't expect to take on the responsibilities of an adult at eleven. The odds were that anybody else outside the car that night wouldn't have rescued Charlene, either. In fact, others *had* been there and hadn't rescued her. He'd been placed in a position no child should be placed in. And what if, asked the psychologist, who was a kindly but rather tight-lipped middle-aged woman with prematurely graying hair, what if he'd gone inside the car and it had burst into flame with Charlene *and* him inside? Wouldn't that also have destroyed the family? Nothing he heard or said in the counseling sessions alleviated any of Zak's guilt or changed his basic perception of the world.

Oddly enough, as a firefighter, every time he made a successful entry into a wrecked car it made things worse, because each entry was an example of how easy it could be.

After his father left and his mother drowned herself in religion, Zak figured it was his fault. When she drowned herself in drugs— his fault. Zak even blamed himself for his mother's cancer. Hadn't scientists tied disease to stress and despair, and wasn't it possible his mother's torment had altered her body chemistry enough to invite the cancer in? As many times as Zak told himself he couldn't live other people's lives for them, he was sure the total disintegration of his family had been all his doing.

And now Al was living with him, and although he paid rent, on those months when he came up short, Zak did not press him. Nor had he asked his sister for money. He felt it was a privilege to take care of his father and sister.

Until a few minutes ago Zak hadn't viewed his history squarely.

He hadn't thought of taking in his father and sister as penance for a crime he'd committed at eleven. He hadn't thought of himself as trying to rebuild the family unit he felt responsible for destroying. He hadn't fully realized that every time he responded as a firefighter to the scene of a car accident, he was not only trying to prove to himself that he wasn't a coward, but also trying to change the outcome of that first car accident in his life. It was a shock to realize how blatant his penance was and how blind he'd been to it. He was twenty-eight years old and was still trying to atone for an event that had taken place when he was eleven. All these thoughts had been rattling around in his brain for years, but it wasn't until now, on a day when there was a good chance he might die, that they began to make sense.

Zak listened to Giancarlo snore and to Stephens as he tried repeatedly to get his cell phone to work. Somewhere in those minutes he realized he'd fallen into a light sleep and was actually listening to himself snore, too. It was hard to know how long he'd been dozing when the walkie-talkie crackled. *"We've got them."*

"What did you say?"

"Commando Two to One, we can see them."

"You're not supposed to be on the air."

"Come on down. We're watching them right now. They're in some sort of pit below us."

"Have they spotted you?"

"If they have, they're not moving."

Muldaur was the first to speak. "Just everybody don't fuckin' twitch an eyelash. Just stay where you are."

"Everybody hear that?" Zak asked. "Everybody awake?"

Stephens and Giancarlo grunted.

"Can anybody see them?"

"No, but I'm going to move around now," Muldaur said. "Real slow. The rest of you stay still. This could be a bluff."

Stephens said, "What if it isn't?"

"Then we'll find out soon enough."

Remaining flat on his back, Zak listened to Muldaur as he ambled over to the bikes. "Okay," said Muldaur. "I see them. They're up the hill where that old road cuts across the mountain above us. Don't anybody look. He's got binoculars on us."

"Are they going to shoot?" asked Giancarlo.

"I don't see a gun, but that doesn't mean there isn't one. There are two of them. I think it's the guy and the chick."

"They must have driven up the main road right past this place," said Zak.

"I vote we get the hell out of here," said Giancarlo. "If they leave somebody with a rifle up there and send another vehicle to the mouth of this road, we'll be finished."

"Before we move, we gotta decide where we're going," said Muldaur.

"We're sure as hell not going up," said Zak. "Because they'll be coming down."

"It's been almost two hours since we were down at the lake," said Muldaur. "It's going to be a lot smokier now."

"I don't see any other option," said Giancarlo. "Unless you want to shoot it out with them right here."

Before they could move, the walkie-talkie hissed again. *"Do you have a rifle on them?"*

"Yep."

"Think you can hit one?"

"Absolutely."

"Then hit one. We're going to drive down. If we see them on the road, we'll run right over their stinking bikes. I didn't want to do it this way, but they haven't given us any choice. We'll never get out of these mountains alive until we eliminate them."

"When do you want me to shoot?"

"Anytime, Fred."

They were scrambling for their bikes when the first bullet whistled into the mine pit. Zak grabbed the walkie-talkie, slung the CamelBak hydration pack onto one shoulder, and was sprinting while pushing his bike through the saplings on the overgrown road when the second bullet ricocheted off the rocks a few feet behind him. The slug made a pleasant whirring sound as it ricocheted into the hot afternoon air, sounding like a wind chime being tapped lightly by a pencil.

46

Zak ran his bike down the mining road behind the other three. By the time he swung a leg over the saddle, Stephens had already reached the main road and was sprinting down the mountain. Burdened by the rifle across his handlebars, Muldaur was quickly overtaken by Zak, while Giancarlo was already out of sight on the descent. Giancarlo was slowest on the way up and the swiftest on the way down.

As they sped down the mountainside, Zak could hear a truck not far behind. Instinctively he scrubbed off speed and waited for Muldaur.

"Go ahead," Muldaur screamed. "Don't wait for me."

"Dump the gun!" Zak yelled.

"Like hell."

The sound of the truck's tires and brakes on the dirt road was growing louder. "Can you stay in front of them?"

"I'll have to, won't I?"

"Remember before the corner at the bottom there's a drainage ditch. If you get across that ditch okay, you can carry your speed onto the flats."

"Where are you guys going when you get to the bottom?"

"No idea."

"Hopefully, I'll be right on your tail." Zak had gained so much distance on Muldaur during their conversation that he could barely make out his last words.

Behind them the truck skidded on a patch of gravel. They could hear the tires sliding, then some banging as the vehicle struck rut after rut on the unimproved road. Zak still didn't know which truck it was, or whether Scooter was hanging out a window with a rifle, but it didn't matter. He could feel the hot wind on his face and in his hair. In their rush to leave, all except Stephens had forgotten their helmets at the mine.

At each of the shallow rain-diversion culverts engineered across the road, Zak dropped his weight down onto the shocks and jumped up at just the right moment to hop the culvert at full speed. Stephens and Giancarlo were both out of sight in front now. The shallow rain ditches that obstructed the road every couple of hundred yards would play havoc with the truck's undercarriage, while a good cyclist with some nerve could jump them without losing any speed at all.

The descent took longer than Zak thought it would, but then time played funny tricks when you thought you were going to die. Even though the events around him seemed to have sped up, this descent was taking forever.

When Zak whizzed down the last leg of the hill and carved the curve that fed onto the flats, feeling the g-forces as he hit the dip, he spotted Giancarlo far ahead. Between them Stephens was glancing back over his shoulder.

Zak caught Stephens in the woods on the Lake Hancock plateau, Stephens pulling in behind, drafting, letting Zak do the work. Zak pedaled hard for a good minute before swinging to his right so Stephens could take a turn, but Stephens pulled over with him and remained in Zak's slipstream. Giancarlo had been too far out in front for Stephens to catch, so Stephens had waited for Zak, who now put his head down and steamed along, towing him up to Giancarlo in less than half a mile. Muldaur was closing in, too. It showed just how strong Muldaur was that he could make up that much distance once they hit the flats. The truck was still out of sight.

It was smokier and windier than an hour earlier when they'd last been on this plateau—bad enough that the air seared Zak's throat with each breath. The poisons would affect his legs if they hadn't already, slowing him down and making the ride even more painful than it already was.

They passed the cutoff to the lake in a blur and were heading through thick woods toward the three-way intersection near the edge of the mountain. The road was flat in these woods, so the bikes quickly lost any advantage they'd had over the chasing truck.

Zak heard the truck reach the bottom of the hill, tires slapping at the potholes. It was coming right up on them. It was going to run over them.

All four cyclists were bunched together now, Giancarlo in the lead.

As the truck grew louder, Giancarlo detoured into the woods on a single-track game trail Zak hadn't noticed. One by one they veered into the woods. Closing in fast, the truck sounded as if it were going a hundred miles an hour. The driver was clearly determined to kill them. Zak followed Giancarlo, while Stephens, who'd been behind Zak, grew anxious about escaping the road in time to avoid the truck and came up alongside him on the narrow trail, nearly forcing Zak into a tree. The clumsy maneuver came close to bringing them both down.

Once in the woods, Zak stopped and watched Muldaur dive off the road a split second before the Porsche Cayenne rushed past at around fifty miles per hour. The SUV missed Muldaur by three feet at most. Obviously, the plan had been to run him down—to run them *all* down. The Porsche braked hard, skidded in the dirt, and reversed. By then the first three cyclists had traveled thirty yards into the woods. Muldaur, who'd gained a mere ten yards, threw his bike down and stood behind the bole of a tree, the rifle braced against the tree and trained on the road. When he fired, the gunshot was incredibly loud in the woods. For the longest time, nobody moved, the Porsche idling in the road in a skein of dust and smoke. The bullet had shattered the rear windows on either side.

After some moments, the Porsche raced away. As they took off, Scooter shouted out the passenger's window, but it was impossible to distinguish what he said.

When Muldaur caught up, the others were quiet. "Those guys are crazy."

"God, that was close," said Zak. "I thought they had you."

"They almost killed you," said Giancarlo.

"I think I felt static electricity on my shorts when they went by."

"Even so, you shouldn't have fired at them." Stephens was in the lead, and, because he'd stopped and the trail had narrowed, the others were forced to halt behind him while he spoke.

"I shouldn't have fired?"

"No," said Stephens.

"Why not?"

"Because now we're as bad as they are. The police are going to see that blown-out window and, well, they're going to think we were the, uh, aggressors. We don't have any evidence it was otherwise. I mean, think about it. We were more or less guiltless until you did that."

"Are you kidding? Everything that happened today was their doing. Jesus, Stephens." Muldaur tried to brush past him, walking his bike with a leg on either side of it, trying to push through until the butt of the rifle caught on Stephens's Iron Horse handlebars. "If I didn't know better, I'd swear you were blind and deaf both."

Zak pushed through the trail on the other side of a tree and got in front of Stephens. "If he hadn't fired, they'd be gunning us down right now."

Venturing south-southeast, they made their way through the woods, pushing their way through a couple of sections of heavy underbrush, where they were forced to carry their bikes on their shoulders. After several hundred yards they came upon an overgrown road at the same time as the walkie-talkie in Zak's rear jersey pocket began squawking. *"They shot at us! Those bastards shot at us."*

"You shouldn't have let them have your gun," came the weaker response.

"Screw you, Fred."

Another voice came on: Kasey Newcastle. *"Fred? You and Jenn and Roger be careful when you come down. They're in the woods near the lake. They blew out one of my windows."*

"Don't forget to leave a couple for me and Jenn."

"You want them tied up with a bow, or do you want them loose?"

47

Kasey steered through the intersection and headed down the mountain. In all the smoke and confusion, he wasn't entirely sure where he was, but he had the feeling this was the road that led to their camp. He and Scooter hadn't spoken to each other since the shots from the woods. It was a first for both of them, having someone fire a gun at them. Scooter still claimed the popping sounds that morning from the cyclist's camp had been gunshots, but the more Kasey thought about it, the more he believed the pops had actually been firecrackers. He even found what appeared to be tattered firecracker wrapping papers on the ground afterward.

Half a mile down the first slope he located a pullout and, knowing how rare such pullouts were, swung in and parked. Scooter jumped out with the rifle and, using his good arm, laid it on the roof of the Porsche Cayenne. He'd been drinking beer and popping Valium to dull the pain in his shoulder; his eyes were wide and glazed.

"What are you doing?" Kasey asked, as he surveyed the damage to the Porsche. Square pebbles of broken glass littered the blanket covering the corpse in back. Hot, smoky air had been whooshing inside the passenger compartment while they were driving, and the backseat was covered with dust.

"The minute they pop into sight," Scooter said, "they're dead."

"You think you can do that with one hand?"

"They'll be sitting ducks."

Kasey was relieved the damage had been only to the windows because, compared with a hole in the sheet metal, they would be easy to replace. His eyes were watering from the smoke, though. It was smoky everywhere, but more so on this downslope, and with the back window gone the air conditioner was no longer filtering out the bulk of it. Now that he'd had some time to reconnoiter, Kasey recognized the road as the one they'd taken that morning when the chase began, the one where they'd cleared the downed tree.

Standing on a stump, Kasey was able to peer through the treetops and out over the forest of Douglas fir that grew alongside this section of the mountain. "You better not scratch the roof with that rifle."

"Your windows are all shot to hell. I wouldn't be worrying about the roof."

"I've got clear coat on there. I don't want you messing it up."

"Yeah, yeah, yeah."

Kasey drank from a can of beer as he gazed out over the valley. The view was limited, but what he could see worried him. The gap in the mountains looked due west and revealed more smoke in the lower valley than the last time he'd looked. In the distance he saw a helicopter towing a huge bucket. The rest was all smoke. He couldn't see along the flanks of the mountain, but massive banks of smoke were billowing in from that direction, enough to obscure the view for thirty seconds at a time and enough to convince him the two fires they'd started below were growing at a massive rate. Once or twice while he was watching, the wind changed and the smoke rushed up through the narrow fissure where he was standing.

The first time it happened, Scooter started coughing. "What the hell?"

"It's getting worse."

"Tell me something I don't already know."

"It's close, too. I think this smoke is from the one you set."

"I didn't set shit, man. Fred's truck set it."

"You set the other one at their camp when we came through the second time."

"Whatever."

"I'd hate to be on a bike in all this. Those imbeciles."

"Maybe we should tell them to flush those bastards down this way. A pincer movement."

"The last time we saw them they didn't appear to be in the mood to be flushed."

"There aren't that many places they can go."

"Chase them," Kasey said on the walkie-talkie. *"Chase them hard. We'll be waiting when they come by."*

"Where are you going to be?" It was Jennifer.

"I'm not going to say on the air. Just chase them."

"We're working on it."

Kasey thought about taking Scooter's place with the gun, but the more he mulled it over, the more he realized he didn't want to shoot anybody. Better to let Scooter handle that. Today he'd already seen three dead bodies and had been driving around for six hours with a cadaver in the back of his Porsche. Wasn't that enough?

48

It was at the south end of the lake on the narrow, flat road where they got caught with their pants down.

The smoke over Lake Hancock was growing thicker by the minute and seemed to be affecting Stephens the most. He had asthma and had brought an inhaler with him and had stopped several times already in order to take a hit of albuterol.

They'd been heading toward the long, agonizing climb out of the basin at the south end of the lake, where Muldaur's helmet had been clipped by a bullet, choosing that direction because none of them could think of anywhere else to go. There were three possibilities, two up and one down, and nobody wanted to climb back up. They weren't sure there wasn't another truck waiting for them or coming down on them. They knew the lower they went on the mountain, the thicker the smoke would get and the greater the likelihood of running into fire, so they vetoed another downhill run, too. They might have continued to hide out in the trees, but the woods weren't very deep, and anybody who launched a serious investigation was bound to find them without trying too hard. It was also one of the first places they would look, since that was where they had last been seen. Zak had visions of Kasey and the others toting rifles as they walked through the woods side by side.

Five minutes after they got back onto the road, they heard a truck behind them, and the sound sent a spurt of adrenaline through Zak. All four of them managed to get into the trees before it arrived, but barely. The white Ford pickup truck with its enormous wheels and tires didn't slow even a little as it passed their hiding place.

Jennifer was driving, Bloomquist beside her, Fred standing in back in his muscle shirt, strapped in with belts or loops or something, wearing shooting glasses and a backward baseball cap, the rifle looking like a toy in his brawny arms. Both Fred and Jennifer were looking at the road; otherwise they might have spotted the bikers' colorful jerseys through the sparse underbrush on the south side of the road. After they passed by, Giancarlo said, "That was close. What now?"

"We stay here," said Muldaur. "The others will be right behind them."

"No way," said Giancarlo. "Listen. There's nobody else there."

"They might be lagging a minute or two behind just to fool us."

"I don't think so," Zak said. "And the ones who just went past, once they get around that corner and head up the mountain on that narrow road, there's no turnaround. They'll have to go all the way to the top. This is our chance to double back."

Muldaur looked around the group. "Okay. Let's go."

They were taking a gamble, because it was a long, flat road alongside the lake, maybe three-quarters of a mile back to the three-way intersection. They might run into one of the other trucks head-on. Or the Ford might turn around before the road started up and catch them from behind. Either way, it was dicey. They began to push their bikes back out onto the road.

What they hadn't counted on was the better view afforded Fred as he stood in the back of the truck, now eight or ten stories higher and almost directly above them on the slope.

When he saw the others looking up, Zak followed their eyes and spotted Fred sighting down his rifle at them. As they scrambled onto their bikes and sprinted along the road, the first bullet thunked into the hard-packed road between Zak and Giancarlo. The second slug whizzed past Zak's head. Zak was in the lead, standing on his pedals in a full-out sprint, the hardest and fastest he'd ridden all weekend, maybe all summer. He thought this must be the same feeling a deer had as it sprinted for its life with a hunter on its heels.

Astonishingly, when he looked down through his legs at his rear wheel, he saw somebody else's front wheel only inches behind. Good. He wouldn't have to slow down to let somebody latch on. The idea was for each of them to draft, for them to work together as a single unit. Four riders trading turns at the front was faster and far more efficient than one cyclist riding alone. Another bullet splatted into the dust in front of him.

Without uttering a word, Stephens came around and, instead of passing in a smooth motion that would allow Zak to slip in behind, powered away. Fifty yards behind them Muldaur was pacing Giancarlo. Zak and Stephens should have been working together, but instead Stephens had used him as a launching pad, and now continued to accelerate away. It was the type of move one used against an opponent, not a teammate.

Zak jumped hard on the pedals and sprinted harder. Then harder still. He could feel the smoky air burning his lungs, his legs aching. The whole thing pissed him off, the shooting, the fact that they were running like mice in front of a cat, and most of all the fact that Stephens was trying to ditch him. He'd been giving Stephens a free ride all day.

He saw Stephens glance back at him and then speed up again as if purposely trying to make it difficult for Zak. Clearly Stephens had been feigning weakness for the past six hours so he could take advantage of them when it came to the crunch. After almost a minute of hard pedaling, Zak got close enough that he was able to avail himself of some of the draft behind Stephens. Even ten feet behind another rider made it easier. When he was eight feet back, he felt an appreciable advantage, and because of that respite was then able to close to within eighteen inches.

The sound of Zak's bike hitting a pothole must have alerted Stephens to his presence, because he pulled over, signaling with his hand that he wanted Zak to take a turn at the front. Zak was so angry that instead of pulling ahead at a measured pace, he stood up and sprinted again, putting every ounce of effort into it. It was a mean thing to do and he could feel his heart about to implode, but he was pissed. He powered for fifteen seconds, breathing deeply and feeling the dirty air as it scoured the deepest recesses of his lungs. When he finally sat, he continued pedaling as hard as he could, checking between his legs to see if Stephens was drafting. Within a minute, he was.

"I thought we were supposed to be working together," Stephens gasped.

"Look who's talking, asshole."

"Sorry. I didn't mean—"

"The fuck you didn't."

They were riding hard, but because they weren't working together Muldaur had caught them, Giancarlo riding twelve inches behind his rear wheel, sitting in. Now all four of them were in a line. They crossed the small bridge at the head of the lake, and then as they approached the three-way intersection, Muldaur pulled into the lead and led them into the woods. There was no path. He simply veered off the road. The other three followed, bouncing across a log and negotiating a pair of shallow ditches, trying to maintain speed. Muldaur stopped 150 yards in and said, "Okay. What's going on between you two?"

"He's been dogging it all day," Zak said, still breathing heavily. "He was faking it. He's as strong as any of us, but I don't think he's taken a single pull all day."

"I'm not as strong as you guys," Stephens said, gasping for air. "I mean, uh, you guys put in like eight thousand, ten thousand miles a year. I don't do half that."

"Okay, okay, okay," said Giancarlo. "Let's settle down here. We shouldn't be squabbling."

Zak knew the tension and exasperation and probably the fumes from the fires were getting to him. On the other hand, if Stephens was withholding valuable support, they were all at risk. He was like a man in a life raft hiding bottles of fresh water from the others.

"I'm trying to conserve energy so I have something left if it comes down to a race," Stephens said, looking to the others for reinforcement.

"Zak's right," said Muldaur. "From now on you do your share or stay off my wheel. Got it?"

"Sure. Sure. I didn't realize you guys felt that way."

"How else would we feel?"

"As long as we're having a bitch session," said Giancarlo, standing in front of Stephens, "maybe now's the time to ask how Morse got my gun."

"What?"

"You know what I'm talking about. You were the one who first came up with the plan to turn the gun over."

"Hey, uh, Morse did what he wanted. He was that kind of guy. He was decisive. When he thought something needed to be—"

"You waited for us to leave, and then you egged him on, didn't you?"

"I didn't . . . well, I mean, I'll be straight with you. I thought it was a good idea. With his negotiating experience it should have been a piece of cake. I mean . . . it makes me sick to think what happened to him."

"You told him to take the revolver," said Giancarlo. "And just to make sure you weren't taking any of the risk yourself, you let him go alone."

"One guy was a whole lot less intimidating. They should have seen that. I'm sure you'll all agree no reasonable person would put the blame for what's happened on me."

A warbler burbled a song nearby. Smoke drifted through the trees. Zak watched as a beam of sunlight sliced through the smoke, looking nearly solid.

Giancarlo kicked Stephens's front tire lightly and said, "We oughta break your fucking neck."

It may have been the first time Zak ever heard Giancarlo curse, and it was certainly the first time he'd ever seen him unleash vitriol onto another person.

"Listen, guys," Stephens said, looking contrite. "I made a mistake. You can't . . . We've all made mistakes. You think I feel good about this? I'm the one who's going to have to tell his wife. I'm the one . . ."

Just then the white Ford became visible through the trees as it raced up the road, skidded in the center of the three-way intersection, reversed, and took the right-hand leg toward the cabins on the lake. At the speed they were traveling, they would soon clear the road and turn back.

"We can head back to the climb they just came down," said Muldaur. "There's no reason for them to think we would go that way again."

"That's because we wouldn't," said Zak. "If we go that way and they come back, next time they'll be checking along the side of the road. It was a miracle they didn't see us."

"We can conceal ourselves in the cabins," suggested Stephens.

"That's one idea," said Muldaur. "But right now they're between us and the cabins."

"We could head down," said Giancarlo. "See what's down the mountain."

"We know what's down there," said Zak. "Smoke and fire."

The walkie-talkie in Zak's pocket crackled. *"They must have gone down the mountain. We've been on all the roads up here and can't see them anywhere."*

"We heard shots. Did you get one of them?"

"Not yet."

"Well, they didn't come past us."

"Then they had to have gone down."

"Repeat. They didn't come past us. Check in the woods. They were hiding in the woods before. Flush them out and chase them this way."

The Ford came speeding past again, stopped in the center of the intersection, and then careened back along the south side of the lake, where they'd recently shot at the cyclists. "Now!" said Muldaur as he pushed his bike across the tinder-dry forest floor.

49

Zak had forgotten how far the beginning of the downhill run was from the intersection. At least a minute of riding on the flat, maybe two. He could hear the white Ford speeding up. Once again, they found themselves in an all-out race for their lives. This time Muldaur took the first hard pull, towing the four-man pace line for twenty seconds, pulling so hard he strung the other three out behind him, each seeking as much shelter behind the man in front as possible. When Muldaur signaled and moved to the right to avoid a pothole, so did the rest of them in a syncopated rhythm like a caterpillar. They were traveling in excess of twenty-eight miles an hour, no mean feat on mountain bikes.

As Muldaur swung wide and dropped toward the rear of the queue, Zak took the second pull, putting his head down and dropping his chain to a smaller cog in the rear. Behind, he could hear the Ford gaining. Feeling he couldn't trust Stephens, whose turn would be next, Zak took a longer pull than Muldaur's: he was determined to get them to the top of the hill before the Ford caught them. After that, they would be in free fall. Zak was breathing so hard he thought he was going to break a rib.

"This is a pretty good workout," Muldaur shouted from behind. He barely had enough air to speak.

"Great workout," gasped Zak.

"Maybe we should do this every year."

"What? Hire guys with rifles to chase us?"

"Yeah."

Before Zak could think of anything else to say, he heard a shot from behind them. There was too much wind in his ears to hear anything else, but he knew the Ford was closing in. Then suddenly the four bicycles careened down the beginning of the long descent. True to form, Giancarlo surged into the lead and was soon sixty yards in front.

Zak and Muldaur rode side by side. They could hear Stephens's bicycle behind them as he lost ground. Zak heard a clattering and cocked his head to one side, thinking somebody had fallen. "Lost the rifle," said Muldaur, pulling ahead.

They sailed down one long stretch of road and turned a corner to the left, all four of them picking up speed.

Zak didn't see Scooter until Scooter fired at them.

In fact, he caught only a quick glimpse of the Porsche and Kasey in the background, and then they were behind him. Muldaur, who had been in front of Zak, had aimed his bike at Scooter, who, probably because of his earlier experience with Zak, fired just the one shot and then dived away from the road frantically lest he get run over again. It was enough of a distraction for them all to get past unscathed.

The road was straight for almost two hundred yards, and Zak heard more gunshots behind them. Then the road arched to the right, and Zak, taking advantage of the arc, pulled to the far right-hand side of the road to get out of sight as soon as possible. It was getting smokier and smokier.

They sped down the mountainside in a loose phalanx, aware that there were at least two SUVs chasing them now. All in all, Scooter had gotten off three shots, but nobody seemed to be hit. Muldaur was a couple of bike lengths in front. Zak could hear Stephens's bike clanking behind him as the chain slapped the chain stay, and when he cocked his head he could hear the trucks; otherwise the wind in his ears blocked all sound. He was well aware that there was no chance of a powwow and even more aware that they were now weaponless.

Zak knew from the night before that this descent would take at least ten minutes, probably longer because of the smoke. As they wended their way along the treacherous roads, the smoke grew thicker until at one corner they almost piled into one another, Giancarlo only five or six feet in front of Zak now. At one point on one of the tightest switchbacks on the mountain, he caught a glimpse of the Ford and the Porsche, both with their headlights on, the Porsche running its windshield wipers. Shortly after that, smoke blotted out everything behind them.

"This is getting crazy," said Stephens.

"I know," Zak said.

"Maybe we should slow down!" Stephens yelled.

"You want to get shot," Muldaur shouted over his shoulder, "*you* slow down."

"We're all going to crash."

At the next bend it became a moot point, because the air cleared up and they were able to increase their speed. By the time the trucks came into view, the cyclists had picked up considerable distance on them, approaching one of the steepest sections of the mountain, a part of the road that seemed to drop almost straight down, arching to the right as it fell. As Zak recalled, it would get less steep around the corner. The two men in front of him actually accelerated. And then Zak did, too. It was foolhardy, and he could hear Stephens losing ground behind them as he griped about their recklessness. Then Giancarlo was skidding off to the right. Muldaur skipped to the left, and Zak found himself on a collision course with a three-point buck standing in the center of the road.

Zak missed the deer by inches, close enough to catch fleas. In front, Giancarlo continued to slow and so did Muldaur, because the road was filled with animals. A rabbit. A squirrel. Three more deer staring at the cyclists as if in a hypnotic trance.

All four riders ended up within feet of one another, standing in a bank of rolling smoke. Giancarlo was coughing the loudest, though Stephens wasn't taking it well, either. "It was a miracle nobody hit that deer," said Muldaur.

"What deer?" said Stephens, in between coughing bouts. Zak could barely see Stephens and couldn't see Muldaur at all. He could see the rear wheel on Giancarlo's bicycle, but Giancarlo's torso was a smoke-shrouded blur. The ambient temperature at the lake had been in the low triple digits, but it had increased significantly down here.

"You think there're more clear spots?" Muldaur asked nobody in particular. "Like if we went forward it might clear up?"

"I think there's more smoke," said Zak.

Zak heard the sound of Stephens's inhaler. And then, farther down the mountain, the fire crackling like a dinosaur snapping two-by-fours in its jaws.

"How close do you think the fire is?" Giancarlo asked.

"I think it's close," said Muldaur.

"Okay," Giancarlo said, turning his bike around and walking it up the hill. None of them would be able to remount because of the pitch. "I don't care what happens up there, I'm not riding into a forest fire."

Without further discussion they turned around and hiked back up the hill, pushing their bikes, coughing, and trying not to inhale too much smoke. Zak and Muldaur pulled their jersey necks up over their faces to filter out the worst of it.

"This is fucked," said Muldaur.

"Anybody read *Young Men and Fire*?" Giancarlo asked. "It's about the Mann Gulch Fire in Montana back in the 'fifties. A group of smoke jumpers got caught out in the open with a fire coming up a slope the same way this is coming at us."

"The ones who survived were the ones who could run uphill the fastest," said Zak. "The slower guys got caught and died."

50

Because they'd been proceeding blindly into the miasma, the unspoken assumption among the four cyclists was that the trucks behind them had turned around, too. In addition to the smoke and the almost unbearable heat, the winds had picked up with gusts Zak estimated at close to sixty miles an hour, perhaps as high as eighty. At one point a large stick blew across the road from somewhere and jammed into Stephens's rear wheel and derailleur; it took two of them to dislodge it. They'd been in the smoke longer than they should have, and Zak had doubts that they would be physically able make it back up the hill. He guessed they'd descended to within half a mile of the camp, which meant they would be climbing for at least half an hour longer to reach Lake Hancock again. Descending had been a bad move, but given the choices they'd been facing, there hadn't been anything else to do.

For all they knew, this was the end of their lives. Zak could see it in the faces of the others, and he was afraid they could see it in his. It wasn't something he wanted to show. Firefighters took a great deal of pride in maintaining an appearance of nonchalance under all circumstances, and Zak knew he and Muldaur had been full of bluster all day. Now the smoke was incapacitating them.

They heard a loud crash above them, and then through the

smoke Zak saw the outlines of the two vehicles, driver's doors winged open. The vehicles were only thirty feet away. The Porsche had rear-ended the pickup truck, and both were more or less blocking the roadway. An air bag had deployed from the center of the steering wheel in the Ford, and there were droplets of blood on it. Jennifer was sitting on the ground outside the truck, while Kasey remained in the driver's seat of the Porsche holding his bloody nose in one hand, a pair of broken sunglasses in the other. Scooter was on the ground on the far side of the Porsche, rocking back and forth in agony. His airbag had deployed also, and judging by the way he was acting, it must have whacked his broken collarbone pretty good. Bloomquist was sitting dismally in the back of the Porsche like a child in the time-out corner.

Zak reached inside the pickup and turned the motor off, then knelt beside Jennifer, who was sitting on the rocky ground as if she'd been thrown there, while Giancarlo walked to the far side of the Porsche and stepped back with a rifle in his hands.

"You okay, Jenn?" Zak asked.

"I'm okay."

"You get thrown out?"

"No. I stepped out and just sat down. I don't know why, but I'm having a hard time getting up."

"It's the smoke. It makes you sick."

"What happened to my face?" Jennifer touched her upper lip, which was beginning to swell.

"Air bags deploy at a hundred eighty miles an hour. Don't worry. It's minor."

Jennifer stared at Zak as if he were a creature she'd discovered at the zoo. "You guys shouldn't be here."

"Too late now."

As they spoke, a gust of hot wind whistled through the area and lifted the smoke enough that they could see one another clearly for the first time. Fred was in the bed of the pickup with his rifle held at his waist, while Giancarlo, in the road below him, was pointing the rifle he found at Fred's chest. Fred's teeth were limned with blood. The ropes and belt he'd used to lash himself into the back of the truck had tangled so that he had a loop over one arm and another around his neck. Even if he wanted to, he wouldn't have been able to react in time to keep Giancarlo from shooting him. "You just throw that out of there," Giancarlo said, "or I'll shoot it out of your hands."

"You don't shoot that well."

"I think he does," said Muldaur. "He's been hunting since he was eight."

Oblivious to his surroundings, Scooter was still writhing in pain on the ground. Jennifer was sitting below Kasey who'd bounded out of his Porsche, probably so everybody could see he wasn't armed. Bloomquist was cowering in the backseat of the Porsche. None of them had expected to see the cyclists up close, and now the only weapons in sight were the rifles Fred and Giancarlo wielded.

While the nine of them waited for something to happen between the two men with guns, a mature elk clambered up the hill, hooves clanking on the rocky road, snorting and lumbering past Muldaur as if he were nothing more than a fence post. The elk's big brown eyes took them in momentarily, and then the animal continued up the road without missing a step. The smoke began to thicken, and Jennifer coughed. So did Scooter. Zak could hear Stephens wheezing. A fierce wind filled with debris and cinders swirled around them and almost blew Zak's sunglasses off. Several hot cinders hit his bare skin. As if stung by a hornet, Jennifer slapped at her leg.

"The fire's too close," Zak said. "We gotta stop screwing around and get out of here."

"Tell him to put down his gun," Fred said.

"You put yours down!"

As they waited for the drama to play out, they heard a loud, whooshing noise like a freight train barreling through a desert town in the middle of the night. Everyone knew instinctively that the fire was getting close. Too close. Zak didn't know a lot about wildland fires, but he knew they created their own geothermal systems, and frequently the winds surrounding them were fiercer than any native winds, capable of causing the fire to behave in unpredictable ways. Spinning around as if in a cyclone, a large, dark object flew over their heads. Moments later the wind died, and the object fell to the earth with a clank. It was part of an old, rusted car body. It would have killed anyone it hit.

"Jesus," said Jennifer.

Zak helped her to her feet; her arms felt warm and moist. He thought she held him for a second too long, as if she needed something from him or was trying to impart a message.

"We need to get the hell out of here," said Giancarlo, who hadn't moved the rifle from his shoulder. "Call a truce and get out before we're dead."

"Fine with me," said Fred. "A truce."

"Then put the gun down."

"No fuckin' way, man. You killed my brother."

"I didn't have anything to do with your brother. I was in camp when that happened."

"Okay, *they* killed my brother. You're part of it."

"We didn't do anything," Zak said. "Scooter knocked him off that bluff by accident. If they both hadn't been half drunk, it wouldn't have happened."

"He wasn't drunk," Jennifer said, stepping away from Zak. Any coalition they might have formed was gone now. Fred began to swing his rifle in Zak's direction.

"You put that gun on my friend and I'm going to pull this trigger," said Giancarlo.

Fred stopped moving. "You guys killed my dog."

"Yeah, well, your dog took a piece of meat out of Giancarlo's leg the size of a sandwich."

"Truce! Truce?" Kasey stepped forward. "Okay? Okay, you guys? Before we all look like broiled knockwurst? I don't know shit about forest fires, but I think we're in trouble here."

"He's right," said Giancarlo. "Put the gun down."

"I put it down, you'll shoot me."

"Give me a break, knucklehead. If I was going to shoot you, I would have done it by now. I need you to put your gun down before I put mine down so we can be sure you don't shoot us."

"Fred," said Jennifer. "Put it down."

Scooter was on his feet now, eyes full of tears. "Don't let them buffalo you, Fred. Put a bullet in him. He doesn't have the nerve to shoot back."

Before Fred could make a decision, the wind picked up again, and they all heard a horrendous crashing to the south. On the other side of a knoll that blocked their view of the valley and the fast-encroaching fire, they heard sounds that resembled a beast with feet as large as trucks, snapping branches and cracking rocks.

Jennifer tried to climb into the cab of the truck, trembling so badly she couldn't coordinate her movements. "I'm getting out of here."

When the crashing noises in the forest began to sound out to the north, too, and they saw flames fingering into the trees a mere fifty yards away, Fred flung his rifle into the road. "Don't shoot, you bastard. Just don't shoot me."

Giancarlo picked up the rifle, ejected the cartridges, flung the gun into the woods with one hand, then did the same thing with the rifle he'd been holding. He collected his own pistol and tucked it into his jersey pocket.

"Just for the record," Muldaur said, "we didn't push Chuck. And that revolver Morse had wasn't loaded."

Scooter climbed into the Porsche. "That fucker was going to kill us all. Why else would he pull a gun?"

"He was *giving* it to you," Zak said. "As a peace offering."

As he stepped into the Porsche, Kasey Newcastle gave Zak a look of incomprehension. Zak could see the horror in his eyes as he momentarily considered the possibility that the morning's hostilities had been spawned by lies, that Scooter had been lying to him all day.

Jennifer was trying to maneuver the Ford, which had less damage than the Porsche, but it was clear to Zak they wouldn't be able to turn around on the narrow road. Both vehicles would be forced to make the return trip up the hill in reverse.

Stephens was already two hundred yards up the mountain, pedaling steadily.

The Porsche and the Ford began driving up the hill backward. Higher on the mountain, Muldaur and Giancarlo pulled over as they were passed by the trucks. When Stephens was overtaken, Zak could see him talking to the occupants of each vehicle as they slowed to pass.

51

Stephens turned around and realized he was the only one who'd left the accident scene. Had they not seen the bull elk rampaging up the road? When a wild animal disregards the presence of human beings, something is seriously askew. And those winds? Stephens had never experienced anything quite like them, the logs and debris flying through the air. The winds were easily 120, maybe 130 degrees Fahrenheit. Everybody was sweating heavily, even Jennifer, whose tight T-shirt Stephens noticed was wet down the spine and below each breast.

This was what it was all about. This was what he'd been saving his energy for. He knew the others had been making vigorous efforts unnecessarily, while he'd been conserving every last watt of power for the time when it would count. The race went not to the swiftest but to the smartest. The swiftest man in the race rode hard, but the smartest man was on his wheel ready to lunge past after the front man wore himself out. Of course he'd been drafting, and in doing so had banked up a fair amount of reserves. He realized the others were in better shape than him by virtue of having put in more hours on the bike, so it stood to reason he had to do what he could to even the odds. Stephens was reasonably sure if they had to ride to the top of the mountain at speed right now, he would beat the others handily.

The first section of the road was steep, but it leveled out a tad and passed through an uphill vale with trees on either side. Soon it began climbing in earnest in a long, steady grind, trees and steep slopes to the left, the treetops and occasional drop-offs to the right. Stephens found himself on a long, sweeping right-hand turn, where he was able to peer down the mountain.

The sight that greeted him made his mouth go dry.

Almost everything Stephens could see below was either on fire or had already burned. When he could pick them out, individual trees looked like burning match heads. All of the green they had looked out on this morning during their first trip up this road had been replaced by smoke, char, and blackened upright snags that had once been trees.

He caught a glimpse of the fire maybe a third of a mile to the south as it raced up the face of the mountain at an alarming rate. He was almost certain the near-vertical slope didn't connect to this road, but if it did the road would no longer be viable. The fierce winds would waft flames across it like a blowtorch. There was no way he or any of the others would make it if the flames encroached on the road. He didn't like going this hard, but if there was ever a time this was it.

He pushed on, feeling the pain in his legs, wondering if he was going to cramp. Last year after the RAMROD, Stephens had suffered a cramp that left his quadriceps sore for a month. When the Porsche and then the white Ford approached him, Stephens moved to the side of the road. He'd planned this carefully, knowing if the four of them requested rides at the same time they were unlikely to be effective, but if he could get up the road and negotiate by himself, he had a chance of success. As usual, the spoils went to the victor, and the victor was the smartest. He was well aware that there was a certain amount of ego involved in outsmarting others, and Stephens wasn't immune to it, although he certainly did his best to project humility, unlike some others he was too generous to name. In fact, part of his mind was rehearsing how he would tell this story to his wife when he got home without sounding like he was bragging.

"How about giving a fellow traveler a ride?" Stephens said amiably as the Porsche came abreast. He would show them he wasn't cut from the same cloth as the others. "I know you've got room for one."

"Fuck you," said Scooter.

"I'm not like these others."

"Who are you kidding?"

"They're firefighters. I'm a chief financial officer. I know Fred's father."

"Jesuuuuuuuus . . ."

When the tall Ford reversed alongside him a few moments later, he looked up at Fred, who was sitting next to Jennifer. "I know you're both reasonable enough to give me a ride."

"Screw you."

"I'm not with those others."

"The hell you aren't."

"It was my plan to make peace between the two camps."

"You're soooo full of crap."

"Just give me a ride. I can help you with those guys. I know what could put them in trouble."

"They're already in trouble. And so are you, asshole."

It was only after the trucks began to fade in the haze that Stephens was shocked to find Muldaur and Zak twenty yards behind and closing. He hoped they hadn't heard his pleas for a ride. Stephens put his head down and focused on the section of dirt and rock three to four feet in front of his front tire. He was going to stay in front of them as long as possible. His lungs hurt. His legs were aching. Even his butt muscles hurt. Despite all his efforts, these two were passing him. Looking at the bright side, he knew once they got in front, their pacing would help, and each time they reached one of the flatter spots on the road, Stephens could draft.

"What'd they say?" Zak asked.

"They wanted to give me a ride, but I didn't think it would be right if they wouldn't take you guys, too."

"Sure you weren't begging for a ride for yourself?"

"Not without you guys."

"Right."

Stephens began pedaling harder in an effort to stay with the two more polished cyclists. He dropped his chain to a smaller cog on the back and pushed for a few strokes, then thought better of it and went back to a lower gear. Even with all his efforts, he was barely hanging on.

"Hey, Zak?" Muldaur was speaking now.

"Yeah?"

"I just found a better way to work out. Better than having guys with rifles behind us."

"You mean getting chased by a forest fire?"

"Right."

"Excellent. I don't know why I didn't think of that."

The fire had jumped the road and was crawling up the mountain behind them. It would take only a small change in direction for the wind to blow it at them. Stephens had no way of estimating how fast it might be closing in, but he knew the climb was going to take another twenty or twenty-five minutes. This was no time for any of them to be making ridiculous jokes. Didn't they know? A gust of wind. A slight variation in terrain. A flat tire. A broken chain. Any piece of defective equipment, and one of them would be a goner. So far nobody'd flatted and nothing had broken on any of the bikes, but if it did the affected rider would be kindling. A few minutes later they hit a relatively flat spot, where Polanski and Muldaur took turns in front and Stephens remained behind. Astonishingly, just before they started the next climb, Giancarlo caught them. When Stephens turned around to take a look, Giancarlo's face was blank and pale, and he was breathing even harder than Stephens.

"Can you stay on, Giancarlo?" It was Polanski. Nobody'd asked Stephens if *he* could stay on.

"Not at this pace. Just go on."

"We can slow a bit."

"Don't you dare."

The winds, which had been boiling over their heads the last few minutes, picked up. For a time they were blowing from directly behind them, coming out of the north. Then they were gusting from the west, hot and full of smoke and projectiles, twigs and pinecones and burning debris. A gust almost knocked Stephens over. They climbed together for thirty seconds before Giancarlo dropped back.

Incredibly, Stephens found himself next to Polanski, who forced him to fight for the smoothest sections of the road; Muldaur was somewhere behind. Whoever lost each of their small battles fell behind slightly when he had to ride the rougher section. And then another blast of filthy air crept up their backs, and Stephens felt something sting his arm. The air was swirling with hundreds of tiny burning cinders.

The heat began increasing at a phenomenal rate. Tiny cinders singed his neck, and one even burned through the sleeve of his jersey. By now Stephens had lost twenty bike lengths on Polanski. He cocked his head to one side and saw Giancarlo another hundred yards down the hill, pedaling in a labored motion, zigzagging from side to side.

A wall of flame rose up behind Giancarlo, and he was limned by yellow. It was hard to judge how close the fire was, but Stephens guessed the cyclist below him would be dead in a minute or less. Forty yards in front of the trio the top of a Douglas fir burst into flame, and one by one they gravitated to the other side of the road as they passed it, each feeling the radiated heat from the flames.

52

Surely the cyclists had to be lying when they said Morse came to them with an unloaded revolver. Kasey had been having misgivings about the incident all day, but no matter how many times he replayed those few seconds before Finnigan shot Morse, he could not honestly view it as a peace talk. What he remembered most was Morse trying to gull them into complacency seconds before he pulled out the gun.

Actually, now that he thought about it, Morse had been somewhat limp-wristed with the pistol. But then, after he got shot the first time, he raised the gun again, and that was when Kasey knew he'd meant to hurt them all along. In addition, had not Scooter checked afterward and found the revolver loaded? Why would Scooter lie about that? As he drove up the mountain in reverse, Kasey decided the cyclists were the true liars. They had to be.

"They don't have the balls to shoot us," Scooter said. "That guy this morning tried and choked. That's what gave Fred the edge."

"I don't know about balls, Scooter. You saw the way they killed Chuck's dog."

"That wasn't pretty," said Roger Bloomquist from the backseat.

"It *was* loaded, wasn't it?" Kasey asked.

"What?"

"That revolver you took off the guy Fred shot. It *was* loaded?"

"I said it was, didn't I? Besides, even if it wasn't, a guy pulls a gun, you have every right to shoot. The cops would."

"I'm not sure he wasn't trying to hand us the gun the way he said he was."

"Don't believe that for a minute. It was the perfect con. He was going to shoot you. You go back down that road and you'll find the bullets. I can show you exactly where they are."

It was an odd assertion, Kasey thought, because this morning only moments after he supposedly tossed them, Scooter hadn't been able to locate them, or didn't want to.

"Hey. I have an idea. We're going to be passing those guys in a minute. Let's bump them off the mountain. We could make it look like an accident."

"I don't think so," Kasey said.

"It's a long ride up this hill on a bicycle," said Bloomquist. "They're not going to make it to safety before the fire gets them."

Kasey didn't pay a whole lot of attention when they passed the first three cyclists, and despite Scooter's urging to do otherwise, he drove with care. So did Jennifer. People had been injured and killed, but so far Kasey had accomplished none of the damage, and he was beginning to see the percentage in keeping it that way.

On top of the mountain, trees were blowing in all different directions, some of the younger firs bent almost to the ground. The Cayenne rocked from side to side in the winds, hot smoke blowing around the interior. Several times Kasey had been forced to slow because of the smoke in the road. They should have picked up the cyclists, he thought. Kasey didn't want to think about it too much, but he had an idea that under conditions such as these, it was tantamount to murder that they hadn't.

53

Zak knew Stephens had been dogging it all day, but the tenacity and courage he showed now that they were all spurred by flames was unbelievable. It was amazing how strong he'd become, falling off the pace for a few hundred feet, then making a gargantuan effort to get back on and succeeding repeatedly. Now, as they headed up the final stretch of mountainside, Stephens was right on their tail.

Twice now they'd seen a wall of fire behind them, and each time it looked like Giancarlo was pedaling out of it, bobbing and standing up at times, even though it was awkward and dangerous to stand while pedaling on these steep gravel and dirt roads. Zak had a dreadful feeling in his gut that Giancarlo was going to be overtaken by the rolling inferno.

Incredibly, by the time they arrived at the last leg of the ascent, Zak was thinking about giving up. It was the first time all day he'd seriously considered getting off and quitting, and the notion startled him. Of course his legs had been aching all along, and his lungs weren't processing the smoky air well—he and the others had been bringing up globs of dirty phlegm for the past half hour—but the rest of his body hurt as well: his shoulders, wrists, and palms, the soles of his feet. Even the muscles in his face felt tight and cramped.

He was having a hard time holding his head up. He wasn't the only one in trouble. For the past two hours he'd noticed a tic playing under one of Muldaur's eyes and what appeared to be a weakening of his left leg, his knee flicking out to the side in an odd way at the bottom of every pedal stroke. He'd thought Stephens or Giancarlo would be the first to crack, but now he wasn't so sure he or Muldaur wouldn't be the one.

This last stretch of road ran up the mountain in a straight line, and several times in the last mile the howling, gale-force winds had come close to knocking one of them over. Zak moved ahead of Muldaur to take another pull at the front just as the wind began rif-fling the tops of the trees in a way he hadn't seen until now, whipping the tallest trees and bending them almost to the ground. Zak found himself expending an enormous amount of energy just to keep the bike upright and stable.

For a while the wind grew so loud he couldn't hear anything else. When it finally died down, Muldaur was cursing. Zak wanted to turn around to see if Stephens was still with them or if Giancarlo was in visual contact, but he didn't dare loosen his grip on his handlebars or even cock his head for a look.

The heat came over the treetops first. Then behind the treetops a large, quick tongue of flame shot into the sky. It frightened Zak, but it must have terrified Stephens, because he pulled alongside and, a moment later, began inching away. He was breathing like a steam engine. Another tongue of flame revealed itself, and instead of disappearing as the first one had, it scoured the treetops alongside the road, setting them alight one by one like a giant blowtorch. Oddly, the winds were so gusty that about a third of the treetops were snuffed out as soon as they ignited. Zak had never seen anything like it.

The winds continued to grow more violent. At times they would blow from directly behind to help push them up the hill. Twice, Zak dropped his chain down a cog or two into a higher gear ratio to take advantage of the wind assist.

It was only with a superhuman effort that Zak was able to get on

Stephens's wheel. Once again Stephens had remained behind for long periods and then took advantage of the energy he'd been saving to leap forward and save himself. When Zak or Muldaur took the lead, they always came around with a slow acceleration so the others could get used to the new pace without being dropped, but Stephens continued to launch himself up the road as if purposely trying to lose them.

Muldaur had been flagging for the last half mile and was now cursing as Zak towed him back in line behind Stephens. Even though they were only making seven or eight miles an hour and sometimes as little as four or five, because of the thirty- or forty-mile-per-hour wind in their faces the second and third man in a pace line received enormous benefit. There were lulls in the fire-induced hurricane, too, which made Zak nervous, because it was impossible to guess from which direction the next gusts might issue.

As the fire to their right began working its way up the mountainside in front of them, they could hear what sounded like the crinkling of giant plastic wrappers. Aside from the occasional tongue of yellow leaping into the air over their heads and then vanishing into the atmosphere, they saw little flame. The fire was like a monster behind a door and seemed to be marching up the gully alongside the road faster than they were traveling. For almost a minute the noise was fifteen yards in front of them. Zak's greatest fear was that the fire would suck all the oxygen from the road and they would suffocate. He didn't mind dying, he told himself, but he wanted a fair shot at outrunning the fire, not that anything about this day had been or was going to be fair. Still, if they could get back to the level of the lake, they might have a chance.

It angered him when he thought about the two vehicles making it to safety without them. Kasey and the others were probably up to their necks in icy lake water right now. Zak had been so hot for so long that a dip in a snow-fed, ice-cold lake seemed like a slice of heaven.

At any moment the fire speeding alongside in the trees might cross the road and block their exit. Should that happen, investigators would find four charred bicycles, eight melted tires, four corpses. The only reason they weren't getting scorched now was that the winds were carrying the heat in a hundred directions, and most of the heat was on the far side of the trees. Even when the flames bore down on them once or twice, all they felt was the same hot wind they'd been suffering all day.

They were riding faster now, the three of them in a line, Stephens pedaling with a ferocity Zak had never seen from him, wobbling from side to side and running off the smooth sections on the road in his haste. If there had been any doubt before, there was none now—they were riding for their lives, and Stephens seemed to know this better than any of them. Zak remembered having once read about studies done concerning airplane crashes. Scientists had wanted to discover who survived and why, and it turned out that in order to survive a cabin fire in a passenger jet you needed to be one of the strongest men on board—the survivors were almost always men. It didn't take researchers long to figure it out. If someone is on fire, every ounce of gallantry and any other civilized trait go out the window. The brain reverts to the Neolithic when survival is on the line. Zak knew they were getting to that place, if they weren't there already.

They had an eighth of a mile to go to reach the crest.

Suddenly Zak's legs found renewed strength. Muldaur's must have, too, because together the two of them chugged up the road like a matched team of plow horses. The wind was howling in their faces, so Zak let Muldaur take the first pull, then when he swerved to the side, went through and rode in front for as long as he could hold it. They continued to switch off, working together until—in less than a hundred yards—they left behind the last of the burning treetops. Without meaning to, they also left Stephens, but they couldn't worry about Stephens any more than they could worry about Giancarlo.

For the last eighth of a mile Zak and Muldaur rode side by side, moving faster and faster, each waiting for the other to crack. In the end Muldaur pulled ahead, and, when he did, Zak cast a look over his shoulder. Stephens was two hundred yards back, but oddly there was no evidence of fire behind him; just the smoke that had been molesting them all along. There was no trace of Giancarlo. Absolutely none.

54

Still breathing almost as heavily as they had been while they were climbing, Muldaur and Zak stood astride their now motionless bicycles and rested their forearms on their handlebars. They were safe, at least for a few minutes. Zak propped his forehead on his arms and stared at the ground. They'd both shot up over the top of the mountain, ridden fifty yards farther, then turned around and pedaled until they were close enough to see the grade.

Even though saving his own butt had been the number one priority during the dash to the top, Zak felt now as if his life depended on how Stephens and Giancarlo fared. For six years Giancarlo had been one of his best friends, and he couldn't imagine how bad it would be to lose him like this; nor could he imagine telling Giancarlo's wife how they'd left him to the flames, or what it would mean to Giancarlo's family. Surely this would haunt Zak for the rest of his life in the same way that his sister's death haunted him. And even though Stephens continued to irk him at every turn, Zak certainly didn't want to see him hurt. It was all too horrible to contemplate.

"He's coming," Muldaur said, gasping for breath.

"Who's coming?" Zak was too tired to lift his head off his forearms.

"I don't know. It's still too smoky to see for sure."

Zak looked up for the first time since they stopped and in the distance recognized Stephens by the subtleties in his riding style. It took a painfully long time for the man to reach them, casting glances back over his shoulder to see if the fire was closing in. Zak couldn't believe how relieved he felt. When Stephens reached the flat part of the road, he pushed only hard enough for his bike to glide to a halt next to Muldaur's, then unclipped, put a foot down, and sipped from his hydration pack, gasping for breath. "You didn't wait for one second."

"We didn't wait for Giancarlo, either," said Muldaur. "But that doesn't mean we don't care."

Stephens coughed up some phlegm and spat onto the road, "I don't get it. I thought it was overtaking us. I mean . . . uh, I really thought we were finished. Like it was going to jump up through those trees and grab us."

"It almost did," Zak said. "We were lucky. You get mixed up in something this screwed up, half the time it's luck that saves you."

"Or doesn't save you," added Muldaur.

"There he is," said Muldaur. All three of them peered down the mountain at a figure riding out of the smoke, Giancarlo being chased up the mountain by a wall of orange. Maybe they had outrun it, but Giancarlo hadn't, at least not yet. It was hard to tell how close the flames were to him, but they could see the effect the heat was having on his efforts. Flames were consuming trees and brush on either side of the road now, but, in addition to the burning vegetation, a sheet of yellow seemed to be running up the road on its own.

"Don't die, Giancarlo," pleaded Zak, "just don't die."

He was 150 yards from the top now—the fire right behind him—riding like a demon, head low, pulling up on the pedals with his cleats as well as pushing down, working the handlebars with his muscular arms and shoulders, using every part of his body to get more power into the cranks.

"I think it's going to get him and us both," Muldaur said, making motions as if to ride.

"I'm not leaving."

They waited for what seemed like half a lifetime, watching Giancarlo compete against a wall of flame three times taller than man and bike. Zak knew there was some point at which, if they didn't leave, it would be too late, that Giancarlo might go down and they might go down, too. He didn't know where the point of no return was, and although he tried his damnedest to calculate where it might be, his brain simply refused the assignment.

"Come on, Giancarlo," Muldaur screamed, his voice hoarse from the smoke they'd been inhaling all afternoon.

Together they cheered Giancarlo up the last hundred feet, then turned and began riding with him. Zak pushed him from one side, while Muldaur stretched out a hand and pushed from the other. Giancarlo was heavy, and to make it harder he ceased pedaling as soon as he crested the top. Through the palms of his fingerless gloves Zak could feel the heat radiating off Giancarlo's back. Parts of his jersey had melted. His hair was singed. The back of his neck looked sunburned, but he was intact.

"You okay, buddy?" Zak asked.

"I've been better."

"We couldn't wait for you."

"I know. Don't worry about it."

"We wanted to, but . . ."

"Hey. I wouldn't have waited."

"We thought you were finished," Muldaur said. "I thought *we* were dead, and then we made it and turned around, and truthfully . . . I never expected to see you up here."

"It died down just long enough for me to get away."

"Maybe there *is* a God," said Zak.

"You know there is," said Giancarlo. "He just pulled me up that hill." Stephens was in front in the drifting smoke, having left the lip of the mountain before any of them.

Zak had never seen Giancarlo this tired. The dressing on his leg was filthy with blood and ash. His face was sooty. There was a dried ring of white around his mouth, probably salt. He wondered how much more riding they would have to do and whether Giancarlo would hold up. Then he wondered whether *he* would hold up.

55

Headlights bright, the white Ford came plowing through the bank of gray and almost struck Stephens, who swerved at the last moment; and then the truck braked to avoid the sudden apparition and went partially off the road. It was hard to tell who was more stunned, Scooter, who was driving now, or Roger Bloomquist who was sitting beside him. "You're not headed back down?" asked Zak. "We were just down there, and it wasn't pretty."

"We know there's going to be some flame," said Scooter, addressing Stephens instead of Zak, "but we'll just have to blast through. We've been watching the fire line. It's not very deep. We can get through."

"People have tried to get through that kind of flame in a vehicle before," said Zak. "It never works."

"The hell."

Before they could say anything more, Scooter gunned the motor, and the Ford shot dirt out from beneath its tires, heading for the brow of the hill. Zak could see that although their warning had hardened Scooter's stance, it had weakened Bloomquist's to the point that he looked near tears.

"I wonder where the rest of them are," Muldaur said.

The walkie-talkie in Zak's jersey pocket began squawking.

"Scooter? We're at the south end of the lake, and it doesn't look good. Did you check the north side?"

The cyclists proceeded slowly through the smoke so the next vehicle wouldn't hit them. Zak began to rethink his tentative plan to jump into the lake. It wouldn't do much good to escape the flames if they smothered in the smoke. "We've already taken enough smoke," Muldaur said, as if reading Zak's mind.

"You thinking about the lake, too?"

"It seemed like a good idea while we were climbing."

Zak drank from his hydration pack until he'd sucked it dry. It held a hundred ounces and had been full an hour ago. He tried to think through their options, but rational thought eluded him. It was a sign of how much the smoke, the exertion, and the loss of water weight through sweating had confused his brain. He knew there were a limited number of paths they might take off this plateau, and he knew they were approaching a three-way intersection, but no matter how hard he tried, he could not wrap his brain around where the various roads led. It was frightening to realize just how badly his cognitive processes had failed. It would be the second or third time they'd gone through the intersection in the past hour.

Without the threat of a major forest fire on their tails, the others—except for Stephens, who had disappeared in front again—were riding a whole lot slower now, each feeling this was a time to reassess and, if possible, recover.

They heard the accident before they saw it. The bike had bounced off the Porsche's front fender, but Stephens, who had rolled to the side of the road and was already getting up, didn't appear to be too injured. The headlights of the Porsche looked bright yellow until Zak took off his sunglasses.

Fred was already out of the Porsche and screaming at Stephens. "Why don't you watch where you're going? You were in the middle of the road!"

"I'm not trying to get in your way," Stephens said, picking up his bicycle. "I'm really not."

"Well, you *were* in our way!" Fred towered over Stephens but backed off when the other three cyclists converged on them. Jennifer got out and stood beside the passenger's door. Kasey winged open the driver's door and stood with one foot on the packed earth and the other inside the vehicle. It occurred to Zak that perhaps because they were now weaponless, these people were afraid of them, two men and a woman, sans guns, facing four cyclists who had every right to be madder than hell at the way they'd been treated all day. Large as he was, even Fred showed signs of being intimidated. What they didn't know was that a couple of fourth graders could have pushed all four of the cyclists over with a broom.

Before anybody else could say anything, the walkie-talkie in the Porsche and the one in Zak's rear jersey pocket rattled in unison. *"Commando Two to Commando One. We're in trouble. Commando Two to . . . don't—"*

It was Scooter's voice, but the message ended in a trail of static. Kasey grabbed the walkie-talkie from out of the Porsche and tried to raise his friend. Fred gave the four cyclists a look that indicated the stolen walkie-talkie was clear evidence that every accusation they'd leveled against them was valid.

"They were headed down," Stephens said.

"Which way is down?"

"You boys turned around?" Muldaur asked.

"Which way is down?" Kasey repeated.

"Tell us what you found up the mountain, and we'll tell you which way is down."

"Fire," Jennifer said. "We found a ton of fire creeping down the side of the mountain toward the lake. The road to the south is impassable."

"Down is back there," said Zak. "We warned them not to go."

The three of them climbed into the Porsche and slammed the doors. Jennifer locked hers.

Muldaur said, "Fuck you," and pedaled past them. Zak and Giancarlo followed. As they rode, the radio in Zak's back pocket sizzled when Jennifer tried to raise Scooter and Bloomquist. It was the only noise any of them heard. Even the whirring from knobby mountain bike tires on the road seemed softened by the smoke.

When they reached the intersection, it became apparent that Stephens wasn't with them. "Hey, where is he?" Giancarlo said. "I know he's not in front this time." They rode in circles in the road for half a minute, calling him and giving him a chance to catch up.

"We can't wait," said Muldaur.

"He's your friend," said Zak.

"No, he's all of ours. But we can't wait."

56

Prior to this morning, Kasey had only seen one dead body in his life, his grandmother at her funeral, so he wasn't happy about any of this. The fact that they'd started two of the fires that were now chasing them up and down the mountain had become a nagging kernel of guilt he was doing his best to bury. The fires were fingering their way up the mountain, one from the site of the wreck and a second from the camp. Kasey knew the fire at the camp had swelled to become the torrent of yellow that was charging at them now.

The squabble came after they'd reversed up the mountain and turned around at the viewpoint near the top. Scooter and Bloomquist climbed into the bed of the tall Ford for a better look at the fires below them. Scooter swore the road was passable and all they had to do was drive down the way they'd come up, but Kasey knew he couldn't possibly see enough of the road to know if that was true. Jennifer said she was not going down. Bloomquist sided with Scooter in wanting to descend. "The quickest way home is the way we came," he said. Fred wanted to go down, too, but only to find the rifles the cyclists had thrown into the trees, so he could reload them from the boxes of ammo he still had in the glove box.

In the end they decided Scooter and Bloomquist would drive the pickup north, while Kasey, with Fred and Jennifer as passengers, would head south. Whoever found a way out would radio the other team. If all else failed, Scooter might try going back down, but not before okaying it with Kasey.

Thinking they would climb into some cleaner air once they reached the next grade, Kasey drove Jennifer and Fred around the end of the lake through dense smoke, but by the time they got to the south end of the basin they could hear fire raging above them. "I'm not going up," Fred said. "No way."

It was when they drove back through the intersection that they struck the bicyclist.

It was a shock to realize Scooter and Bloomquist had apparently gone down the mountainside without telling them. That they had to get this information from the cyclists galled Kasey. After they made it clear they weren't giving them rides, three of the cyclists pedaled off into the smoke, their faces sooty and their eyes embodying the thousand-yard stare of men who knew they didn't have long to live. It was a measure of their weariness that they didn't put up too much of an argument.

Kasey still hadn't decided quite which direction to drive when Stephens, the remaining cyclist, walked around and rapped on his window. "Don't roll it down," said Fred.

Kasey pushed the button and lowered his window, but only halfway. It was hard to hear what Stephens was saying over the stereo and the ineffective air conditioner, which was running full blast. "I said I know you, uh, you fellas don't want to give me a ride, but . . . well, it would be worth your while if you did. There are going to be inquiries. The county sheriff's office is going to be looking into what went on out here. Accusations are going to be hurled."

"And?"

"Basically, it's going to be your word against theirs."

"We don't mind if you all end up in jail," said Fred from the backseat.

"A very good case can be made for their side," Stephens said. "Chuck falls. You shoot at us. We send a guy down to talk things over. You shoot him. Twice. We light off some firecrackers and run. You shoot at us again and pursue us."

"Those really were firecrackers?" asked Kasey.

"Of course they were."

"But you guys busted the gate," said Fred.

"I don't know anything about the gate."

"Fuck you," Fred said.

"No," Kasey said. "Wait a minute. So what's your point, Stephens?"

"It's just . . . I feel I have so much in common with you guys. I mean, those firemen . . . they stick together, but we're . . . from a different segment of the population."

"Which segment is that?"

"We're in the top one percentile. Your family is. I am. I should be in here with you guys."

Kasey thought Stephens's salary couldn't possible be anywhere close to the Newcastle family income, but that wasn't his concern right now. "Look, buddy. We don't have a lot of time. Try putting it in English."

"Okay. Yeah. Sure. You leave me here with these guys . . . there's no telling what might happen when the police ask questions. I can see things both ways. They have some valid points. But so do you. I can see your side of things, and it would make your case unbeatable if you have me to back you up."

"Just tell me one thing," Kasey said, casting a sidelong look over his shoulder at Fred. "That revolver your friend had this morning. Was it loaded?"

"Well, right now . . . I'd have to say it was."

"Was it really?"

"Don't ask him shit!" Fred tipped forward in his seat, bellowing into Kasey's ear.

Kasey said, "So you're saying if we give you a ride, you'll help us put those guys in prison, where they belong?"

"I don't owe them any loyalty."

"What if we give you a ride and you renege on the deal later?"

"That's not going to happen. I don't renege on deals. Ask anyone."

57

Zak, Muldaur, and Giancarlo decided to go back and check on Stephens. It irritated Muldaur that they were being forced to retrace their progress in this smoke, because their time on the bike and maybe their time on earth was going to be limited by the volume of smoke they inhaled. It was having a palpable effect on his leg muscles, his throat was thick with it, and he could almost feel it nestling in his lungs.

In the solid wall of gray, they spotted Stephens's bike on a mat of pine needles beside the road. Just the bicycle: no Stephens, and no sport utility vehicle.

"Stephens!" Giancarlo shouted. "Stephens!"

They set the riderless bike upright against a tree to better mark the spot, then pedaled back to the three-way intersection and headed toward the lake and the access road to the cabins. Muldaur had one of the worst headaches of his life and attributed it to the vast quantities of smoke he'd inhaled in the past hour. His head throbbed so badly he was afraid he might be on the verge of a stroke. Muldaur had come into this weekend feeling he was the strongest rider in the group, but Zak had been taking measured pulls alongside him all day and was beginning to look stronger by the minute. He'd been training hard this summer, and despite the smoke it was showing.

They took the narrow game trail that led to the lake, dodging low branches in the smoke, until they found the short stretch of beach eighty yards from the road. The water's edge was barely visible in the murk. Despite the fact that they needed to get organized and keep moving now that the lakefront didn't look viable, Zak got off his bike and waded into the water, scooping handfuls of the lake into his mouth, removing his hydration pack and filling it with water.

"You drink that, you're going to get giardiasis," Giancarlo said.

"How long does it take to start?"

"Good point."

Giancarlo dropped his bike and stepped into the water, too, while Muldaur picked up a series of shiny brass rifle casings from the sand. He'd hoped to find a layer of clean air clinging to the water, but the glassy surface attracted smoke like a hooker in church attracted unwanted looks. Zak waded into the shallows until Muldaur couldn't see him, though he was no more than twenty feet distant. He sank down into the lake until only his head was showing. "What if we just sit here? I mean, if we don't do anything else. Just float. What if we do that?"

"We'd die from smoke inhalation," Muldaur replied.

"What if we don't give a damn?"

"I don't believe you don't give a damn."

"What if I don't care what you believe?"

"We've got to get away from here and you know it. We've been through worse than this in the fire department."

"Have we?"

"Well, maybe not. But we'll make it out of here. Zak, if I really believed we were going to find good air out there somewhere on the lake, I'd be the first one in."

"I'm just so tired I think I'm going to drop dead."

"Me, too," said Giancarlo. "But the deal when you get in a situation like this is, you keep going until you drop. And then you get up and go some more. You *never* quit."

"Let's get going before we talk ourselves to death."

Once they were moving again, Muldaur was sorry he hadn't taken a dip with the others. Their shoes were squishing and their Lycra shorts were shiny with the wet, and he envied the coolness they must be feeling, however temporary. The road that headed north out of the Lake Hancock basin climbed sooner than he remembered, and the heat from their work began to build quickly. Giancarlo had already disappeared in the smoke above them, while Muldaur and Zak rode one in front of the other as they had been doing most of the day. Muldaur had a queer feeling in the pit of his stomach that Zak's unwillingness to do another climb put him a leg up on Zak if things got desperate again, which made him also feel that if only one of them was going to die, it would be Zak. He immediately felt guilty for having the thought.

Once they began climbing, his legs felt wooden. Earlier, he'd strained every muscle in his calves, quads, and buttocks, and had been pushing through the pain with each pedal stroke, but now he felt as if he were made out of wood.

By the time they'd ascended five hundred vertical feet, the smoke on the road behind them began to get sketchy. They were catching glimpses of Giancarlo up ahead, and astonishingly he was holding his own; he may even have gained ground since they began. Was it possible Muldaur and Zak had shot their wad on the earlier climbs and Giancarlo was now beating them the way Stephens had been?

Without speaking about it, Zak and Muldaur both stopped at one of the drainage canals cut diagonally across the road. He knew these mountains probably received 150 inches of rain a year; the shallow ditches were important for preserving roads that otherwise might be washed away by rainwater. Breathing heavily, they stopped and angled their bikes so they could see down the hillside. The sky showed some blue, but it was mostly a gauzy pale gray. Below, over the lake, a thick residue of smoke lay in the basin like a deformed cake. On the opposite side they could see fires burning on the far mountain. They had only one option, and the fact that they were on their way cheered Muldaur just a tad. The plateau behind them had acted as a buffer, but sooner or later the fires would be coming up this road. The most troubling aspect of this route was that if the fire sneaked up behind them, they would have no recourse but to race it to the top of the mountain.

"How far to the top of this?" Zak asked.

"You don't remember?"

"Do you?"

"I was thinking thirty minutes from the lake?"

"I was going to say forty."

"Ballpark."

For a while the road was clear of loose rocks, and they were able to ride side by side. When a helicopter passed overhead, Muldaur said, "Too bad we don't have a flare gun. We could signal." Having a possible source of rescue so close at hand while finding themselves helpless to attain it was dispiriting.

Fire began approaching from below and to their left. They couldn't see it, but they could see the smoke pushing up over the ridge in front of it, moving at twenty-five or thirty miles an hour, the smoke dark and heavy and carrying embers, some of which were large enough that Muldaur was worried about running over one and flatting a tire. Higher up, he could see the hurricane winds roiling the landscape. The more he saw, the more depressed he became. By the time he finally heard the Ford truck racing up the slope behind them, Muldaur was just about ready to quit.

58

Stephens knew he would eventually win out, and he had, because his three former riding companions were pedaling in the smoke while he was comfortably ensconced in the backseat of a vehicle costing, with the turbo option, full leather, and GPS, well over a hundred grand.

"So why did your friends kill my brother?" Sitting next to Stephens, Fred slapped the tire iron into his palm.

"Well, now, I don't know that I would call them friends, Fred. They're people I went on a weekend ride with. You know them as well as I do."

"You didn't answer my question."

"Which question was that?"

"Don't play dumb. Why did they push my brother off the cliff?"

Jennifer turned around in her seat and looked at Stephens with an intensity that seemed close to psychotic. He had always been able to charm women, particularly the ones who were dependent on him for raises and annual evaluations, and he wondered why he hadn't been able to win over this young woman. She'd been as adamant as Fred that he not ride with them.

"I don't know any more about it than you do. Just what they

said. I was just waking up when they were chasing Scooter through the camp."

"They were *chasing* him?" Kasey asked.

"That's what it seemed like."

"They wanted to get rid of him so there would be no witnesses, right? With no witnesses, they would have told us Chuck and Scooter both fell off, one of them trying to save the other."

"All I know is they said it was an accident, and Scooter caused it."

"That's bullshit and you know it!" said Finnigan.

"Well, uh, yes . . . it probably . . . I'm just relating . . . because they're saying it, doesn't make it true. Hey, look. I barely know those guys."

Suddenly Stephens was aware that the Porsche was pointed down the mountain. "We're not going down, are we?"

"Take a look."

"You're making a mistake."

"Who's driving? Me or you?" Kasey stopped the Porsche in the middle of the road. Although the smoke wasn't as thick or settled as it had been half a mile back on the plateau, they could see only 150 feet now.

"I don't see any fire," said Fred.

"Oh, it's down there," said Stephens. "Look at those scorched treetops."

"Whatever was here is gone now."

"I'm telling you, it was . . . the flames were thirty feet high. Fifty feet high. I don't mind admitting I've never been so scared in my life. It's completely unpredictable. Why take a chance?"

"Where'd it go?" Kasey asked.

"I'm not sure. At one point it was in front of us. The wind was blowing every which way."

"If it was in front of you, you'd be dead," said Fred, matter-of-factly. "Jesus. You guys are all liars."

"Why don't you call them?" Kasey said, handing a walkie-talkie to Jennifer. "See what Scooter found down here?"

While she tried to raise Scooter, Kasey let the Porsche roll down the hill.

"I can't raise them," said Jennifer.

"Jesus!" Fred Finnigan exclaimed. The Porsche slid to a halt.

Bursting through a cloud of smoke, the Ford pickup was speeding up the hill backward, slewing from side to side on the narrow road. Beyond the pickup a large, dark cloud was chasing it up the mountain like something out of a cartoon. In another fifteen seconds the Ford would collide with the Porsche, and the cloud would overtake them all. Kasey pushed the gear lever into reverse, wrenched around to look out the back window, and floored the accelerator.

When they got to the top, Scooter rolled down the window in the Ford and yelled at them, "Did you see that?"

"See it?" Kasey yelled back. "It almost caught all of us."

After they turned around and were racing along the level roads in the woods, Stephens twisted around to evaluate the luggage space behind the rear seats. If they weren't hauling too much gear, he would importune Kasey to stop and pick up his bicycle. There was no point in leaving a three-thousand-dollar machine out here where the fire would destroy it. He pulled one corner of the storage cover up. "Jesus Christ! What's he doing here?" Morse's eyes were open, and his head was twisted to one side, grit and pebbles imprinted into both cheeks. His dull, dried-out eyes appeared to be staring directly at Stephens.

Fred looked over his shoulder casually and said, "Kasey likes carrying him around. We were thinking of mounting him on the hood when we drive back into town."

Nobody else spoke. Still turned toward the back, Stephens peered out the rear window. Flames had come up the hill and were licking the opening to the woods behind them, highlighting the dark tunnel of trees alongside the road with a brilliant burst of flame. They were actually being chased now, and by a fire that had traversed a quarter mile in only a few minutes.

"Jesus!" Stephens said, surprised by his own profanity. "Let's get the fuck out of here."

Stephens was no longer in control of his own destiny, and it was making him feel increasingly uneasy. He was riding in the back of a car with a man who detested him and who may or may not have been drinking all day—the floor was littered with empties—and panic seemed to have overtaken the driver in a way he hadn't witnessed in any of the cyclists. That was the attribute he admired most about the firefighters, the fact that they were able to take every adverse circumstance in stride, although their gallows humor was certainly annoying and even puzzling. At least they were never on the verge of losing their minds the way these people seemed to be.

Several times the Porsche strayed to the side of the road in the smoke, and either Jennifer or Fred had to scream at Kasey to get him back on track. On top of everything else, the engine was beginning to misfire. "Maybe we should stop and take out the air filter," said Stephens. "It's probably clogged from all this smoke in the air." Kasey's reply was to slam his foot on the accelerator. The flames in his rearview mirror had scared the wits out of him. Stephens himself was shaking, more frightened now than he'd been all day. Fred's nostrils were tinged with soot. The interior of the car was full of smoke. If he didn't know better, Stephens would have thought Fred was whimpering.

They were past the lake now, heading northeast. It was the same road he'd ridden up with the others before resting at the mine, and Stephens knew that once they reached the loose network of logging roads that crisscrossed the top of the mountain, they would most likely be safe. The only problem would be getting there. What worried him was that if the Ford stalled in front of them, there wouldn't be enough room on this narrow road for them to maneuver around it. In other words, they would all be on foot, all six of them. After half a mile when they broke out of the smoke, Fred and Stephens both turned around so they could peer back down the mountain. Flames had burst through the lumpy mound of smoke that had been sitting over the lake. It was hard to tell how high they were, but Stephens estimated some at a hundred feet or higher, dancing up through the smoke at intervals before dying back down. The road they'd been on only minutes earlier had turned into a death trap.

Some of the trees behind them were tall—a hundred feet or so— and he knew how dry they were and how fast they would burn once ignited. Every year after the holidays, he burned his Christmas tree out behind his house, and it never failed to go up like a Roman candle. They were driving up an entire mountainside of them. As if to emphasize the point, a gust of wind dropped a chunk of burning material in front of the Porsche.

Kasey ran over one of the rain-diversion culverts at speed, and their heads all bumped the roof. Stephens bit his tongue. Fred cursed. Jennifer cried out. Kasey slowed enough to regain control of the vehicle, then sped up again. "Watch out for my friends," Stephens said. "They're probably on this road."

"I thought *we* were your friends," Fred said, elbowing Stephens hard. Stephens tried not to stare at his enormous arm muscles or at Fred's hair and eyebrows, which were bleached from too much sun.

This was, he thought, a weekend of curious allegiances: first to the cyclists, because his commonality with them was their commitment to physical fitness, exercise addicts who congratulated themselves on their addiction, telling themselves how fortunate they were not to be addicted to something worse, like booze or drugs or gambling. His connection to Newcastle and these others had more to do with class than behavior. They were all of the same class, some by virtue of birth, but all by virtue of income. While it was true that each of these people, except perhaps Jennifer Moore, had been born to privilege, Stephens had accumulated enough money and investments during the past fifteen years that he felt at ease, if not at one with them.

Stephens knew by the amount of dust flying around on the road in front of them that they were gaining on the white Ford. If that was true, they were gaining on the cyclists, too.

The smoke had thickened and was blacker. The wind was picking up. From the way the road arched around the face of the mountain, Stephens realized the fire they were running from might soon be alongside them. On this stretch, they could not see far enough through the trees to know where the blaze was for sure, but judging from the smudges in the sky, it was on their left and moving forward quickly.

"There's one now," said Fred, leaning forward until his nose was nearly touching Jennifer's earlobe. "Run him down. Run that murdering bastard down."

Kasey increased his speed as he passed the cyclists, and for one terrible moment Stephens thought he was going to hit them, but Kasey made no move to sideswipe the bikes. As they overtook the first cyclist, a sweep of heat, smoke, and jagged orange flashes reached up through the trees on their left and licked the roadway. Stephens began to feel the heat from the flames through the broken-out rear windows.

They drove through the gauntlet of burning trees and kept going, and as they did so it grew deathly quiet inside the Porsche. It was clear to everyone that they were leaving the cyclists to die.

No matter how hard he tried, Stephens couldn't stifle the thought that they were *all* going to die. He'd been scared earlier in the day, and a couple of times he'd been close to panic, but until this moment he'd never felt he might not make it. He wasn't sure what Kasey and the others were thinking, but they were all as stiff as he was.

While they were traveling faster than the cyclists, this narrow and treacherous road didn't allow them to travel over twenty-five miles per hour, so as they passed them, each biker was able to get a gander at Stephens inside the Porsche. He hadn't been counting on that. The first was Muldaur, who seemed to be suffering as much as any man could. The look of shock on Muldaur's face when he recognized Stephens in the Porsche was exceeded only by the bitter look Zak gave him a moment later. Giancarlo, unexpectedly the lead rider of this trio, had the temerity to flip him the bone. Stephens knew they were disappointed that he'd circumvented their group negotiations to make a deal for himself, but hey . . . there was survival and then there was everything else. If they weren't smart enough to figure that out, it wasn't his fault.

And then it happened. The eventuality Stephens had been warning the others about for some minutes now. The white Ford in front of them had stopped in the middle of the road, was actually rolling down the hill backward. The brake lights came on and the engine, which had stalled, roared back to life. Momentarily. Then a cloud of black smoke poured out the tailpipe, and the truck stalled again.

There was barely enough room for the Porsche to squeeze past, and even then its driver's-side wheels were bouncing over the rocks that rimmed the road. Kasey swung out even farther. The driver's door on the Ford popped open, then closed when the driver realized the Porsche was about to take the door off.

After they were safely in front of the disabled Ford, Stephens turned around and saw Bloomquist and Scooter climbing out of the tall cab. Behind Scooter, maybe two hundred yards down the mountain now, a stand of trees burst into flame. The three cyclists were in front of the flames, but only barely. Stephens couldn't take his eyes off them. They were about to be roasted. He couldn't believe it.

Bloomquist and Scooter yelled for the Porsche to stop, but the Porsche engine was running rough, too, so maybe Kasey was afraid if he stopped and let it idle it would quit, that they would all die. Or maybe he was afraid that if he stopped, the fire would overtake them in those few seconds. Or the cyclists would. It was hard to know why he floored the accelerator, speeding into a bank of black smoke that had drifted onto the road, but he did. Stephens felt sick about it, but still he was glad they hadn't stopped.

"Slow down," Jennifer yelled. "We need to pick them up."

"You're going to crash," said Fred. "Can you even see?"

Stephens could feel the rocks under the car as they edged off the road. They rolled sideways and then hit a tree and came to rest, rear wheels spinning, the Porsche canted at a forty-five-degree angle. Now they'd done it. Now they were on foot, too. Without knowing how, Stephens found himself on the road blundering through a web of smoke, running. He couldn't see the fire racing up the mountain behind them, but he could hear its dull roar.

All six of them had been relegated to climbing the mountain on foot. And, of course, the cyclists were so far back they were all probably dead by now.

59

Zak was surprised to see Stephens in the backseat wearing a smug look of satisfaction. It took a couple of seconds for it to sink in, but when it did Zak found himself enraged to the point that he actually felt a wave of energy run through his limbs. Good. Anything to help propel him to the top of the mountain in front of the fire. It was the first shot of adrenaline he'd felt in a long while, and it perked him up. It was one thing to get chased up a mountain by fire, another to die while one of your erstwhile friends gloated over it. Zak would have ridden through hell to wipe the self-satisfied look off Stephens's face.

Flames began licking at their backsides. Zak hadn't noticed that the fire was so close until he rode into the ditch and then quickly back out. He'd felt the heat on his back at the same instant he locked eyes with Stephens, which added to his fury. Now he pedaled harder and felt his quads and the little muscles directly over each knee begin to cramp, felt a glow on his backside like sunburn. If it got even the tiniest bit worse, he was going to go down. All he could do was suffer until he died. That was all any of them could do. Then the heat backed off just a fraction.

Even though Zak would have sworn neither of them had any more strength in their legs, he and Muldaur continued to speed up.

It took a superhuman effort, but they caught Giancarlo and passed him. "Come on, Giancarlo," Zak said. "Stick with us."

"I can't. I went too hard. I'm cramping."

"You can make it."

"When you guys get out, tell my wife I love her."

"The fire's right behind us," Zak said. "You have to keep going."

As they spoke with Giancarlo, Zak heard the flames behind them creeping through the trees. As near as he could tell, the fire was traveling slightly faster than they were. It would take down Giancarlo, and then it would take them down. They'd slowed after overtaking their friend, and now, if they didn't speed up again, the fire would roll over all three of them in a minute. Zak knew exactly how it would happen. They'd wilt from the radiant heat before the flames even touched them.

"I know, I know," Muldaur muttered when he saw Zak glancing back down the mountain. "We've gotta pick it up."

"I'm not sure I can go any faster."

"You can, and you will."

The wind began blowing on their backs, hot and breezy, scouring the road until they could see the disabled Ford in the center of the track. For a split second Zak feared it was an ambush and that Scooter and Bloomquist would come running around the side of the vehicle with rocks to smash their skulls, but as they steered around the truck he saw that the occupants were gone.

As they rode into another bank of fast-moving smoke that had filtered up through the trees, Zak veered to the left. "Look out. Runners."

The first struggling runner was Roger Bloomquist in shorts, sneakers, and a Hawaiian shirt flapping around his waist. Zak didn't think he'd ever heard anyone breathing so hard. "Back off a bit. You keep going like this, you're going to collapse."

"Jesus Christ!" Bloomquist gasped. It took him several seconds to find enough air to finish the utterance. "I am *trying* to back off."

"Try walking," Muldaur said as he came past. "Walk and run.

Get your breath back. It's a long haul to the top." It was an eerie feeling, Zak thought, to be giving encouragement to someone he was
pretty sure would be dead in a few minutes.

Scooter was 150 yards in front of Bloomquist, scuffling along in
a lopsided gait no doubt contrived to protect his broken collarbone.
He looked as haggard as Bloomquist. As Zak recalled, they still had
a long way to go, at least ten minutes on a bike, twenty or more on
foot. As they closed in on him, Scooter began zigzagging in a deliberate effort to keep them from passing.

"On your left," Zak said, but Scooter cut to the left, and then
when Zak moved to the right, he swerved in that direction. After
several attempts, Zak pulled alongside, and even then Scooter tried
to match Zak's speed.

"Fuckers," Scooter hissed through clenched teeth.

"Slow down. Pace yourself," Zak said. "You keep going this
hard, you're going to blow up. You need to maintain as even a pace
as possible."

"What I need is for you to . . . die . . . fucker." Scooter's words
came out in gasps as he approached a steeper portion of the road.
He'd taken all of his fear and anger out on Zak. Just for a moment,
as they made their way up the steeper section, the wind died and
everything grew quiet except for the sound of Scooter's footfalls
and Zak's tires on the road, their breathing, and the flames crackling
in the woods behind them.

"Fuck you, chump!" Scooter said, as he accelerated away from
Zak.

"Slow him down," Muldaur said, from behind. "He's going to
kill himself."

"I'm trying."

As the grade grew steeper, Scooter took more distance out of
them until the wind shifted and he vanished ahead of them in another cloud of smoke. They began coughing as the smoke grew
denser. Far behind, they could hear Giancarlo coughing as well.
After a few minutes the smoke thinned and the grade eased and Zak

was able to drop his chain one cog in the rear and raise his tempo. Though wheezing now, Muldaur remained on his tail. They both knew once a rider lost touch with another rider, his pace dwindled significantly, so it was good he'd remained in contact. Whoever didn't keep in front of the fire would go down. There would be no begging and no second chances. Actually, Zak thought, there might be some begging.

They continued to ride in tandem, Zak and Muldaur, and as the road grew less steep Zak spotted the Porsche up ahead in the ditch, two wheels in the shallow depression, two wheels in the air but just barely touching the road. Both the front and rear passenger's doors were ajar. Not far up the road Zak saw three figures running.

The next runner they caught up to was Fred, who, as Zak watched, slowed from what had been a staggering lope to what was now a laborious walk. Behind them, Zak heard the fire roaring to life again. He heard shouting, too. There wasn't anything he could do to help those he'd left behind, as a cloud of smoke and ash passed overhead and scores of hot cinders began speckling the branches of nearby firs, setting them alight. Once again he found himself overtaking Scooter, who appeared out of nowhere in the smoke. As weary as he looked, Scooter made a crude attempt to reach for Zak with his good arm. Zak pedaled out of reach before he could fasten on. Behind, Muldaur said, "Don't even think about it." Scooter had done exactly what Zak warned him not to, and was now for all intents and purposes finished. He was stumbling, his lungs making a noise that sounded like a loose air fitting.

With the fire getting louder, roiling gusts blowing in various directions at once, and the speed of the wind picking up so that he had to work to hold his front wheel steady, Zak realized the fire could go anywhere. It might jump ahead. Or it could sweep over them from behind, as it had been threatening to do. Muldaur came abreast and, after drinking it dry, unleashed his CamelBak and dropped it to the road. He chucked a half-full water bottle that had been in a holder on his down tube, too. Zak followed suit, draining his hydration pack and letting it drop to the road, along with the walkie-talkie and virtually everything else he was carrying. The less weight, the better. At this point a few ounces might cost them their lives.

Keeping a steady focus, Zak sighted Jennifer jogging with determination. She looked as if she had enough strength in her legs to carry her to the top at her current pace. He caught her at a point where a little-used secondary road led off to the right and seemed to flatten out. Zak knew both roads would have the same elevation gain if they ended on top of the mountain, so the flattening would be temporary, but he could see where it would be tempting. The temptation proved too much for Jennifer.

Zak spotted Stephens fifty yards up the side road, resting with his hands on his knees, cocking his head to watch Zak.

"Don't do it!" Zak yelled. "You don't know where it goes."

"It has to go up," Stephens shouted.

"Does it? The quarry road was a dead end."

By way of reply, Stephens turned his back and began jogging away, trailed by Jennifer, as two deer galloped across the road between Jennifer and Zak.

"I don't like it," Muldaur gasped.

"Not much we can do."

"God, it's windy."

After they passed the spur road, the mountain grew smokier, and soon they were riding in smoke so thick and dark it turned the day into night. Here the main road followed the natural contours of the mountainside. As they pedaled, they got a sense that the flames were paralleling them in the woods on their right, which meant the fire must have at some point crossed the road Stephens and Jennifer took.

"Holy shit, what is that?" Zak asked, glancing into the woods below them. The roaring fire sounded like an army of giants marching through the woods. Forty yards distant, a dark orange glow shone through the trees.

"It's right there."

"Jesus."

"Speed up, man."

"You think I can go faster?"

"Giancarlo?" Muldaur yelled. "Giancarlo? Hurry." Zak turned around and saw that Giancarlo was out of sight and too far back to hear them.

The smoke lifted as more wind came down on them, and Zak saw flames leaping sixty feet into the air to their left. There was howling on their right, but fire was coming up the mountainside from below, too. The immediate heat on his left shoulder forced him to steer to the right side of the road as far as he dared. He could feel the growing heat on his bare left arm and leg. For a moment he wasn't sure whether to stop or keep going. Or whether to turn around and take a dive down the mountain. He turned his head so his face would be the last part burned. What an ugly pass they had come to when he had to decide which parts of his body he wanted burned last. Then the heat dissipated, dying down as suddenly as it had revved up, though his left side still felt hot. When he turned his head, the flames were gone and the wind was blowing smoke lazily down the mountain instead of furiously up.

"Are you okay?" Muldaur asked.

"I guess." The hairs on his left arm were singed, and his arm looked sunburned. "You?"

"I think it burned all my curlies. I won't have to shave my balls for a year."

"You shave your balls?"

"My wife likes it."

"I'll have to remember that if you don't make it."

"Yeah. You do that. What does Nadine like . . . in case *you* don't make it?"

"Nadine likes a guy with a pure heart."

"Shit. I'll never be able to fake that."

Even after Zak reached the top, it took a few moments to realize his odyssey had finally concluded. As he struggled with the fact that he was now safe, two wildland firefighters strode out of the haze on the plateau like an apparition and asked him if he was all right. He said he was.

He wasn't going to get shot and he wasn't going to get broiled, and as he stood beside the two firefighters, watching Muldaur work his way to the top, he allowed himself some water from a canteen the woman offered, marveling at how feeble and weakened Muldaur appeared, at how wobbly his bike was, and how he looked as if he was about to fall over with each pedal stroke. Was it possible that Zak had looked that bad?

Then, as he and Muldaur waited for what seemed like an eternity alongside the two firefighters, Giancarlo came out of the smoke like a wraith and poured on the power. As he watched his friend climb, Zak wondered whether Stephens and Jennifer had been forced to backtrack to the main road and, if so, whether the flames had caught them and cut them down. He wondered if the shouts he'd heard as they were climbing hadn't actually been screams. He wondered whether Bloomquist, Scooter, and Fred were going to make it. And Kasey. Where was Kasey?

It wasn't until that moment that he realized he hadn't seen Nadine's brother outside the Porsche. He'd seen everyone else on the road, but not Kasey. "You see Kasey running?" Zak asked.

"Not me," said Muldaur.

"I didn't see much of anything," said Giancarlo, who'd reached them by then. Remarkably, he didn't appear to be burned.

Zak suddenly had a vision of himself having to explain to Nadine and her skeptical family how all this had happened. He would have to detail every action and decision of the day again and again, not only to the authorities, but to the family. It was going to be hard enough to account for the three deaths he knew of already, but if Nadine's brother came up missing or dead, it would mean the end of Zak's already tenuous relationship with her.

It took a series of radio transmissions between one of the firefighters and her supervisor, who was apparently somewhere to the east of them, for Zak to get the full picture. Stephens had made contact with another firefighting crew. He was safe. He did not know the whereabouts of the others, and the last time he'd seen him, Kasey was in the Porsche. In fact, word was relayed from Stephens that he didn't recall seeing Kasey get out.

"Shit," Zak said.

"What is it?" Muldaur asked.

"Kasey's still in the car. He probably thinks that's the safest place. I'm going down."

"You'll never find him in all this smoke," said Muldaur.

"If you go down, you'll never make it back up," added Giancarlo.

"I have to go. He's stuck in the car."

"Maybe he *was* stuck," said Muldaur. "But he must have gotten out by now."

"I can't take that chance."

The way Zak saw it, things boiled down to Nadine and how badly he wanted to spend the rest of his life with her. If her brother died up here, Zak would lose her. Until he met Nadine, he'd never understood the expression *wanting to grow old with*, but this was the woman he wanted digging in the garden outside his window when he was creaky and aching and his digestion had gone bad . . . although to be truthful he had no idea whether Nadine liked to garden or not.

"Where'd the fire go?" Zak asked. "Why didn't it keep coming up?"

The second wildland firefighter, a reedy young man who had been looking nervous since the moment Zak first saw him, said, "We've been watching it all day. These mountains have magnified the effects of the wind. There's no telling. There's no telling where it's headed next. I mean, it's just as likely to hit a section as it is to skip over it. You get anywhere close to it, and it's going to be like a blowtorch. Down below, they had winds of almost sixty miles an hour. One direction. Then another. It's the weirdest fire we've fought all summer. It's a bellows effect of the pass that keeps changing things so quickly. You got wind coming through there like a hurricane. They had to close I-Ninety this morning because of the winds."

"What about the helicopter? We saw a helicopter earlier."

"They've got engine trouble. They're back in Fall City working on it."

"So there's no truck or anything up here?"

"Not unless *you* brought one."

"Don't do it!" Muldaur said.

He got up to speed in fifty yards, and then, as soon as he hit the smoke, he held his breath for as long as possible, finding his first intake of smoky air even more foul tasting than he remembered. As he descended, the smoke continued to grow thicker.

There were alternating patches of burnout on the mountainside, so that half a mile down he found a huge charred area, both sides of the road scoured clean, timbers smoldering, and then a quarter mile later the trees were green and unspoiled again. He went through two clean sections and two burned ones. Then the smoke thinned and the wind picked up, and he found himself with a death grip on his handlebars. He knew the fire came right behind the wind and that he was coasting into the most dangerous area.

The mountain had an indentation with a small gully on the right that the road builders had filled in and which became a crease as it climbed the mountain on Zak's left. It was on this section where Zak found the first body. The fire had roared up the gully, burning everything he could see below and most of the trees in the crease above. The body was facedown in the center of the road, and he couldn't tell who it was until he turned it over. The clothing that had been pressed against the dirt had kept almost all of its original color, and unless he'd given his Hawaiian shirt to someone else, this was Roger Bloomquist.

Zak let the body sag back to its original position and remounted. On the trip down the mountain he'd been gulping air when there *was* air to gulp, but now he was holding his breath for the simple reason that he was in shock. He'd been a firefighter for seven years, but aside from photos in some early training sessions, he'd never seen a burn victim, at least not a dead one. As he coasted into the bowels of uncertainty, he tried to think about what Bloomquist must have gone through in his last few minutes. He wondered what his last thoughts were, and he wondered, too, what his might be when he got caught by the flames.

The second body was within shouting distance of the first, and had it not been obscured by smoke he would have seen it while he was still bending over the original corpse. He began crying, more at the futility and senselessness of these deaths than anything else. He never cried on the job, but this was different. He'd known these people. And their deaths had been so needless. They might have driven to the top of the mountain a long time ago if they hadn't tried to go back down through the fire. The second corpse was curled into a ball, arms extended as if picking berries. Closing in on the body, he braked to a stop. How odd that this person had a history and a memory and maybe a thousand or so people who knew his name, and now with only a slight change in wind direction he'd become a lump of charcoal.

He stared for much longer than he probably should have, trying to identify the body without touching it. Eventually, he recognized the leather sandals. He looked for and could barely see the tattoo of a dollar sign on his ankle. Scooter. All of his crap had finally led to his own death. Had Scooter been willing to take Zak's advice about slowing down, he might have made it out on foot, but in the end even the hideously out-of-shape Bloomquist had overtaken him.

It was hard to believe how far down the mountain he had to coast in the violent winds to find the Porsche. The area around the SUV was untouched, the trees covered with soot and tinted by smoke, but still ripe and awaiting ignition. Ironically, had Scooter and Bloomquist hunkered down here, they might still be alive, because this area was relatively unscathed.

The vehicle was in the ditch where he'd last seen it, both passenger's-side doors ajar. Because of the extreme tilt, he couldn't see in the passenger's-side windows, nor through the windshield, which was starred and partially buried in the dirt and rocks.

Faint music flowed from inside.

Dropping his bike in the center of the road, Zak called out, "Anybody in there?"

He lifted the front door, propping it open with one arm while he peered into the cockpit, which appeared to be empty. An air bag had deployed out of the steering wheel. "Jesus," Zak said aloud as the implications of this fiasco struck home. He never should have come down the mountain. There were loud crackling sounds nearby as the woods began exploding. The fire, which had skipped over this area on its first pass, was beginning to nudge it again, and the odds of outrunning the flames a second time were infinitesimal.

Just as he was pulling away, he saw what appeared to be a pile of clothing in the driver's foot well.

The pile began moving.

Kasey was bent almost double, prying at something near his feet with a large, bone-handled knife. His face was stained with tears, and he looked as despondent as anybody Zak had ever seen. "I thought you guys were gone."

"We thought *you* were gone."

"My foot's jammed."

"Think two of us can get it out?"

"I don't know." Suddenly Kasey looked like a kid on Christmas morning. He was twenty and had been facing this alone, and now he had help.

"Just a minute. I need to get something to prop this door open." Zak clambered off the side of the Porsche and looked around for a limb or a rock. Below their position he could see flames leaping over the tops of trees, dying down, then leaping up again. It was the same fire that had chased them up the mountain, returning now to complete the chore.

All he could do now was pray he had the guts to dive in and get

Kasey out, pray that the panic that had paralyzed him at the earlier wreck didn't return. He knew he was stalling, and every minute he stalled was putting him and Kasey a minute closer to death. He was all too aware that this wasn't a fire department operation, that he didn't have people backing him up, that he wasn't wearing any protective gear. He felt so unbelievably vulnerable with his arms and legs bare. He knew that, should the fire overtake them, nothing burned faster or hotter than the interior of a modern vehicle with its plastic dash and console and synthetic carpets and seats. Even without the gas tank, which almost never exploded except in movies, car fires were hot and dangerous. Everything around them would light up like a small sun.

He hadn't been away more than a few moments — at least he thought it was only a few moments — when Kasey began yelling. "You still there? Christ, you didn't leave, did you? You stupid bastard."

Zak peered into the doorway. "Try to keep the excitement level down to a dull roar, would you?"

"I thought you left."

"Nobody's splitting. We go out of here together."

"It's too weird. You pulled my sister out of a car. Now you're pulling me out."

It was weirder than Kasey knew. He'd rescued Kasey's sister, but seventeen years earlier had failed to rescue his own.

He'd cheated death when he was eleven; he'd always known that. His destiny had been to crawl inside with Charlene and not come out. He wondered if he was going to cheat death and destiny one more time.

Zak walked around the rear of the Porsche and stooped to pick through the rocks at the edge of the road. When he thought he saw a pair of cycling shorts inside, he stood on tiptoe and peered through the broken rear window. It was Morse. These guys were murderers and liars, and, when this was over, their thousand-dollar-an-hour attorneys were going to blame the deaths on Zak and Muldaur, but all morning they'd been hauling around the body of the man they'd murdered as if it were some sort of trophy.

"Where are you? Are you still there? You're not making any noise."

Zak picked up a piece of broken rock and jammed it into the door hinge. "Let me look at what's going on."

Thinking it was a miracle he hadn't been overcome by panic already, Zak slithered into the Porsche, lowering himself past the gearshift console and Kasey Newcastle, who reeked of sweat and fear and the sour smell of old beer. His guess was that a formation of rocks in the ditch had bit into the sheet metal like a fork and jammed his leg.

Zak pulled gently on Kasey's bare leg. "That hurt?"

"Hell, yes, it hurts. You don't think I've been trying to yank it out?"

Zak was lying half across Kasey's hips, feeling his body heat against his own already hot flank, their voices close and soft like lovers. "Give me the knife."

It was dark in the bottom corner of the Porsche where Zak was working, but he quickly calculated what needed to be done. The sheet metal had popped inward and grabbed Kasey's ankle like some sort of metallic flower so that the bloody flesh and bones of his lower leg were gripped tightly. Using the blade of the knife, Zak began prying the metal out of the way, using a second rock he'd brought with him for leverage.

"Shit! What are you doing to me? Ouch. Shit."

As he worked inside the Porsche, Zak had to admit he felt safe swathed in all the leather and luxury. Even knowing there was a cadaver in the back didn't bankrupt the false feeling of refuge.

"I hear the fire," Kasey said. "How close is it?"

"Close enough that you're going to have to run on that ankle after I get you out of here."

"Run on it? I can barely feel it. Maybe if we close the door? Maybe it would go over us."

"The fire gets anywhere close to this rig, it'll go up like a road flare."

"I know you're a fireman and everything, but are you sure?"

"Yes."

"It sounds like it's right outside. Hurry. Damn it, Zak. Hurry."
It was the first time Kasey had ever used Zak's name.

"Okay. You're free. Pull your leg out."

When Kasey scrambled out of the Porsche, he actually used parts
of Zak's body like rungs on a ladder. Zak backed out. By the time he
reached the road, flames were close enough that he could feel them
on his jersey.

Kasey was already flying up the road on foot.

Because the fire was fingering through the trees on either side of
the road, Zak knew this had turned into another footrace. For a moment the fire seemed delayed, yet the instant it gathered some momentum and began marching up the mountain with any sort of
certainty, they would both be dead.

Zak picked up his bike and began running alongside it, wondering if he should abandon it. He and Kasey were running at almost
the same speed, Kasey 150 yards in front, though he had yet to turn
back to see if Zak was okay. And then, as he pushed the bike up the
hill, Zak began to lose ground. On Kasey and on the fire.

Running put new stresses on his already overtaxed leg muscles
and, as he ran, Zak's legs began to cramp. If he could get on his bike,
it would be better, he thought, as shadows from a cloud of black
smoke scudded up the mountain over their heads. He heard an explosion behind him: probably the Porsche's interior as it reached ignition temperature and burst into flame.

It didn't irritate Zak that Kasey was ahead of him. What irritated
him was that Kasey hadn't turned around, hadn't given Zak a second
thought. It made him sick to watch panic manipulate people, knowing it could just as easily manipulate him. Ironically, they were running toward the bodies, seeking refuge in what had already proved
to be a deadly trap for Kasey's two friends. The bike began to feel
heavier and heavier. He had the feeling that without the additional
burden of the bicycle, he might be able to run himself into a groove,

and perhaps the stiffness in his legs would ease up, but he didn't let go of the bike and consequently was forced to slow down. He could hear trees crackling like distant gunfire. His shoulders and the backs of his legs were beginning to grow hot. So this was what it was like to get chased down by a forest fire. This was what it was like to die alone in the woods. At least he would be able to stop moving. He'd been moving all day, and he was so tired . . . At least he'd be able to rest.

As he pushed his bike up the mountainside, he began thinking about his own impending death. He knew Nadine would eventually go on to marry somebody else. In years to come, he would be the firefighter boyfriend she had that one summer. By the time she had grandchildren, she might not be able to recall his name. There would be a hole in the world where Zak had been, but it would be a very small one, just as in the grand scheme of things, with billions of people on the planet, most humans left rather small holes when they died.

As Zak ran, Kasey cast a glance back over his shoulder for the first time. It was clear from his movements that he wasn't checking to see how Zak was doing but was instead gauging the distance to the fire.

Sighting a small boulder on the left side of the road, Zak ran toward it, pushing his bike, vaulting up onto the rock and leaping onto the saddle. He'd already put the bike into the second lowest gear in expectation of something like this and was able to power through the dead spots at the top and bottom of his pedal stroke as he slowly picked up speed. As soon as he got into a rhythm, the fire leaped forward and began roaring down his neck. He'd gotten just enough distance by hopping on his bicycle that the heat didn't take him down immediately. He could smell hair sizzling. No matter what happened, he wasn't going to give up. He would ride until the tires on the bike exploded. He wasn't going to give up.

The wind picked up and began blasting him from left to right, just hard enough to take some of the heat off him.

Deep down he knew if he stopped for even a second or two the fire would overtake him and he would drop onto the road like the others. Getting back onto the bike when he did had been a stroke of luck. He no longer felt his legs cramping. He was now in a position he'd assumed for hundreds, if not thousands, of hours every year, and his body knew it well.

He quickly gained enough ground on the fire so that he was no longer breathing superheated air. The atmosphere around him remained hot and smoky, but at least his lungs could extract minimal amounts of oxygen. He was now moving at the same speed as the fire. Without realizing it, he'd been growing more and more hypoxic. His legs ached, his lungs burned, and he felt as if he was going to faint, but he kept riding. With all his troubles, he was reeling in Kasey, who increased his tempo as they both crossed from the dry ground to the previously charred section of the mountain where the two bodies lay.

When Kasey came upon the first body, he slowed momentarily, stared in disbelief, then picked up speed. Like a child rushing past a haunted house, he bypassed the second body without looking at it and kept running through the charred tunnel of smoldering, stick-like snags. At this rate it wasn't going to take long for him to reach the untouched part of the hillside, where he would once again be vulnerable to the escalating firestorm behind them.

By the time Zak caught him, they were only yards from exiting the charred section. "Stop," Zak shouted. "Stop right here." He knew that there was no fuel here, that the fires had already consumed everything they could. Kasey was not going to stop.

Pulling alongside, he overlapped his handlebars with Kasey's hips and began leaning against him until they both veered toward the right-hand side of the road, wobbling and tilting. Together, they went over in a heap, Zak's bike on top of the mess. "What the hell are you doing?" Kasey screamed, as he fought to extricate himself.

"Stay here!"

"Like hell. Are you nuts?"

"Are you?"

"Did you see those bodies?"

"They got cooked from the burning trees. You see any trees here with the potential to flare up?"

Kasey ceased struggling. "Trees?"

"There's nothing left to burn here. We go up where all those live trees are and we'll end up looking like charcoal briquettes. This is perfect. It's like we set our own back burn."

"What?"

"There's no fuel here. Nothing left to burn. Now sit still, and maybe you'll live through this."

60

Six hours later

He'd been dozing, drifting in and out of consciousness, in one of those patient gowns with the open back. His left shoulder had enough white Silvadene cream on it that he could just glimpse it with his peripheral vision. He hadn't been here long, because there were no get-well cards or balloons, just a half-open door. For a long while he lay still, taking in his surroundings, listening: visitors traipsing up and down the hallway, a wheeled cart rolling past the door. He knew he'd taken a helicopter ride. He knew men in brown uniforms had asked questions and he knew he'd closed his eyes without replying. Vaguely, he remembered that the doctors and nurses at Harborview had been fussing over him because he was a firefighter. Somebody had asked if he needed pain meds. He couldn't remember how much he'd taken, but it was enough that he could barely feel his burns. He could barely feel anything.

He was wondrous and grateful to be out of the mountains, even more wondrous that he was still alive. He'd never been so grateful, and questioned whether it all hadn't been somehow enhanced by the drugs freewheeling through his bloodstream. It took many long minutes to realize he had a line in his left arm and a nasal cannula pushing oxygen through his nostrils. Down the corridor he heard a television playing the evening news. Somebody turned the sound louder. The story involved people being rescued from the mountains in the middle of one of the worst fire seasons in western Washington history. He knew he was one of those people. The only part he caught before a car commercial was "officials have verified at least two deaths. There may be more."

Which bodies had they found? he wondered. There was no telling how many died in the end. The fact was, he couldn't recall for sure whether Muldaur and Giancarlo had made it. He knew they'd reached the top of the mountain, but that didn't mean they were alive now. The fire had been so entirely unpredictable.

A dark figure stood in the doorway for half a minute before Zak took cognizance of it. The figure had Silvadene smeared over various parts of his body and was draped in an oversize hospital gown similar to Zak's. "Hey, buddy. Through with your nap?"

"They must have doped me," Zak said, tasting the dryness in his throat. He wondered how long it had been since he'd spoken.

"If I remember right, you were asking for the formula so you could mix up a batch at home."

"Was I?"

"You were dopier than hell. You and Kasey, I guess, ended up hiding in some hot rocks when it blew over the last time. You got some contact burns from the rocks on the road, but other than that it's just smoke inhalation for the both of you."

"Is he all right?"

"Don't worry. Your girlfriend's brother made it. He's up the hall telling the county sheriff's investigator all about us. They keep looking at me. They came in here once, but we got the doctor to throw them out. The doctors were going to put you in the hyperbaric chamber for smoke inhalation, but at the last minute decided against it. Actually, I believe they only have one chamber at their disposal, and it's already full."

"Who's in it?"

"Stephens. Jennifer. And a nurse who's looking after them."

"Jennifer made it?"

"Yeah. Stephens. Jennifer. Kasey. They all made it."

"Anybody else?"

"You, me, and Giancarlo."

"You're going to have to help me out with the math here."

"There are six dead or missing. Chuck, Morse, and Ryan Perry we already knew were dead. Bloomquist, Fred, and Scooter are missing, but they found two bodies they haven't identified. So we're not sure who else is dead."

"What's Kasey telling them?"

"They won't let me close enough to listen."

"You talk to them yet?"

"The sheriff? Yeah. It was a little tense. Apparently our story doesn't match up with everything else he's been hearing."

"What happened with Stephens?"

"I heard a couple of the deputies talking, and I have a feeling he's aligned himself with the other side."

"Saying what?"

"I don't know."

"How's Giancarlo?"

"A few burns and smoke inhalation like the rest of us. That man's got the constitution of a horse."

"He was like that in drill school, too . . . You haven't talked to Stephens?"

"No. He and Jennifer went on the first flight. Giancarlo and I went later. You and Kasey didn't get picked up until way late. For a while there, we all thought you were dead."

"Were you sad?"

"I had to ask for a second box of Kleenex to wipe my eyes. Why'd you go back?"

"I didn't feel I had a choice."

"There's always a choice."

"Not if you're me."

"Zak, you're a better man than I am. No way was I going back down that mountain. I just couldn't believe I was watching you disappear into that smoke again. A little while after you left, the fire blasted up the road like a blowtorch, and I figured it had taken you out. Then on our way out we flew along the road, and there were two bodies facedown in the road. I thought one of them had to be you."

"It was probably Bloomquist and Scooter. They were in the middle of the road. They got caught trying to outrun it. I'm guessing Fred did, too. Probably up the spur road."

"Thought you might like to know, Nadine showed up awhile ago. She's down the hall with her brother and the rest of the family."

"I don't know if I'm ready for her. Six dead. Jesus."

"Yeah." Noises in the corridor grew louder and then receded. A minute later people passed by speaking in whispers. Zak recognized Nadine's voice. Muldaur was fumbling with the controls for the television to search for news reports about the fire when a figure darkened the doorway: Nadine Newcastle in tennis shorts and an off-white blouse, her hair pulled into a ponytail. The three of them looked at one another wordlessly before Muldaur said, "I'll leave you alone."

"That's not necessary," Zak said.

"See you later." Muldaur squeezed past Nadine, letting in more light as he swung the door wide. After they were alone, Nadine pushed the door closed with her fingertips.

"I want to thank you for what you did for Kasey."

"Did he tell you?"

"Actually, I pieced it together. He hasn't said anything about that part of it. You were safe, and then you went back down and got him, didn't you?"

"Yes."

"Whatever else takes place, I want to thank you for that. From the bottom of my heart. Zak, you've got more guts than anybody I've ever met."

"Not really."

"I'm just so glad he made it. And you, too."

"Yeah."

"I'm so glad you're here." Close to tears, she clasped her hands in front of herself and watched his eyes. It was a long time before either of them broke the silence.

Finally, Zak said, "What?"

"I just . . . I just want to know where I can kiss you where it won't hurt."

Zak contorted his face in what he hoped was a humorous way and pointed to a spot on his cheek until, grinning, she came close and planted a kiss. As soon as she pulled away, he pointed to another spot, which she kissed, then another. The game went on until she got Silvadene on her lips and had to wipe it off with a corner of the bedsheet. At that point she took his hand, sat in a chair beside his bed, and glanced at the doorway with a fleeting look of guilt. "I can't stay."

"You just got here."

"Kasey's going to find out where I am and throw a fit. My father's out there trying to make sense of it, but Kasey's story keeps changing in subtle ways. The sheriff says it doesn't match what you guys said. They're . . . they're calling you guys liars and all kinds of other names."

"I bet they are."

"Zak . . ."

"Would you like my side in a nutshell?"

"That's what I was going to ask."

He gave it to her, thinking it through slowly as he tried to get his brain engaged with the process. The longer he spoke, the more rigid and tense her body became. When he was finished, she didn't ask any questions. He wasn't sure if that was a good sign or a bad one, though he'd done his best to include all of the pertinent details and head off any questions she might be entertaining.

"They're talking lawyers and jail time for you guys and, if criminal charges don't pan out, civil suits. Kasey said you're the reason Scooter is missing."

PRIMAL THREAT ▲ 345

"Scooter's not missing. He's dead."

"Oh, my God. Are you sure?"

"I saw him. He's dead."

"Oh, Lord. We knew he was missing, and we knew there was a good chance he was gone, but . . . Oh, my God."

"Nobody wanted anybody dead."

"No matter what Kasey says, I know you didn't do anything wrong. And you went back for him. Anyway, I came to tell you nothing between us has changed in my mind. At least I don't think it has. But I have to think all this through. I have to hear the rest of Kasey's story."

"Nadine, I love you."

"I know you do. And I love you."

"Your family's probably going to—"

"Shush," she said, touching a finger to his lips.

"Nadine?" The voice from the hallway was her mother's. "Nadine?"

She stood up beside the bed but didn't turn away. "Nadine," he whispered. "I want to spend the rest of my life with you."

"Oh, Zak." She held his look for a long time. "I'm not sure that's going to be possible."

After Nadine left, a sheriff's deputy spoke to Zak. "I know it was confusing up there, and from what I gather your two groups were pitted against each other," said the deputy, Tom Mathers, a tall, reedy young man who'd walked into the room bouncing on the balls of his feet. "The way I'm seeing it, their stories are going all over the place—especially this guy, Stephens—but you three have remained constant. To me that either means you got together and rehearsed a script, or you're telling the truth."

"It's the truth," said Zak. "I'm a little too dopey to be remembering lines. The truth is all I've got right now."

"I'll tell you one thing. And you can bank on this. You boys ever get involved in anything like this again, anytime, anywhere, I swear

I'm going to come and dog you. You won't get away with it a second time."

"We didn't get away with anything the first time."

"Maybe. Maybe not. We're still looking into it."

When Stephens caught them at the nurses' station the next morning, Muldaur's wife, Rachel, was alongside them. The plan was for Rachel to drive Zak and Muldaur to North Bend, where they would recover their parked vehicles at Stephens's house and caravan back into Seattle. Stephens was still in a hospital gown; Muldaur and Zak were in clothing brought by Muldaur's wife.

Stephens had dark circles under his eyes and Silvadene cream on his ears and along one side of his neck. Other than that, he appeared in perfect health, probably the result of a night in the hyperbaric chamber. "What'd you tell the deputies?" Stephens asked.

"Nothing but the truth, the whole truth," Muldaur said, giving a salute and lapsing into his Hugh voice. "Why? What did you tell them?"

"Well, uh, of course . . . I told them . . . the story of what happened, obviously. I'm just wondering. I mean, *exactly* what did you tell them?"

"*Exactly?*" said Muldaur, still posing as Hugh. Rachel, who was almost as tall as her husband, gave him an indulgent look. "*Exactly?* That would be good . . . to know exactly. Wouldn't it?"

"I think so," said Stephens.

"Okay. We'll tell you what we said. *Exactly.*" Muldaur stepped back and crossed his arms.

After a few moments, Stephens said, "Well?"

"You first."

"Me?"

"Yeah. You tell us what you said—*exactly*—and we'll tell you what we said. *Exactly.*"

"Well, I, uh . . . you know. I told them what happened. You

know . . . pretty much . . . yeah, I told them the whole story from beginning to end."

"That's what I thought," said Muldaur, turning his back on Stephens and walking away. Zak and Rachel followed.

Stephens called after the trio. "We'll have to get together in a week or so. You know. Talk things over. Compare notes. Go out to dinner with our wives." He looked at Zak. "Bring your girlfriend."

"You've got to be kidding, right?"

"Well, fine. Yeah. How about you?" Stephens looked at Muldaur.

"I don't fucking think so."

The next day fire crews on the mountain recovered six corpses. Within twenty-four hours the medical examiner's office determined that Chuck Finnigan's blood-alcohol level at the time of his death would have qualified him as a drunk driver if he'd been in a car. Scooter and Fred Finnigan had been drinking all day, too, because they were both legally drunk when they died almost eight hours after Chuck.

The case against Zak and the others crumbled after the autopsy results. The prosecutor's office said it came down to one very coherent story matched up against another set of stories that had already diverged in several instances and was obviously heavily influenced by alcohol. He didn't believe a jury was going to buy their claims. The prosecutors said if they'd been inclined to prosecute at all—which they weren't—they would have built a case against Jennifer Moore and Kasey Newcastle, the only survivors from that camp, for accessory to murder. But they didn't.

61

A lot of things happened in the next few years.

Zak continued to work alongside Lieutenant Muldaur on Engine 6 until five years later, when Muldaur retired and he and Rachel moved to Montana to bike, ski, and take up fly-fishing.

Giancarlo Barrett was introduced to trail running, and while he never announced that he was quitting the bike, he parked it in the back of his garage—and several years later, when he realized both tires were flat and the shocks were leaking, gave it to the Goodwill. It didn't surprise Zak that Giancarlo never wanted to ride a bike again. Zak never saw Stephens after that morning in the hospital. Zak continued to ride and sometimes to race. He got married. They had two children, both girls. Ten years after that weekend in the mountains, when the girls were in first and second grade, they received word his wife's brother had died.

It was a sunny Saturday afternoon in autumn when Zak found himself sitting in a large Episcopal church in Clyde Hill. The trees all across the city were turning colors. Hard feelings in the Newcastle family had decreased to the point where Zak almost felt comfortable sitting in the same pew with Mr. and Mrs. Newcastle, Nadine on his left, their two children on the either side of them.

Zak listened to the priest and then to the speakers, who, one by one, extolled the virtues of the deceased Kasey Newcastle. After college Kasey worked for his father for a couple of years, then got an offer to run a consortium of real estate companies back east. He'd worked and lived in New York City, marrying and divorcing once while amassing more wealth in just a few years than his father had in forty. Then one rainy night in Connecticut a semi crossed the centerline and plowed into Kasey's luxury SUV, and despite all the best safety systems he'd died on the spot.

Zak wondered sometimes whether Kasey ever got over losing five of his best friends in one day under circumstances that were cloudy at best—and at their worst must have burdened him with at least some measure of guilt, as they did Zak. Several years earlier at a large, family Christmas party where he'd had too much to drink, Kasey cornered Zak and went off about how the biggest injustice of the last century was that Zak and the others hadn't done prison time over what had taken place that weekend. When Nadine asked why, if Zak had been intent on killing him and the others, Zak had returned to save his life, Kasey reacted as if the thought had never occurred to him. Or as if Zak hadn't returned.

Other than that single drunken holiday rant, Kasey was always polite to Zak in the way that only a man who thinks you're capable of murder can be. Once Kasey made the move to the East Coast, Zak and Nadine received most of their information about him through Nadine's parents. His return visits to the West Coast were brief and infrequent. He died at thirty-one, ironically in an accident similar to the one that had killed Zak's sister.

In recent years at weddings and funerals and birthdays, Kasey, who'd once relentlessly avoided Zak, sought him out, looking him in the eye as if the two of them knew something wicked nobody else in the room could ever realize. Zak couldn't tell if Kasey's stare was meant to be a challenge or if he was attempting to forge some sort of blood bond. Either way, Zak didn't take the bait and now would never know what Kasey had meant by it. Because Kasey had been cremated, there was no procession. Outside the church, people commiserated with the family. Zak and Nadine had two girls they both adored, six and seven, and except for sporting Zak's jug-handle ears, they were otherwise near clones of their mother. After most of the mourners had gone, the girls played on the grass in the sunshine with the children of Nadine's cousins. Zak found himself alone with Nadine, who turned to him and said, "I loved him so much."

"I know you did."

"After we became adults, we were just never as close as when we were growing up. When we were little he used to protect me at school."

"Big brothers are good for that," Zak said, surveying the snow-covered Cascades in the distance and thinking that at this time of year biking up there would be impossible.

Zak put his arm around his wife and pulled her close. He'd been lucky in life. He'd fought hard for that luck and knew the fighting was the single biggest factor in it. He knew whatever luck Kasey had been born with had run out at Panther Creek; the material fortune Kasey enjoyed for the rest of his life had been tainted with what he'd done or not done back there on the mountain.

Forty feet away Zak and Nadine's daughters shrieked and turned cartwheels on the grass, the long funeral pushed out of their minds by the reunion with second cousins. The afternoon sunlight shone through Nadine's dress, silhouetting her legs, still strong from ten-nis and from jogging in the park while the girls rode bikes.

Zak couldn't help thinking about how Nadine's tearful mother had wrapped her arm around his waist an hour ago and said, "Well, at least we still have one son left." He knew she didn't really mean it, but was grateful for the gesture. Nadine, sensing he was lost in his own thoughts, gave his hand a gentle squeeze.

ABOUT THE AUTHOR

EARL EMERSON is a lieutenant in the Seattle Fire Department. He is the Shamus Award–winning author of *Vertical Burn, Into the Inferno, Pyro, The Smoke Room,* and *Firetrap;* as well as the Thomas Black Detective series, which includes *The Rainy City, Poverty Bay, Nervous Laughter, Fat Tuesday, Deviant Behavior, Yellow Dog Party, The Portland Laugher, The Vanishing Smile, The Million-Dollar Tattoo, Deception Pass,* and *Catfish Café.* He lives in North Bend, Washington.

ABOUT THE TYPE

This book was set in Galliard, a typeface designed by Matthew Carter for the Merganthaler Linotype Company in 1978. Galliard is based on the sixteenth-century typefaces of Robert Granjon.